Other books by the author:

Nobody Knows How it Got This Good (stories)

PETROCHEMICAL NOCTURNE

AMOS JASPER WRIGHT IV

Livingston Press

The University of West Alabama

Library of Congress Control Number: 2023934465

Typesetting and page layout: Joe Taylor, Cassidy Pedram
Proofreading: Jack Estes, Scott Robinson, Brooke Barger,
Cassidy Pedram, Savannah F. Beams, Jacob Dial
Cover art: Shutterstock
Cover design: Amos Jasper Wright IV
Cover layout: Joe Taylor

PETROCHEMICAL NOCTURNE

"Fear death by water." — T.S. Eliot, The Wasteland

The Pink Flamingos of Spanish Town

In the waning, autumnal days of the Obama administration, eight *yes we can* years gone in a flash, but still very much anthropocened in the mental slave ships sailing downriver, I tuned the radio on the table before me to *Radio Free Dixie*, which you will not be able to pick up anywhere outside of Louisiana, which you will find is not a place on the official maps, which have all been redrawn by unreconstructed stone Generals who will not surrender, for the maps here are out of date the very moment of their mapping. The Mississippi River has twitched again, snaked into the Gulf of Mexico's ever-growing and metastasizing Dead Zone, the omnigenous nothing where nothing can live, like the bucking flexuous filigrees and extravagant arabesque architectures of Fisk's meander maps imagining the many hypothesized paths the daimonic river has taken over the course of human-less millennia, for the river is not satisfied with taking but one path — as we are bound to by the necessitous manacles of our lesser nature — no, the river must take all possible paths, as in Fisk's maps. Down at the levee earlier that day, where I sometimes go to contemplate the polymorphic biographies of the river, I alone saw the petrochemical epiphenomena of things unseen: the strangely colored toxic chlorine clouds in chartreuse and dead salmon or moribund, putrid cantaloupe, the hazmat clouds merging into a coherent sentient mass of chlorine gas ghost ships sailing downriver on Fisk's myriad Mississippis.

That mosquito evening, while the pink flamingos nested and the ExxonMobil plant met its production quotas for toxic cloud manufacturing and I leafed through the mesmeric illustrations of extinct birds in *The Birds of America,* a familiar voice on *Radio Free Dixie* recited lines from "For the Union Dead," which had a message for stone Generals who will not surrender: "Shaw's father wanted no monument except the ditch, where his son's body was thrown and lost with his men," the crackly voice casting an autumnal disquiet over the courtyard. I had long grown used to the abysmal air quality in the courtyard, the hellish fumes of holy ghost benzene and disincarnate naphtha, the air almost flammable, like some mephitis leaching from a basement morgue. And besides, in Baton Rouge, there is nowhere one can go to escape the petrochemical plant's ubiquitous pall of toxic vapors and chemical paramnesias. As the autumnal season was just commencing — the insectivorous vesper bats of the equinox and for miles around black smoke from the cane harvests drifted eastward in stateless ghost ships over Fisk's river, storms of formaldehyde ash falling in lethal fugues — at that time when all is most in flux and the maps are most futile, I thought little of the unnatural commixtures of the plant's petrochemical molecules and the smoky cane harvest, the verses echoing throughout the tribal streets of Spanish Town and Standard Heights. All year long I had been resisting premonitions of an epic struggle between the opposing factions of an undecided conflict, of mendacious monuments to dead symbols toppling into rivers of wormwood. A great siege was about to begin, the windows boarded up on Osage Avenue. Actors deep in the past are trying to liberate us from the Angola of the present.

The *Radio Free Dixie* broadcast was disrupted by the plangent peel of tocsins resounding like last trumpets from the Exxon-Mobil plant, the refinery's aural warning of a chemical leak or noxious release to the remaining tatters of the community languishing in the empty spaces around the plant, but mostly heard during the monthly tests that punctuated time like chemical church bells. I was then living a short walk — through Veteran's Memorial Park, by the cannon aimed at the ExxonMobil plant on the north shore of Capitol Lake — from one of the world's largest petrochemical and refining operations, not that I am bragging about keeping such toxic company. One gets used to the sweet gasoline odor of benzene — once used to decaffeinate coffee; one more reason not to drink decaffeinated coffee, I thought — burning on the wet air, detectable at 1.5 to 4.7 ppm. One Angola in parts per million. One wormwood in parts per million. One Standard Heights in parts per million. Sometimes autumn in Louisiana, that vanishing point on no map, when the cane is burning down like a match put to an old plantation in the fields, can feel like spring, and the winters are confused with summer, but the sinking of the land into the sea and the sea's ascension — meeting the land loss to erosion halfway, as it were — is not to be confused with levitation or other forms of modern resurrection. *Radio Free Dixie* broadcasts poems of resistance and Maafa, the lugubrious astronomy of the nocturne that was heard in

Standard Heights over the plant's public address system — a test simulating an industrial accident or the strident harbinger of the real thing. Explosions and accidents are all part of the plan, all factored in ExxonMobil's balance sheet, nothing to be alarmed about. The sobbing of the autumnal violins referred to in "Chanson d'automne" — I once heard it read in French by someone in Haiti over *Radio Free Dixie* — were heard on the river bluffs before the Battle of Baton Rouge, one of the first campaigns in the coming siege, the barges' doleful fugue of foghorns blowing on the present river, the loss of which we mourn in the dying fig trees, the meteors in the satsuma, the dead star of wormwood embittering the waters, the sickly green hebetude of the banana trees strewn with cheap plastic beads.

Every spring, the annual Spanish Town parade, known for its politically incorrect ribaldry and the not totally inaccurate caricatures of elected officials, necklaces the magnificent trees with silver, green, purple and gold beads that drip decadently from the branches on windy days long into the summer. This is known as Peak Bead Season. The cheap plastic beads clicking in the wind, party trinkets draping the branches in long scintillating ellipses like Saturn's rings, leaching toxic lead into the soil. Spanish Town is the unnatural habitat of an endangered species of plastic pink flamingo, nesting in Capitol Lake. Yards flocked with flamingo-shaped woodcuts painted pink. Flamingos in bowties and top hats, dressed in fine black tuxedos like petrified bacchants, their long serpentine necks decorated with beads and disposable plastic throws. One scholarly-looking flamingo eyes the ExxonMobil plant from behind a smart monocle. A family of flamingos in purple LSU football jerseys. This species of pink flamingo is found nowhere else but Spanish Town and a few pioneer death-wish flamingos that have strayed north into the No Man's Land of Standard Heights, returning to the ExxonMobil plant's otherworldly cloud manufacturing operations where they were born, as some species will migrate to the spot of their naissance to complete the closed loop of their lifecycle.

Before flocking in pink flamboyances beneath the bead throws of Spanish Town, the plastic pink flamingos start their strange lives as petrochemicals in the ExxonMobil refinery. After processing, the raw feedstock is shipped in cargo tanks to offshore manufacturers, the infinite protean possibilities of plastic, its amorphous will to take on any shape is injected into flamingo molds, whence the kitschy lawn ornaments that plague Spanish Town. The rings of Saturn and the moons of Jupiter might also be made of petrochemical plastics. The invasive bird has been banished by the area's more conservative homeowners' associations — it's too tacky, they say, or the birds like to have too much of a good time; this isn't Florida, they say.

The plastic pink flamingo, designed in 1957 by Don Featherstone, while working for Union Products, won the Ig Nobel Prize for art, a parodic award sponsored by the *Annals of Improbable Research* to recognize trivial, humorous scientific achievements such as research on the five-second rule, cryogenic sex research, and a paper, rigorously researched and cited, that black holes qualify on technical and theological grounds for all the criteria of perdition, as conceived in the popular Judeo-Christian tradition. The plastic pink flamingo — an invasive species that won the same parody award as the five-second rule for its contributions to public health — established its habitat upon suburban lawns and gardens across the country. Then on November 1, 2006, Union Products ceased production of the pink plastic flamingos and their extinction seems all but a foregone conclusion now, though these pink flamingos, before becoming endangered, flamboyantly multiplied: a few Lazarus specimens can be descried by the discerning eye hiding from hunters and petrochemical taxidermists in Spanish Town and Standard Heights.

Today when I open Audubon's *The Birds of America,* that awkward gangling pink albatross questions, from its single dimension on the printed page, my right to exist. Audubon studied and sketched the bird in its natural habitat before thoughtfully killing it off with a fine shot to reduce damage to the specimen. Something about this bird, the way it gracefully yet torturously balances on the rock like an embalmed gymnast, disturbs. Audubon has so ambiguously conjured the toxic marshy atmosphere of the barren Cancer Alley landscape in such a way that I cannot say whether this is a primeval, Jurassic world before the petrochemical revolution, or maybe some poisonous post-apocalyptic planet long after civilization has ended in a self-inflicted vanishing point — a black bloom lush in the dark that must not be disturbed, not for water, not for sunlight. An indistinct industrial haze lingers over the flamingos in the background. The smoke of the cane harvest is thick in the air this time of year. Audubon's flamingo is bent at the neck, the sinuous, curvilinear stalk evolved to drink water from shallow pools, the bird's boomerang beak simulating the curve of the rock: the formerly animate echoes the inert. The first time I saw Audubon's pink flamingo print in this collection of taxidermy birds — it was a day when the benzene and naphtha were especially odorous, a day not unlike the barren taxidermy landscape depicted in Audubon's flamingo world — I mistook the downward curve of the neck for a headless body, the bird decapitated by some unseen blow. Of course, there are hunters in this Sportsman's Paradise — the state nickname — who will kill such a magnificent bird without so much as a single rue in parts per million and they will not use a fine shot. Audubon's birds were life-sized — to fit the flamingo into the cage of the print, Audubon was compelled to artificially arrange the flamingo in a contorted, misshapen fashion that is uncomfortable to see. Even dead, the flamingo must be subjected to torture to satisfy an aesthetic vision. In the background of this print, behind this graceful pink bird and beyond the scope of alien marshes and mud flats, rise the lambent spires and steeples of the petrochemical infrastructure, the birthplace of these cadaverous, resplendent plastic birds of Spanish Town, the ExxonMobil plant expulsing airborne particulates in toxic gaseous belches polluting the flamingo's habitat.

    I closed the pages of *The Birds of America* on the taxidermy flamingo, and tried to locate the sirens in the indeterminate unmapped space north of Capitol Lake — that No Man's Land where the streets are named for lost native tribes. It was just a test, I reassured myself, a safety simulation, though I hardly believed this. Sometimes a test is the real thing. Quaint, colorful little Spanish Town would be erased by an industrial accident at the ExxonMobil plant's cloud manufacturing facilities or in the schematic chambers where the feedstock for the pink flamingos was produced. The plant's warning siren intensified in volume. I was losing the transmission of

Radio Free Dixie, that broadcast from the past warning us of toxic events in the Angola of the present. No longer able to hear "For the Union Dead," I turned the radio off, listening with growing alarm to the plant's warning siren expand into the silentious black nightfall.

There is only the one window here, in the small apartment building where I lived at the periphery of the plant's domain, but I have been grateful for its view overlooking a courtyard softened by a furious, subtropical garden. Hibiscus and no birdsong. I had started the evening out in the courtyard, then relocated indoors when the mosquitos became too bloodthirsty and the air quality declined — one warning siren in parts per million — and I was unable to breathe the cane harvest ghost ships sailing inland off Fisk's river. From behind this terrarium glass, I watched as the mailman inserted the ExxonMobil community newsletter into each mailbox of the apartment building, the corporate literature extolling the plant's good works. And dreaming in the distance, the smoking towers of the plant nod, a petrochemical Versailles. Giraffes gambol and flamingos frolic, the thousands dead at Bhopal. A pink plastic flamingo on holiday beneath a flowering hibiscus bush. I never knew the pink plastic flamingo was modeled on a real bird, I thought it was another of the fictive mythical beings, the werewolves and *lusus naturae* synthesized in the cryptozoological laboratories and oneiric manufactories of Petrochemical Modernism, Toussaint said, that day he showed me the vacant lot in Standard Heights where the family house had been before the Christmas Eve explosion and the last of the cash buyouts. What other petrochemical monsters might the ExxonMobil plant have created? Toussaint asked, looking towards what must have been a fond childhood memory of a view, even though there is no view of anything but counterclockwise bad memories here.

Petrochemical Nocturne

Cancer Alley's chemical plants and refineries upon nightfall are the black sparkling skylines of forbidden cities, bejeweled crystal palaces glitzing darkly on the present river, the stereochemical spires of industrial cathedrals and chemical basilicas, the petroleum temples of a prehistoric god, like a cemetery snatched from the dead.

Paraffin oil lamps burning black flames on industrial altars. Black chandeliers of hydrocarbons dripping petrol on the temple floor. At night, the refinery emits an alchemical afterglow, hums an artificial, infrastructural sunset that etches a spectral graph of luminous color above Fisk's river, which may not exist except in myth, a bouquet of fireworks falling over a ghostly city in Whistler's black and gold nocturne. The carnivorous animal fog on the river distorts the refinery complex like the diluted, brushy watercolors of J.M.W. Turner's watercolor conflagrations. From a riverboat, or the western shore of the river, the refinery could be Venice twinkling softly and mutedly through gaseous brume, the magical glow of romantic gas flares reflected in the Stygian lagoon, and the night tormented by the burn off of flammable gases released by pressure relief valves. On the river's black rippling surface: a watercolor study of a besieged city, the smokestacks and cooling towers like the spires of some aspirant metropolitan eidolon.

If there is even a future after the Age of Oil, an epoch that cannot end soon enough, art historians will have to answer for why no impressionistic or photorealist painter has deployed her skill to render these petrochemical temples, capturing them as Audubon captured the pink flamingo — in oil instead of formaldehyde. If I were a painter I would take the oil refinery and all its hellish infrastructure as my infernal subject, and do for the ExxonMobil plant what Monet did for haystacks, the railway station and water lilies; what Van Gogh did for the sunflower and olive trees; what Cezanne did for the still life of fruit; what Warhol did for the soup can and the car crash; what Ed Ruscha did for the Standard gas station. If ExxonMobil were treated as a subject for landscape painting or still life, as so many other manmade landscapes of this synthetic country have been, there would be no room for human figures, or for Toussaint, as in the paintings of the *vanitas* artists where only macabre mementos and small tokens of remembrance remain, like the random bricks strewn in the vacant lots where the family home once stood. Toussaint and I, still life figures in Cancer Alley, would be but Stymphalian birds in a hurricane against the inhuman scale of the petrochemical plants, our modern leviathan, the signal-to-noise ratios all denominator in the violence of the warning sirens — another industrial accident to investigate, another dot on the TOXMAP. For those like Toussaint who grew up in the carcinogenic shadows of the plants, aestheticizing these industrial hellscapes of Cancer Alley, whether in words or pictures, is a death mask privilege and a seldom luxury.

The musical name — nocturne — implies pianos and saturnine strings percolating in a minor key, heard on quiet dripping evenings in Spanish Town, a melancholy dirge set to the Doppler peel of the plant's warning sirens — a test, a simulation of another industrial accident or the real thing. I call this hideous, stridulous, engineered music the petrochemical nocturne, and to hear it one must have an ear like a pack of bloodhounds, no beeswax in there, a canorous amalgam of industrial electronica and sub-bass dubstep, U.K. Grime, and the tinkling minor piano of Chopin and Satie. The nocturne is audible in the florid, mephitic color of the gas flares lighting the present river like cult flambeaux, and in the plant manager's voice resonating in admonition over the radio waves of *Radio Free Dixie:* the oscillations of radio frequencies and the physics of occult petrochemical processes mix in an unregulated register of Cancer Alley locusts fed on a bad memory diet and the violent roar of river water rushing through the Spillway in flood season.

In Baton Rouge, the Houses of Lords and Commons burn every night, glowing lambent and holocaust on the Mississippi. Turner's *The Burning of the Houses of Lords and Commons* depicts the burning of Parliament as witnessed by thousands of awestruck Londoners from the Thames River's south bank, nocturnal and conflagrant impressions hastily sketched *en plain air* from the foredeck of a ghost ship while the seat of government burns away in aesthetical fires. The resultant sketchbooks were bequeathed to the National Gallery in the Turner Bequest and are now in the collection of the Tate Gallery — far from Cancer Alley. Even the Westminster Bridge is there, like the Interstate 10 bridge in Baton Rouge, spanning the bank of the Thames to the west bank of one permutation of Fisk's Mississippis.

But it is J.M.W. Turner's *Fire at the Grand Storehouse of the Tower of London, 1841* which most nearly simulates the infernal self-spectacle of the ExxonMobil plant burning on the nocturnal river. I am trying to make this petrochemical mosque understood in the hazmat hieroglyphs of its own terms, which are less transpicuous than one might think. Beware the aesthetic cult of pyrolatry, lest the cathedral collapse on the heads of leprous supplicants. To the painting's left, in the realm of the deepest black, Turner has scratched out in gouache a white light burning in the window of a tower, a vertically oriented, fuzzy white rectangle floating in the gloom: the conflagrant window flashing in the Christmas Eve explosion. And though the carnivalesque epiphenomena of Fisk's rivers have established the unreliability of eyewitness testimony, on November 2, 1841, *The Times* newspaper ran an eyewitness account of the events of October 30, right around the time of the cane harvest burnings on the west bank of Fisk's river, which account I reproduce here in full:

[Sergeant] Edwards ['of the 1st Battalion of Fusilier Guards'] states, that while he was in the Nag's Head public-house, in Postern-row [opposite the north side of the Tower], he perceived, to his great surprise, a light through one of the windows, just above the bomb proof part of the Bowyer Tower. He went out and crossed to the railings at

the top of the moat by which the Tower is surrounded, and watched the light for a minute or two. At first it appeared but little larger than the glimmer of a candle, but it suddenly increased to such an extent, that no doubt was left upon his mind that the place was on fire.

The glimmer of a candle must have been how the Christmas Eve explosion was catalyzed, such glimmer rapidly increasing to such an extent that no doubt was left in Toussaint's father's mind that the plant was on fire. Turner was painting the ExxonMobil refinery burning at night on the Mississippi River: the Cambrian black matter drilled below the seabed traveled the reticulated network of pipelines from the Gulf worming through the swamps and bayous, elevated over levees and highways, and into the refinery plant where it produced pink flamingos. Our own skeletons become fuel energy for some future post-human species' internal combustion engine, when that doomsday device is reinvented after the collapse of our own insatiable civilization at the Age of Oil's unmourned end.

Unlike Toussaint's genealogy, which he received in piecemeal installments from his father — the slave revolts in Haiti, the bloodhounds, the German Coast Uprising — and in incendiary fragments from his mother — the slave ship *Clotilda* porting in Mobile, the Colored Entrance, the bombing of Osage Avenue — the genealogy of ExxonMobil is documented in exquisite detail, and the petrochemical plant where Toussaint's father worked (production of adhesives, liner for rubber tires, isopropyl alcohol, pink flamingos) until the Christmas Eve explosion can trace its origins back to the Standard Oil Company of New Jersey and the Standard Oil Company of New York, one of the Seven Sisters oil companies, the miscreated oligopoly that monopolized the global petroleum industry for much of the mid-twentieth century, controlling almost ninety percent of the world's petroleum reserves.

On November 30, 1999, just as the last Millennium was grinding down like an internal combustion engine running out of fuel, while the planet was distracted by the impending self-made doom of the Y2K Bug, Exxon merged with Mobil in a $73.7 billion agreement — thus was born the ExxonMobil Corporation, a monstrous supercorporation. Boardroom applause and premium champagne for the newborn. ExxonMobil's corporate personhood was created and guaranteed under the same equal protection clause that would have applied to

Whipped Peter and other natural persons had the law been more than due process for petrochemical chimeras. Over time, the plant facility and oil refinery operations expanded around Standard Heights, devouring more and more land for the unknowable, poker-faced processes contained within: the ExxonMobil plant is proportionate to 250 Superdomes, because in Louisiana things are measured in Superdomes on the spatial scale, and in hurricanes on the temporal scale.

This merger, partly metaphysical and partly commercial in nature, of Exxon and Mobil was characteristic of the irrational exuberance that characterized the dotcom bubble, when the country underwent a euphoric technological mania akin to the Dutch's tulip mania when the price of a *Semper Augustus* tulip bulb fetched extravagant sums in the speculative bubble of the Dutch Golden Age. But you will never see a tulip willingly grow in Standards Heights. The merger of Exxon and Mobil reunified Standard Oil's two largest remaining companies, a bicephalic Janus-faced *lusus naturae* in the petrochemical bestiary. Economies of scale, consumer demand for a galaxy of petrochemical products, and the company's price-earnings ratio rewarded investors while those families living in the contaminated shadow of the plant counted their returns in ratios of births to funerals, Christmas Eve explosions to suicides-by-cop.

ExxonMobil is a city-state unto itself, with its own body of rules and oral traditions maintained by an order of petrochemical priests, and Toussaint dwelt in the Capital of that petrochemical city-state, the provinces of the industrial Versailles. A city-state once ruled by Trump's erstwhile Secretary of State, CEO of ExxonMobil, Rex Tillerson. ExxonMobil's Baton Rouge Refinery — one of the largest in the world and the first commercial fluid catalytic cracking plant — has an input capacity of 502,500 barrels per day, the material basis of the petrochemical feedstock that created Spanish Town's pink flamingos, and all other plastic immortalities that shall outlast us all.

From oil barons and petrol patricians such as Frank Phillips, of Oklahoma and Phillips Petroleum, and Herbert Henry Dow, of Cleveland, Ohio and Dow Chemical, which were like the mom-and-pop of the energy sector, arose the petrochemical plantations on which Toussaint's father worked, no less than his ancestors had worked the cane and rice plantations up and down another of Fisk's rivers. I cannot say for sure where Toussaint was on November 30, 1999 when the supercorporation ExxonMobil, that bicephalic juggernaut of the Mississippi River, was endued with corporate personhood and transformed the river into a Gordian knot twining and snarling around the bloody red stick that founded Baton Rouge, though he must have felt the electrostatic changes, the frequency distortions then occurring on the river side of Scenic Highway, behind the razor wire fencework defining the doleful edges and skeletal borderland of Standard Heights.

When the *Radio Free Dixie* broadcast suddenly ceased that mosquito evening in a hurricane of black static, and I heard now what had been there all along, layered beneath the Union dead poem: the faintly distant — but growing more urgent in its volume — warning siren issuing from the plant, a voice of corporate disquiet in the monster of petrochemical personhood that sent an odd-numbered flamboyance of pink flamingos scattering for cover into the green shadows of a banana tree. The plant was armed with several warning systems that were triggered during an emergency event, a haunting siren echoing in the mind long after it was gone, a sinister nocturne reminiscent of the air raid sirens wailing during the London Blitz when death rained from the sky. And, living in Spanish Town, so close to the plant's volatile and sphinxlike operations, one never knew for sure if this was a test or the real thing, but it was safe to assume the siren was not warning of a simulation of the Christmas Eve explosion that sent Toussaint's father west of the Mississippi. Sometimes the warning siren was accompanied by the loudspeaker voice of some overtime plant personnel, almost like an industrial aria, though I could never discern the words — repeated minatory mantras or petrochemical spells without much coloratura — of what must have been an inauspicious libretto. Ignore the warning sirens at your own peril.

I put down *The Birds of America*, turned to a ripped page, a print of the now extinct passenger pigeon, and tried to locate the provenance of the warning siren in the No Man's Land north of Spanish Town. I performed this echolocation each time the siren resounded through the still stagnant air, rupturing the humid quietude, but never accurately placed the siren's location, the warning seeming to shift with the direction of the wind and the currents of the present river. It was just an unspecific shrieking lament and automated ululation somewhere in the matrix of petrochemical space north of Spanish Town.

Although I often counted myself the only one, I have long

been a proponent of *solvitur ambulando* — it is solved by walking. What cannot be solved by walking is unsolvable. I have attempted to solve many problems walking the levees and deserted streets of Baton Rouge, and created many more problems in the solutions, have walked the humid miles to Tiger Stadium to see Alabama shut out LSU on a hot night in autumn. That was the year LSU fired head coach Les Miles and it felt like the city had lost a godfather. The city was still recovering from the flood of 2016: the continual righteous dismay of flooded homeowners when water flows where they do not want it, into the inconvenient places where they think it should not flow, as if water has ever obeyed the squandering freak whims of a species that decided it was a good idea to build his castle out of hydrocarbons. Every year the floods that fall are worse than the floods before, and I foresee no end to it. The land sinks a little more, a football field's worth into the vanishing point every 100 minutes. Flooded cars abandoned on the roadside, claims adjusters wandering through the damage and inspecting the havoc with a ruler, and the sodden and moldy interiors of homes turned out on the curb, the mountains of sheetrock and ruined building materials. I have been shown the past by the ghost of Huey Long, and the ides of our future by the ghost of Alton Sterling. I have heard the wolf-whistle in the toxic wind. I have seen the red stick driven into the heart of the Mississippi. I have heard the shrieks of vesper bats in the Pentagon Barracks, their black mass circling the Capitol tower at nightfall, their pings and clicks echolocating the movements of invisible armies in the Battle of Baton Rouge. I have walked around miles of yellow police tape, a body in cruciform on the bloody street. I have seen the river reverse course and twitch like an electroshock patient. I have seen rivulets die in the gutters, and the crucified river drown in its own blood. I have lost Toussaint, maybe forever.

But on this occasion, I did not follow the haunting sirens' petrochemical nocturne. I turned riverward down Spanish Town Road, the muscular branches of live oaks and magnolias dripping fresh notes of rainwater, passing two parrots in cages that recited the Union dead verses. Trashy, colorful beads were splashed around the thick stone neck of the statue of Huey Long, which I used as target practice for footballs — an immobile receiver running slow motion dream speed routes — until I learned that the Kingfish populist himself was buried beneath the monument after his state funeral on the Capitol lawn. The low cloud cover reflects the radiance of the refinery's mephitic splendor, that sulfurous black rose blazing just north of the State Capitol, and in the sage trees I feel the cooler oracles of wind coming inland off the present river — the waterline was high, a sign of the river's swelling avulsions. Rarely on these walks did I ever encounter another soul, except the statue of the assassinated Kingfish populist; downtown — a more desolate and blasted, postlapsarian wasteland has not been discovered — I walked by a homeless man holding a cardboard sign, written in jagged, zigzag letters: *I used to be someone.* Then again, maybe nothing is solved by walking — only meandering.

The riverfront at Istrouma Bluff has seen ships sailing under the flags of many nations, Native Americans, British, Spanish and French colonial ships, and the Republic of New Afrika. That was a day with many unexplained anomalies and unorthodoxies, not the least of which was Hunter Gracchus' death ship docked in the Port of Baton Rouge, right alongside the *USS Kidd,* a decommissioned Fletcher-class destroyer dry-docked on the east bank of the Mississippi as part of the Veterans Museum. An American battleship docked on the river — what was it but a preparation of naval forces for the coming siege which I felt to be on the cusp of tipping over into the vanishing point of no return? Of course, the Hunter Gracchus needed someone to whom he could unburden himself of the story of his hunting accident, and Baton Rouge — where the bloody red stick was discovered by explorers in the days when birdsong could still be beard on the banks of the river that was not yet bitter from the fallen star poisoning its waters — was a logical place to disembark and reconstruct the industrial accidents which were still recurring in Toussaint's cognitive map, as though the retelling could halt their recurrence. I was soon to be that person for Toussaint who seemed condemned by petrochemical forces beyond his control to wander endlessly between New Orleans and Baton Rouge, caught in the regressive mechanism of an industrial process flow diagram, retracing the stations of each restless ancestor, from one end of the self-repeating river to the other, and all the taxidermy rivers — present, past, and future — which could ever flux in Fisk's maps: a cartographic recordation of the total river's collective profluent memories, the millennia compressed into a single map image, from the day Pierre Le Moyne d'Iberville and his men came upon the red stick crucifying the river and fixing it in place to the timeless ice ages when woolly mammoths and dire wolves and extinct megafauna roamed the land which is now owned by the ExxonMobil supercorporation.

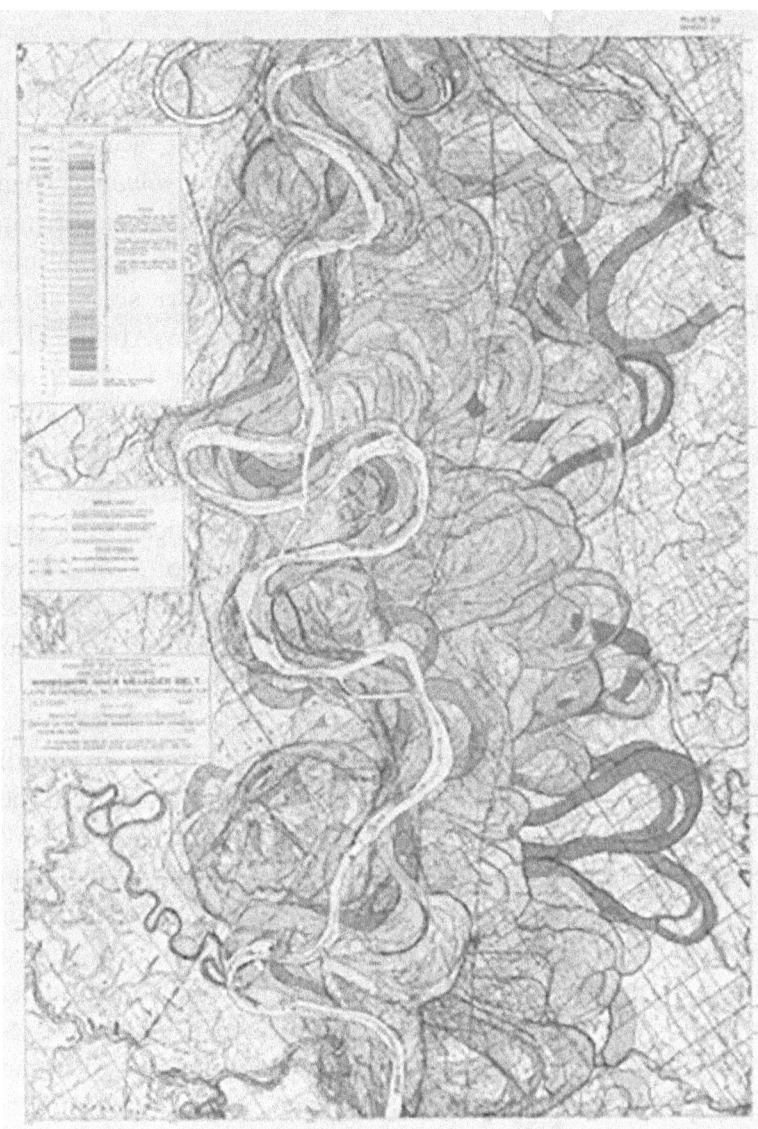

Every time I went to the present river, drawn as I was by the vivid permutations and cacophonous arabesques swirling in Fisk's meander maps and the wormwood fugue of the tugboats' doleful foghorns, I was startled anew, as if I had never seen them before, by the metal silhouettes of impressionistically humanoid figures arranged in strange attitudes and fixed postures suggesting agents who had an important message to impart and, at the same time, a necessary withholding of that immemorial message. The Baton Rouge riverfront was the sacred ground of a tribe of cast iron and aluminum androgynous figures, creations of the Icelandic artist Steinunn Thorarinsdottir, under the name of civic improvement or public art. Those figures cast in iron were a rich patina of rusty river brown, and those cast in aluminum glinted a strident silver that was harshed almost blinding white in the setting sun. Some of the figures sat apart or in couples, staring ahead with unseeing, vanishing point eyes at the down-flux of the present river to the Dead Zone in the Gulf of Mexico, where the ExxonMobil plant's toxic effluvia discharged, or catching the river by surprise when it reversed course and flowed against nature upriver; or those humanoid figures on the levee's green park benches who never took their alien eyes off the shadowy lands on the river's western bank where the casualties of the nocturne go.

This metallic tribe of sculpted hollow humanoids appears at politically sensitive sites all over the world, such as the United Nations headquarters in New York City, and they appeared in Baton Rouge in the tumultuous hazmat days after the Alton Sterling police shooting. But one of the cast iron figures had recently gone missing — a 400-pound statue, bolted to the bench, now at the bottom of the river, perhaps, or marched off in shirts versus skins phalanxes to fight the good fight. A nontrivial cash reward was being offered for the statue's return; so far as I know it has never been claimed.

While I sat on the empty levee bench, where the missing cast iron figure had once been, I was joined by a man — I recognized him as the same man I spoke with on Basin Street where Storyville and the Iberville Projects once stood — deboarding a riverboat that had just docked, taking his place among the sculptural metal humanoids. The riverboat was a bright sickly white with red trim and draped with patriotic flag bunting, the decks' Victorian scrollwork like spider webs or dreamwork jungle filigrees, the giant red paddlewheel in the rear dripping with wormwood river water. Other than a solitary figure avoiding the sun beneath a black umbrella who did not leave his post at the ship's stern, Toussaint was the only passenger to disembark at Baton Rouge, and it was not till later, standing with him outside of the abandoned, ghostly Charity Hospital, that he told me why he only traveled between New Orleans and Baton Rouge by riverboat, inefficient and inconvenient as that must have been for him: his ancestors had been imported here — like commodity cargo, like bananas, like contraband and fenced goods — aboard slave ships from Haiti and West Africa, and by riverboat through Mobile. What is more, as one of the few passengers on the riverboat, he was sure not to be pulled over and arrested, or worse, for "driving while black" on Interstate 10, patrolled by the grand goblins and dragons in the state police who seemed to think every passing vehicle was a white Bronco, the name on his license — Toussaint — an unwelcome relic from the region's French colonial heritage, a time before the Louisiana Purchase's Americanization when the tribes in Standard Heights' native street names were not yet at the vanishing point.

Rush hour traffic was at a standstill on the Horace Wilkinson Bridge, from which Ophelia jumped into the river. The Horace Wilkinson connected the east and west banks of the Mississippi, like cantilever steel stitches gathering two sides of a wide and universal wound. A man on the bridge, looking down at the long barges and tugboats passing on the water below, might not be jumping, he might be reading a eulogy for the pink flamingo or epicedium to the river, which died when the ExxonMobil plant's first chlorine gas ghost ship set sail. I watched the west bank subsistence fishermen angling for mutant catfish, wondering what piscine heresies from the wormwood bestiary they could possibly be catching. A flock of surveillance drones hovered over the river, the thousand distributed eyes of the petrochemical intelligence monitoring Toussaint's movements through the black gold refinery kingdom — drone videos of the river traffic would later be posted on YouTube, the machine wraiths and apparitional locusts that floated over the river from the purgatorial lands west of Standard Heights where Toussaint's father disappeared after the Christmas Eve explosion.

If what's past is prologue, then — ah, but one must beware these tricky if-then statements: sometimes the river will flow between *if* and *then*, separating cause and effect forever. The east bank of *if* on which Toussaint searched among the hazmat flotsam and jetsam for some particle of meaning among the diversiform probable primary causes of the Christmas Eve explosion, and the west bank of *then* where the disaggregated effects appeared and disappeared, backward and forward without any reference to a logical flow. I often suspected Toussaint, this riverboat man, was not born in the right time, but of course this can't be true, the time you are in must be the right time, necessarily and counterfactually, as the Mississippi has taken the only path possible given the countless permutations of geological variables, out of obeisance to the same ineluctable natural laws that governed the petrochemical processes effected inside the ExxonMobil plant, but Toussaint would say there is no right time for a black man, and he would be right, whether he lived under the regime of Petrochemical Modernism or some other.

I was standing between two of the anthropomorphic sculptures, one cast iron representing   black, and the other scintillating aluminum representing white, trying to determine to which of the two metal tribes represented by the two figures I belonged, as Toussaint approached from the dock, picking up the thread of our conversation, unhesitatingly, right where we'd left it on Basin Street, having parted ways there before being drenched by one of the abrupt and violent rain bombs that seem to be getting more frequent with every year's passing.

I travel between New Orleans and Baton Rouge exclusively by riverboat, just as in former times before the internal combustion engine, Toussaint was saying, as we walked, unconsciously in the direction of the ExxonMobil plant, along the hot black asphalt path of the levee top. I try to stay off the land in Louisiana as much as possible, he was saying, I can feel the land sinking millimeters at a time beneath my feet, subsiding infernally with my every step, it's very discombobulating to move across an apparently hard, resilient ground surface only to have it sink beneath your feet, there is an integrity to the flow of the river that I do not find in the land here, I used to feel something adjacent to grief for the land loss, for the unnatural passing of a natural system, but the river is transparent about its flux, the river says *I am transitory and deciduous*, whereas the land is only a verisimilitude of stability, the mendacity of the trickster land says *I am solid earth, I am stone and rock* but is no more permanent or everlasting than the dismal stone from which General Lee's monument in Lee Circle is quarried or the dream puffs of steam forming in ephemeral, pareidolic patterns over the ExxonMobil plant, Toussaint said.

Even as I write this, South Louisiana has completely disappeared in the petrochemical hauntology, as birdsong has been drowned out in the plant's warning sirens. All that remains of the Mississippi is Fisk's meander maps, the actual river with its industrial traffic of barges and tugboats subsumed by fictive cartographies, consumed and exhausted by the ExxonMobil plant, swallowed whole in one go by the quenchless Dead Zone.

Instinctively, I followed Toussaint, walking at his side as if we had agreed upon a destination or route before he deboarded the riverboat, and this harmony of action coordinating our independent movements — along the desire paths cut through the dead grass as if someone had single-handedly dragged many corpses across the ground — towards a distant but common terminus as we discussed the mechanics of process flow diagrams and the theories of thinkers such as Frantz Fanon or Albert Murray, two men whose writings have had lasting impressions on my way of thinking about the petrochemical regime. We walked up River Road towards the casinos, the State Capitol towering above the trees, turning inland away from the present river at a point Toussaint seemed to know in the depths of his memory palace and through the portal of the Pentagon Barracks — the courtyard centered by a waterless fountain. A strange geometric fort in the shape of a pentagon, which had been the site of official visits from Robert E. Lee and Abraham Lincoln when the fort was under the flags of the Confederacy or the Union, and before that still ambivalent conflict the site had been used by the Spanish, French and British in holding the river, for the flags here are as notoriously unstable as the river itself; I sometimes went to the Pentagon Barracks alone, pteropine metamorphoses flickering among the gas lamps, when I needed to get away from the warning sirens, though they were still audible of course, I could never wander far enough away from the warning sirens to silence them, or to see which flag was now flying above the fort, fat green lizards climbing the glowing white plantation columns.

I followed Toussaint out of the Pentagon Barracks, crossing through the English gardens growing wild and unfunded beneath the Capitol skyscraper tower, and north through Arsenal Park where antebellum blonde girls in white dresses pose for spring pictures, proms, engagements, graduations, all the ritual events marking passage from one of life's phases to the next. A few ragged palms and other torpid tropical flora seemed to list languidly in an underwater wind. Children threaded between us on the concrete path, playfully ringing the Liberty Bell, tolling the petrochemical hour, an uncracked replica of the real thing in Philadelphia where Toussaint's mother lived until the Siege of Osage Avenue. The replica Liberty Bell was aligned on the path so that the viewer, in order to contemplate liberty and all the highfalutin patriotic feelings that were supposed to be inspired by this uncracked replica, could not do so without the State Capitol building, Huey Long's populist tower in the swamp bayou Art Deco style, the limestone edifice looming in the background, and often wherever I went in Baton Rouge I felt the State Capitol building's panopticon effect, that I was seen by the governmental eyes in the tower's cupola but could not see them.

I followed Toussaint to the top of the earthwork Indian Mound, a sort of earthen bump or monticule in the park like the oyster middens gradually constructed by pre-contact coastal and island communities, which once served as a lookout point across the river, those from the *if* of the east bank to keep the eye of the Hand and Eye Motif open for hostile movements of the warring tribes from the *then* of the west bank. Now that the tribes were no more than forgotten street names, the elevated point in Arsenal Park provided us with an unobstructed vista of the ExxonMobil plant's cloud manufacturing operations reflected in Capitol Lake. From the elevation of this mound, with the warning siren wailing, I have seen the extinguished tribes rise from the cooling towers in the broken treaties of steam. The Indian Mound, eroded by time, must have stood a story or two higher than it is today, commanding a more exalted view in the past of a pre-petrochemical landscape, before the levees were built and Fisk's protean rivers were fixed upon a single course, all but lost to us now. A cannon points over the small Capitol Lake, the mouth of the weapon aimed at the ExxonMobil plant — ready to fire at the proper signal. It was atop the Indian Mound that I told Toussaint about the poem I'd heard that evening broadcast over *Radio Free Dixie.* He recited the rest of the poem's verses from memory, and when he got to the final verses, the ones about the Aquarium being gone and a savage servility sliding by on grease, our voices blended together into a univocal recital. Toussaint descended the Indian Mound first, children running up the mound on either side of us to play with the cannon, riding it like a horse and mouthing cannon fire explosions, and I too descended after first checking that the cannon was not loaded; for the rest of the way we talked about the sometimes refluence of recorded events that we thought were finished, Christmas Eve explosions that keep on exploding, how the Angola of the present can be as unstable as the land loss Toussaint had by now learned to stop grieving, interlacing our histories in a helical bond with a tropical provenance in the Haitian Revolution, the island from which Toussaint got his name.

Not till we stopped in Standard Heights, where Toussaint is perpetually re-arriving, vacant acres of unmown grass and open ditches, did I realize where he was taking me, this impromptu *Tiergarten,* a reserve of patchwork forest in the middle of the city strategically planted with hardwoods and deciduous trees that explode in livid color in late autumn. The rampant verdure of Standard Heights, the mature and spirited trees, each with its own charismatic or despondent personality, enveloped by miles of blasted concrete and heavy industry, reminded me of my hometown's Olmsted Plan, *A Park System for Birmingham*, the failed master parks proposal, an exercise in imaginary landscapes that was never built, the myopia of the city's business interests sabotaged any chance of having nice things. The scabrous streets of Standard Heights are little more than minor apocalypses of asphalt rubble, a decaying carcass like dead alligator skin, the broken glass littering the streets releasing a musical sparkling crunch underfoot. An epidemic of illegal dumping, shredded tires and bloody mattresses like distressed cries for help. Fire ant mounds that towered up to a man's ankles. In all the years I have been in Louisiana — so long now that I have forgotten why — since leaving my native Alabama, despite repeated efforts I have failed to pinpoint the refinery's exact location on the TOXMAP myself, only Toussaint with the refluent blood of Fisk's multitudinous rivers flowing in millennia of oxbows and a petrochemical jazz of motley loops through his veins could lead me through all the chlorine gas and the benzene and naphtha miasma to the petrochemical plantation. A tall security fence topped by silver helixes of concertina wire, but there is no sight of the refinery, which only shows itself at a distance, as if the closer one gets to it the more it disappears into a vanishing point of its own making — the most dramatic views are from the west bank of the river, in Port Allen, or from the Huey P. Long Bridge and the Horace Wilkinson Bridge, colossal aging infrastructures connecting the *if* of the east bank and the *then* of the west bank.

Toussaint showed me to the spot where the family home once stood, an overgrown area two blocks east of the ExxonMobil plant, that immortal crystal city, an emerald and mechanical metropolis from which emanated dire voices and siren warnings. I was raised by the concrete, he said. This is where the small room I shared with my brother once was, Toussaint recalled, pacing out the perimeter dimensions of the room in the grass, maybe ten feet by ten feet, a small suffocating room reconstructed from memory, and suddenly the walls of that house, a house which even in its afterlife still trapped Toussaint, rose up around him, and though we stood on dreams of grass Toussaint and I were instantaneously transported to the interior of that house, the walls enclosing us, and I could smell his mother's home cooking in pungent buttery wafts from the kitchen, a Saints game on the television, down by three points in overtime, the Saint-sations cheerleaders in glittering black and gold outfits on the side-lines and Toussaint's father no longer sitting in his chair now, instead standing in the middle of that remembered room between the kitchen and the television waiting for the Saints to inevitably disappoint him once more — the innovation and creativity the Saints exercised in losing a contest that favored them were a masterclass in snatching defeat from the jaws of victory, yet Toussaint's father could not turn the game off, he had to bear witness to the loss down to the last second, in case a miracle happened and the Curse of the Saints was finally exorcised.

The concrete was my father and the falling ash was my moth-er, Toussaint said, the one implacable and unflinching, the other tox-ic and dust-haunted. Each time I return to this house in memory, it subtly changes and morphs, in perpetual flux like the river — noth-ing unnecessarily disorienting at first, no profound changes to the overall concept, but still something is off as if someone has rear-ranged the house in my absence, a window set in a different wall, a door is moved, a floorboard that once creaked no longer speaks to me, a wall is painted a lighter or darker shade of off-white or stale cream, the light falling at a new angle, these remodeling transforma-tions are imperceptible at first, Toussaint said, but the additions and alterations, and in some cases subtractions where a door, window or even a whole room has been closed, begin to announce themselves in the aggregate as costly forfeitures of recognition until the family house is so unrecognizably altered by the heartlessness of flux that I no longer know my way about the rooms, he said, and I become lost, a stranger in my own house. I must be prepared, for the day may come when I am no longer able to locate my memory of the family house in Standard Heights at all, so that in order to preserve the original memory of that domicile as intact as possible it may be that I have to cease remembering it, each remembering also an alteration, a renovation — a door moved, a window bricked up, a room gone — as fingering an old photograph, even one in color, will cloud and ultimately erase the image one wished most not to forget, Toussaint said.

The family house faced the backside of a dead-looking strip club, Toussaint continued, channeling my attention in the direction of a low, ash-colored windowless cinderblock building silvered with arabesques of razor wire like shark teeth on a double helix, the girls dressed in little more than bathrobes and fishnets coming and going at all hours, hustling girls barely women named after girly drinks, Brandy, Martini, a girl whose actual name was Sex on the Beach, their hair in leopard print bonnets, their gaudy bedizenment like the multitudinous sapphires of the plant glittering in the night. I watched these otherworldly creatures from the family house's front window, the extravagant brawls in the parking lot over little more than an imagined offense to honor, sometimes a shoestring scuffle or less-er peanut rumpus that escalated into an all-out battle royal, a knife slashing in the sulfurous light, the blue and red police lights flashing on the cinderblocks, and my father forbidding us under unspeak-able lumps to ever go there. We were not to so much as look in the direction of the strip club, much less gawk at the fishnet girls and their nocturnal commerce. Long-haul trucks shipping strange and venomous chemicals to and from the ExxonMobil plant parked there overnight, he said, and were always gone by morning.

I waited for Toussaint to continue, to keep walking, but he was now, after so much planetary nomadism and digressive unset-tlement, where he needed to be, here in Standard Heights, at the location of where he grew up and the omphalos that centered his up-river and downriver meanderings, those intricate disentanglements of memory as wayward as the river was before it was chained up in the levees. Then I realized something about myself: if Toussaint had continued walking, to New Orleans, or even into the Gulf of Mexico's Dead Zone, I would've followed him. To Africatown or Rwanda, I would've followed him, to Osage Avenue or the aban-doned rooms of Charity Hospital and onto the dissection table in the autopsy amphitheater.

Often while waiting to deboard on the deck of a Mississippi riverboat, I think of the peregrinations of John Francis, the African-American environmentalist, banjo player and legendary walker, Toussaint said, though he was not always such a zealous ideologue of walking, there was a catastrophic event which he witnessed, changing his mode of movement forever: on January 17, 1971, Francis witnessed two Standard Oil Company tankers collide in San Francisco Bay, spilling 840,000 gallons of oil into the Bay, an environmental emergency, though some may call it an accident, that traumatized him and he vowed to never ride in an automobile or anything that used an internal combustion engine again, not even a city bus or in the back of a hearse. From that day forward he walked wherever he was going, like everyone did, rich or poor, before the invention of the automobile and its omnivorous appetite for the black gold in the ground. In a society which has almost forgotten how to use its legs, John Francis became a pedestrian pariah. The Christmas Eve explosion was like that for me, Toussaint said, that was my John Francis moment, as I call it, though I could not have known it at the time, two Standard Oil Company tankers colliding on the Mississippi River and irreversibly igniting an unchecked chain reaction of toxic events that patterned my life after the petrochemical personhood that was not of my choosing. Some people, those who have too little imagination perhaps to be compelled to change their lives by anything in the sublunary world of changeable and fickle elements, have what the churchy called a Coming to Jesus Moment — I had a Coming to John Francis Moment, Toussaint said.

Though Toussaint's birth was elsewhere, having been born downriver in the very hospital in which his father's autopsy was conducted after the Christmas Eve explosion, he grew up in the Standards Heights neighborhood of North Baton Rouge, just north of Spanish Town and the State Capitol tower, close enough to the plant to believe the smokestacks were the towers of a forbidden city. In all his meanderings away from the petrochemical center, Toussaint lived for a while in Atlanta, he said, a few blocks from the Ebenezer Baptist Church, and later in Houston's Fifth Ward working as a ghostwriter for hip hop artists, SoundCloud rap and vaporwave and the chopped and screwed sounds from the wards of Houston, eventually ghostwriting too for bigger names like Kodak Black,

Smokepurpp, and 21 Savage — all had lyrics ghostwritten by Toussaint, he'd been acquainted with Boosie in Baton Rouge before the rapper went to prison, and then from Houston he returned to Baton Rouge in time for the Alton Sterling shooting and Black Lives Matter after a Creole palm reader in Houston's Fifth Ward Frenchtown — settled by Louisiana Creoles displaced by the Great Mississippi Flood of 1927, an event that served as the catalyst behind the grandiose make-believe Rube Goldberg system of levees and spillways required to protect the petrochemical palaces in Cancer Alley — showed him the tarot card of the drowned Phoenician sailor.

I spent the next years working among the New Black Panther Party, Toussaint said, issues like voter intimidation and the announcement of a bounty for the capture or life of George Zimmerman, the murderer of Treyvon Martin. At the Triple S Food Mart, in my hometown, I watched the portrait mural of Alton Sterling going up, the gold grill glittering in his mouth like the smile of an ancient pharaoh, a memorial bouquet of dying flowers and rotting teddy bears piling up on the curb. A sort of shrine with votive candles burning for Alton's pointless death, the Triple S Food Mart is the last place on earth I would want to die, in the parking lot of a convenience store. Photographers from New York and New Orleans came to North Baton Rouge and took pictures of the place, so the rest of the world could see the crime scene and the blank, dead eyes of the teddy bears, but we had to live here. Technically, the Triple S Food Mart is not in Standard Heights, you have to cross the No Man's Land beneath Interstate 110 and dodge through some neighborhoods that are so down-and-out they have never seen better times, but we used to go there and shoplift, my brother and I, nothing that was Angola-level looting, whatever would fit into our hoodies, Toussaint said, pretending we were fugitives on a great heist, tiny hands swiping candy bars and canned sodas and Skittles because I was entranced by the rainbow colors, taking little fistfuls of the multicolored candies and eating them in the order of Roy G. Biv.

When I needed inspiration for ghostwriting, I read the works of the founding members — shall I call them founding fathers? — of the Black Panther Party, Toussaint said, Eldridge Cleaver's *Soul on Ice,* the beautiful and sad prison letters of George Jackson, which should be copied and pasted into the New Testament in lieu of Paul's pious whining — to me these were our true founding fathers, the founders of the Republic of New Afrika, not those cantankerous slave-owning white men of the so-called Enlightenment like Jefferson or Madison who founded some dystopian haunted carnival cruise line they called America, when tribes like the Osage were already here, he said. This is a country that tried to cast Julia Roberts as Harriet Tubman in a biopic of the Underground Railroad's heroine, so what do we expect? I wear the scalps of dead presidents, their blood trickling down my face and into my eyes, blurring my crimson vision. Stabbing others in the back, shooting myself in the foot. By indigenous techniques of lyrical détournement, I humble-braggingly reroute the satanic energies unleashed by the petrochemical nocturne. In these lyrics, I have borne witness — as if I had only been born to bear witness to things beyond my control — to the barbaric execution of not just Alton Sterling in the parking lot of the Triple S Food Mart, but Fred Hampton, the great Black Panther organizer slain by the Chicago police in a pre-dawn raid on the Panther's Monroe Street apartment. Again and again, as if unable to control themselves, the police reveal which bank of the river they are really on. The soul does not keep long on ice, not like Emmett Till's faceless body or the stone corpse of General Lee rotting at the eye of the storm that is Lee Circle, Toussaint said, looking south and downriver towards New Orleans. If General Lee's undead neo-Confederate bootlickers woke up, day after day, in a dingy rented room like Fred Hampton's, bullet holes in the wall, blood on the mattress, they might think twice about the terms of surrender.

From recurrent nightmares of the statue of General Lee in Lee Circle peeking above the high waterline of the flooded city, I myself have awakened in that very bed, where Fred Hampton lay dreaming his last dreams of founding a Republic of New Afrika, the wall behind me perforated with bullet holes like bloody constellations, the bare mattress sticky-wet with fresh black blood, and were it not for the bullet holes one might be so naïve, so American as to mistake the bloody mattress for a grisly post-coital, a botched birth, or just a prolific menstrual cycle. But the bullet holes in the wall belie the whip. Nothing is more American than a blood-soaked mattress and connect-the-dots bullet holes in the wall, Toussaint said, looking at the spot in the vacant lot where his own bedroom once was and he lay, beneath the bullet hole stars, on a salvaged mattress dreaming of distant, uncontaminated republics.

While the house danced and vibrated to the bounce music at the strip club, I connected the bullet holes into cosmic patterns of mythic asterisms, African warriors of the Gigantomachy forming alliances with the Osage or the native tribes of Standard Heights in the good fight against the petrochemical regime: the three bullet holes in a series forming Orion's Belt — Alnitak, Alnilam, and Mintaka — and Betelgeuse in the upper left, above the lamplight, and Bellatrix faintly shining to the upper right, the blood-soaked mattress black as the night above Standard Heights. I thought I saw the North Star twinkling in the bullet hole, but no one who grew up in Standard Heights ever followed a bullet hole to any kind of freedom that was not the afterlife freedom sung about in ancestral spirituals.

By the time the Saints football team had racked up twenty losses in only their second season, Toussaint said, my father was closely following the cases and fates of the Chicago Eight, for the disruptive mayhem they allegedly incited at the 1968 Democratic National Convention in Chicago, mostly to find out what would happen to Bobby Seale. My father was then living in Iberville when the verdicts of the Chicago Seven (Seale's case was dropped in a mistrial) were announced over *Radio Free Dixie*. Jubilee is a time you cannot possibly understand, Toussaint said, looking at me. Later, in my own time, we followed the cases and fates of the Jena Six. Always a city's name and a number. The Central Park Five. The Martinsville Seven. The Angola Three. The Standard Heights One. The Curse of the Saints.

My mother was more concerned than my father probably should have been that some of my crayon doodlings on the brown paper bags our crawfish came in resembled the courtroom sketches of the Chicago Eight. Unskilled portraits of the family in uncontrolled, digressive loops and writhing lines and crayon convolutions of whorled diagrams and impossible process flow diagrams. More than the unflattering family portraits, she was frightened by the crayon gripped in my tiny melted Skittles-colored hand because, although I didn't know at the time, these crayons in so many rainbow colors were made from paraffin wax, a soft colorless solid derived from hydrocarbon molecules that originated in the ExxonMobil plant. I drew how I thought the ExxonMobil plant must work, a child's sincere but simple engineering, phantasmagoria of pipes and chimeras of chemicals, all draining the life from Standard Heights and turning the river bitter. Only, at that young age, I'd never seen Franklin McMahon's charcoal drawings, adding acrylic watercolor effects later, of the trials of the Emmett Till murder and the Chicago Eight, Bobby Seale bound, gagged and shackled, facing a charge of contempt of court after being denied his constitutional right to defend himself. Seale is drawn full-bodied, with a corporeality missing from the ghostly curvilinear silhouettes of white courtroom factotums no more substantial than ExxonMobil's manufactured cloudworks. The proceedings had to be drawn because a courtroom photographer would keep judge and jury on ice. These transparent bodies, composed of shadowy squiggles and spineless loops — nightmare incubi of nooses and coffins writhing with venomous snakes. Every child in Standard Heights, born with a gag in the mouth, understands what it means to be handcuffed to a chair, unable to move even as the water rises to one's neck.

After the big city photographers went home to their big cities, I left copies of Fanon's *Wretched of the Earth* and *Black Skin, White Masks* at the Triple S Food Mart memorial to Alton Sterling. The cops needed them more than I did. The Department of Justice had not yet announced whether charges would be filed in the sacrificial killing of Alton Sterling, but I didn't need them to make any such announcement, I already knew the outcome. So I returned to the memorial again at Triple S Food Mart, this time leaving a copy of Huey P. Newton's *Revolutionary Suicide* in the arms of a rotting teddy bear. I was trying to decolonize my own mind, Toussaint said, at no time did I ever forget that Louisiana is the backwater province of a failed colonial empire sold to the United States though it wasn't theirs to sell. Stay cock-diesel. Blood will burst from turnips. The King of Zulu blows chemical bubbles from a golden trumpet. No pale faces behind the concertina wire. The graveyard shift is 24/7 in Standard Heights. I got out of Houston before Hurricane Harvey hit, haven't been back since, but the next one, a petrochemical storm like the eye of Jupiter — they should name it after Alton Sterling or Fred Hampton. Hurricane Sterling, Hurricane Hampton, the ensemble of spaghetti models forecasting major landfalls of wormwood storms and chlorine gas ghost ships in Louisiana, he said.

Toussaint's restive meanderings — Houston, Baton Rouge, Atlanta, Boston — were a personal decolonization process, like John Francis' dromomania — how could he not when Standard Heights and Iberville were reduced to rubble? Less than rubble: rumors of rubble. The petrochemical regime's work here had been so thorough that no place existed to which he could return home except the memory palace crumbling in his mind, the windows of the palace boarded up, bullet holes in the wall, the street strewn with dumped tires and bloody mattresses — but the indestructible petrochemical plant where toxic chlorine gas ghost ships and pink flamingos were manufactured endured long after the Christmas Eve explosion.

We never opened the windows, Toussaint said with a finality suggesting he still did not open windows. Opening a window in the house was the worst possible offense against my father's adoration of order I could have committed, and at any rate, even if I wanted to open them, the windows were either painted shut with a viscous black paint or sealed forever with the ultimatum of my father's no. In springtime, when the air was a heavenly balm and not the putrid Book of Job boil it normally was in the long hot summers, it didn't matter, the window stayed closed, not even in August when it was so hot the walls sweated did they open. For a long time I didn't know that windows could open, Toussaint admitted, had never felt the whispering zephyrs blow through the house on a crisp, cool day, those rare times — despite their rarity the memory of them is sharper than the muggy, sluggish, sultry days that never seemed to end — when the humidity was at a humane level and the thin, wispy almost translucent scritta pages — for when I held the pages up to the sunlight the fiery words on the following page bled blackly through like a secret message written on wet toilet paper — of the Bible I read outside on the porch did not warp and dissolve in my fingers, and when I saw other houses, mainly those outside of Standard Heights, for all the other families in Standard Heights obeyed my father's rule, with their windows open I was both in awe of this transgression, but also terrified by the freedom, Toussaint said, stepping around a homeless man on Hiawatha Street. There was, of course, a reason for my father's prohibition against the windows, but I was not yet old enough to understand it.

I have returned many times to Standard Heights in search of the house Toussaint says he was raised in but the neighborhood he remembers eludes me like a zero-sum game of hide-and-seek. From Spanish Town, he who would find Standard Heights must first pass through Arsenal Park, the sentinel oaks seeming to menace and follow you with their arboreal underworld shadows, thence to Capitol Access Road by the Governor's Mansion, turning north on West Highway Drive, passing the mid-century neighborhood where political lobbyists and state representatives' homes overlook Capitol Lake, turning briefly riverward on Leesville Avenue, then brusquely north again up Sorrel Avenue through a frightening industrial area; from there one carefully crosses a series of three railroad tracks and athwart Choctaw Drive, continuing north on Sorrel, then east on Chippewa Drive where the streets are named for vanquished Native American tribes and chieftains, and the fences crowned with silver lacework of concertina wire around the ExxonMobil plant begin and some security guard in a windowless room watches your every move on a grainy little monitor with video input from the plant's surveillance camera network. But these are just the directions, by cardinal points, through the physical environment and are of no use in navigating the nonlocal metaphysical infrastructure which so transfixed Toussaint. Anyway, as he said, the family house where he grew up in Standard Heights is long gone.

ExxonMobil has succeeded in buying out the houses of every last family in Standard Heights, Toussaint said, except east of Interstate 110 where the blocks of houses are mostly intact, these houses were spared the strategic buyouts and the bulldozer when ExxonMobil's engineers' assessments concluded that Interstate 110 would act as a mitigating barrier in the event — only a matter of time — of a catastrophic failure at the plant. An explosion, a meltdown, a revelation. But for those who were bought out of their homes in Standard Heights, resettling elsewhere, some sticking around Cancer Alley and others leaving the state for good, though the payout was more money than they knew what to do with, like those casino gas station ticket scratchers winning the Powerball, many of these refugees from Standard Heights were what is now known as *unbanked*, and so the buyout, which at first appeared a once-in-a-lifetime windfall, a ticket out of Standard Heights and away from the warning sirens and the storms of chemical ash, was only the first setback. One householder fell to his death from the roof of the Ace Hotel in New Orleans. Another drowned in the Mississippi, his bloated body found wrapped around the ghostly pole of a dead cypress tree. One went blind staring at a solar eclipse. Another killed in a grisly hunting accident in Devil's Swamp Lake. One taken by flesh-eating bacteria after swimming at Grand Isle. All scales are deadly here, the microscopic as well as the macroscopic, bacterium and celestial mechanics — even with the ExxonMobil payout in hand, the plant's noxious jurisdiction never let the former residents of Standard Heights go, Toussaint said.

Standard Heights was not decimated all at once. That would be too noticeable. The removals and buyouts were phased over many years. A house here, a house there. No one but the remaining families — and they were fewer by the time I was old enough to be aware of the world on the other side of Fisk's river — notices the vanishings. An entire Standard Heights block planted with sunflowers, the giant cycloptic yellow and gold crowns the only blots of color in that industrial moonscape. The ExxonMobil buyout program, funded with endless cash flow, commenced the planned evanescing of the neighborhood, one house at a time. As the families moved out, physical and administrative geographies changed; the census tracts enlarged as the population density decreased. Broken Windows Theory was practiced and made real by the buyout's managers who had never been to Standard Heights themselves, had never seen the Mississippi River except maybe from the window of a private jet. The buyout created vast hazard zones, a No Man's Land where man's self-important presence was a monumental absurdity, an illogical folly, like Flanders Field, which all these years after the wartime imperialist destruction was wrought has bloomed with red poppies. Flanders Field's trees, the ground stripped of all vegetation or green signs of life, were like the ghostly poles of dead cypress trees in the backwater swamps of Fisk's rivers, Toussaint said, his dispossessed gaze drawn now towards the river on which we heard the low, melancholy notes of tugboat horns.

No more the intrepid, noble Age of Heroes I read about in the State Library, from Hercules to Saints quarterback Drew Brees, an age superseded by the Age of Oil and the Age of Plastic, the age of inconsequential and imperishable taxidermy, Toussaint said. In this way, in the stygian shadow of the ExxonMobil plant, which also supplied the distant and more privileged cities of the East Coast with gasoline, we lived at the point of origin, the generative cradle of our petrochemical civilization, where all of Petrochemical Modernism's *vanitas* products, gadgets, gizmos, appurtenances and consumer goods were manufactured from the raw crude inputs drilled mercilessly from the dead ancient seafloor: diapers, chewing gum, makeup, ink, upholstery, bicycle tires, dresses, cassettes, motorcycle helmets, compact discs, curtains, vitamin capsules, skis, tool racks, mops, umbrellas, roofing, denture adhesive, speakers, tennis rackets, nylon rope, water pipes, shampoo, guitar strings, antifreeze, combs, heart valves, enamel, anesthetics, fan belts, refrigerators, floor wax, sweaters, dishwashers, caulking, food preservatives, cortisone, dyes, life jackets, car battery cases, yarn, toilet seats, linoleum, rubber cement, candles, hand lotion, luggage, football helmets, toothbrushes, balloons, crayons, pillows, artificial turf, movie film, golf balls, ballpoint pens, boats, nail polish, petroleum jelly, basketballs, purses, deodorant, pantyhose, rubbing alcohol, shag rugs, epoxy, insect repellent, fertilizers, fishing rods, ice cube trays, electric blankets, milk jugs, trash bags, roller skates, paint rollers, aspirin, ice chests, sunglasses, parachutes, artificial limbs, folding doors, soft contact lenses, shaving cream, toothpaste, football cleats, insecticides, fishing lures, perfumes, shoe polish, footballs, oil filters, hair coloring, lipstick, dice, house paint, soap, shoes, transparent tape, shower curtains, tents, telephones, cameras, bandages, drinking cups, ammonia, and the toxic hosts of other petrochemical products that were supposed to make our lives easier, safer, more convenient, more fun, more fulfilled, more and more and more, Toussaint said.

Even the ink — here I am on the rim of saying *the word of God* — used to print the gospels was processed in the ExxonMobil plant, and the Bible's pages were the same stuff on which the profane words of the Christmas Eve explosion accident report were written by engineers and industrial safety consultants who had not been there themselves, working the midnight shift — mother did not like him to call it the graveyard shift — in the plant as my father had. This ink could be used to write a revelation, a suicide letter, an affidavit, the text of the petrochemical nocturne, he said.

Toussaint named all these phantasmagorical products as if reading, in the somberly metered cadence of a eulogy, names of the dead from a ledger, and as I knew he wasn't enumerating all the possible products of our petrochemical civilization, a cosmic bazaar without beginning or end, by the latent mechanism of some reflexive association I recalled the dark wall of the dead chiseled into the Vietnam War Memorial where I had once been to see the total effect of so many names for myself, my own defamiliarized features reflected through them in the black granite, the names repeating like binary code till they were no longer the names of individual people, but inert matter and senseless loss, a claustrophobically oppressive sensation of dumb numeracy not unlike the rising stultification of the sheer gravity of all those recited petrochemical products weighing mightily on my conscience — many of them I had used with unthinking convenience that very day — like the crushing water above a sunken shipwreck, the words chiseled layer upon layer in the black stone like unregulated garbage in a forgotten landfill.

Of all those mysterious products, some utilitarian and some fanciful, which began their lifecycle within the industrial dreamworld of the ExxonMobil plant, the product which stood out the most, Toussaint said, was ink. Without ink — no Treaty of Dancing Rabbit Creek, no Emancipation Proclamation, no signed surrender at Appomattox, no novels of James Baldwin. I looked around myself, Toussaint said, and the sphere of influence of the plant and Standard Heights expanded to encompass the entirety of the observable ecumene. ExxonMobil's reach was inescapable, even after they bought out the house and the family split up and moved away, I was still surrounded by an inarticulate and baleful requiem of petrochemically derived objects, the linoleum floors you walked on, the very clothes on your back, the tires on the car you drove to get as far away from here as possible, the movies you watched to escape it all, the drugs you took to forget everything, the fishing rods you used to catch poisoned fish to feed yourself, the sweater you pulled over your head for the cold snap, the football you threw into the mists, the used washing machine my father bought my mother to make her life a little easier, the particolored polish she applied with a small brush to her nails, the toothbrush we used to make our teeth gleam white in our skulls, Toussaint said, all were made inside the plant.

The ExxonMobil plant was apotheosized into a generative, ubiquitous godhead from whose agonies and throes the world as we know it was formed, producing the plastic wrap rage that plagues the Occident every time a consumer tries to open a plastic-wrapped good — in vain, as few of life's petty frustrations will more quickly and vividly trivialize the human project than wrap rage, the nugatory futility of wrestling with heat-sealed plastic blister packaging and hinged clamshell containers bursting with raspberries and blueberries, fruits that looked juiced up on steroids. Sometimes the plastic packaging fought back, and my mother once cut herself trying to open a tamper-resistant plastic package of light bulbs to replace the bulb that burned out over the kitchen sink. She had a reputation around the house for breaking the light bulbs in these wrap rage struggles with the plastic packaging and my father kept heavy tin snips to cut open such recalcitrant packaging, but they'd recently been used to cut sheet metal for house repairs and were nowhere to be found, my mother resorting to a boxcutter to surgically remove the bulbs from their mortuary plastic, slicing her fingers open and bleeding all over the bulbs. Why do they wrap things this way so that they're so hard to open? I asked my mother. So you can resist the temptation to shoplift, she said. To put you in your place, my father said. The red lipstick my mother wore — what must that have tasted like the only time I ever saw my father kiss her? The black pantyhose that covered her legs for the only time I ever saw her wear them at my father's funeral just after the New Year. It was as if my mother was a female mannequin chemically constructed by the petrochemical imaginary, Toussaint said, everything we had originated behind those malign miles of security fences delimiting the ExxonMobil plant from Standard Heights, and in this way the plant's petrochemical products were value-added into the most intimate places of our family life, the end users in the planned product lifecycle, and the language of value *chains* and consumption *chains* and supply *chains,* when I first heard these slave master phrases of corporate catechism uttered by buyout managers, all betrayed that our own lifecycle was just one feeble link in these abstractly modeled chains, chained as we were to the petrochemical perpetual motion machine, Toussaint said, stopping now to listen to a portentous voice he had picked up on, with his Standard Heights ear, long before I had noticed it.

A dystopian, mechanical voice resounded through the hollow streets of Standard Heights, and only by deep listening was I able to locate this voice as issuing from the plant's public address system. Some superintendent or plant safety officer releasing another warning to plant workers. It was this disembodied, technocratic voice that first evoked the sinister homologue between Standard

Heights and Thereseinstadt, as I'd then been reading H.G. Adler's *Theresienstadt 1941-1945: The Face of a Coerced Community*, in the pages of which Adler describes the bureaucratic expropriation of assorted property for a concentration camp: "The property entered in the title registries and land tables…will be expropriated with suitable compensation…and after 31 May 1942 will become the property of the emigration fund for Bohemia and Moravia. [Exceptions are made for real estate and furniture holdings belonging to the Reich or the Protectorate and] property that directly serves the practice of religion. [Compensation will be made] for expropriated property and businesses, for resettlement costs, and for unavoidable loss of income connected with the resettlement. The compensation will be paid in cash if not otherwise agreed." Compensation was duly made. Adler goes on to cite the source of the compensation, as it appears that in this zero-sum world one gains anything, or otherwise nothing at all, only at the expense of another: expropriated Jewish property.

"The orders necessary to carry out, implement and supplement this order are to be issued by the Reichsprotektor….The commander of the Security Police for the Reichsprotektor…will take the measures necessary to construct the Jewish settlement, through administrative channels. He can issue orders that deviate from the laws of the Protectorate of Bohemia and Moravia."

Oh, those ominous ellipses — what lies between those elisions, the triad of black dots, what horrors has Adler spared us from? When I shared these disturbing parallel passages of Adler's study with Toussaint, he seemed to be remembering some traumatic episode from the time when the family home was still standing, for ExxonMobil's Reichsprotektor had visited the family home one day, during dinnertime, to make a buyout offer, issuing orders that deviated from the laws of Louisiana and the United States. Once a flourishing center of Jewish culture, Thereseinstadt was ghettoized for propaganda purposes, a sort of Potemkin legerdemain for the Nazi's true activities of extermination in more remote corners of the Reich. The camp was touted as a spa town for older Jewish retirees, a terminal point beyond which no one would be transported, where they could live out their days in small town peace and rustic comfort. The Reich completed the illusion by reserving this ghetto for more illustrious and prominent Jews whose disappearance the Reich could not risk on account of attracting too much international attention.

Composers and professors and musicians and the like from the professional and intellectual classes. As Adler's ominous black ellipses grew more strident in the plant's warning sirens and metastasized into the chemical symbologies of the manufactured cloudworks and toxic ash from the smokestacks, I wondered what petrochemical legerdemain was behind the ExxonMobil buyout program of the family homes in Standard Heights.

What the other expropriated families of Standard Heights did with the buyout money I cannot say, Toussaint said, but as the area became cordoned off by tall perimeter fencing with hostile warning signs yelling exclamation points and tortile concertina wire one certainly felt enclosed within a concentration camp, a coerced community at the very least, and I remain as convinced now as I was then on the question that presented itself by all this razor security wire: was ExxonMobil trying to keep intruders and trespassers out of the plant or ensure that no one in Standard Heights ever escaped, except the feedstock for all those petrochemical products I saw in the stores, everything individually and brightly packaged in unending cavalcades of functional units, Toussaint said.

I must have been fiddling with my camera for too long — I was planning a shot of the spot in the vacant lot where Toussaint said the family house had once been before the expropriations — for when I looked up Toussaint was gone. This was his way, coming and going at a moment's notice, the river's doppelganger essence of flux. I was now alone in Standard Heights, in the middle of a vacant lot, and soon it would be too dark for taking pictures.

I cannot reproduce for you photographs of the ExxonMobil facility as they would have appeared from the vantage of Toussaint's memory-reconstructed house that day we rendezvoused at Fisk's river and I followed him to the stark green void of Standards Heights. Turner's *The Burning of the Houses of Lords and Commons* and *Fire at the Grand Storehouse of the Tower of London, 1841* must suffice as illustrations of the plant's soul — a crippled, spidery silhouette encircled, as by a magic circle, with barbed wire. For anyone who has not seen the ExxonMobil plant up close, all of this must surely strain credulity, but nothing can be done until the petrochemical police policy changes: photography of the plant was forbidden, enforced by a network of surveillance cameras and a private security patrol that would seize your camera and destroy the film, so it should come as no surprise that all the digital photo-documentation — if you Google image search the refinery — are aerials or taken from a safe distance. In a state of widespread, unexplained industrial accidents, this is no accident.

Despite the prohibitions against photographing the plant, still I tried to get as close to the petrochemical facility as I could. I followed Scenic Highway — there is nothing scenic about this highway, demarcating as it does the industrial world of the plant where Toussaint's father worked from the residential sections of Standard Heights — passing Chippewa and Osage Streets, Navajo and Mohican, the magic names of the vanished tribes. I turned towards the river, onto a private street — an aggressive alarm sounded and the security gate through which I entered closed behind me. A police officer stepped from an unmarked vehicle and approached me in that slow, authoritative crawl of southern lawmen who can take their time. I looked much like Van Gogh in his self-portrait of 1889, the blue phantasmagoria of unhinged arabesques and oneiric swirls in the background, the intensely honed gaze stalking the viewer, and so if a police officer saw such an unlikely man meandering the grounds of a heavily guarded petrochemical plant integral to the nation's energy infrastructure security, he might be justified in stopping to ask him what he was about. After aggressively searching and photographing my satchel, which I always carried with me, finding only some papers and books, the officer filed a written Homeland Security incident report, noting that I was a writer — he'd never heard of me — and a few weeks later I received a call from the FBI's New Orleans Counter-terrorism Division. The plant's private security detail had escalated my case. The FBI investigator was much more civil than the ExxonMobil cop, but I knew this to be an investigate method to make me comfortable enough to open up to a faceless authority, to yield my secrets and everything Toussaint had told me. After all, I could have been interested in the plant, not for historical or academic reasons, but because I was an environmental terrorist, one of those "tree-hugging nut jobs" who sabotage industrial equipment to take us all back to the Stone Age. Tree hugging, I would say, elevates hormonal levels of oxytocin, releasing a unique chemical blend that contributes to holistic sensations of wholeness, repose and belonging. After an airless and awkward pause that was long enough to sound fishy, I took the phone to the window of my apartment in Spanish Town — I had been flipping again through the pages of *The Birds of America*, studying the contorted taxidermy pink flamingo when I received the call from an unknown number — and noted that the pink flamingos in the courtyard had moved and were now facing away from the warning sirens then playing the regular evening petrochemical nocturne. Without saying anything that would implicate myself, I listened to the nocturne, wondering if he could hear the warning siren on the other end of the call, from his bureau office down in New Orleans. Photography of the plants is strictly forbidden, he reiterated. Something about critical infrastructures and the security of energy supply chains. Remembering what Toussaint had said about every child in Standard Heights being born with a gag in his mouth, I explained my business at the Exxon-Mobil plant to him, that I was looking for evidence of a ghost ship. He rendered all the correct verbal cues of cordial and professional assent but sounded unconvinced, maybe he thought I was a little crackers, but the FBI agent let the matter rest without further inquiry.

The Dreamwork of Petrochemical Modernism

It wasn't long before I saw Toussaint in the New Orleans Museum of Art — yes, it must be him, I thought; no one else has that dignified profile, the way he held himself like the proud son of a pharaoh — standing quietly and pensively before a glossy photograph of brightly colored consumables whose chemical constituents might have been processed in Standard Heights, where the streets are named for vanished native tribes. The museum tombstone label, at the bottom right, identified it as the work of Andreas Gursky, one of a series of large format c-print photographs of supermarkets and big box retailers' interiors, the shelves lined and arrayed like so many geological strata, the spectral and meticulous Tetris patterning the splashy puerile color palette of a children's jungle gym or playground equipment, because we're all children at heart, and because marketing mavens on Madison Avenue still believe that bright colors encourage us to buy things, comforting us in the long vacuous hours between a need and its fulfillment, an omnivorous need which can never be satiated by all the commercial clutter produced Petrochemical Modernism. Like an insentient liquid, we fill the limits of the container we occupy, a consequence of over-built, overly roomy houses: too many spaces whose voids must be filled with the clutter and surfeit of a material culture now on the brink of self-destructive insanity. Neither was the unchecked clutter unique to the middle-class of south Baton Rouge, Toussaint had said that first time I followed him from Fisk's river through Arsenal Park to Standard Heights, even the unbanked and pauperized of Standard Heights, in substandard houses bandaged in Tyvek wrapping and sheet metal had second-hand junk spilling out onto the yards and forming vast territories of rusting junkyards like a transfer station for the Goodwill and the Salvation Army, there were houses on our street, Toussaint said, so replete with the crappy miscellany and derivative rummage of the second-hand economy that we did not know who lived in them, the front door was inaccessible, the front yard was part cemetery, part landfill, medical equipment and car parts strewn everywhere, a manmade labyrinth of unusable junk, the most impractical futility one could imagine, and for which there is no known cure, my advice would be to put down *The Wall Street Journal* or *The Complete Tweets of Donald J. Trump* and take seriously the nightmarish claustrophobic vision documented in *Life at Home in the 21ˢᵗ Century*, a study of the material culture of petrochemical suburbia, lest we asphyxiate on mass produced rubble, Toussaint said.

I knew exactly the material culture he was describing, had grown up in its midst in Alabama's taxidermy museum of rural dialectic, the dentist chair on the front lawn, the engine block beneath the magnolia, the random mélange of tractor parts and unserviceable farm equipment, all kept for some obscure purpose, a junkyard of means without ends. I stood next to Toussaint, spellbound by the gaudy petrochemical aura of this mesmeric but deadpan photograph for some time before he noticed me, the photograph taken from a slightly elevated perspective hovering like a ghost over the store aisles, though nowhere is the store's floor visible, two shoppers — cut in half at the torso by the top shelf — lost amid the rabble of riotous color, though almost lost to the viewer as well, vanquished as they are beneath the onslaught of merchandise and impedimenta, all the chattel of Petrochemical Modernism's frenetic output, the photographic frame squeezing center and periphery into a single unified but fraught shot, visible to Toussaint and myself, standing outside the photo, but to the shoppers on the supermarket floor the center and the periphery were concealed. Nor was it apparent to them that there was any way out of this commercial maze: the shelves appeared as steps of a ladder one could climb out of the picture only to the viewer. The aisles' endpoints, the exits are curtailed by the photo's borders, cutting off any means of ingress or egress, rendering the aisles inescapable, and the two shoppers, alone on their islanded aisles, unaware of one another, are trapped in the shopper's solipsism of gross domestic product. Petrochemical Modernism has engineered the ultimate particolored labyrinth. The photograph was colossal, the freighted supermarket shelves scaled up to the dimensions of 19th century landscape paintings or the epic tableaux of classicism, the canvases depicting great battles and coronations, or episodes in the history of the Roman Empire — some 6 feet in height, 10 feet in length, so that one could walk along the floor of the museum gallery at the painting's edge, just close enough that the guard would not stop one, as if walking the aisles of the store depicted in the photograph, however I noticed in the reflection of the photograph — a glossy acrylic surface that blackly echoed our translucent shadows moving over the store — that while the museum guard did not prevent me from peering closely at the photograph to examine its intricacy of detail and the colorful texture at close range, so close that center and periphery evaporated in the totality of a single item on a shelf, shadowed by my own hooded silhouette, scrutinizing the c-print for some flaw or evidence of brushwork, as I do before any painting, she did step in and, though she asked civilly enough, requested that Toussaint please maintain a respectful distance between himself and the photographic surface.

At first, Toussaint froze, his shadow no more than a cobweb falling over the aisles of petrochemical products. This was no polite suggestion or neighborly request, it was an institutional command disguised as a recommendation, an *or else* backed by the museum guard's hip-holstered sidearm. I knew that if Toussaint did not treat the guard's ultimatum as an invitation to regard the photograph from a more correct distance, a request that was not made of me, the museum's security apparatus of guards and art world thugs would be mobilized and I would find myself alone in the museum gallery. I thought of the ExxonMobil security guard, the prohibition against photographing the plant — ostensibly for the purpose of national energy security, to keep the GDP flowing — and wondered what they were hiding. Though a part of me — that part which also wishes to knock all the gleaming petro-products from the shelves of Gursky's supermarket — did not want him to, Toussaint wordlessly complied, stepping back from the hanging photograph at the same time that his reflected, darker other took a step deeper into the store aisles, retreating from the center and back into the unmapped peripheries.

Embarrassed, I forthwith walked away from the photograph, as if leaving the supermarket itself after a bitter altercation with the manager — the price of a banana — or another customer — the scarcity of the final banana. Gursky's photo elicited in me something beyond plastic-wrap rage, to run down the aisles, both arms out like a child trying to fly, swiping all those goods from the shelves, sending them scattering by the thousands out of the frame of the photograph in an avalanche right at the feet of the museum guard just as I had wanted to take a picture of the ExxonMobil security guard before surrendering my camera. I wondered: had we been in an actual supermarket, and not looking at an artistic photographic representation of one, and Toussaint had approached the shelves' stock in a menacing way, perhaps violating some unspoken code by getting too close to inspect the label on a bottle of soap, to examine the ingredients of a stick of deodorant, or any of the other petrochemical products whose supply chains passed through the ExxonMobil plant, would the store's security forces have asked him to take a step back, to not get too close, implying some veiled threat, lest he find out something that was supposed to be kept secret from the consumer at the supply chain's other end?

Toussaint remained fixed before the supermarket photograph, at an exaggeratedly safe distance, a mockery of compliance, unable to read the labels or inspect the ingredients of the products on the shelves from so far away. The photographic image of the store tantalized, promising nothing more than what glimmered on the surface, no unplumbed depths, no profound mysteries, but somehow that was enough: sometimes the surface contains plenitudes. The security guard would not leave the gallery, Toussaint reluctantly moved on from the photograph of the store aisles, and in the next gallery, of the dozen or more pictures hanging on the wall, he selected but one and instinctively made a beeline for a dark painting of Native American refugees marching through a familiar landscape of swamplands. Spanish moss hanging from the trees, the humidity palpable in the air. The Native American at the march's vanguard carries a European musket over his right shoulder, perhaps traded in exchange for beads or pelts, items made by hand, nothing mass produced in petrochemical supply chains. Not our plastic Mardi Gras beads either, but handmade beads. Toussaint leaned forward to read the painting's title, *Louisiana Indians Walking Along a Bayou, 1847*, exhibited at the Paris Salon in the year 1848, at the Académie des Beaux-Arts, the museum label said — never before had Parisians, the   cosmopolitan beneficiaries of colonization, seen the human costs of their North American empire.

I've seen this painting many times, Toussaint said, and despite this repeated exposure I still cannot completely plumb the totality of its meaning, though I know why the natives are marching, I do not know from where they are coming nor where they are going, nor what they expect to find when they get there, and though the climate and landscape could not be more different from this Boisseau painting, I think of Franklin's lost expedition, all those white Europeans wandering aimlessly through the Arctic, all because they desired so insanely and as if possessed by satanic energies to discover the coordinates of that mythical Northwest Passage, the navigational shortcut from Europe to the Pacific Ocean and on to the Orient, but aren't shortcuts always like that? Aren't imaginary shortcuts always fatal and disastrous for the shortcuts' believers? The Franklin expedition ended as every venture of white Europeans did: in calamity, fiasco, and cannibalism, every endeavor undertaken by white Europeans has flopped and ended in a bungled farce or a hecatomb of nightmares, the crew aboard the *HMS Erebus* and the *HSM Terror* only a microcosm of what goes on in the greater Occident, the anthropophagy of the crew crystallized the cascading failures, over many centuries, of the Occidental experiment which is now in its most decadent phase in Petrochemical Modernism, as you can see for yourself in what little remains in Standard Heights, and these Native Americans in *Louisiana Indians Walking Along a Bayou, 1847*, one of the natives armed with a European firearm, wandering through the bayous that in the next century would be irreversibly polluted with the skull and crossbones effluvia and toxic discharges of the petrochemical industry, flee the material pressures of a rapacious and unconscionable new way of life, Toussaint said, one built on supply chains and manacling the river in levees and transforming everything before it into process flow diagrams. No wonder the native at the front of the march carries a European musket for self-defense against the cannibalistic urges of the very European who traded the weapon.

Toussaint's voice — speaking so authoritatively and blithely of cannibalism, of white Europeans eating one another in the cold out of the insane desperation of hunger that drives one to consume the flesh of one's fellow proto-capitalists — the serious tenor of this voice, speaking of such direful things, again drew the attention of the security guard, who was indeed armed like the European who traded the musket to the marching native, as in our era of mass shootings I often find myself unconsciously assessing the location of exits and reading the room for who may or may not have a weapon, and so we left the natives to continue their interminable march and I followed Toussaint to the next picture on the wall, the west wall of the room I believe it was, the picture was Alfred Boisseau's *Flood on the Mississippi* depicting the rescue by rowboat of a family stranded on the roof of their house, a painting which is dated 1896, the museum label indicated, many decades before the construction and celebrated opening of the Spillway, the engineering marvel that was supposed to protect us from the *Flood on the Mississippi*.

Before painting *Flood on the Mississippi*, Alfred Boisseau left Paris for the New World, settling in New Orleans, we read on the painting's wall placard. Why anyone would leave Paris for Louisiana is a mystery to me, Toussaint said. Richard Wright and James Baldwin fled to Paris because they knew the cannibals were constructing the petrochemical labyrinth around them and that if they tarried even a moment more it would be too late and there would be no way out. Now, it's too late, the exits have been sealed. The rooftop of that flooded house could be any house in Standard Heights, Toussaint said. What was constructed by the oil company could also be deconstructed. Standard Heights was a company town built for workers by Standard Oil at the turn of the last century. Standard Heights is over for me, no one has any reason or desire to ever go there again — a vile place that should never have existed, as it is not true that the world is better off with such places existing, another mendacity of the petrochemical psychology, as so many of Standard Heights' survivors will have you believe. I never believed either, as my superstitious father religiously did, in the Curse of the Saints — they were just a poorly coached, average football team that made a living snatching defeat from the jaws of victory. Voodoo dolls of head coaches like Rick Venturi with a .125% win percentage accomplished nothing but they made you feel better about another preventable loss. The Curse of the Saints is a bogeyman like the jigaboo specter of the black superpredator created by white abnormal psychology — too much benzene in the brain — to frighten their children, Toussaint said.

After another comically bad Saints loss, my father once told me about one of our forebears, he loved more than anything to talk, mostly to himself, about the storied deeds and derring-do of those who came before him, an enslaved person named Gordon from the west bank of the river — a region unknown to me at the time — who because of the severity of his whip scars became known as Whipped Peter, Toussaint said.

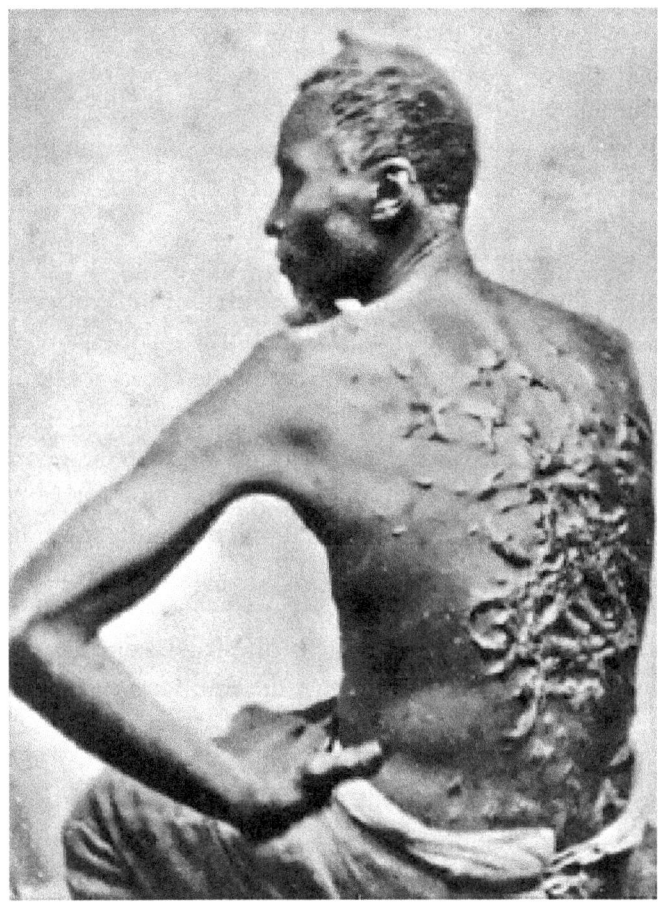

In the days before the petrochemical plantation engulfed the globe in plastic, Gordon escaped from a plantation on the west bank of the Atchafalaya River in St. Landry Parish, a Parish still run by the plantation mentality, and to evade detection by the slave hunters' bloodhounds — the master's minions of the multi-headed Cerberus guarding the underworld to prevent the dead from escaping — he masked the scent of his trail with the stink of raw onions, so that my mother could not chop or cook onions without conjuring for me the snarl and menace of those hellish, nasty bloodhounds. I hated the dogs more than the slave owners. Even the stray dogs that hung around the back of the strip club, rutting and fighting, I avoided, systematically. If the madeleine was for white people with prodigious memories, then onions were for escapees who could not forget too soon. Three months after the Emancipation Proclamation, when freed slaves were joining the conflict, Gordon enlisted with the Union Army, offering his services as a guide through the Confederate swamps and bottomlands, rising to the rank of sergeant in the *Corps d'Afrique,* then perishing in the Siege of Port Hudson. I have no idea how my father knew so much about so distant a forebear, but his deportment during these recitations of family history was such that it was understood he was as serious about this as he was the Curse of the Saints. Before my father acquainted me with Gordon from the river's west bank, I could not believe we were afterbears of enslaved persons — I could not say the word *slave*. My tongue could not utter the basic units of the word's sound, the phonemes and morphemes that when put together in the right combination were a man deprived of his liberty by another man. Others of our enslaved ancestors, my father said, Toussaint went on, turning again to the Boisseau painting of the Mississippi flooding its banks, could be found buried in the Kugler Cemetery, at least when the Spillway was closed — when the Spillway was open millions of gallons of the Mississippi River flooded their gravesites, a small price to pay, the Spillway engineers reasoned, to save New Orleans and other Cancer Alley settlements from catastrophic flooding, Toussaint said.

For a long time, I was transfixed before Boisseau's flood painting, a white church steeple peaking above the dark floodwaters like the mast of a sinking ship, and as Toussaint told me about Whipped Peter and then the Spillway and the incredible force of nature he witnessed crashing the control gates, I thought I saw active ripples or currents circulating in the painted floodwaters, no longer a static surface, yes there categorically were watery movements on the surface, and I saw the water rising steadily and immeasurably up the white church steeple, Fisk's river filling the frame with unstoppable and nonnegotiable floodwaters.

You've never seen water till you've seen the Bonnet Carré Spillway opened after a seasonal upriver event that triggers the opening protocols, my father said. When my father took me for the first time to see the Spillway opened I realized water is a mercenary, unsentimental, and matter-of-fact state of nature, a force unto itself bordering on the metaphysical and more than the rusty brown discharge that coughed from the tap at home. Floodwater trivializes everything in its way, Toussaint said, looking in the direction of the river's west bank where Whipped Peter and Charles Deslondes rested. Tamed in a glass, water is the last naught of summer. The drowned Phoenician sailor's body washing ashore. They say water is supposed to be the source of life, but in Louisiana water will kill you, whether by flood or flesh-eating bacteria, poisoned waters for which there is no alexipharmic bearing toxic sludge and waste, the great dead zone in the Gulf of Mexico that is gobbling up the sinking land of this state one centimeter per year — Louisiana is a place where a worst-case scenario can come true and everyone throws a block party. I grew up at the edge of the Gulf of Mexico, by a bipolar river that fed the Dead Zone, growing larger by the year, yet did not see the Gulf until the mouth of the river spat me out like a bad taste in its mouth. From the barrier islands, barely above sea level, I was horrified by the offshore oil platforms, floating cities burning in the night, islands of infrastructure ringed with fire, the air shredded by the cacophonous sea shanties of the seagulls. For the first time, I saw the infernal infrastructure that drilled the oil and sent it upriver to the ExxonMobil plant to be processed according to the flow diagrams in the Christmas Eve explosion accident report, Toussaint said, the alpha and the omega, refining half a million barrels per day.

The Spillway has left nothing untouched. The ground surface upon which these ancestors — a mythical people like the Alaskan Yupik or Choctaw — walked is now buried under several feet of muddy, nutrient-rich sediment. Other times, when the Spillway was not scheduled to be opened, we walked those enigmatic grounds, and I imagined that I could feel their suspirations and putrefaction beneath my feet. I imagined the Spillway opening without warning while my father and I were yet in harm's way, the great and mighty waters crashing the control gates and overtaking and burying us with these enslaved ancestors of whom my father spoke with more familiarity than he talked to his coworkers at the plant about his own family.

To construct this Spillway, which required the planned flooding of the enslaved persons' gravesites, the Army Corps of Engineers expropriated the land on which our ancestors grew sugarcane for the Hermitage Plantation, while the levees blocked the ancient view of the river from the floodplains so the sugarcane workers' descendants like ourselves could forget about the river, one could live one's entire life on the former grounds of the Hermitage Plantation and, unless one climbed to the summit of the levee, the highest point for miles around, never see the river. The engineers constructed amnesiac levees to make us forget that the river existed, and that black bodies bound in chains had been transported on it, Toussaint said, taking note that the Boisseau painting's water level was rising to precarious levels inside the frame.

Since it was built, the Spillway has been opened a total of eleven times — in 1937, 1945, 1950, 1973, 1975, 1979, 1983, 1997, 2008, 2011, and most recently in 2016, Toussaint said, and I have no doubt that as the earth continues to undergo anthropogenic adverse changes to its weather systems the Spillway will be opened many more times, maybe even a day will come that the Spillway is never closed and my ancestors' gravesites are permanently flooded. My father traveled from Standard Heights down to St. Charles Parish each time the Spillway was opened, a ritual event which like solar eclipses and comet returns came only once every decade or more in periodic cycles, and he considered it a sort of familial rite of passage to take me with him down to St. Charles Parish — a place I could've lived without visiting — not only to see the Spillway opened, and the floodwater roar over our enslaved ancestors' gravesites, but to *hear* and *feel* the powerful onrush of voluminous water crashing the bays like undead horses out of Revelations. The Spillway waters, once unleashed, rushing headlong and ineluctable just as designed, washing away every antediluvian thing before it, like history itself in one vicious torrent filling Lake Pontchartrain. And unlike the river, the Spillway's linear release could not flow backward, the whole point of the engineering was to channel the floodwaters unidirectionally into the lake. The violence of such water is difficult to fathom, like scores of Trojan Horses.

He instructed me to close my eyes — I did — and see the Spillway flooding the slave cemetery not with the facile sense of sight, which shackled us no less than the levees manacled the river, my eyes the same color as the Mississippi, limiting our vision to only what Petrochemical Modernism allowed us to see, but with some superior, ancestral, and transcendental sense that aspired to whatever working man's conception my father possessed of art: Hokusai's woodblock print *The Great Wave off Kanagawa*, the crest of the wave's claws bearing down on the Japanese fishermen, Mount Fuji — there are no mountains within sight of the Spillway or Standard Heights; the earthen levee, built by the Army Corps of Engineers is the most mountain-like piece of topography I had seen up till then — framed within the wave's circular crest and utterly dwarfing the distant mountain, the print capturing that fragmentary instant of the wave's finale before it crashes, never to reappear, yet leaving incalculable destruction in its wake. The opening of the Spillway that day — and that opening would not be the last time, as the river fattened and surged on my father's blood that leaked in the funeral home accident — only confirmed for me that an indignant, rogue deity dwelled in the Mississippi River and sometimes his ire caused the river to crest and spill over its banks and flood the ancestral cemetery, Toussaint said.

I don't remember exactly the year my father took me with him in that rite of passage to see the opening of the Spillway, whether it was 1979, or 1983, but it could not have been 1997 as that would have been too late, by then I would've been too old to have any interest in watching so much river water diverted through flood-protection gates to save the sinking city where my father grew up in the Iberville Projects, and 1950 was out of the question as a temporal impossibility, all I know is that I was young, and they opened all 350 of the bays, moving 350,000 cubic feet per second of water, Toussaint said. I could not fathom that much water. You expected archangelic opera to play as the gates opened. The whole spectacle of the opening is an overly melodramatic curiosity for the local community, a sideshow, as morbid rubberneckers will gawk at a grisly car accident or gunshot victim drowning in his own blood on a street named for some Catholic saint or extinct native tribe. The engineering itself is fairly simple, basic enough for a child to understand: the opening is accomplished by lifting 7,000 wooden beams arranged in 350 linear bays with a rail-mounted gantry crane that slides across tracks on top of the concrete Spillway structure. Several thousand people assembled across the concrete slopes of the outlet, sitting in foldable lawn chairs, grilling and barbecuing, like tailgaters revving up at an LSU home game. A second line brass band played familiar jazz numbers. As the first needle or pin was pulled from the Spillway structure, and a gash of water trickled out, the crowd cheered and applauded — finally something manmade in Louisiana worked as it was supposed to. The opening of the Spillway was a public event of complex emotions for my father, exultant and somber, and with his lapsarian personality this was not simply an engineering event happening in Cancer Alley, but a Biblical inundation about which mythic hymns would still be sung millennia hence. My father expected me to feel something in the presence of this manmade deluge, which happened so seldom, but the truth is I felt only a mild interest and hunger for a hotdog, Toussaint said while I inspected Boisseau's painting for any changes in the waterline rising up the little white church steeple, the painted waters now pressing and surging at the painting's frame like floodwaters challenging a levee. I looked around to determine whether the security guard had noticed the threatening floodwaters rising inside the painting, but this alarmed her less than Toussaint's proximity to the Gursky supermarket photograph. The volume of water in flux through the Spillway causes it to vibrate and tremble violently, Toussaint said, still feeling those vibrations rattling the dice in my bones today, and there are those among the onlookers gathered on the levee who thought — some no doubt hoping — the Spillway structure might collapse, that the Michoud fault would awaken and topple the Spillway. Even the levees, Toussaint said, which protect the living from the angry riverine deity, are burying grounds. The Irish excavated the canals in New Orleans, slaves were too expensive to lose to yellow fever or malaria, and when the Hibernian levee-builders perished, the dead were buried in the levees, which became flat-topped mass graves, in this way the dead, in the most literal way possible, defend the living from the fate of those in Alfred Boisseau's painting of the deluge, but the dead defend the living from death by water only at a dear price, Toussaint said.

Whipped Peter was not the last of my father's amateur genealogy, his endearing efforts to make himself feel better after a Saints loss. If my father's allegorical family histories are to be believed, we hailed from a family of resistance fighters, renitent souls who fought the good fight with the 25th United States Colored Infantry, defending New Orleans from being retaken by Confederate zombie forces, and the 54th Massachusetts Infantry Regiment, authorized by the Bureau of Colored Troops, General Orders No. 143, for there must be a bureaucratic protocol even for the inclusion of armed Negroes in the battle against the Confederacy, though this could be a screen memory masking another subsurface memory, like photographic negatives overlaid one on top of the other, obliterating the identifiable individuality of each image, contaminated memories playing games with one another to hide from their accusers, hiding from the hellish bloodhounds so as not to be found out and reconciled with the officialdom of an all persons fictitious disclaimer, and I came to realize that perhaps my father's idea of ancestry was more fantastical and ecumenical than my own, but he would not have thought it was the son's place to judge the father. But in all other things he was a very literal man — when he said don't open the windows, he meant don't open the windows — and what he said was meant to be taken with the literalism that the fundamentalists and evangelicals brought to bear upon the more outlandish passages of the Bible, interpreting Ezekiel's vision of the floating wheels as demonic spaceships or ancient UFOs. Things that were not to be believed under even the best of circumstances, not even in the best of all possible worlds, which was worlds away from Standard Heights, Toussaint said.

Of everything my father told me, I believed nothing but the most rudimentary surface contact with cross-referenced, fact-checked truth — that our ancestors were buried beneath the floodwaters of the Spillway; that Whipped Peter was a forebear, much less that he ever existed; that he escaped from captivity and disguised his scent from slaveholders' bloodhounds with onions; that he joined the Union Army and fought against the Confederates; that he endured and survived all those whippings — until I discovered tucked into the pages of *The Negro Motorist Green Book* a reproduction of the glass plate portrait of Whipped Peter, his back deformed with ridged keloid scars that reminded one of the cratered, scarred surface of the moon or the industrial canals cut through the swamps and marshes below New Orleans. This *carte de visite* of Whipped Peter was utilized as fodder for the Abolitionist cause, and I was haunted by the savage cicatrices on his back, often dreaming of them spelling out some cryptogram on my own back. Even the pictorial realism of this reproduction I began to doubt, until I found bureaucratic, enumerative proof of Gordon's existence: Gordon was enumerated among the plantation's male chattel slaves in the 1860 census, and the census record, written in a white man's handwriting, in facsimile form in the State Archive, the original either long lost to time or moldering in archival storage in Washington D.C. Records of the deed of sale of forebears such as Gordon and Deslondes had to be somewhere in the State archives too, Toussaint said, but I never found them. For the deed of sale, for a black man searching for his beginnings, is the moment where an ancestor is born through formalized bureaucratic recognition, nothing is real in this country unless it can be deeded, a recorded exchange between buyer and seller, prior to the deed of sale there is only the ghost ship's manifest, unless it can be tabulated and counted in columnar form for all time it does not exist, before tabulation there is only the scattered entropy of runaways and spillways, Toussaint said.

The Boisseau flood painting could no longer contain the storm surge and once the frame gave way like compromised levees the painted floodwaters poured from Boisseau's painting and onto the museum floor, carrying the white church steeple with it, spreading and pooling across the gallery hardwoods, then rising up the walls in petrochemical watermarks, filling my shoes with wormwood floodwaters and draining away through the floorboards as quickly as it came.

When the security guard who had shooed Toussaint away —
like a fly from the dessert — from the Gursky photograph stopped
watching us as if we might somehow assist the Louisiana Indians in
armed revolt, or shoplift all we could from the supermarket shelves,
as if on cue we evacuated to the next gallery, leaving the floodwaters
on the floor for the guard to mop up. The Boisseau flood painting had
not stopped leaking out of the frame and there was some concern we
might be washed away in the floodwaters. Again, I followed Toussaint instinctively, attached by an invisible umbilical, this time to an
anthropomorphic sculpture like one of the Mardi Gras Indians of the
Seventh Ward. Behind us, I could hear the Boisseau painting's floodwaters surging onto the museum floor, a natural sound amplified
by the echoing stillness that is unique to museum galleries, almost

cadaverous in their quietude, rendering the softest movements into uncommonly vivid shotgun blasts. A velveteen footfall amplified to an almighty stomp. A creamy and satiny swish of a skirt magnified into a hurricane-force wind. The susurrus of one's breath before a masterwork heard as if blown from a final trumpet. The dilation of a pupil before a well-lit painting becomes a solar storm.

The security guard had followed us into the next gallery, leaving the floodwaters to inundate the floor — Toussaint pausing before a work titled "TM 13," one of Nick Cave's bizarre Soundsuits: full body sculptural costumes recombinantly hybridized from a ghillie suit, a space suit, and shamanic headdresses, some covered in coruscant beads and others patterned like the quilts of Gee's Bend. This sparkling anthropological artefact — an excavated and restored ceremonial costume from one of the hundred and more tribes of the Mardi Gras Indian Nation.

Cave's first Soundsuit, the museum label informed the viewer, was created in response to the 1992 police brutalization of Rodney King, an event that, like the O.J. Simpson police chase, every child of my generation remembers — my earliest memory of what the police state's lackeys like the ExxonMobil security guard can do even with the cameras rolling. The security guard eyed us with cynical misgiving, as if at any moment Toussaint might put the Soundsuit on and overthrow the art museum in some radical black power uprising against the museumification of Petrochemical Modernism.

I lived in a world of rambunctious color and lurid pattern on the edge of a brown river, Toussaint said. I remember the old men of Standard Heights at Mardi Gras wearing similarly outlandish homemade costumes out of found objects and castoff materials, though of cruder construction than the finessed products of Nick Cave, their entire bodies covered in polychromatic buttons and beer bottle caps from the beers they'd drunk all through the previous year, Toussaint said. My own father started a Mardi Gras costume like this, of beer bottle caps and other fun-looking junk salvaged from around the empty lots of Standard Heights, though he did not get a chance to finish it before the Christmas Eve explosion, Toussaint said, his voice ringing discordantly in the empty gallery.

Against all reasonable evidence, the juxtaposition of Toussaint against the Soundsuit so violently unnerved the museum security guard that Toussaint was finally asked to leave. Instead of worrying about the museum filling up with floodwater released from Boisseau's painting, the guard was escalating our case to the museum's central security desk, having decided that Toussaint was a threat to the Soundsuit, just as the ExxonMobil security guard had escalated mine to the FBI's Counter-terrorism Division. Maybe Toussaint had, when I wasn't looking, put on the Soundsuit — I didn't see any such thing, but I could not let Toussaint be expelled alone from the art museum, so I followed Toussaint out of the museum and into City Park, under the dappled dark cooling beneath the storied Dueling Oaks, so-called because of the Creole swordsmen who met there to defend some droll and daft code of honor. One of the museum's miniature red trains passed by, a child in the last train car pointing knowingly but without any discernible reason at Toussaint. In the museum's sculpture garden, walking in the footprints of others pressed in the crushed gravel paths, we passed by a bronze sculpture of Botero's corpulent and opulent women, the surplus cellulite on the petrochemical body. We stood beneath the bronze and steel abdomen of a nightmare-sized spider arching over us on eight spindly legs, and I thought I saw the legs twitching, the spider ready to eat us. City Park's immensity only strengthens the illusion that one is not in a city, but in a sylvan surrealist painting. Darkness was growing in the trees, and museum staff were corralling visitors through the gates of the sculpture garden. A few token stars blistering the firmament, and one loses any sense of the terrene. I turned to say as much to Toussaint, but he had vanished down a gravel path beneath ancient mossy oaks and was gone from my sight, disappearing into the swirling fog coalescing into an armada of chlorine gas ghost ships.

The Petrochemical Symbols of the Hazmat Placards

One azure afternoon in the fall — the Saints had lost yet another embarrassing, lopsided game — my mother caught me rubbing wild onion on myself, Toussaint said. She stopped me at the door of the house, sniffing the air with suspicion, Why do you smell like onions? she asked, Toussaint said. I hadn't thought she could smell it, so deadened generally were her olfactory senses by the pervasive naphtha and benzene odors permeating Standard Heights. What do you think I said was my explanation for the onion-rubbing? Bloodhounds, I told my mother, Toussaint said, and she looked at me as if I'd said the n-word itself. Wait right here, she said, and I knew what was coming. This was worse than opening the windows. For the windows could be closed again, the genie put back in the bottle, but the bloodhounds could not be thrown off the scent of my 14th-amendment-created person; after that my mother whipped me so hard with an orange electric cord that I could not sit down without pain for days, and I walked awkwardly across the ExxonMobil-cleared lots as if straddling a horse. Thought the whipping left no permanent physical scarring, only emotional river wounds, this was my transformation into Whipped Toussaint.

While my mother made gumbo or hung the soppy wash from the clothesline, our clothes hanging like sodden ghosts in the moonlight, I memorized the ideographs of the Globally Harmonized System of Classification and Labelling of Chemicals, that system of hieroglyphs for oxidizing liquids, corrosives, explosives, compressed gases, acute toxicity, skin corrosives, skin irritants, aspirant hazards, environmental and aquatic hazards, and the transport pictograms for flammable gases, liquids and solids. I mused over these arcane chemical symbols and badges of Petrochemical Modernism's occult hazards like the motifs of Southern Death Cult tribes I'd seen in the State Library: the encircled swastika motif, the quincunx motif, and the Hand and Eye motif — an open eye gazes critically and unsentimentally out from the palm of a brown hand.

Brooding from the closed window of a shared bedroom, or if my father wasn't home the cracked window of the living room, which later doubled as a parlor and grieving room for the funeral, I counted the trucks muscling through Standard Heights with, in the place of the usual U.S. DOT hazmat placards featuring the chemical symbols, the motifs of the Southern Death Cult on the back of cargo tanks that drove in and out of the ExxonMobil plant. A cargo tanker with the Hand and Eye motif placard parked on Mohican Street from the 21st to the 23rd of December the year of the Christmas Eve explosion. The skull centered in the diamond diagram also appeared on the hazmat placards on cargo tankers and trucks that dieseled through the Native-American streets of Standard Heights in the gelid, stinging days after the New Year celebrations, a nocturne of fireworks shimmering in descending dying embers on the black river. Mere coincidences perhaps, but with the river separating the east bank of *if* from the west bank of *then* where the slave hunter's bloodhounds waited to snarl at runaway enslaved persons, cause and effect were as confused in disorganized entanglements as the different layers of Fisk's rivers.

I began tabulating the symbols' appearances and assigning meaning to them, Toussaint said, the symbol for oxidizing liquids was like a flaming hoop through which circus animals jumped; the exclamation point was the sudden mark of punctuation after God's statement to Abraham to bind and sacrifice Isaac, the only Biblical story my father knew to threaten me with if I ever opened the house's windows; the symbol to the diagonal left of the death's head was the hand of the Hand and Eye motif being corroded with acid wormwood, Charles Deslondes' amputated hands; and the symbol to the left of the skull was the planet exploding after taking a direct hit from Halley's Comet, Toussaint said looking up at the sky-colored welkin densely knotted with thunderclouds. I saw the Hand in Eye motif spray-painted on the wall of a building on Osage Avenue, and placed my own palm over the hand and the motif fit like a glove, and when I pulled my hand away the eye in the hand's center opened and blinked, and I saw what my father meant for me to see when he instructed me to close my eyes and envision more than could be seen with them open: the Spillway flooding the cemetery wherein the bones of our bones lay.

Certainly, the Osage tribe placed this ancient motif on the brick wall of the housing projects where my mother once lived, so that I might find it and, in the placement of my hand over the motif's hand, see what the Avenue's Osage saw in the final moments before the wave of Manifest Destiny crested and they were annihilated. But not only at Osage Avenue: the Hand and Eye motif appeared as if branded into the flesh of the black-streaked stone of Charity Hospital, like the branded hand of Captain Jonathan Walker whose palm was scarred with *S.S.* which I believe stood for Slave Stealer, as a reminder, every time he opened his hand, of his involvement in a conspiracy to smuggle slaves out of Florida to the West Indies, Toussaint said.

For my part, I wondered whether I would ever do anything noble and doughty enough to warrant having *S.S.* branded on my hand, I said to Toussaint.

Again and again, Toussaint said, on the native streets after the Christmas Eve explosion there passed an endless exequy of hazmat trucks — these trucks were elevated so high above the ground that a child such as myself could not see the drivers, so that they pursued their destinations as if driverless, like the headless horsemen of Standard Heights — bearing, in the place reserved for the government-required chemical placard, the Chi Rho christogram and the Hand and Eye Motif, mysterious messages in petrochemical hieroglyphics from the river's west bank.

Although I have spent most of my life sweating for no reason as if paying penance for the villainies of others, freeze events do occur at this subtropical latitude, reminding us that water, not always liquid, can form in more than one state. On the night of the Christmas Eve explosion, my first thought was for the Spillway freezing. And in the night, encrusted with crystalline moonlight, the petrochemical plant was coldly, whitely transformed into a twinkling Winter Palace, residence of the murdered Russian monarchs I read about in the school library. I should have known that the bullet hole stars were aligned in malign asterisms, because it snowed the night of the Christmas Eve explosion, fat flakes descending like white shadows in the bitter breath of the dark, which I interpreted as a validation of the glacial cosmogony of Hanns Hörbiger's *Welteislehre,* which posited ice as the most basic element determining all cosmic processes, one of the more improbable theories I had encountered in a book about Aryan mysticism — crazy shit white people believe — but the night of the Christmas Eve explosion made me fear that Hörbiger had been right in his gelid suppositions. At first, we thought the whiteout of snowflakes must be the chemical ash that so often fell upon Standard Heights, blown into the sky from the smokestacks of the plant, except this whiteout melted before my father's body had even been identified — the deathless chemical ash did not melt.

You may know the common states of matter as solids, liquids, plasmas and gases, Toussaint said, but the states of matter in Standard Heights are not so simple. Four states of matter felt too limiting and did not correspond with what I knew about the river, there must be a fifth state that was being produced in the petrochemical experiments inside the ExxonMobil plant, some Frankenstein that was part solid, part liquid, part plasma, part gas and part some fifth state of matter as yet unknown, petrochemical superfluids and liquid plastics, unearthly plasmas that behaved like solids, and gases that behaved like ghost ships, exotic commercial applications of Bose-Einstein condensates and degenerate matter, quasi-particles and quantum fogs, in some phantasmagorical petrochemical brew for even more fantastic goods than the plastic pink flamingos of Spanish Town or the supermarket products in Gursky's photo. But something had gone wrong, Toussaint said, very wrong, somehow this petrochemical experiment in new states of matter had suffered a grave miscalculation or human error and caused the Christmas Eve explosion.

I saw the Mississippi River in all four states of matter: a turbid brown liquid churned by barges in the industrial summers, a polyvalent plasma when it was aflame with the setting sun, a gaseous wraith when the chlorine gas ghost ships drifted from the west bank, and a cruel and impassive solid when it turned to ice in the winter freezes. Christmas Eve, in my state of anxiety that the *Welteislehre* might be coming true, I imagined the Spillway like an engineered ice sculpture, the rushing roar of water frozen in midair like the strings of a hyperborean harp suspended as musical icicles. Don't worry about the Spillway, my father said, thinking of an event even more improbable than snow falling on Standard Heights, the story repeated just as his grandmother told it, albeit with more ice than a glass of sweet tea from the governor's mansion, about how the Mississippi River froze in 1899, for she had been there in St. Charles Parish, not far from the *Mandingo* plantation, on the levee that wintry Valentine's Day, which happened to be Mardi Gras that year, to see something which had not been seen since the last Ice Age when mastodons roamed Orleans Parish: icebergs floating down the river from St. Louis, where upriver Mississippians, as my father called those who lived on the river whether they lived in Mississippi or not, walked on water from the east bank to the west bank of the river, the icebergs sliding in glacial glissandos by the river towns — Memphis, Natchez, Vicksburg, places that to me sounded like imperial palaces, the ship-sized chunks of frozen river passing too the historic world-changing spot where the red stick was found at Scott's Bluff, the sugar cane plantations in the shadows of their frozen oaks, the icebergs floating unbelievably beneath the cathedral spire in Jackson Square and reversing d'Iberville's voyage all the way to open water in the Gulf of Mexico, the icebergs melting into the ever-growing Dead Zone.

Whenever my mother felt in the Middle Passages of her bones the imminence of a hard freeze, which came in January or February, we rushed to swaddle the banana trees and fig trees in anything we could find: plastic trash bags, tarps, bedsheets, sweaters, quilts, blankets and towels. We wrapped the pipes with bedsheets or home-made blankets and left the faucets dripping. My brother had a habit of disappearing when it came time to prepare for the hard freeze, and to make up for this absence I took my mother's preparations for the severe cold a step further, wrapping the trunks of ExxonMo-bil's oaks with bedsheets and quilts that I had never been told were the Quilts of Gee's Bend, passed down to my mother from relatives in the hamlet of Gee's Bend, Alabama, the sharecropper women who quilted bedcovers for warmth in the unheated shotgun shacks of Wilcox County. The ExxonMobil trees — beeches, oaks, syca-mores — all wrapped at the trunk with these colorful, errant geo-metric patterns. The hard freeze, prolonged by a moody planet, may have contributed to the Christmas Eve explosion, as the cold that winter sealed pipes and conduits in an icy vise that was not calculat-ed in the system's design parameters. That was the winter the birds of Standard Heights were gone for good. In one of the lots cleared by ExxonMobil, the house was long gone, but they left the sundial and a bird fountain standing in the yard. The gnomon of the sundial tracked the diurnal movements of the empyreal lamp, and at night the moonlight so refulgent that a triangular midnight shadow befell the moondial. When vernal temperatures warmed that March the block of ice in the bird fountain melted but no birds returned in the spring.

My moral universe was defined by righteous prohibitions de-lineating the contours of Standard Heights, a place rendered nonsen-sical without the protective order and composed, stormless system of this paternal governance. I wanted to open the window to see what would happen, of course I did. Any prohibition has the effect of creating opportunities for the behavior it is intended to prohibit, as surely as ExxonMobil was bound to explode sooner or later. I was then — by the moondial — more than twelve years old and had never opened a window in my life, and I lived with such superstition against the opening of a window that I began to believe all sorts of things: that I would be sucked through the window by a violent-ly pressurized carcinogenic gust and never seen again, sucked into the benzene atmosphere; that the opening of the house's windows would permit the entrance of ghouls and the Creole and Cajun bo-geymen one heard about from the Standard Heights AARP crowd. I could not so much as open the windows when the house strangled us with smoke from a burning king cake, or to get a whiff in spring of the soft beckoning fragrance of nocturnal flowers. Following the Christmas Eve explosion, days of agonized indecision would pass, while my father's body was drained of its lifeblood, the rooms cluttered with fatherless dread well into the New Year, before I ventured to open the window over the kitchen sink. The family prohibition against ever opening the window, any of the windows, was passed on from my father as if it were the Eleventh Commandment, firmly established on the proverbial "for want of a nail," but when my father did not return home after the Christmas Eve explosion there was no stopping me, Toussaint said.

I looked out the open window, which had opened too easily, almost of its own accord. No blood moon. No seismic quaking. No trumpet blasts. No toxic gust swept me away to the bloodhound netherworld west of the river. For years after leaving Standard Heights I opened windows — wherever I was: a hotel room, a highrise apartment in a strange northern city — with the greatest unease, and the rueful pang this wrought on my conscience, that I was in violation of my father's Eleventh Commandment, lingered acutely for many days after. The Christmas Eve explosion substantiated the moral imperative of his Eleventh Commandment: opening windows had the power of reverse causation to cause explosions. The explosion dropped the doors from their hinges, and blew the glass out of all the windows so that we could not walk barefoot indoors. The aftershock elongated into the next day. Men from ExxonMobil and EPA were seen around Standard Heights in white hazmat suits like spacemen roaming the plant and the emptied lots with blinking meters and detection equipment. We never saw their faces, though beneath the white hoods, in lieu of a human face, was the skull and crossbones in the center of the chemical symbols diagram. One of the ExxonMobil men, in particular, I remember because he did not wear a white hazmat suit like the others, but stood off on his own, with an official air, beneath one of the live oaks, methodically opening and closing a black umbrella. The Christmas Eve explosion had been so loud and so final, a petrochemical ultimatum to those who lived in Standard Heights, that I can still hear it ringing and exploding in my ears, in quiet and unquiet alike I hear that ultimatum like a last laugh, and the aftermath just keeps on happening, there is no end to the aftermath's chain reaction, the awful residuum and causatum all jumbled in a hydrocarbon requiem. The strangest thing happened to me, Toussaint said, when the explosion came with its impartial ultimatum, it was like the explosion had already happened, had happened many years before my birth and maybe since the hemic red stick crucifying the river was discovered by pale men in giant ships, and everyone in Standard Heights was just catching up to it, we had been living inside this Christmas Eve explosion all our lives and we didn't know, but now there was no going back, now the explosion was our present, past and future. The Christmas Eve explosion was, for me at least, the end of time. Plaster fell in white snow from the ceiling. The ExxonMobil trees held their breath. The stars flickered out like window signal candles on the Underground Railroad. The window glass remained unswept on the floors well into the next year, the shards of the windows twinkling like ice and snow in the bitter, frigid light.

The Christmas Eve explosion ignited other chain reactions in the very structure of Standard Heights. The earth, which has a poor reputation as it is among those forced to live here in the Middle Passage between birth and whatever awaits after the second line is over, has been carved up like a Thanksgiving turkey into arpents, parcels, lots, plots, tracts, acreages, and subdivisions into legal units of ownership in a way that was unthinkable to the Osage and the other native tribes in the street names of Standard Heights. But in Standard Heights the earth was not being so carved or plotted, the gridded platting that the Standard Oil Company used in the founding of Standard Heights was being reversed, and the verdant uniformity underlying Standard Heights' neat rational system of blocks and lots, the yards we played games of pickup football in were reassembled and pieced back together into larger and larger tracts of something they called the *greenbelt*, which because of its name I associated with *The Negro Motorist Green Book*. I was not at all certain I wanted to live in a greenbelt, some industrial rendition of Sutpen's Hundred. To escape the greenbelt, I would need more onions than the earth could provide, Toussaint said.

ExxonMobil, through the expropriations of their greenbelt program — needed to create the *Lebensraum* for the plant's future expansion projects and a buffer of safety for future explosions — has been avariciously buying up the family homes in Standard Heights for years, a sort of anti-urban acupuncture, a semi-voluntary program valuing the homes through certified appraisals — all the appraisers were white folks from across town where the Christmas Eve explosion, if it was felt at all, was little more than a disheveling, an innocuous stridor in the local papers — and in the cleared lots, after the demolished houses were trucked to landfills, ExxonMobil planted native live oaks and Shumard oaks whose shade cast a rich, benevolent twilight over us. The first deciduous tree — a Shumard oak that turned a violent explosive orange every fall — I ever saw was planted by ExxonMobil, as if autumn itself was one of the plant's petrochemical inventions. ExxonMobil had been reforesting the cleared lots to reduce liability and community exposure in the event of an industrial accident, when the plant did not behave according to its schematic control diagrams, but it was really as though they were planning an attack, not preparing the prevention of an accident. Our house was the last holdout on a block that once had twenty homes on it, each home the lively center of a family descended from the diaspora spread across Gondwana, Toussaint said.

I remember the police cruisers that parked in the ExxonMobil's trees' shade, the engine running, the cars apparently empty, faceless behind those sinisterly dark tinted windows. Sometimes strip club girls in spidery black fishnets and strange lingerie approached the cruisers, spiking their way in impossible heels across an empty lot, taking something from a window that rolled down, and then spiking away, some of the girls with the same native street names. Skull and crossbones girls called Pocahontas and Navajo, below average life expectancy, some dying on the police tape streets named for the chieftains of lost Native American tribes, many of them of the Hopewell tradition. I can still recite the names. Powhatan Street. Winnebago Street. Navajo Street. Calumet Street. Pocahontas Street. Huron Street. Hiawatha Street. Tecumseh Street. Osceola Street. Geronimo Street. Pontiac Street, which I knew as the General Motors car. I knew only that the Native Americans of these streets, like the Navajo, lived out the afterlife of their tribes on reservations not unlike the greenbelt of Standard Heights. The greenbelt program spared nothing in its expropriations. Even the Star of Bethlehem Baptist Church was gone. High modernism in Standard Heights took the form of an annihilative question mark, a basketball bouncing itself in the street. Bicephalic deer wandering around dazed and foaming at the mouth like a creature on codeine.

Luminous swarms of fireflies coalescing into a single glowing body the size of a dragon and whirling and gyrating around ExxonMobil's greenbelt trees, which possessed their own personalities and temperaments; some trees were cheerful and sanguine, others brooded balefully over Standard Heights, lugubrious crapehangers and ornery patriarchs, casting a vector field aura like that felt around sentient intelligence, engendered by the conjunction of all the trees' individual details which, concerting together, created an impression of the trees' stable personality: height of the tree, color and morphology of the leaves, circumference of the trunk, color and texture of the bark, distance of the branches' tip from the trunk, the color of the light filtering earthward through its green, yellow and brown branches.

The oldest of these ExxonMobil trees were taller than the power lines and razor fencework around the plant, Toussaint said. In the longueurs of summer, light penetrated the tree canopy easily, greenly dappling the vacant blocks of grass, the tree shadows vibrating in the wind, but as I got older, and the trees matured, darker quarters of Standard Heights developed where light never penetrated and the ground beneath was greenly lightless at all hours, until nightfall when the humming streetlights cast artificial prison yard light yawning at oblique sulfuric angles, iodine slices of triangles and trapezoids, tragic luminous geometries surrounded by gnat-blown humid darkness in which gunshots ricocheted. The great banquet and democracy of moths and other nighttime fliers' transverse orientation confused by the streets of artificial moons. I remember hearing the replica bell in Arsenal Park ringing viciously on such nights.

I climbed into the green crowns of the ExxonMobil trees to get a better view of the plant and its sorcerous operations hidden behind the security fences, where I suspected the plant's priesthood of burning the Fisk maps, covering up the evidence of environmental crimes. Many times I had been warned to stay out of the ExxonMobil trees, that what went on on the other side of the security fences was none of my business, but climbing the trees was the only way to make sense of the chemical symbols on the hazmat trucks that motored down the native streets day and night, as it is beyond the powers of any Standard Heights mortal to achieve anything like a vista or elevated perspective in the flat alluvial plain of the Mississippi, which has a democratizing, leveling effect on the denizens of the Delta: neither the immiserated poor nor the petrochemical plutocracy enjoy anything like the views of Queen Anne in Seattle or the Rocky Mountains in Colorado, the spectacles of nature divided out by class and market segments. The head football coach of LSU was at the same elevation relative to sea level as my father working the nightshift at the plant. On the banks of the present river, all differences in topography, the matrix of landscape asymmetries were flattened millennia ago by floodwaters and the seasonal depositions of ancient sediment, a natural process that has been interrupted by the manacling of the river in the levee system. And though, summoned at the gunshot hour by my mother when it was too dark for even shadows to be out, my body eventually came down from the ExxonMobil tree, my heart-mind never did, attempting as I was to climb to the same altitude as the smoking spires of the petrochemical cathedral and the cupola of the State Capitol tower, from which it was rumored you could see the Republic of New Afrika and Gondwana, but from the spy tree's highest accessible branch I could still see no limit to the petrochemical city's domains that metastasized in smoking towers and chemical-glowing infrastructure up and down the sinuous spine of the river, Toussaint said.

I did not yet fully understand what went on inside the plant, Toussaint said, that unmapped zone of industrial witchcraft where my father spent so much of his time. I thought the earth's clouds were manufactured by ExxonMobil. And if, over time, one grew acclimated to the   plant's smokestacks gushing exhaust plumes in every shade of gray and white it was not an unreasonable hypothesis, steam vapor rising day and night from the tall cooling towers that, in their withering decay, appeared as old as the church towers of medieval Europe, or the mysterious minarets of the Ottomans. The ExxonMobil plant was the stuff of legends and the greasy folktales told by the lunch countermen at the crawfish shack. This unremitting cinereous message of steam billowed out and mixed interchangeably with the clouds, which did not appear bound to the earth, divagating and descanting like a gaseous and supernal jazz improvisation above the river. And so ExxonMobil's cloud manufacturing operations, headquartered in Standard Heights, cranked out the clouds that occluded the sun and thereby the ancient timekeeping device, a sundial, which was not cleared along with the house to which it once belonged. The ExxonMobil cloudworks, whiter and purer when set against the dark blue-gray sky of a summer storm coming in from the west bank, the metabolic output from synthesizing new states of matter from the river water, had an opulent substantiality and individualized identity generally denied to Standard Heights, where even your neighbor's house could be gone by morning.

And so we lived in this eerie, industrial forest next to a sprawling factory complex that synthesized clouds, Toussaint said.

From afar, I heard the cheerfully competitive shouts of horseplay — the trees voicing their dissonant personalities. I moved in the direction of the arboreal voices. Through the columns of dark tree trunks, I came upon a game of pickup football in a treeless lot recently cleared of a home belonging to a family whose breadwinner was found face down in the Mississippi. His arms out like the crucifixion. My father and the other fathers in Standard Heights, on a day when they should've all been at the plant working, cut a casket made from one of the dead ExxonMobil trees. The mother had no choice but to sell and ExxonMobil, petty as it is, wasted little time in making a widow an offer. I will not say it was an offer she could not refuse — refusal was not an option. That was not the game ExxonMobil played. The pickup game's playing field was strewn with construction debris from the recent removal; if you were tackled in the rubble, you might cut yourself on a brick shard from the piers supporting the wall of a bedroom or kitchen. The other boys ran a deep pass play about where the house's small living room was once the scene of Demetrius accidentally shooting his older brother in the head. The boys on this pickup team were the only heroes I knew, each a sporting *homo ludens*. Jesse Owens showing Hitler how fast an Alabama black man can run was a slow motion roly-poly next to the greased lightning of my brother sprinting out the front door, our mother yelling after him not to run in the house, to catch a perfect spiral from Demetrius' twin. Muhammad Ali is a bantam next to Shaquem Jaxson who was the first of many to give me a bloody nose, tackling me so hard I saw stars and felt my brain impacting my skull. That Jaxson played football for East Mississippi Community College and never turned pro is quite beside the fact. He saw the field, and that's all that matters, huddled in his purple and gold uniform beneath the stadium lights and caught a deep ball in the end zone, keeping the game ball as a memento of fourth and goal. Then there was Marshal Mayday with the rectitude and rhetorical flair of a Frederick Douglass, and that he later went to prison for victimless crimes is just how it was around there. George Washington Carver and Booker T. were schoolhouse fictions, mythical strongmen beside the good fight boys of Standard Heights. While the crewcut white boys across town, safe from the Christmas Eve explosion, still wanted to be Robert E. Lee and Stonewall Jackson when they grew up, we ran the ball up the gut, fearless and never keeping score, like a hundred mini O.J. Simpsons pounding the rock. We designed our own custom plays called the Benzene Bomber and the Petrochemical Power Play. We were each the Black Power Ranger, Zachary Taylor. Da'Ron Treadwell was our star running back and he was never afraid to lower his head and take a dirty hit. No referees called fouls or sissy penalties. That he died diabetic with a bad case of gout is no fault of his own. Demetrius Shelton's readiness to sacrifice his body for the game exalted him into our Charles Deslondes. My brother was an athletic cipher known as Big X, running the route trees like a prodigy, his hands always coming up with the ball out of thin air like a magic trick. The Crown Royal was in the purple bag and all our fathers suffered from contagious impostor syndrome, Toussaint said.

We played shirts versus skins smashmouth pickup games of tackle football in the greenbelt lots grassed by ExxonMobil, dividing into Team Exxon and Team Mobil. Exxon usually won. These games were often interrupted mid-play, and we paused in the middle of a route or a block to look up at the sky — something we never did — as a commercial jetliner from Houston or Atlanta banked serenely like a dinosaur overhead, aligning its flight path with the runways at the Baton Rouge Metropolitan Airport, the airport that connected our little chocolate metropolis to distant and exotic places, Toussaint said sighing with something like future-facing nostalgia for anywhere but here. After Exxon took the title against Mobil, we played The New Orleans Saints versus the Dallas Cowboys, The New Orleans Saints versus the Atlanta Falcons, The New Orleans Saints versus the New England Patriots, the New Orleans Saints versus the World, and — against all the rules of collegiate and professional sports — the New Orleans Saints versus Louisiana State University, which often as not ended in a tie.

The Curse of the Saints took time off. The year the Saints won Super Bowl XLIV, though Standard Heights was by then long behind me, I remembered replaying the game in which Tom Dempsey kicked an NFL record-breaking 63-yard field goal to trounce the Detroit Lions 19-17 in the game's final seconds, a feat billed as the Saints' greatest achievement, and in the estimation of my father also humanity's, and I remembered especially that as Dempsey's kick sailed through the yellow uprights that was the first time my father hugged me with a joy so genuine and pure it was not to be believed, he clasped me to his chest and would not let go, lifting me off my feet and squeezing my diaphragm so tightly I thought I might faint, Toussaint said, still feeling the lingering effects of that victory hug. If that was his reaction just to a field goal, he would've hugged everyone within hugging distance, even the ExxonMobil plant managers, for the Saints' Super Bowl win over the Indianapolis Colts, 31-17, had he not been working at the plant that Christmas Eve, for the Saints winning a game was a win against the world for the people of Storyville, the people of Iberville and the people of Standard Heights, losing was a loss for him personally and a loss for Iberville, a loss for all of Standard Heights, a loss for good in the battle of good versus evil. When the Super Bowl's game clock hit double zeroes and the confetti fell, he would've been there, had it not been for the Christmas Eve explosion, to join with the rest of Standard Heights pouring into the native streets to celebrate, fireworks popping off, championship gunshots at the full moon and the bullet hole stars, hugging and kissing strangers like an armistice had been declared in The Battle of Baton Rouge, the Curse of the Saints exorcised at last, except that in the meantime the expropriations of the ExxonMobil buyout program were nearly complete and there was nothing left of Standard Heights by the time of Super Bowl XLIV. No one in Standard Heights knew how to count those Roman numerals, XLIV, like the date of some great historic event carved in the immemorial white marble of an ancient monument or temple ruin, Toussaint said.

Then Toussaint showed me his tattoo — the Roman numerals XLIV in Trajan typeface — on his upper arm, black numbers on a brown monument in memory of the joy his father never had, stolen by the Christmas Eve explosion, the Curse of the Saints exorcised without him, the date of ultimate victory carved in human flesh as black bodies have always been branded by those who do not wish them to forget.

The black and gold Saints jerseys, Toussaint said, seemed to me like the martial uniforms of some elite, ancient pharaonic fighting force, but after the years of so much losing the Saints fans wore paper bags over their heads and the team was renamed The Aints. For much of football season, in the years before the Curse of the Saints was lifted, on Sundays my father — who attributed the Saints' losing streak to the curse of the Superdome, built over the Girod Street Cemetery — wore a brown paper bag from the grocery store over his head, we laughed, drawing cartoonish frowny faces and grotesque carnival expressions with a black marker on the bag, but my mother was not amused. The paper bags drawn with the vaudeville faces of the Hiawatha Street funny man or some actor like Stepin Fetchit or Willie Best. And with this paper grocery bag on his head he recalled, talking through a knife slit for a mouth, with some pigskin heartsickness, the day the Superdome opened, back when Archie Manning was the franchise quarterback, zipping up and down the stadium ramps, the dome smelling like a new car. The Republican National Convention was held under the same domed roof the Saints players later kneeled in protest against the Angola of the present. And the Curse of the Saints affected more than the black and gold home team: the night the Superdome's lights went out in the middle of Super Bowl XLVII, between the Baltimore Ravens and the San Francisco 49ers, my father was laughing with his brown paper baghead on the west bank of Fisk's river, Toussaint said.

The Christmas Eve explosion also violated the principle of one man, one vote: not only did my father not get to see the black and gold Saints in Super Bowl XLVI or the game-saving on-side kick in the fourth quarter that became known as The Ambush, nor a year earlier was he able to exercise his Fifteenth Amendment rights in the election of Barack Hussein Obama II, to see a clique of educated, mostly coastal white people in the big blue cities cheer on a black man who was not a stand-up comic or a pro athlete, the boxers, basketball players, and football players we imitated in the vacant lots of our pickup games won sports contests but not elections. Nor would he have believed that Oprah Winfrey was contemplating a bid for the same high office, though a dead man's vote would not be so supernatural as it sounds in a spooky paranormal state such as Louisiana where dead men have been on the voter rolls since before Pinchback was governor. But downriver in Iberville, just before construction started on the Superdome, he did hear Robert Kennedy's May 27, 1968 speech on *Radio Free Dixie*, a month after King's assassination at a Memphis motel, my father could still recite it word for word, as he did that evening when I came home late from a pick-up game in the dark, bloodied, bruised, having caught a perfect pass between the two ExxonMobil greenbelt trees marking the end zone. We won, I told him, Team Exxon won. That's good, he said, that's terrific, you better keep on winning, because a black boy is only allowed to win on the gridiron, victory can be yours if you stick to the 100 by 53 yards of the football field, no more, he said, that's all you get, 100 yards this way and 53 yards that way, that's the little sandbox allowed for your winning.

To the man who during the Curse of the Saints' losing streak religiously wore a brown-paper baghead on gameday, the election of a black man to the presidency was a risible futility and impossible practical joke, "There is no question about it," the attorney general said, my father quoting the assassinated attorney general while my brother and I thought, after too many nights on the graveyard shift, the old baghead had gone mad, "In the next 40 years a Negro can achieve the same position that my brother has as President of the United States," the attorney general said to sixty plus countries through forty radio transmitters over the Voice of America. The entire free and unfree world heard this white boy from Massachusetts, my father said, say that a Negro could be president, and half the country laughed and the other half cried, and not just any old Massachusetts, not Lowell or Lawrence, or even Roxbury or Dorchester where the suicidal Negroes live on fatal blocks abandoned by the Jews, or someplace like that, but Jewish Brookline, Massachusetts, and here I am in Standard fucking Heights, of Baton fucking Rouge, Louisiana, sweating my black ass off, and busting my black balls at the plant, and I ain't seen nobody yet in that whitest of White Houses who looks like me, talks like me, walks like me, farts like me, fucks like me, don't even die like me, don't do nothing that nobody from Iberville or Standard Heights do, and so what Bobby Kennedy is saying, my father continued while my brother had stopped listening, what this Massachusetts man who got shot just like King is saying is, if you know how to interpret this peckerwood doubletalk and read between the lines, is that if the Negro is a good boy and behaves like the white man wants him to — talks straight, acts right, stands up straight, stops all that hooting and hollering out there in them streets, keeps his teeth and his mind clean and behaves like a white boy from Brookline who would never dare throw a brick — for the next half century then maybe the White Power Brokers will let him throw his hat in the ring with the rest of the Harvard Yard boys. You hear that boy, he said to me, you hear what Bobby Kennedy is telling you? You be a good boy now, stay out of them streets, no gangbanging, no drugs and no premarital sex, Toussaint and one day you can make your pappy proud and be President of the United fucking States of America. I hope I make it to the fortieth anniversary of that Bobby Kennedy's promise about the Negro president, my father said, because I sure am going to hold that dead man to it.

The Christmas Eve explosion made certain that he would not live to see Robert Kennedy's Negro president prophecy come true at the polls in 2008, and only Whipped Peter and the captain of the chlorine gas ghost ship know whether he held Bobby Kennedy to his promise when he met him on the river's west bank where the bloodhounds prevent the dead's escape from the underworld plantation. But when Jesse Jackson's presidential campaign failed to put a Negro in the White House and George H.W. Bush was elected as the 41st white president, the jaded old baghead said Bobby Kennedy was a peckerwood liar, a false witness and worse, to which my mother sensibly replied, but it hasn't been forty years yet, and because my father was not one to let anyone else have the last word, well it feels like 400 years! We've been in the wrong place at the wrong time for the last 400 years!

Such fulminating baghead lectures from my father were singular events, but their singularity I think represented his innermost thoughts, his private Standard Heights worldview as it was shaped by a grow-up-quick childhood downriver in Iberville. Generally, he went to work at the plant and came home, and race politics were not much spoken of, though I knew he fantasized about foreclosed futures issuing from lesser and greater roads he'd not taken, the myriad forking paths one picks from each day, seemingly trivial at the time, but with orders of magnitude of consequences, indeed reaching far beyond the visible horizon of anyone's lifetime, the brachiating manifold of possible but dead futures in which we, his family, did not exist, as such exercises in futile imaginings, bloodlettings of the spirit, require the negation of all that is before you, but perhaps the negation of Standard Heights and ExxonMobil and the Curse of the Saints was the whole point, Toussaint said.

Maybe the fulfillment of Bobby Kennedy's pronouncement would not have mattered. Obama might not have been black enough for him; he didn't go to Southern University, Xavier, Dillard, Hampton, Tuskegee, or Howard or Morehouse, or any other of the other HBCUs, but the same too-big-for-your-britches school as the Kennedys, Toussaint said. I've been to Brookline, whose leafy, shady, salubrious streets and buttoned-up Brahmin houses are the perfect place to bring up statesmen, scholars, and scientists without them having to breathe benzene and naphtha and develop that petrochemical cough that plagued my mother. And in Brookline, real snow whirling about my face, not the toxic snowfall of chemical ash that coated everything in Standard Heights, I understood that my father would not merely roll back the lamented choices of his lifetime, but undo the decisions of his predecessors all the way back to the Big Bang; he would be Joe Louis and then the first fight between a black American and a Nazi pugilist would not have required a rematch; he would have been Charles Deslondes and the German Coast Uprising would not, in his telling of it, have ended the way it did — with inglorious hecatomb.

Though he could not have known, consciously, of the specious correlation he'd created, my father miscited the attorney general's quote as occurring in 1968, placing the fulfillment of Kennedy's prognostication of a Negro president at the year 2008, the exact year of Obama's election, but the son must fact-check the father, the *Radio Free Dixie* quote too was contaminated to fit the timeline of my father's calendar, which flowed backward or forward like the river: Bobby Kennedy in fact said a Negro could be president "in the next *thirty or forty* years," a much more flexible and uncertain timeframe, and by 1968, the year my father erroneously cited, Bobby's brother John Kennedy had been dead four years, after being allegedly shot by a lone gunman in Dealey Plaza, Dallas, Texas, for the historical record, once examined without baghead prejudice will show that Bobby Kennedy's speech took place in May of 1961, closer to the time when my mother left Prichard and spent two sleepless nights in the Gaston Motel listening to homemade bombs go off like the detonations of some immemorial and unfinished conflict between belligerents who no longer remembered what the fight was all about.

The Good Fight

More or less at random, as I was then trying to be less predictable in my habits, I'd gone to a bar on Chartres Street, paid the surly doorman for the cover charge, and through the mashed throng of hyped bodies, mostly white frat-bro types and their blonde ratchets, pumping fists and cheering for McGregor to whipsaw Mayweather, where I descried at the back of the bar, beneath the eerie, otherworld-ly incarnadine glow of the emergency exit, Toussaint alone, staring up at the television screens depicting Floyd Mayweather, a boxer who after more than thirty years at the sport had perfected his craft as much as one could ever hope to, in the first round of his bout against the pugilistic parvenu McGregor, an MMA fighter, who had never fought a professional boxing match before in his life and who had probably never been this close to a black man before either. I bought drinks for both of us and joined him in the shadowy smoke beneath the red emergency exit light.

My father was not a Bible thumper, Toussaint said, and though I could barely hear him over the beery din and the biased cheers for McGregor, some drunks chanting *Great White Hope, Great White Hope,* Toussaint did not raise his voice much in competition with the bedlam, but my father relied, Toussaint said, like everyone else in Standard Heights, upon the Good Book to make sense out of the hand we'd been dealt, and a pugilistic quote I heard often from him, especially as it related to his time at the ExxonMobil plant and his baghead fandom, was, "I have fought the good fight, I have finished the race, I have kept the faith," from 2 Timothy. As he got older, and the Christmas Eve explosion drew nearer, the quote became simply, "I have fought the good fight." No more the race, no more the faith, just the good fight, Toussaint said as McGregor connected a series of deft, offensive punches on Mayweather. As if running out of time, my father felt constrained to abbreviate such verses. He encouraged us to do likewise, to fight the good fight against invisible armies of enemies. After fact-checking his timeline on Bobby Kennedy's prophecy of a Negro president within the next forty years, which had sewn doubt in my mind, I went to the Bible for myself to estab-lish the textual authenticity of my father's Biblical memory. I read the full quote in the pages of the Second Epistle to Timothy — a valediction from the Apostle Paul to his spiritual son, Timothy, as he anticipates his own destruction, though no one knows for sure the circumstances of Paul's death, but he was almost certainly martyred, sources as renowned as Tertullian and John Chrysostom diverging on the details, but dovetailing reliably in the most crucial detail that

Emperor Nero had Paul put to death, Toussaint said. But my father had omitted something crucial, the words just preceding my father's quotation were elided — "For I am now ready to be offered, and the time of my departure is at hand" — so that the entire unredacted verse, without my father's omission of valediction, I read aloud in the same room where I later found *The Negro Motorist Green Book*, "For I am now ready to be offered, and the time of my departure is at hand. I have fought the good fight, I have finished the race, I have kept the faith."

I could not help incanting this valedictory verse, from spiritual father to spiritual son, while watching, at a crowded Chartres Street bar in the French Quarter, this fight between a black, orthodox style super welterweight and a scrappy upstart white southpaw from Ireland. The outcome of the Floyd Mayweather Jr. versus Connor McGregor fight would have interested my father very much, Toussaint said, certainly more so than our pickup football games in the vacant lots of Standard Heights. Though it was obvious why white fans should pull for McGregor, this fight benefited from none of the race-baiting of fight promoter Don King — still the race of the fight's pugilists was impossible to ignore, however it was marketed, when McGregor was patronizing Mayweather to "dance for me, boy," and the Irishman's wicked braggadocio cut below the belt too: "I'm half-black too, from the bellybutton down." The verbal pugilism continued for months leading up to the fight, and Mayweather counter-punched: "I want him to call me monkey again so when I knock him out I can say to him, get up monkey." A black man had fulfilled Kennedy's prophecy almost ten years before, when McGregor was twenty years old, and yet these two boxers were talking about monkeys, Toussaint said, as if the scars on Whipped Peter's back were still fresh and unhealed. The boxers were being held to double-standards, the press covering with a proclivity for editorial favoritism Mayweather's convictions for domestic violence or the ostentatious flaunting of conspicuous wealth, his gold chains and luxury cars and serial bankruptcies, while McGregor's selfsame out-of-the-ring character flaws — the pencil-dick bravado, the swaggering ostentation — were brushed aside as the shenanigans of Irish youth and the jocular capers of a pugnacious, darling Irish rube, the same people who had constructed so many of New Orleans' levees, for McGregor was a Hibernian caricature of Floyd's "Money" Mayweather persona, the media willing to varnish it, I believe, because it came with an unintelligible but winsome Irish accent, Toussaint said, and then the bar crowd roared as McGregor connected an early-round punch on Mayweather's chin, scoring for the Great White Hope, and for a moment I began to worry about Mayweather's chances in this unorthodox brawl. Mayweather's record — 49-0 — going into the fight was perfect, and hundreds of millions of dollars were being bet against him, I thought. But letting McGregor land a few *pro forma* punches in the early rounds, tiring him out, seducing him into a false sense of security was a survival tactic in use since Whipped Peter and Charles Deslondes fought their own good fights.

And then I realized who my father had in mind when he enjoined us to fight the good fight against an unspecified enemy: the Great White Hope, Toussaint said. The invisible enemy was invisible because he was all around us, a circumambient combat. The Great White Hope fight in 1982 demonstrated, a decade or more before the O.J. Simpson trial that would rivet and haunt my baghead father, to my brother and I how the good fight was to be fought, if not won. For days leading up to the fight, it's all he could talk about, my mother could not come to see the point of boxing, white or black, two men in shorts smashing each other in the face till the other one dropped to the mat and a bell rang, and some bookies shook hands and paid their bets. She could see the same thing between people she personally knew right here in Standard Heights in the lots on Hiawatha Street. No better than the dogfighting or cockfighting one could see in the front yard for no charge and a minimum of inconvenience, no booking fees, no parking problems, as the century's problems more and more center around the availability of parking. But the neighborhood dogfights my father said, were not held in Caesars Palace, but in the vacant lots expropriated by ExxonMobil or the crumbling parking lots behind the bounce beat strip club, the dogs barking all through the night and sometimes the maimed bloody body of a dog found by children in a dumpster the day after the fight, Toussaint said, taking a moment to raise his drink.

My father, could he afford them, would have purchased tickets for the Gerry Cooney versus Larry Holmes fight at Caesars Palace, never mind the white supremacist clowns in the audience threatening to shoot Holmes, not just to see the fight — he wanted to tour Las Vegas and the Seven Wonders of the Vegas Strip: the Eiffel

Tower, the High Roller, the Statue of Liberty, the Fountains of Bellagio, the Mirage Volcano, the Grand Canals at the Venetian, and the Mountain at Wynn, plus the Egyptian pyramid and sphinx, and the Excalibur castle. Why, I can hear him say, go to New York, Venice, Paris or Cairo when you can go to Vegas and see them all in the same place? The Seven Wonders of Petrochemical Modernism.

If my father was not present at the Holmes fight, though he wished to be, instead watching it on a coworker's television, through the screen of which all the great events then occurring outside Standard Heights seemed to be mediated, the Joe Louis versus Max Schmeling fight took place so long ago that he was only able to relate secondhand accounts of it to me in the aftermath of the Holmes fight, Toussaint said, and so the contest that set an African-American man against a *bona fide* Nazi in Yankee Stadium came to me, as it were, third-hand: the Nazi pugilist defeating Joe by the twelfth round with a blitzkrieg of jabs that disoriented Joe and giving him his only knockout of the prime of his career. No riots followed Louis' loss to a Nazi, though Langston Hughes was in the audience at that fight, reflecting sadly in his autobiography that, "I walked down Seventh Avenue and saw grown men weeping like children, and women sitting in the curbs with their head in their hands. All across the country that night when the news came that Joe was knocked out, people cried." When Mayweather came off the ropes punching at McGregor's smarmy face he punched straight through McGregor and all the way back to Max Schmeling, Toussaint said.

But most did not see the contest for themselves in Yankee Stadium, instead crowding around crackling old radios in rural whistle stop towns and rusting jackwaters across the South like Maya Angelou who said of the fight, "my race groaned. It was our people falling. It was another lynching, yet another black man hanging from a tree…this might be the end of the world. If Joe lost we were back in slavery and beyond help. It would all be true, the accusations that we were lower types of human beings. Only a little higher than the apes." Now you will see why, Toussaint said, if Larry Holmes lost to the Great White Hope everyone in Standard Heights would be chased by bloodhounds across the Mississippi, and why if Mayweather lost to the loudmouth Irishman we would be monkeys in a cage. We expected a son of a bitch and failed artist like Hitler to send flowers and a message of congratulations to the Nazi boxer's wife, my father said, when Joe lost the first match, but the American media too, even in its praise of Joe Louis' vindication of democracy against the Reich's fascism in the second match, could not rise above peddling in the little bigotries of the day: Louis was "a jungle man, completely primitive as any savage, out to destroy the thing he hates." Mayweather was no jungle man — he was the jungle, Toussaint said, looking up to the televisions now just in time to see "Pretty Boy" Mayweather connect with a vertiginous blow to McGregor's temple. There were so many screens above the bar, not all of them synchronized, that we saw Mayweather smash the Irishman and then smash the Irishman again.

For reasons I will never understand, my father did not believe Joe Louis challenged Max Schmeling to a rematch and won by knockout in the first round, nor did he want to be shown the picture of Louis and Schmeling, old men now, embracing each other like long-time friends who have not seen each other after being separated by many years and bouts, Toussaint said. As far as the sentimental picture was concerned, it was staged, coerced, theater. The score, in his mind, was not settled by a simple rematch and the Great White Hope still held out too much hope of winning. For all his protestations, he preferred to see a black man take on a white man in the ring. Of the Rumble in the Jungle fight — George Foreman versus Muhammad Ali — he said, if I wanted to see two Negroes fight each other I'd throw a dollar out the window on Rampart Street. The Fight of the Century, matching Joe Frazier against Muhammad Ali, did not interest him in the least, he did not wish to pay to see a match between two black boxers, and he said he'd seen enough of two brothers smashing it out while white men in suits counted their cash not in bills or wads, but in the number of suitcases. My father openly loathed Don King, the unscrupulous promoter behind the Thrilla in Manila and the Rumble in the Jungle, a fight requested by Zaire's dictator, Mobutu Sese Seko, for exploiting race in his fights for monetary gains, Don King was an Uncle Tom carnival barker who would sell out his own race for better seats to a lynching, was involved in organized crime, and smiled for the camera while holding an AT4 rocket launcher, though he perversely reveled in the terror instilled in white people at the sight of a black man wielding a rocket launcher, Toussaint said as Mayweather connected on a hard haymaker to the Irishman and the booing of the bar briefly drowned him out.

Cooney, like McGregor, was Irish, and my father never understood why the white folks left it to the ragtag Irish to defend their gimcrack claims to racial supremacy. President Ronald Reagan had a phone installed in Cooney's locker room so he could make an immediate presidential phone call congratulating him if Cooney defeated Larry Holmes — no such phone was installed in Holmes' locker room, and even had there been, I doubt Holmes would have answered the call. I would've picked that phone up and told Reagan and his evil empire and trickle-down economics to kiss my black ass, my father said. The lack of a phone in Holmes' locker room was not the only cheap shot. A ceremonial precedent was not followed: the introduction of the fighters was reversed. Normally, the reigning champion is introduced to the ring last, and the challenger is introduced first, but in the 1982 fight, George Cooney, the Great White Hope of his generation, and the challenger to Holmes' title was introduced last, and Holmes — the reigning heavyweight champion — was introduced first, an insulting reversal of protocol that so displeased my father, but confirmed all his expectations about where the black man stood in the ring of 1982, that had the Christmas Eve explosion not, he would not have trusted the optics of the boxers being introduced in the proper order for the Mayweather-McGregor fight: first, McGregor wearing an Irish tricolor flag as a scarf, and then Mayweather, his face covered in a black ski mask like a bank robber. There was no flag for Mayweather's nation, Toussaint said, a man without a country has no flag except the color of his skin.

The 1982 fight was a big money made-for-TV reprise of the original Great White Hope: James Jeffries versus Jack Johnson, a fight scheduled with deliberately cruel irony on Independence Day, 1910. James Jeffries — the Great White Hope of that era — was summoned out of retirement on his California alfalfa farm to vindicate the master race against the Curse of Ham in a Manichean bout during an era when, in every town across the defeated but unrepentant Southland, the chambers of commerce were constructing and dedicating the Confederate statues we are today tearing down, Toussaint said looking in the direction of what I thought was Lee Circle. Jack Johnson was, by far, my father's favorite boxer, not least because Johnson was arrested under the Mann Act, for traveling across state lines with white women, a fact which did not go unremarked by my mother. Jack Johnson sought to do to James Jeffries what every Negro ever had wanted to do to his white overseers, white masters, white bosses, white authority, Toussaint said. Knock him flat on the mat. In the Great White Hope's ring, sportsmanship too was segregated: Jeffries refused to shake Johnson's hand before the match. Imagine that, my father said, being such a chickenshit peckerwood that you'll step into a ring with another man, hit him in the face, let him hit you in the face, back and forth like that until one of you passes out, but you won't shake his hand?

Looking back, in a continuous line from Mayweather to Johnson, it was as though we'd been fighting the same good fight for a hundred years or more, always against the same omnipotent opponent, the Great White Hope, who lost every time, but could not be compelled not to return to the fray. The Great White Hope was also paranoid about his blood, Toussaint said, that he might have some of the enemy within him, the bloodhounds might sniff him out and chase him out of the ring. George Cooney had his DNA tested years after the fight, to determine his ancestry — his grandfather's mother was African-American — the Great White Hope had been fighting himself all along. We told y'all so, said the grown men weeping like children, and the women sitting in the curbs with their head in their hands, Toussaint said, we done told y'all so.

My father withheld his blood from these genetic ancestry tests, Toussaint said, they were not accurate enough to pinpoint the tribe or village from which his forebears were stolen back before even Whipped Peter, and the political boundaries of the nations created since Africa's liberation meant nothing, these genetic tests were another means for the Great White Hopes to prove they were not black, that the enemy was not within them. Even the fighting styles were correlated with race: Jeffries, like McGregor, deployed a fatiguing swarming style of total aggression and panicked fury, summoning all the fighting Irishman within him, while Jack Johnson made use of the same patient, methodical defensive style as Mayweather, the same style blacks used to survive outside the ring in the South for centuries. Yes sir, no sir; and then a brisk counter-punch. Yes, master and then — knockout. Because a black boxer must first let the Great White Hope think he has a chance and let him throw his hat into the ring, like Jack Johnson more than a hundred years before, "Pretty Boy" Floyd was a master of false hope: after shrewdly timing his strategy based on calculations of McGregor's average endurance in short MMA fights lasting twenty-five minutes,

Mayweather let McGregor linger into the tenth round, toying with a fatiguing opponent in a cat and mouse game; Johnson too in his fight against the Great White Hope, fearing the repercussions of an early knockout, backed off his wearying opponent but scored three knockdowns by the fifteenth round when Jeffries' corner intervened and halted the fight, white fans rushing the ring, and Johnson's entourage forming a protective barrier around him — once the outcome of the fight became known, violent race riots broke out across the country. If a black man was going to knock out the Great White Hope in the ring then the country must burn. When Trump posthumously pardoned Jack Johnson for his violation of the Mann Act, I knew what this was really about: the Great White Hope is motivated by an unspoken need to forgive Jack Johnson for humiliating him before the world, to display the limitlessness of his largesse, and for taking his white wife to Montreal and having a ball in exile in South America, Europe, and Mexico beyond the reaches of the petrochemical sirens. An immortal in the ring, Jack Johnson died in an automobile accident after visiting a diner that refused, on the basis of his skin color, to serve him a meal, so that in the final bout the Great White Hope still brought the big man down, Toussaint said.

McGregor picked up some fouls punching Mayweather in the back of the head, soliciting absonant cheers from the bar crowd.

Petrochemical Nocturne

But sneaking cheap-shot fouls could not go the distance for Ireland. The mood in the bar turned glum as it became evident that McGregor was winded, outmatched and outclassed. After ten rounds of defense and vicious counter-punching, methodically and patiently wearing his opponent down, the referee declared Mayweather the victor, McGregor trounced due to technical knockout as Confederate statues are being toppled or dismantled in courthouse squares, as Robert E. Lee is now being dethroned in Lee Circle. This time no protective entourage had to surround Mayweather for protection, but Mayweather was not Ali or Jack Johnson, fighters who transcended the sport, weighing in on the exigent social and political issues of their times, Mayweather and McGregor cynically conspired to play the race card in order to market the fight to the prejudicial bugaboos of a country that could not win a rematch against its own Confederate statues, but in the end Mayweather kept his perfect record, and made himself a millionaire again — the prize purse estimated at over $100 million.

Rarely have I seen a black man happier than Mayweather, Toussaint said, as he held the Money Belt: a bespoke Italian-made alligator leather belt encrusted with 1.5 kilograms of 24-karat gold, 3,360 diamonds 600 sapphires, and 300 emeralds. My father would not have wanted to believe Mayweather's announcement, during the post-fight interview, that he was done with boxing for good, retiring from the ring, implying that he had fought the good fight, finished the race, and so forth, and that his faith had been kept: there would be other Great White Hopes to defeat, Toussaint said.

Now that the fight was over, and the lucky Irishman had lost, the bar resumed normal operations. The barman swept broken glass off the floor. Some belligerent McGregor fan had thrown a bottle at the wall when it became evident that Mayweather had been sand-bagging the Irishman all along, strategically suppressing his skill in order to gain a competitive advantage in later rounds after the Irishman had worn himself out, mostly tilting at windmills, as the Great White Hope always has. Done tried to tell y'all, I heard someone say. I settled the tab, feeling that McGregor had got what was coming to him. Get up, monkey. Before Toussaint and I left the sports bar on Chartres Street through the rear emergency exit and into an alleyway, we saw money exchange hands for lost bets — I thought of Jesus' cleansing of the Temple — and the last thing Toussaint said to me, as he walked off in the neon whirl of Canal Street, the post-card palms rising like spidery sentinels above the vintage streetcar in which a brass band played jazz funeral music, was fight the good fight and forget the faith.

The Curse of the Saints

Boxing might be my father's suffering passion, second only to his love of the Saints, but my mother believed it would lead to fighting, unemployment, jail, gambling, broken bones, nose bleeds, a bad character, and worse, so she did not stand in the way of the pickup football games, a benign pastime compared to the vices attributed to boxing, as if boxing was more malignance and contagious disease than a sport, but when I try to recall those pickup games they are a cloudy, indistinct blur of improv plays and broken bones scrimmages — the river fog mixed with the plant's toxic effluvia to form a nefarious smaze that drifted over the playing fields — like watching a game from afar, pseudomorphic fog oozing off the river so thick and opaque that the opposing team and one's own teammates were lost in the gray murk, but I could hear them shouting, indeed can still hear them shouting as if I stood immersed in that sightless murk this very moment, and so we played more by ear than by sight like a team of bats, a symphonic orchestration of grunts, epithets and halloos, orienting ourselves by this athletic-musical echolocation, the plays developing bizarre and lawless configurations unseen in any coach's playbook, defenders hiding behind trees, wide receivers in the trees. Secret trick plays called by desperate quarterbacks. These were trick plays to end all trick plays, named for the bits and pieces of history we knew. The Annexation of Puerto Rico. The Battle of Baton Rouge. The Battle of New Orleans. The Standard Heights Scarab. The English Turn. The Creole Dingdong. The German Coast Uprising. The Spillway. The Ratchet Thot. The Strip Club and the Bombing of Osage Avenue. Plays that when called allowed us to alter the outcome of history, right there on the fields of Standard Heights. The quarterback lobbed the football in the direction of the shouts, hoping for the best, and in this way many interceptions were thrown, and after every interception we tackled the intercepting player as hard as we could to force a fumble, the ball slipping out, the play living a few moments more as we recovered the ball and then ran it back in the direction of the imagined end zone between two ExxonMobil trees, and the boy who recovered the fumble was in turn tackled by the intercepting team, forcing a second fumble. The football did not want to be kept. This to and fro fumbling could go on all night, keeping a play alive longer than was natural until the quarterback — a boy who I heard was shot and killed by police in the same winter of the Christmas Eve explosion — lobbed the football into the foggy murk and the ball did not return to earth. The football was raptured, we said, it had served its time on earth and ascended into the heaven of the Sportsman's Paradise. Though we looked, we never did find that ball, Toussaint said, lament and loss in his voice.

After the pickup games, still wrangling over the final score, disputing the legality of a play, we banged on an old Coke machine plugged into the outside wall of the service station, the glass bottles tumbling out and as we had no bottle opener to pry the metal top off the glass bottle we went to superhuman lengths to get at the brown, sugary elixir, some of us going at the tops with our teeth, breaking a tooth in the process, bashing the bottle with a rock, breaking the bottle in the process, Coke and glass splashing everywhere, until an older boy taught us to pop the top off by placing the bottom rim of the metal top on the right-angled edge of a cinderblock wall and hammering the top with the meat of a closed fist — the top popped off with no resistance and rolled around on the ground, Toussaint said. We were gobsmacked. This utilitarian reliance on intermediary devices and instruments such as bottle openers were not always needed to get what one wanted, sometimes the environment provided what was needed, even if it was a cinderblock wall with no other salient purpose than to pop off our glass Coke bottle tops. The Coke machine was of another era, Standard Heights was a time machine that still got its coke in glass bottles; other parts of town had Coke machines with new plastic bottles, the tops screwed off easily, no bashing or hammering on a cinderblock wall was required, you simply twisted the cap off and swigged down the dark brown, saccharine liquid and disposed of the plastic bottle and never thought of it again, Toussaint said.

The football games of fall ended as the houses of my friends and playmates vanished — there were not enough of us left to fill out a squad. Team Mobil was down to five players, three of them linemen. The homes in Standard Heights were small enough and shoddily enough built that they could be vanished in an afternoon, putting up little resistance before the bulldozer: in the morning a dear friend's house, in the rooms of which I had played, was by evening a patch of dirt and unidentifiable rubble picked over by stray dogs and blackbirds. I watched these razings from behind the windows I was forbidden to open, helpless to stop them. I grieved blackly, seething to see my friends and their families expropriated and pushed off the land like the tribes in the native street names, but I was too paralyzed and nerveless to halt ExxonMobil's bulldozers. The bulldozers munched the houses with a sickening appetite, leveling Demetrius' house like a teepee in a Category 5. Standard Heights' greenbelt forests expanded lot by lot until ours was the only house left ExxonMobil hadn't bought out and demolished for the plant's safety clearance and liability reduction area, an area from which the supercorporation wished to monopolistically remove all uncertainty and manage all liability, the risk of any and all explosive entropy. The primeval forest enclosed us in greenbelt, snuffing out any possibility of escape. Bloodhounds with rabid red eyes lurked behind trees. ExxonMobil was a petrochemical wave eroding the shoreline of our island, grain by grain of sand, and the plant's luminous corona out-dazzled the night sky so that even the immemorial myths written in the constellations were confused and shrouded in vapors of poisonous light. No other such light exists, Toussaint said, the light of a petrochemical plant or refinery at night, no painter's work has ever come close to approximating that chemical bombast and luminous holocaust which was really a non-light, all of Petrochemical Modernism's attempts to illuminate the bogeyman darkness are done so with non-lights, the plant borrowing its daimonic energies from the orange-red glare of the flames from Jesse Washington's immolation I read about in the hazmat hieroglyphics.

But before the bulldozers mauled them I explored the empty houses, Toussaint said, many of them unlocked, the doors standing open as if the families fled some imminent nameless catastrophe in the night, meandering about the disheveled rooms, testing my father's Eleventh Commandment by opening the windows of these abandoned buyout homes — nothing happened. In a way, I was disappointed, I had wanted some consequential effects, a requital for every house bulldozed, hoping the windows were connected to the plant by invisible wires and that opening the windows would trigger a chemical chain reaction and destroy the plant with its own process flow diagrams.

Of course, ExxonMobil was unable to buy out every house before other natural and unnatural catastrophes claimed them. Some houses succumbed to electrical fires or gas explosions, acts of God, *force majeure*. A cigarette left burning on the crack house floor. A house was bulldozed — the occupants still inside — when the husband discovered his wife cheating on him with his brother. Another house too succumbed to flames for insurance or love. Then a hurricane made landfall late that summer, the swirling, rotating evil eye on the path for a direct hit, and Standard Heights was transformed overnight into an encampment of tents and FEMA trailers as the Blue Roof Program transformed New Orleans into a tessellation of blue-tarped rooftops. Though he often spoke about taking me to a Saints game, I never set foot inside the Superdome till Katrina, the storied gridiron on which my favorite players performed superhuman athletic feats converted into a storm shelter for the thousands upon thousands of displaced persons seated in the stands, not as fans gathered for a football game, but like a marooned colony of stateless persons fleeing a conflict at the borders of the petrochemical ecumene, and when it was all over and the floodwaters receded and the Army went home, the Superdome was graced, if that is the word, with a pile of garbage and debris at the fifty yard line.

Before the wormwood floodwaters came through the compromised levees, we agonized in a heightened state of suspense waiting to see where the storm — named for a bitch-beautiful woman — was going to make landfall and delay the Saints' football season. For days the rain slashed sideways in unrelenting world-without-end torrents, playing minor scales on the metal miles of infrastructural pipes and chemical conduits, dinning out the petrochemical nocturne on the native streets. After the catastrophic flood that deluged the city in late August, unyielding rain a month after the Rodney King riots, the city began leasing the vacant greenbelt lots from ExxonMobil for landfills. The floodwaters had ruined so many thousands of tons of drywall and other building materials that the municipal landfills were full and could not receive the flood debris fast enough, and we watched with growing alarm as the storm trucks unloaded more wet wreckage like a burnt offering to the plant: chairs, refrigerators, recliners, outdated computers, a piano soundboard, mattresses, couches, sinks, cabinets, drywall, flooring, windows — all of this inert mass, byproducts of Petrochemical Modernism, rotted with a thriving culture of flies madly swarming the truckloads of garbage dumped by the elephantine trucks that came and went at all hours on the native streets. An entire shotgun house was dumped on Hiawatha Street and a front porch and gable with ornamental scrollwork were left to rot on Winnebago Street. The Standard Heights stragglers picked over the salvage and reused what they could, and as the flooded flotsam became integrated into the household economies of Standard Heights that garbage heap, higher than anything I'd ever seen except the plant's cooling towers, became as sacrosanct as the Mount of Olives, some of the holy rollers proclaiming in their supernatural seriousness this hurricane trash pile was Jerusalem's mountain from which Jesus was said in Acts to have descended into heaven like the clouds manufactured in the ExxonMobil plant and at the very peak of which trash the Resurrection of the Dead would begin, not soon enough for some of them, though for my part I never figured out why Jesus wanted so badly to return to a planet that every night in my hydrocarbon dreams I saw lashed with flowing whip-rivers undulating like the serpentine scars on Whipped Peter's back, but I guess He had His reasons, Toussaint said.

The one-in-a-million find from the flood landfill was a recovered Drew Brees Saints home jersey, black and gold, we took turns wearing it, convinced whoever wore the landfill jersey would be endowed with superhuman athletic abilities during our pickup football matches in the cleared lots, and the jersey attracted enough attention around Standard Heights — no one had the money to buy a licensed football jersey — that spectators turned out for our trick plays and fourth and forevers, the audience growing to such proportions that there was nowhere to sit. Some of the holy rollers looked at the Mount of Olives trash and said, the Lord provides. From the flood landfill, we pulled out the discarded furnishings — chairs, tables, a sofa, a crawfish pot repurposed as a stool — and arranged them facing a busted television, and then rows of ratty recliners and patio furniture like bleachers in a stadium facing the cleared lots where we played brutal games of tackle murderball — the first luxury gameday suite in Standard Heights.

It wasn't the Superdome, but that luxury gameday suite was all we needed to feel like real pros on the greenbelt gridiron, though it was not at all unusual for a neighbor to put his entire living room set out on the front yard: tatty old sofas and bloody, soiled mattresses appeared overnight on the curb all the time, even the bullet holes themselves were removed from the walls and tossed out for garbage collection, the blood stains drained down the gutters. Car seats were torn out of totaled and unregistered vehicles and set on four corners of cinder blocks around a grill or barbecue pit in the yards of Standard Heights' other families — my father forbade furniture in the yard, said it made us look like white trash. This isn't some trailer park like Prichard, he would say, winking at my mother. This is Standard Heights, the living room furniture belongs indoors, he said, not out on the lawn like some kind of peckerwood ghetto. Standard Heights has to live up to its name, he said.

The vacant greenbelt lots where we played our dauntless games, tackling each other as if the game was refereed by the Old Testament's eye for an eye, abutted a landfill of empty oil drums, Toussaint said. This oil drum landfill had been there longer than the strip club and maybe longer than the native streets and the river it-self. This nightmarish mountain of rusting oil drums, which no holy roller dared called a Mount of Olives, grew to fantastic proportions over the course of my childhood, we marked the passage of time by the drums' unrelenting growth, and as the drums piled up, and the base became less and less stable, the drums moved and slipped in the night, the mountain morphing like a slow motion metal river made of macroscopic oil drum molecules, so that from one day to the next it never presented the same aspect, a metabolic metal amoeba ani-mated with strange shapeshifting sentience and secretive serpentine purposes, one of the great wonders of the world of Petrochemical Modernism. Could this be the famous mountaintop which Martin Luther King Jr. said he'd been to and from the heights of which he had seen the Promised Land? I tried to remember a time when the oil drums were not there, the drums rusting like the insane screeching of oxidizing bats, and the oil drum mountain predated the community elders — mostly toothless and infirm people born without the right to vote — the only things about the mountain that changed were the ever-growing number of drums and the extent of the metal mountain claimed by the absolute sovereignty of rust, the same bloody reddish brown as the trickling water filling the claw-foot tub in which our mother bathed us, a claw-foot tub that in petrochemical dreams came to life as an obese man-eating hippogriff.

Petrochemical Nocturne

Before the floodwaters had fully receded, with the sunlight filtered through the diaphanous essence of naphtha and benzene, Team Mobil's quarterback overthrew the football on a desperate Hail Mary into the pile of drums — Jesus himself could not have caught that deep and high ball. At that time, it was our only football. No one else wanted to climb the drums in search of the football, so I volunteered, approaching the monotonous horror of the drum pile so as not to disturb the sleep of a fairy tale giant. There were two ways to go about recovering the football: analyze the possible footholds and handholds of the drum pile, then meticulously pick my way over the pile one drum at a time, all while keeping an eye out for the football; or, like quarterback Drew Brees doing a flying superman over the top of the defensive line, leaping headlong and with no fear of tetanus over the petrochemical horror and coming up miraculously with the football for a game-saving touchdown. I put the one-in-a-million black and gold Brees jersey on and tried to focus on my superhuman athletic abilities: If I could somehow do the superman over the top I would find the missing football, except there were millions of disposed oil drums, rusted and leaking, with gashing edges and shifting like sand, and I'd never had a tetanus shot. In the end, I'd had to accept vanquishment by the oil drums and give up on another lost football, Toussaint said.

When it came to be my turn to wear the black and gold Brees jersey — a day that I anticipated more than the day I would leave Standard Heights — I did not make it past the front door before I was stopped and questioned by my father. Where did you get that Saints jersey? he wanted to know. I found it in the hurricane landfill, I said to my father, and he glowered at me as if I'd stolen the jersey from Drew Brees himself out of the Saints' locker room. He demanded that I take the jersey off and turn it over to him, and when I balked, something I rarely did, he tore the jersey off of me by force — it was as if the wind ripped the jersey from my body in one swift efficient movement over my head. I never saw the Saints jersey again and it was not among his things after the Christmas Eve explosion. I began looking for that jersey before my father's corpse had even been drained of its lifeblood. Mother, while boiling potatoes for mashed potatoes, said he did not like me wearing the Saints jersey because Brees, the franchise quarterback, was a white boy from Texas, and he played for Purdue, a team he despised because their mascot was a Boilermaker, and so my father's loyalty to the Saints was a complicated one, though this theory of my father's hatred for the landfill Saints jersey does not quite hold up to scrutiny, Toussaint said, I don't think she understood any more than I did why my father had ripped the special jersey off my body and done away with it, but she could not let such a rash thing go unexplained. He would have to look on passively as Doug Williams, the first black man to win the Lombardi trophy, quarterbacked the Washington Redskins to victory in Super Bowl XXII — not the Saints and not a black quarterback. Without the Saints jersey, the pickup football games lost their panache, it wasn't the same, the footballs we used deflated after running a few plays and the games turned into a Standard Heights interpretation of rugby inspired by WWF. Shaquem Jaxson and Da'Ron Treadwell smashing each other with lawn chairs. Demetrius Shelton jumping on top of you from the branches of an ExxonMobil tree and calling it a tackle. Marshal Mayday pulling a Mayweather of windmills on everybody within punching distance. Demetrius and Da'Ron chop-blocking you in half. My own brother body slamming me on Hiawatha Street.

In the offseason, distraught over another disastrously losing season, my father obsessed over the black and gold Curse of the Saints, the voodoo in the Dome. He was not a religious man but these sports fan superstitions came naturally to him, and if he met a minister or preacher, as one regularly did in Standard Heights, men who kept angels kenneled in doghouses, he wasted no time in anguishing the man of God with the principal woe of his sports-spiritual life: the Curse of the Saints. This curse was proof that cosmic forces were at work in the deep state boardrooms of the NFL, that some Manichean contest was at stake in each game inside the Dome. The reasons for the Curse were obvious to anyone who had ancestors buried in the Spillway: building the Superdome atop a cemetery, on consecrated ground, had put a hex and a pox on Saints football, even if it was an above-aground Protestant cemetery in Catholic New Orleans: 2,319 burial wall vaults and more than a thousand tombs were displaced by the construction of the Superdome in a city that cannot stop displacing the dead as much or more than it displaces its own living inhabitants, Toussaint said. No other franchise in the National Football League built their stadium atop a burial ground, of course the Saints would build their home stadium over a burial ground, my father bemoaned, imploring the preacher or minister to exorcise the Curse of the Saints from the Superdome, to dispel these restless malevolent spirits from the National Football League, while many of these holy rollers, Saints fans themselves, searched the scriptures for textual evidence that God took an interest in the outcomes of athletic contests. And, as my father never tired of repeating every time the Saints lost another game, there was some exegetical evidence that He did, in fact, take more than a casual interest in what went on inside the Superdome: the story of David and Goliath was oft cited, with particular attention given to Jacob wrestling the angel. But this did not imply that God, who also created the bloodhounds and the bipolar river, was on your team. The season-by-season statistics and record versus opponents are not strong evidence for a benevolent creator if you are a Saints fan.

The Superdome was built on top of a cemetery without any thought for the voodoo that is in the water. These cemeteries were laid out and platted like small metropolises with central arteries and side streets, the marmoreal aisles like the crooked alleys of medieval cities. The dead lived in these elegant marble and stone mansions while many of the living squatted in trap houses, or eked out survival in the suboptimal rat race of the Iberville Projects. A deconsecration of the burial ground was recorded on January 4, 1957, and the interred whites were relocated to Hope Mausoleum in New Orleans and the interred blacks relocated to Providence Memorial Park, which I think is in Metairie, the district that sent David Duke to the State Legislature, Toussaint said, and so what was separated in life and united in death was separated again by life and segregated in undeath, by those who celebrate the day the Gulf of Mexico's hypoxic dead zone was born.

During the football season of the Christmas Eve explosion the Saints' losing streak had gone from comic to tragic. That Sunday, the Saints lost another game and my father put on his Aints bag head. The Saints were a team gifted at innovating spectacular, creative losses, losing games in ways that had never been done before, the Saints were the avant-garde of losing, the black and gold were the Picassos and the Warhols of losing, the Cubists and postmodernists of defeat. The vanguard of snatching defeat from the jaws of victory, Toussaint said. When I think about all the creative ingenious ways the Saints devised to lose a game — this is not a fun game when you can't sleep, thinking of your favorite team's creative genius for losing, like counting sheep — I realize why the other baghead fathers in Standard Heights went to church on Sundays to pray away the curse, instead of watching the game. The game was lost before the fourth quarter, some of them well before halftime. My brother was in the yard, mindlessly tapping on the house with a hammer — the television exploded through the front window and landed in the yard not far from his feet.

The black and gold curse was not restricted to the Super-dome. The Curse of the Saints afflicted the family, my mother miscarrying during halftime. Bedridden for days, we cooked our own dinners of crawfish and corn on the cob, till she emerged one color-less winter morning, cradling her hollow womb, barely with enough strength to hold a cup of cold coffee. But in the yard, close to where the television landed after the Saints loss, she planted a small tree, in remembrance of the unnamed, the unborn, but my father refused to let her grieve — he despised the feminine cult of grief and death over a blood clot, the miscarriage was nature's way, he said, which was his way of saying get over it, it's for the best, the unborn was not ful-ly developed in its human quality, resembling a botched cross-pol-lination of a pig and a fish. Miscarriages were common as fleas and baby-killer roaches in Standard Heights, every family had them, it was almost like acne or smoker's cough, what was so special about her miscarriage that she deserved to memorialize the nameless un-baptized blood clot with a mourning tree in the yard next to the de-stroyed television?

And so he took three shovels from the shed, gave one to me, and one to my brother and ordered us to assist in digging my mother's mourning tree out of the ground, and he blamed the mis-carriage on the Curse of the Saints that was visiting itself upon his family, a curse brought upon us all because I was damn fool enough to wear the Drew Brees jersey recovered from the flood landfill, Toussaint said. Now it seems he couldn't tolerate someone besides ExxonMobil planting a tree in Standard Heights where con-ditions of growth were so feracious that the Mount of Olives landfill and the mountain of rusting oil drums brimmed with a pullulating green miasma, an asphyxia of jungle vegetation. Maybe it was the Curse of the Saints, maybe it was the ExxonMobil plant, no one kept count of the miscarriages in Standard Heights anymore. The halftime holy rollers said it was a divine punishment for being a Saints fan, it was the return of the Monster of Ravenna, that odious misbegotten thing born in Renaissance Italy with a frightening congenital disorder from a grotesque bestiary: a horned head, the letters *YXV* carved on its chest, hirsute limbs, winged like a bat, hermaphroditic genitalia, an evil eye glowing like a lantern in its bony kneecap, the awful creature standing on a single clawed eagle's foot — this monstrous child had been reborn in my mother, the holy rollers said, and it did not deserve a mourning tree, Toussaint said.

The mourning tree would not be easily uprooted, gripping the soil with the tenacity of a tree planted before the mountain of oil drums. We tugged and pulled, hacked at the mourning tree's roots with a hatchet, engaged in our own good fight with Mother Nature, the struggle greater than the end result: my father's moral sense of accomplishment when the tree's dedition at last meant the struggle was over, with a shredding and ripping noise, did nothing to exorcise the Curse. The uprooted tree went to the landfill with the flood debris, and my father warned me to stay away from it. The busted television remained smashed in the yard like the severed head of a robot. My father threw the television out too soon — had he waited he might have seen for himself how the Curse of the Saints turned out.

I watched the uprooted mourning tree slowly wither and expire, the leaves browning, falling off and blowing through the strip club parking lot and across the empty lots of Standard Heights, windrowing against the empty, bought-out houses that had not yet been bulldozed by ExxonMobil. Pouring pitchers of water, stolen from the spigot projecting like a nose from the side of the house, did nothing to rejuvenate the mourning tree, and by now it must be, like the angry man who dug it up, lost to the processes of decay in the same phase of matter as the chemical cinders and alchemical ash that unravel from the septic sky upon Standard Heights.

My brother and I somehow developed beyond the blood clot rejected by my mother's damaged womb, but outside that safe abyssal matrix in her belly we were exposed to more perilous miscarriages of Petrochemical Modernism: endocrine disruptors. The treachery in my rubber ducky bath toy, the yellow bird with the evil red smile, the perfidy in my brother's dolls, the recreancy in the soft, cuddly face of a teddy bear — endocrine disruptors were the omnipresent petrochemical poisons stitched and plasticized into our pseudo-innocuous toys. When I first heard of these endocrine disruptors, they were in the white clouds manufactured by the ExxonMobil dreamworks and they were in the bloodthirsty bark of the bloodhounds from the west side of the river. We played with secondhand toys manufactured with aniline, azocolourants, cadmium, lead, formaldehydes, perfluorinated chemicals, nonylphenol, chlorinated paraffins, phthalates, and triclosan. Endocrine disruptors and lead exposure were the nursery rhymes and mother's milk of our petrochemical childhood, the chemical basis for my brother's attempted suicide by cop, though why he should be in Angola and not me can only be answered by the bloodhounds in our bloodstream.

Children of Whipped Peter's time played with macabre, bellicose toys: guillotines, toy cannons that fired gunpowder, and puzzles illustrating scenes of internecine conflicts, though none contained endocrine disruptors. While we amused ourselves with deflated footballs and loaded pistols, the children on the other side of town played with plastic Ninja Turtles, reptiles that mutated after exposure to toxic ooze, and we raced white Bronco replicas down the streets named for lost tribes, sending them into the path of the hazmat trucks that rolled over the little white Broncos like they were nothing, flattening them into unrecognizable chunks of metal and splintered plastic fragments. The endocrine disruptors came to our front doorstep, and we felt like the anointed of Standard Heights, the chosen few to be so often visited by hazmat truck accidents that spilled liquid asphalt or flammable and corrosive toxic liquids with highfalutin polysyllabic chemical names that burned your lungs and eyes, as if Standard Heights was chosen by the petrochemical gods for punitive plagues. East Baton Rouge Parish, once the hazmat teams in their spacesuits had cleaned up and left us to contemplate the latest chemical spill, used prison labor to clean up the crash debris or the garbage that fell off the trucks, the prisoners in bright orange jumpsuits reboarding the prison transport vehicles — white school buses which we had once taken to school ourselves — bound for Angola prison, a place that I identified with human confinement, unconstitutional tortures and the legendary fall rodeo we heard about from those who drove to Angola to gawk obscenely at convicted murderers and malcontents thrown from a wild beast.

The toy white Broncos we played with the year of the dream speed police chase, Toussaint said, up and down Hiawatha Street making vroom sounds and police sirens with our mouths. My father, in his Aints baghead, obsessed over the O.J. Simpson trial. All anyone in Standard Heights could talk about that year was "The Juice." The trial image of O.J. wriggling his large, running back Heisman hands into the too-tight black leather gloves is forever seared in my mind — a thousand better memories have not supplanted it. The players on Team Exxon threw one black glove of a pair away, and in the pickup games Da'Ron and Demetrius wore a single black glove when they ran up the score, striking Heisman poses and yelling, *if the glove doesn't fit, you must acquit!* My father was certain that Simpson would be convicted and executed, he was charged with killing a white woman, and there wasn't a black man in the history of the United States who was not hung from a tree even for the uncorroborated rumorous supposition of maybe looking askance at a white woman once, much less murdering a white woman *and* a white man in her own house. We awaited the trial verdict's announcement as my mother asked my father whether he thought O.J. was guilty. But guilt and innocence weren't what this murder trial was about, Toussaint said, no more than the staged fight between Mayweather and McGregor was just about the size of the prize purse. I don't care if he's guilty, my father replied, leaving the room, he probably did it, those two had a history of abuse, but I don't care, he said. After so many whites had gotten away with murder since Whipped Peter's time, I think my father wanted to see a black man get away with it too. Even the score. And nothing changed the fact that Nicole Brown was dead. She was deader than the mourning tree and she wasn't coming back. Somehow, a black man getting away with what white men had been doing in daylight before there ever was a petrochemical nocturne was a token of the do-good progress that Kennedy said we would have to behave ourselves for, Toussaint said. Though she would not have known the Gandhi quote, about an eye for an eye leaves the whole world blind — that would've been the non-violent essence of my mother's comeback to his Old Testament jurisprudence: don't open the windows, stay away from the landfill, let Simpson get away with murder to even the score a little, though while he was on the clock at ExxonMobil my father kept his commandments to himself, Toussaint said.

My brother and I — at a neighbor's house, as we did not yet have a television of our own after my father destroyed ours over the Saints' loss — watched with mixed feelings of jubilation and disquietude the low-speed Bronco chase on the Los Angeles freeway lined with a cheering crowd. It was the most incredible thing: all those people cheering on a black man running from the cops, from the bottom of Standard Heights I saw how Los Angeles really was the City of Angels. If I ever reached driving age — not a guarantee — I would drive like "The Juice" on Interstate 10, running from the Louisiana State Police, Toussaint said, between Baton Rouge and New Orleans, after committing unspeakable crimes against the ExxonMobil plant. O.J. Simpson fled the police at dream-like speed, as if he was in no hurry, and in Standard Heights, where the pickup boys scattered at the first sight of a cop, he became a folk hero. In the police chase freeway crowds were people who had been in the Rodney King riots two years earlier when sixty-three people died, the City of Angels' jails filled with more than 12,000 arrested, and 2,300 more were injured after the savage police beating of Rodney King — another black man in a white car fleeing the police in a high-speed chase — on March 3, 1991. Los Angeles seemed to self-destruct after a copwatch videotape made by a private citizen from the window of his apartment unit was released. No one, least of all the Rollin' 30s, forgot the police drug raids of Operation Hammer, nor the black boys who nearly beat a white trucker, Reginald Denny to death on live television at the intersection of Florence and Normandie. I was only a first-grader when the Rodney King riots went down, but I wanted to throw the brick that set off the riots, like a match thrown on the highly flammable mountain of oil drums, Toussaint said. Reginald Denny, bleeding from the head, could've been one of the petrochemical truckers piloting at nightmarish speeds the hazmat trucks with their chemical placards through Standard Heights, disappearing in the plant's truck entrance filigreed with silver miles of razor wire, Toussaint said.

```
00:00:23:26 MAR. 3 1991
00:03:46:19
```

Team Exxon and Team Mobil, we all wanted to evade the police, racing down Interstate 10 to New Orleans or Houston wearing one black leather glove, nothing could stop us. We watched this dream speed police chase, the police pacing measuredly behind the white Bronco, till my mother found out on whose television and in whose house we were watching the made-for-TV chase and made us leave before the outcome was decided. She didn't like us watching what she saw as the valorization of outlawry, this was something worse than boxing. If Simpson was innocent — and he was presumed innocent till proven guilty in the courts by a jury of his peers, my brother reminded us — then why, my mother wanted to know, was he fleeing the police? An innocent man doesn't run from the law. Did Jesus run from the Romans before His capital punishment? O.J. should turn himself in, and then his innocence will be proven in a court of law before a jury of his peers as you say, my mother said, in an uncharacteristic naiveté that galled my groaning graveyard shift father, as a black mother of black sons she knew as well as my brother later would, but not better than my father did at the time of and before the slow motion dream speed chase, that black men's innocence was never presumed by anyone beforehand, his was a conditional innocence that required evidence and the burdens of proof. He's not black, he's O.J., my father said. At that moment, no one but him knew where all the knives in the house were located. If two black men exchange gunfire on Pontiac Street, my father said, and a white person doesn't see or hear it — then did it really happen?

My mother bored quickly with these jaded race riddles, Toussaint said. Though the former athlete (how many of us, when our cenotaphs are written, will be nothing but "former athletes") was seemingly guilty, still my father, who I would not describe as a vindictive man, wanted to see him acquitted. For a while there, acquittal was all he could think about. If the Curse of the Saints could not be lifted, and the Saints could not win it all and hoist the Lombardi Trophy on Poydras Street with black and gold confetti and champagne spraying everywhere, then before the Grim Reaper caught up to him — he did know yet it would be the Christmas Eve explosion — he wanted to see at least one black man get away with murder, with some good downhome country fried all-American *bona fide* honest-to-god homicide, and not just a single homicide, but a double homicide, glove or no glove, Heisman Trophy or no Heisman Trophy, because somehow in his mind the ability to get away with murder was more determinative of one's standing in the world than the right to vote, or desegregation, or where he sat on the damn bus, because it meant that black men had ascended to the plane of angelic übermensch*en* — like white men, they would be beyond good and evil. To get away with murder, and of a white woman, and not just any old white woman from Highland Road or Airline Highway, but Nicole Brown Simpson, a celebrity blonde bombshell, was to eat H. Rap Brown's cherry pie. The whole pie too, every violent slice of it. Despite my father's wish to see O.J. acquitted, the Christmas Eve explosion made sure he was not around to see "The Juice" paroled years later for an unrelated crime, the *State of Nevada v. Orenthal James Simpson, et al.* armed robbery case, O.J. trying to reclaim his fenced sports memorabilia in a Vegas hotel room, in what was in all likelihood a setup, for having been acquitted, O.J. became black the instant the jury of his peers announced the verdict and the judge handed down the sentence of guilty for stealing what was rightfully his, for then his celebrity was tarnished, and he was left with only his blackness and the fading furor of the cheering freeway crowd like some late twentieth century slave insurrection but no one could've known during the chase that O.J. held a gun to his own head while Al Cowlings was at the wheel — 100 million people viewed the chase that day, including the pickup boys from Hiawatha Street, and the common lot of Standard Heights felt we were part of some comprehensive drama, the white Bronco racing down the modern Underground Railroad, running from the blood-hounds, and the low-speed chase was good for business too: Domino's Pizza reporting that pizza delivery sales during the televised police chase surpassed sales on Super Bowl Sunday, Toussaint said.

The reaction to the O.J. Simpson trial in my own community, I told Toussaint, could not have been more diametric to the cheering and underdogging in Standard Heights. The respectable white denizens of small towns with big names like Demopolis, Tuscaloosa, Montgomery, and the smaller towns in between like Greensboro, Lowndesboro, and Hayneville, were horrified that O.J. Simpson might be acquitted, if not exonerated, on account of his sports celebrity, his luminary football persona somehow overruling his blackness, even though many of them had watched and cheered for him when he was a star running back for USC and then in the NFL for the Buffalo Bills and the San Francisco 49ers. The salt of the earth was behind him when he was running on the field, but he was not running from the law as a running back, O.J. ran over 11,000 yards for 61 touchdowns and set numerous NFL records, and they watched the police chase too, tuning into the news and ordering meat lover's pizzas, riveted by the spectacle of a former athlete trying presumptuously as much as uselessly to elude the law as the running back once eluded and juked defensive backs on the field with his wily athletic moves, my own relatives cheering for the cops to overtake the white Bronco, for the police helicopters to open fire and end the police chase in a made-for-TV fireball — this is why they paid for cable, is it not? — the police chase could not go on forever like this, it was an embarrassment to the dog-whistle law and order they saw in the prison stripes of the referee's jerseys. O.J. Simpson's running from the cops, in their estimation, which is worth little, I said, was an admission of culpability, their minds were made up then, O.J. did it, he murdered his white wife and her white male companion out of black jealousy, case closed, after all those years of football "The Juice" had a vile temper and an abusive history, many of them discountenancing the miscegenated marriage in the first place, without ever thinking through the myriad reasons why a black man might run from the police, I told Toussaint. But that did not stop the salt of the earth from picking up the sensationalist tabloids at checkout counters, the *National Inquirer* featuring O.J. and the Bronco police chase on the front cover, and later the indelible lurid image of him squeezing his large, running back's hands into the black leather gloves, and then primly if finitely shocked by the pornographic forensic photos of the jackoff bloodbath of a crime scene, Nicole's head nearly decollated from her neck by the murderer's knife, but then when the House of Spencer's Princess Diana died in a gruesome car accident, these same salt of the earth, who live in a federal presidential constitutional republic, and are no more monarchists than they were believers in O.J.'s presumption of innocence, these salt of the earth were so distraught, so discomposed by the tragic death of a princess that they sent flowers and cards to Buckingham Palace, while O.J. stopped counting the death threats he received in prison, I said.

The Green Book

Drawn by the vacant lots strongly resembling — in the violence of their vacancy, the anti-memory of their erasure — Standard Heights, I found Toussaint, his social security number tattooed on his forearm, at 1208 South Saratoga Street, the address where Robert Charles was gunned down by New Orleans police in 1910. Toussaint stood in a tentative position, neither on nor off the vacant lot, the house in which the standoff occurred now long gone, contemplating invisible essences or some unfinished effects of the turbid histories ensnaring us both, histories personal and continental which we were still making sense of. The day was uncommonly hot, even for New Orleans, and Toussaint and I sweated together; it was not exactly friendship but whatever condition it was was strengthened by the shared experience of profuse perspiration beneath the ultraviolet judgment of a crucifying sun that seemed to expose my every self-conceit in its radical glare. Bells at St. John the Baptist Church tolling the hour were the only indication that time was passing at all.

My father reminded us, Toussaint said, that the Rodney King riots were nothing new for us, terrifying us with the picaresque legends of Robert Charles and the riots he incited after killing four white policemen and several civilians, so that I never quite knew whether New Orleans was the most exciting place in America or the city which most nearly approximated a surreal nightmare. Robert Charles was a local leader in the black emigration movement to return to Liberia, a sort of Negro Free State, seeing with the clairvoyance of one who has already been chased by the bloodhounds what awaited us upriver as well as downriver: the body of the drowned Phoenician sailor floating on the Spillway, the police beating of Rodney King and the Curse of the Saints. The police in New Orleans were a sacrosanct brotherhood — the force of the community would descend upon the villainous thug who dared to attack that brotherhood. Not even ethnic whites were immune from the wrath of the sanguinary mob: Italians were lynched when Police Chief David Hennessy was assassinated by Italian mobsters. 1208 South Saratoga is now a trash-blown vacant lot, indistinguishable from Standard Heights, unmarked by any historical placard to recall what awful things took place here, Toussaint said, gesturing towards the lot. The omnivorous petrochemical nocturne is feeding on the few remaining physical tokens of its crimes, reducing every Green Book address into a vacant lot, devoid of personal memory or verifiable history, through piecemeal amnesia resolving into an asphalted generality. A portable basketball goal post has fallen over. The black and gold and purple lights lit up the Superdome. Though the brick steeple of St. John the Baptist Church commands one's attention up into the quagmire of clouds, it is in the Superdome, rising like a supermoon over Saratoga Street that God still speaks. The low din of traffic and linehaul trucks pounding the Pontchartrain Expressway rattles the bones of bishops in the church crypt, Toussaint said.

My father, who hung around South Rampart and Dryades Streets in those days, claims that he talked the talk with John Howard Griffin, a white journalist from Texas undercover in New Orleans as a black man after a dermatological operation temporarily darkened his skin, Toussaint said. Some sort of sociological experiment to document the black man's experience from the white man's perspective. He wrote about his experiences as a black man in *Black Like Me*, which my father had no interest in ever reading, he did not need some Texas cracker telling him what it was like being a black man in New Orleans. But the man could pass for black, my father said, the dermatological operation worked. This white journalist rancher from Texas' skin was dark as the white man's soul is said to be. He thought it was strange that a white man should wish to become black, as often as folks in Standard Heights sometimes wished for a whitening themselves, but after so many years at the ExxonMobil plant he had stopped questioning anything the white man did. The white-man-turned-black-man's book had a familiar mantra, *Now you go into oblivion*, though my father never read it, leaving for his graveyard shift at the plant he often said this to us, it was his way of saying goodnight. I lived on the other side of oblivion, the side you cannot see, Toussaint said looking at me, like the west bank of the Mississippi River, the cane field smoke through which Whipped Peter ran from plantation bloodhounds. Fleeing the bloodhounds, running as fast as "The Juice" in his Heisman Trophy year, Whipped Peter himself must have run through the rows of wind-rippled cane fields and burned up into smoke himself. I have waded into the cane fields, that wide green sea undulating from horizon to horizon, the thrashing rows crashing down upon me like green waves, and been pulled under like the drowned Phoenician sailor, in search of Whipped Peter, finding only the burning oblivion of the cane harvest. You're on one side of oblivion, Toussaint said, and I'm on the other. Into oblivion like my brother's attempted suicide by cop, into oblivion like poor Leonard Deadwyler, shot and killed by police after speeding through red lights, not because he was running from the law like O.J., but because his wife, who was in labor, needed a doctor. Into oblivion like my father reporting to work for his shift at the plant the night of the Christmas Eve explosion. Into oblivion like the football lost in the mountain of oil drums. Into oblivion like everything the petrochemical nocturne has ever touched. What you must understand is that New Orleans, in the days before the Louisiana Purchase, was a more civilized and racially subtle society than it was after its Americanization, the Southern white Protestants mindlessly imposing the binary racial classification system through which they viewed the universal modulations of skin tone and against which Robert Charles threw himself into oblivion. Petrochemical Modernism cannot operate in a complex world of triads and tetrads and pentads. Only binaries will do, Toussaint said.

Not long after the O.J. Simpson freeway chase, I discovered the only book in the house other than a Bible, my mother's cookbooks, some safety manuals from the plant — a slim, green book that almost disappeared in my hands. The greenness of the cover belied the contents, its significance negated by the volume's thinness.

I lifted the book, open, to my face and inhaled the dust of the Jim Crow era. The title was strange and lurid: *The Negro Motorist Green Book.* I knew from the n-word in the title, a word seldom used except by Standard Heights' grandfathers, that the book must be very old, from another time before the pickup games and maybe even older than the Curse of the Saints, Toussaint said, looking off towards the Superdome and wiping beads of sweat from his pensive brow. My father had never owned a car; in Standard Heights, the plant was so close he walked the few empty blocks to work, passing few people, just the menagerie of hungry strays, mostly cats, raccoons, dogs, and police, the occasional lost ibis or heron blown inland from the river. For our trips to St. Charles Parish to bear witness, as my father called it, to the opening of the Spillway he borrowed a truck from a dead friend. The Green Book was like a survival manual for the world before my own, advising Negro travelers how to navigate America's sundown towns, the segregated public facilities, and find friendly lodgings, gas stations, mechanic shops, beauty salons, restaurants, nightclubs, country clubs, and other wayside amenities where a black man could rent a room, get a flat tire fixed, a meal to eat, a hot shower, a roof over his head, a drink and dance to music, without the worriment of strange fruit. I was shaken by how many unwelcoming places were outside the South. Salt Lake City had not a single hotel that would rent a room to a Negro. Glendale, California; Levittown, New York; Warren, Michigan; Anna, Illinois. Northern cities that I believed were progressive open societies, welcoming of the South's *persona non gratas,* its racial refugees and undesirables, such as by a certain age I knew us to be. Sure enough, there was Baton Rouge among the sundown towns. A town where I had watched the sun go down many times across the river, Toussaint said. And there, among the list of colored motels in each state was a familiar name, the Gaston Motel, in Birmingham, Alabama — a motel I'd heard my mother mention before to my father when she did not know my brother and I were listening through the thin walls of that already disappearing family home. This association then, between the Gaston Motel and the Green Book, meant that my mother had once been a traveling Negro, I realized.

I knew my mother was in the room before she said anything, her presence detectable in the silent scorn of the black words on the page, Toussaint said. You mustn't let your father know you saw that, she warned. But why not? Are we not supposed to travel? She took the book from me, quickly scanning the pages herself, and I cannot say whether she saw the words *Gaston Motel* on the page before her, but she hurriedly clapped the book closed and returned it to its spot on the shelf, disappearing in the dark recess created by the shelf's depth — no light ever seemed to penetrate back there.

The Green Book with its sundown towns and petty little segregations instilled in me a total terror of the world — of which up till then I had only chance and fleeting glimmers — outside Standard Heights greater than, or if not greater, then a degree of terror of quality and quantity certainly equal to the terror I felt when I thought of the punishments that would befall me for violating my father's Eleventh Commandment never to open the windows. Did O.J. Simpson not read this Green Book? Rodney King and Robert Charles? There was no known Green Book instructing us in how to travel within or without Standard Heights, within or without Baton Rouge, within or without Louisiana. We traveled from Hiawatha Street to Pontiac Street at our own risk, Toussaint said. Standards Heights was both a jungle and savannah, man-eating lions roamed the alluvial plains, rabid bloodhounds and ostriches, talking pelicans and peacocks, yet no one had written any travel guide about it. We had potholes the size of lunar craters, and bullet hole stars in the night sky. We played by the rules of our own Green Book, and I promised my brother that when we learned where the streets with native names lead, I would write the Green Book to guide the wandering, lost souls of Standard Heights safely out of the petrochemical plantation, Toussaint said, looking down Saratoga Street as the Superdome changed colors from black and gold to Mardi Gras green, gold, and purple.

My brother and I did not watch the Rodney King videotape when it occurred — my mother would not have wanted us to see it, and no one we knew in Standard Heights had a television in 1991 — though I will never forget — even today I expect the worst when I see one — the white 1987 Hyundai Excel in the background of the video frame, the car from which King and his buddies were forcibly removed by the Los Angeles police: this is why they wrote the Green Book, I thought to myself. If only King had had the Green Book he might not have been bludgeoned with police batons and kicked by their boots, the race riots avoided, maybe he would've driven to safety in the Gaston Motel, but then he would not have become the celebrity figure who loomed over the O.J. freeway chase and the too-small black glove in the trial. My brother said that ten seconds of blurry footage, at the beginning of the tape, showing King charging the officers were edited out of existence. No one knows where those ten seconds of footage went, or what might happen if they were restored, but it felt like years were stolen without those ten seconds.

King was cited for a litany of traffic incidents, and there is nothing the police hate more than a black man who cannot obey basic traffic laws, which for the police represent the simplest expression of his need for law and order: King driving his vehicle under the influence into a wall in downtown Los Angeles; a hit and run of his wife; citation for erratic driving with an expired license; another arrest for speeding and failing to stop at a red light; and driving the wrong way. Traffic citations are offenses against the dog-whistle law and order and the Green Book recognized this. Speeding, running red lights at will, failing to signal — all contraventions that could metamorphose into a German Coast Uprising. Take the case of Leonard Deadwyler, Toussaint said, failing to stop at red lights while driving his wife, who was then in labor, to the hospital. It is imperative to this order that the Negro stay in his lane, stop when told, and not presume to travel between Point A and Point B any faster than his countrymen. The eyes must always be open; closed eyes could be dreaming. Given King's history with the Los Angeles police, knowing firsthand what the police might do to him were he pulled over again for reckless, intoxicated, erratic, or African-American driving, it seemed that King was attempting what my brother also failed to bring to completion: suicide by cop. King's suicidal drinking and driving, so long after the riots named after him — the police had so colonized his mind, as the Baton Rouge police colonized my brother's mind, the colonizer had to be decolonized only by the self-sacrifice of the colonized, like running into a two-way mirror that reflects not oneself but one's persecutors, and on the other side of that mirror, invisibly watching you run headlong at the mirror is a white crewcut cop with a cockroach mustache in a chair, laughing satanically and indifferently taking administrative notes; if he did not seek it out consciously and deliberately, death by cop would come to him ineluctably and as a matter of course by some other means, unconsciously or happenstantially, in order to fulfill the statistical imperative of Clinton's 1994 omnibus crime bill, with its three strikes baseball rule, as prison beds need the bodies of superpredators in them to create cash flow. Even if King's attempts at suicide by cop failed, the Los Angeles police got King — no known relation to Martin Luther — in the end, just as the Great White Hope got Jack Johnson in the end, and as the Christmas Eve explosion got my father in the end, Toussaint said, staring with intense concentration at the vacant lot on Saratoga Street. King was found unresponsive at the bottom of his swimming pool, Toussaint said, the drowned Phoenician sailor. I told you to respect the laws of water, my father said, the Spillway release roaring in our ears. The autopsy report, which like the Christmas Eve explosion accident report delved no deeper than the twilight of appearances, concluding that King died by drowning resulting from cardiac arrhythmia while under the influence of illegal substances. His arrest and beating had nothing to do with it, in other words. Suicide by cop is not yet recognized by most coroners as a legitimate cause of death, Toussaint said.

I attended a high school named after a Confederate war hero, Toussaint said, and because after school I did not wish to return to the vacant lots of Standard Heights, I loitered among the long, foreboding shelves of the school's library, shelves that cast long shadows from the fluorescents humming above like lights on death row, fingering the spines of crumbling books, some with pages moldering, others missing or ripped out. The school library's collection acquired secondhand from the purged books of the white schools' libraries across town where the hazmat trucks never went. Books donated from all over, some from downriver. I opened a book at random and turned to the copyright page stamped with the seal of William Frantz Elementary School, a school that for the black community held terrifying connotations. Most of the library's books were older than the Curse of the Saints. Anything on science was long antiquated. In that school library, the Ptolemaic universe still prevailed in the minds of fish and snails, and the earth beneath was hollow, as in Edmond Halley's hypothesis of an inhabited inner earth core. Phlogiston was the contributing root cause of the rash of arsons — the fires for love and insurance — in Standard Heights.

Forbidden now to read our home copy, I asked the librarian to show me the shelf where they kept the Green Book. The librarian, a woman older than my mother and so very old indeed, slippering around the library with her hipshot gait, much like a scholarly hunchback, weathering our ridicule with equanimity, that she looked at me with the same horrified solicitude as my mother when I ate the satsumas growing wild in Standard Heights. I knew then I was on to something, that it was not just my mother who feared the Green Book's list of addresses for traveling Negroes, Toussaint said, but the librarian was a step ahead of me. She knew which green book I meant, but instead of the Green Book she gave me *Sir Gawain and the Green Knight*, a story I read with the gusto and reverent apprehension I read the Green Book before my mother confiscated it. I read of the green knight mounted on a green horse who enters King Arthur's court, and challenges the assembled guests to an absurd contest: to strike him once with his own axe on the condition that the Green Knight may return the blow a year from the day. The axe bequeathed to whomever accepted the challenge. No other knight but Sir Gawain in all of King Arthur's court arose to the Green Knight's strange challenge, and Sir Gawain raised the Green Knight's axe over his neck and let it fall in one expert movement upon the goliath's monumental green head, Toussaint said.

Every hero, I was learning, must pass a test. O.J. Simpson's test was the freeway chase and my tests, should they come, would not be academic multiple choice, more like the tests in Greek myth, escaping from labyrinths, questing for the Golden Fleece, getting out of Standard Heights alive. But the Green Knight, instead of falling after his head had been chopped off with his own axe, remained animated, undead, picking his decapitated head up off the court's floor and remounting his green steed, the neck hemorrhaging voluminous blood and gore, and the severed head's lips, still empowered with speech, reminding Sir Gawain to meet him at the Green Chapel in a year's time to conclude their agreement. The Green Knight's severed head's lips whispered the dreadful names of sundown towns in the Green Book to me in dreams, and I beheld the beheadings of my favorite Saints players, one by one. The holy roller churches in Standard Heights were all painted a sickly pale green like the legend's Green Chapel where I, like Sir Gawain, flinched at the Green Knight's first axe blow, failing the test, and waking up as my head fell off my neck. O.J. Simpson was a sort of black knight to my father, and had O.J. used the medieval defense oath of compurgation, he might've been acquitted of the crimes for which he was convicted when he tried to reclaim his own sports memorabilia in a Las Vegas hotel room, Toussaint said.

Because the only books we had in the home were the Green Book and the Bible, I asked the librarian if I could borrow a copy of Beecher's Bible, something I'd heard about from a Saints fan known in Standard Heights as an Islamist, and which I took to be some especially radical unorthodox translation of the Bible. The librarian again silently considered my request, shaking her head in tested patience with this tetched little boy asking for strange books, then explained the true meaning of these so-called Bibles. Beecher's Bible referred to the breech-loading Sharps rifles covertly smuggled to anti-slavery immigrants in Kansas, to equip an armed struggle that would earn that state the moniker of Bleeding Kansas, as a result of the Kansas-Nebraska Act's ruling that the matter of slavery in the new state would be decided by popular sovereignty. To me it seemed that all the states were bleeding, especially Bleeding Louisiana, whip-scarred as it was with river wounds like Whipped Peter's back. There are no Beecher's Bibles in this library, the librarian said.

Sir Gawain and the Green Knight was my first baptism in the Biblical story of David and Goliath, a story my father never mentioned unless the Saints were playing that Sunday. And though all knights in shining armor were, without exception in the legends, valiant white men, the precursors of the Age of Exploration's white adventurers and globe-insatiable navigators, such as Captain James Cook and Mungo Park, in those stories, Toussaint said, I dressed in medieval armor and raised the axe over the Green Knight's neck. I too might be a gallant knight in shining armor, Toussaint said, riding golden steeds into the smoke and welter of the Siege of Osage Avenue.

Nothing stopped me from being that knight in shining armor, I said to Toussaint, as we both watched an old woman, resembling a Section 8 archangel, pushing a grocery cart full of fried chicken down Saratoga Street. We may live on opposing sides of oblivion but the knight was a trope that was not forbidden to little white boys in Alabama, I said. I did not yet know of my blood relation to one of the conspirators in Lincoln's assassination, the handsome and charming Powell, his meandering skull with the same underlying structure and features as my own, though like Toussaint, I too attended a public school named in honor of a Confederate war hero, the artillery officer John Pelham who died young and left a handsome corpse, like those sleeping soldiers in Gardner's battlefield photos. No one who went to school there knew who Pelham was, much less the reason the school was named for him. In my own school library, I had modern textbooks on any subject, and I saw the headless pink flamingo body flapping and fluttering as blood ran from the bird's neck in the pages of *The Birds of America*. I could not have known then that the sound of the school bell as it rang and rang like an alarm in that public school named for a Confederate artilleryman was the petrochemical nocturne warning me like the sirens at the plant of coming storms, I said.

The Green Book was the black man's *On The Road*, Toussaint said, a book I read many years later, and one which could only have been written by a white man, for had a black man done even a quarter of the things Dean Moriarty and Sal Paradise did while on the road in the America of the late 1940s he would be just another Treyvon Martin. The school library's collection was haphazardly curated, with books out of order, books in African languages no one spoke, science textbooks that were hopelessly antique, books that had not yet registered the occurrence of some of the century's most newsworthy, momentous events, in which the Cuban Missile Crisis or the Civil Rights Movement had not yet happened. Despite historical inadequacies, these textbooks from the past were a timely escape from the Angola of the present. I devoured travelogues especially. But I never found *The Negro Motorist Green Book*, though I must have read the title printed on the spine of every book in that library. I thought there might be other similar such books — blue books, orange books, red books, black books — in the State Library where I read the memoirs of Booker T. Washington and I read Martin Luther King Junior's *Letter from a Birmingham Jail,* a place I hoped never to go; I read *The Souls of Black Folk* and *Incidents in the Life of a Slave Girl*; *The Mis-education of the Negro* and *The Autobiography of Malcolm X*. I read the *Experience and Personal Narrative of Uncle Tom Jones* and *Twelve Years of Slave* about a New York free person of color who was bamboozled and sold into slavery in Bleeding Louisiana. I read about Harry Haywood, and I read Amira Baraka. I read anything that I thought would aid me in escaping the rabid bloodhounds in the petrochemical labyrinth of Standard Heights, Toussaint said.

But I read other things too, Western history, what white people did to one another and the earth, enchanted with Greek mythology, the petty jealousies and cosmic conflicts. Greek myth divided nicely into three ages: an age when gods dwelt alone in the seas and mountains; an age when gods mixed freely and sometimes comically with mortals; and then a heroic age when the gods meddled seldom in human affairs and great heroes like Martin Luther King and Booker T. Washington, Drew Brees and Mark Ingram defined the heroic age, an age that must have started ending with the corporate merger of Exxon and Mobil into that bicephalic petrochemical monster and really ended with the Christmas Eve explosion. Then a final, tragic, non-heroic age, which we are enduring now like an electroshock patient endures his treatment. Every Greek hero had a relatable hamartia, like the fallible and self-destructive Saints players who fumbled, missed tackles, and threw disastrous interceptions, provoking father into depressive rages and the final defenestration of the television onto the front yard.

I recognized many of those around me as gods: the rape, murder and incest the Greek chroniclers described of their deities not altogether different from what I knew of families in Standard Heights. Sometimes the Greek gods did not behave very godlike, they were awful people immune to disease and injury, laughing at error, and happy to make war. I read with rapt terror of the Gigantomachy, the great battle fought between the Olympians and the race of Giants for control of the cosmos, and the Titanomachy, that ten-year war fought between the Titans and the Olympians to determine which generation of gods would have dominion over human affairs. All around me, on Hiawatha Street and Osage Avenue, it seemed we were still embroiled in these good fights, unrefereed matches between immortals, in the Rodney King riots and the bombing of Osage Avenue still deciding which generation would lord it over the mountain of oil drums.

I studied Greek myths with the same zeal Standard Heights' churchgoers learned Bible characters like David and Goliath, Samuel and Saul, Joseph and Mary, and because I associated Biblical places like Golgotha and Judea with the mythmaking of Christendom, I began constructing my own myths based on local geography and place names. Oceanus lived in the Mississippi, the great infernal river running between Standard Heights and the west bank where the bloodhounds of Cerberus laid in wait for runaways, which to me was the outermost margins of the knowable ecumene, an infrastructural underworld where Whipped Peter, Charles Deslondes, and the heroic dead lived a spectral, cadaverous, adumbral post-existence delighting in Elysium, and in this august invisible company we played pick-up games on the Elysian Fields of Standard Heights' greenbelt lots.

The land west of the river — West Baton Rouge Parish and beyond where the sun flamed down red and orange each evening over the treetops and skeletal trusses of the great bridge — this land was home to the legions of dead. I was certain that Cajun cannibals lived across the river. Franklin's disastrous expedition ended somewhere in West Baton Rouge Parish and in this parish the cannibals had their own currency, elected leaders, a dead language and cannibal holidays, keeping bloodhounds for pets. After the Christmas Eve explosion, I climbed the great churchlike trees along the high bluffs overlooking the river to see the dead I'd read must be waiting on the other side of Oceanus' watery home, which I populated with drowned sailors, heartbroken lovers, vanished natives, and bloodhounds. Whipped Peter, Charles Deslondes and my father too must be there in the afterlife cane fields with Rodney King and all other suicides by cop. The Mississippi was all hot water baptisms of the river dead, and in all this creolization of geographies I could no longer reliably distinguish Acheron from Cocytus, or Phlegethon from Styx, all tributaries of the Mississippi itself which after the Christmas Eve explosion became the Lethe. The dead too climbed the skeleton trees of West Baton Rouge Parish to steal glimpses of those they'd left behind on the river's east bank, back in Standard Heights, and for a long time I believed that if I climbed high enough, higher even than the plant's cooling towers and smokestacks that Whipped Peter and Charles Deslondes would be able to spot me and I could wave in nostalgic greeting at them back into the past — a place more real and full of promise than the future languishing on the river's east bank. From the height of these bone trees I kept vigil for the cane harvest burning in the fall, those immense walls of roiling immolations and cane smoke betokening the ingress of hell, forming a rampart of fire between us and the bloodhounds and the frightful lash of the whip, Toussaint said, stepping out of the way of a police cruiser driving at slow motion dream speed down South Saratoga Street.

But the east bank was not always the real estate that the living cracked it up to be either: Devil's Swamp Lake, a manmade lake but more like the devil's bedpan just north of Standard Heights and the ExxonMobil plant, created to construct Baton Rouge Harbor — a misnomer, as the harbor was a stygian alluvium, a harbor in name only. Timidly at first, out of the hazmat chemical placard depicting a leafless tree and dead fish, spotted on a hazmat truck the day we lost the football in the mountain of old drums, I began developing my very own homegrown thanatology, working through the recreant jitters that speechlessly swamped me, the plant's warning sirens were my threnody. The more superstitious Christians would not boat or fish there. Devil's Swamp Lake was classified as a Superfund, which I imagined was some kind of mutual fund that generated fabulous amounts of money like the blinking casinos on the river and the portraits of Power Ball winners on Interstate 10 billboards. The crawfish netted at Devil's Lake were hideous crustaceous beasts, apocalyptic inesculent anthropods cast out the Garden of Eden, condemned to earth, like the Monster of Ravenna. A few white Christians, for whom eternity was in the lower intestine, told us that the devil lived in Devil's Swamp Lake, a hairy, sulfurous and baleful angel who could not be trusted with the keys to the plantation. For this very reason, and no other, my father took me to fish Devil's Swamp Lake and the fish we caught — eyeless, muculent, half-dead fish-like things, more terrifying than the insane catfish he brought home in a paint bucket — were not the Miraculous Draught of Fish caught on the Sea of Galilee. Far from it, Toussaint said. The Exxon-Mobil plant was wormwood, the noxious star that poisoned a third of the waters. And every time we went to Devil's Swamp Lake, I saw one of the hazmat cargo trucks with the chemical symbol of the leafless tree and the dead fish on it. The Devil's Swamp Lake, before the fish-kills and the Superfund classification, was fished by the red stick natives who drank clear and pure water directly from the earth, cupped in the palm of the hand out of crystalline streams, uncontaminated creeks, undebased bayous, but I was terrified of even drinking the slummy metallic tap water that irregularly flushed from the faucets in Standard Heights like a russet and rancid flatulence.

I feared that if we could not eat the catch or the crawfish from Devil's Swamp Lake we would be forced, like the white Europeans, to the last resort of cannibalism as were the doomed explorers of the Franklin expedition. But it appeared that as yet there was no knockout and no prize money in the Gigantomachy, for a white — the race of the perpetrator is almost a boring tautology at this point — coworker at the ExxonMobil plant shot and killed a plant safety supervisor on my father's graveyard shift and we forgot about the wormwood in Devil's Swamp Lake. Black men get into gang violence, sure. One of the pickup boys might shoot you over turf, hustling the wrong side of Pocahontas Street, but a white man will shoot total strangers. White men become business executives, professional sports franchise owners, senators, serial killers, and workplace shooters: any given day there are numberless angry white men so fed up with women's suffrage and blacks voting and who uses what bathroom that they're one bad day away from shooting up a daycare. Not even rich old white men are any longer safe from the murderous rampages of their fellow rich old white men, Toussaint said.

But the white men were mild compared to the malevolence of their white women. In the opening of *The Devil Finds Work*, James Baldwin was enamored with white women — Joan Crawford and that generation of beautiful, seraphic Hollywood actresses — but I was petrified of them, Toussaint said, the mere presence of a white woman gave me the heebie-jeebies: white women were the mothers, wives, and sisters of the white men who whipped Whipped Peter, the white men who decided it would be a good idea to build the ExxonMobil plant on the east bank of the river, the white cops who beat up Rodney King, they were the bitches to the bloodhounds guarding the west bank of the river wound, and the white women even dabbled in the dark arts of torture and sadism themselves my father said, making creative refinements and little flourishes of their own where their white men lacked the imagination. There was Darya Nikolayevna Saltykova, the bloodthirsty Russian noblewoman who preyed on her serfs. Countess Elizabeth Báthory, the female Dracula, torturing hundreds of little girls in her castle dungeon: beatings, burnings, mutilations, freezings, starvations, biting the soft flesh off a young peasant girl's face. Writhing bodies covered in honey and live ants. Always the girls were of a lower social class than the Countess herself, peasant daughters. On one of these latter fishing expeditions to Devil's Swamp Lake, not long before the fish died off altogether, the last ichthyoid harvest floating lifelessly on the dead swampy surface, drinking whiskey from a half-gallon milk jug my father related to me, Toussaint said, what he knew about the Delphine LaLaurie mansion in the French Quarter, a neighborhood to which at that age I'd not yet been, and which sounded like some exotic and supremely decadent Francophone Sodom and Gomorrah where no one ever wore clothing and peed in the streets. The Delphine, so my father said that day on Devil's Swamp Lake, was accused of having tortured her enslaved persons — we shall not call them slaves, he said, because you can't be a slave unless you're born one — binding them in kinky iron collars and fettering them to the walls, torturing those already held in bondage excited some nefarious colossus that otherwise remained latent in the center of the white reptilian brain. A slave girl died attempting to escape Delphine LaLaurie's subjection, she jumped from the balcony — one of those beautiful wrought-iron balconies green with the hanging ferns from which the krewes launch throw beads and other Mardi Gras trinkets — and died on the cobbles of Royal Street. There are worse places to die I suppose, my father said, reeling in a thrashing wormwood fish that did not want to be caught. We brought five fish home from that final trip to Devil's Lake Swamp, but my mother refused to cook them — she did not want them in the house, a poisonous fish crossing the threshold of the house invited disaster, and she went hungry instead of consuming tainted petrochemical fish, Toussaint said, but my brother and I ate it because our father did.

After the Christmas Eve Explosion, that New Year's Day I went one last time to Devil's Swamp Lake, still no sign of life or fish, an amorphous and oleaginous green-black sheen shimmering in colorful blooms on the swamp's motionless extinct surface. I could smell the devil's bedpan long before I reached it. The flaming river which in my mythological geography had been Cocytus, the river of lamentation, and Acheron, that mythological river separating the land of the living — a brazen lie — from the posthumous lands where the cane harvests blazed. And before the shattered glass from the exploded windows was swept off the floor of the house, I saw Charon ferrying the soul of my father across the dark waters of the Mississippi and into the underworld plantation on the west bank. He did not wave goodbye, Toussaint said.

And neither did Toussaint wave goodbye, in that inimitable way of his departures, abruptly ending a storyline whenever he was through with it, or it was through with him, whichever came first, the way he might have thrown a dead fish back into Devil's Swamp Lake. I watched as he walked towards the Superdome. There was a game that night, and though he did not have a ticket, I think he liked being around the black and gold energy of the fans in Champions Square, remembering his father in an Aints baghead, hoping this might be the night the Curse of the Saints was finally broken, for good. South Saratoga Street was dead and empty, like a postmortem lying on an autopsy table, and the green and gold and purple lights on the Superdome went out, replaced by the Mercedes-Benz corporate logo branding the dome. But then something strange happened — the carmaker logo mutated through a kaleidoscopic series of ancient and arcane symbols, the Hand and Eye Motif and the hazmat transport ideographs for oxidizing liquids, corrosives, explosives, compressed gases, acute toxicity, skin corrosives, skin irritants, aspirant hazards, environmental and aquatic hazards, flammable gases, liquids and solids, one after the other in a rapid contaminated sequence of petrochemical hieroglyphs like the incanted alphabet of the Curse of the Saints on the side of the Superdome where the Mercedes-Benz logo had been.

Later that evening, after the Saints lost the game despite their home field advantage, I thought I saw Toussaint again standing before Delphine LaLaurie's mansion at 1140 Royal Street, his arms crossed over his chest, studying the mansion's third story rooms where LaLaurie's human chattel were subjugated in the cruelty of bondage, that peculiar institution of helotry that yokes the master perhaps more, or if not more, then at least in direct proportion to the extent of his enslavement of another. The Joan of Arc parade — a medieval procession of drunk stilts-walkers and horseback inquisitors — had just passed by, painted harlequins and green knights, a medieval fantasia. Toussaint might have been outside the Royal Street mansion a long time, turning into a timeless and immobile statue himself. Royal Street burned a bold and luculent gray-orange and the sun blown out like candlelight flickering in the watery pavement, as black rain dripped finally from the ironwork balustrade and wrought iron balconies filigreed with hanging potted ferns like the green gardens of a once great and ancient city. Then Toussaint unfolded his arms — I could see his Social Security number tattooed there — and began rubbing his throat with his hands, an assuagement of some phantasmal trauma, as if necklaced with an invisible iron collar.

The Lincoln Theater

On rare days of clement walking weather, I often left Spanish

Town and its plastic flamboyances of pink flamingos to get away from the plant warning sirens, threading downriver along the shoulder of River Road, the river invisibly progressing behind the levee top, catching the wind off hazmat trucks with their cabalistic language of chemical symbol placards. For miles between Baton Rouge and New Orleans, River Road follows the curvilinear meanderings of the many Mississippis, the strange hellish infrastructure of the petrochemical operations, the small communities nestled against tank farms, the road passing beneath overhead pipes that mysteriously cantilever out of the levee and run like trellised bridgework across the road — the landscape of a subtropical Bosch. River Road is fanned by arpents, the old French unit of land area, subdivided in deep and narrow lots that provided every landholder with river frontage and access to the rich plantation lands that grew rice, sugar cane and indigo. The arpent pattern, here and there, is broken up by the industrial aggregations of oil terminals and pipeline stations: the georgic life has been supplanted by the petrochemical. Another hazmat truck passed, this one marked by the skull and crossbones hazard symbol. I turned left onto Ashland Road, and there, beneath the hospitable shade of an aged oak tree, was Toussaint, contemplating the old rundown manor house with its classic white portico centering a gated green lawn — a relic from the river region's preindustrial days when a different type of plantation ruled the river wound and now the perfect set, frozen in time, for filming a movie about Whipped Peter's escape from the bloodhounds or the German Coast Uprising. At first I had thought the human shape a mere fallible effect of the oak shadows dappling the green but then the shadow moved and began to speak. An indeterminable time had passed since I had last seen him on South Saratoga Street at the place where Robert Charles went to the stygian lands west of the river: suicide by cop. A hazmat truck passed between us, and when it was gone, I crossed Ashland Road and turned to face the decaying, melancholy remains of the manor house.

I thought I might find you here, Toussaint said, sniffing around this old plantation movie set. Because theaters in the South were so meticulously segregated, Toussaint began, every African-American community had its own Lincoln Theater, so named for The Emancipator who was shot in Ford's Theater by a deranged Confederate actor. In perhaps one of the only ways that made it like everywhere else, Baton Rouge too had its own Lincoln Theater, closed and abandoned now, the film screens dark and bats in the projection room, where on Saturdays and Sundays I could view black and white films like *Imitation of Life, No Way Out* and *The Defiant Ones.* Nothing new. The Lincoln Theater did not show anything contemporary, the theater was a sort of antidote to the contemporary. For a long time, I would not set foot in the Lincoln Theater's dark amphitheater, fearing I would be shot by a deranged Confederate actor from the 19th century, a zombie century which did not want to die, kept on life support by Petrochemical Modernism.

Sundays at the Lincoln Theater were ideally suited for movie-going because the theater was empty and I did not have to fear being shot by a madcap actor like John Wilkes Booth in my hometown's Lincoln Theater. More often than not, I was the sole theater-goer, able to choose any seat in the theater, and even change seats in the middle of a film if I wanted to get closer for a better look at a particular scene's details, or farther away from the screen when a scene panned out and I needed to take in the totality of the panorama, or when a scene of vivid violence could not be endured from the proximity of the front row. The old man in the ticket booth did not care that I was too young to see such films of the country's racial id. I saw Blaxploitation films like *Mandingo* and *Sweet Sweetback's Baadassssss Song*, *The Black Angels*, about a black biker gang, *Blacula*, which is exactly what it sounds like, *Blackenstein* and *Dr. Black, Mr. Hyde,* the plots of which are also predictable enough, but most poignantly I remember *Mandingo's* Blanche, a beautiful blonde drunk with a terrible, mangy Southern accent, and the counterpoint to James Baldwin's love affair with Joan Crawford, Toussaint said, looking towards one of the upper windows of the old manor house. The racy plot of *Mandingo* is a dazzling trashy blur now, the movie poster in the cracked window of the Lincoln Theater like a miscegenated sendup of *Gone With the Wind*. The slave master of this film — a handsome quarterback type named Hammond — purchases a slave from the Mandinka people of West Africa, Ganymede, played by former boxer Ken Norton, forced to become a prize-fighter to enrich Master Hammond's purse and by proxy defend the master's injured virility, and forced to submit to soaking in hot water to toughen his skin. They were called slaves then, not enslaved persons, because that was the word Master Hammond fashioned for his investment property. I could not see Muhammad Ali soaking in scalding hot water to toughen his skin for a fight promoted by Don King. Blanche and Hammond marry — because this is the South, starring trashy white people, she has been having an affair with her brother, but represented herself to Hammond as a virgin, the very picture of the white trash jezebel — but after discovering a slave girl is pregnant with her husband's child, she blackmails and seduces Ganymede — she will tell the Master that he raped her if he does not comply with her perverse demands. Such is the movie's plot, probably loosely based on a true story, or true in the sense that the chlorine gas ghost ships and the bloodhounds are, Toussaint said. Like Mayweather toying with McGregor for twenty-eight minutes in the ring, each minute worth almost $10 million each, Ganymede spends much of the film's 127 minutes shirtless, muscled as the men in a Michelangelo, and I could not understand why he didn't beat up his oppressors, male or female, but *Mandingo* instilled in me what I already knew from my father's stories of Delphine LaLaurie at Devil's Swamp Lake — that white women are dangerous, and that boxing's origins can be traced back to the plantation. A white man might whip you or make you fight other Negroes to earn your keep, but a cruel beautiful trashy white woman like Blanche will take body and soul. And when I saw the Mayweather-McGregor fight all those years later, the bar packed with a hundred drunk frat-bro clones of Master Hammond, I thought of poor Ganymede and his painful death in a cauldron of boiling water right here on the lawn of the manor house — the Great White Hope of *Mandingo* got Ganymede too in the end, Toussaint said, pausing a moment as a hazmat truck jounced down Ashland Road.

I knew from my readings of Greek mythology in the State Library that Ganymede's homeland was Troy, abducted by Zeus in the form of an eagle, the all-American mascot. Homer writes of Ganymede in the *Iliad* that he was "the loveliest born of the race of mortals, and therefore the gods caught him away to themselves, to be Zeus' wine-pourer, for the sake of his beauty, so he might be among the immortals." Abducted and enslaved even among immortals, to pour the wine of the gods, rather than work the fields of mortals, the naming of the lead slave character as Ganymede was no mere happenstance. Like the myths, Southern plantation life was rife with the petty jealousies and incestuous dalliances and murderous clashes of the Greek heroes and gods, just look at this old place, Toussaint said, referring to the old manor house, a giant blackbird keeping watch from the portico.

Once I saw enough of these films I began to discern the general contours of Blaxploitation's subgenres: martial arts, westerns, horror, prisons, comedy, nostalgia for the Old South, musical, though to me they were all comedic horrors or horrific comedies, and I loved the strange soundtracks of funk and soul and jazz — I had never heard anything but the plaintive dirge of the petrochemical nocturne that resounded industrially through Standard Heights, and so I went to the movies as much for the music as for the Blaxploitation storylines, the plots like the rotting flood debris in the landfill. I first heard the music of Herbie Hancock in the soundtrack for *The Spook Who Sat By The Door* — there was no Herbie Hancock on Hiawatha Street, only the sound of the plant warning system. Remembering the soundtracks more than the storylines, I would return to these films watched alone in the silver darkness of the Lincoln Theater when I began ghostwriting hip hop lyrics in Atlanta and Houston, drawing on sources such as Jean Toomer's *Cane* and Longfellow's *The Song of Hiawatha* for birdsongs and swansongs about being raised by the concrete on Hiawatha Street, Toussaint said.

Sundays were the best for movie-going, the Lincoln Theater was my church: while Blanche interracially seduced Mede on screen, the other side, the south side of town pimpled with expensive white churches, crustaceous steeples and arthropod altars, echoed with the ring of lucre and tithings dropped like bombs from high altitudes into golden pans passed between soft hands, to the accompaniment of — there was never anything as joyous as singing, the human voice prohibited, strangulated, contaminated — bold floral baroque harpsichord music, a Baptist Buxtehude, almost like Halloween theme music, as the churches' mullioned belvedere windows transposed the earthly sunlight like Blanche's breath filtered through essence of lemon zest, and gothic flying buttresses, the tall and narrow lancet windows which strove, in their narrowness, to reflect the minds of the churchgoers and to keep the petrochemical world on the other side from encroaching upon this sanctum of white suburban prayer. While I sat alone in the Emancipator's theater, looking out for John Wilkes Booth and an assassin's bullet zipping through the silver dark, every white church across town, where educated plant workers and chemical engineers believed the Bible came down to Moses from Mount Sinai and directly to a Red Roof Inn bedside drawer and that Jesus Christ walking on floodwater was the only kind of Navy we need, was collecting tithes to pay for cancer treatments.

Overall, while from the back row I watched Blanche and Mede illicitly couple in darkness, the Sunday service took on the air of an expensive funeral. Meanwhile, in Standard Heights, the Sunday services, which I skipped to get churched in the Lincoln Theater, were more like a tailgating party. The black churches in Standard Heights were less highfalutin and less fire and brimstone than the crosstown white ones where Master Hammond would've gone to church, we were more exultant and cheerfully irreverent. Preachers did not wash their hands. We were not afraid of a few germs. We hugged and called those outside of our family brother and sister. That I was not baptized in one of those holy fortresses of gloom is only testament to my father's ability to indefinitely defer something he does not want to do by saying, with real feeling and heartfelt probity, he will get to it tomorrow, which never comes the way you think it will. A master class in temporizing against my mother's lifelong wish to see my soul saved from the various perditions that can befall a Standard Heights boy, but in the end he prevailed so thoroughly that my baptism — which he did not wish to be done with water from the Mississippi, for that would have made me too a *homo sacer* like all the other contaminated baptized boys of Standard Heights, who never made it out alive, baptized or not — was never consummated, and in the same way that baptism was supposed to set one apart from the secular mob, this non-baptism or indefinitely deferred baptism set me apart from my own tribe, Toussaint said, looking away from the old manor house now and in the direction of Fisk's river.

It was while biding my Sundays in the Lincoln Theater that I saw *The Defiant Ones* and though I don't recall whether I saw it before or after *Mandingo* it must have been after, even if *The Defiant Ones* came out decades before, because I remember reinterpreting everything I thought I knew about Ganymede and Master Hammond, for the next time I watched *Mandingo* I saw them in a new light, Ganymede and Master Hammond yoked to one another in iron shackles, invisible to them at the time, and invisible to me the first time I saw it, Toussaint said rubbing his neck and then his wrists as if invisibly shackled himself. And on the screen of *Imitation of Life* I pined for a mother like Juanita Moore, Toussaint said, though my mother shared more affinities with Juanita Moore than I could have known at the time. Having practically horse-traded with ExxonMobil to return my father's remains after the Christmas Eve explosion, I knew at once what *No Way Out* was really about: a black physician performing an autopsy on a white man — a black man was not permitted to see the insides of his oppressor's body — nothing to find there except godless red, white and blue blood and guts, soulless organs and meaningless, scornful viscera like any deer or pig sliced open. I did not feel one way or another about it, but it was probably from these Blaxploitation films in the Lincoln Theater that I developed any sense of *amour-propre*, which was not taught to the pickup boys but we earned it ourselves on the greenbelt gridiron. Certainly, we did not get it from our baghead fathers or the Saints who recorded another losing season that year. Certainly not from my mother's miscarriage or the mountain of oil drums. Certainly not from seeing the autopsy table in Charity Hospital where my father's guts were opened by a white coroner in a blue surgical mask, faceless like the hazmat teams that tested the air in Standard Heights after the Christmas Eve explosion, Toussaint said.

Years later, after the Saints finally won the Super Bowl, in the aftermath of the Aurora, Colorado theater shooting, I'd been right about a deranged white man shooting up a theater when James Eagan Holmes bought a ticket to the late night showing of *The Dark Knight Rises* in Theater 9 of the Century 16 multiplex and opened fire on the theatergoers, as if armed white men had a special evil affinity for attacking people while they escaped the troubles of this world by participating in the vicarious experiences of a fictional world, perhaps one with different rules or outcomes than this one. Sitting in the darkness of the Lincoln Theater, in the movie light of *Mandingo* or *The Defiant Ones*, this had been my worst fear. Holmes, like Booth, believed himself to be an actor: he'd even dressed up like The Joker character from the movie, his freakish hair dyed red-or-ange, wearing enough full-body armor to be victorious in the Siege of Standard Heights. In a parallel universe, the Aurora theater shooting occurred during a showing of *Django Unchained*, with Holmes dressed in costume as Dr. Schultz or the Monsieur Calvin J. Candie. Each Sunday, while the holy rollers got high and mighty on resurrection, I saw the same actors die, Ganymede in the cauldron of boiling water, wondering how actors like Ken Norton survived the filming and depiction on screen of their own deaths. I would no longer watch movies if I were an actor, Toussaint said, I couldn't stand to see myself die on screen, over and over, at the hands of a belligerent and demonic white man like Master Hammond.

This may have been around the time of the Mandela Effect, a mass delusion believed by hundreds of thousands, many of them white, on all continents that Nelson Mandela died in prison some-time in the 1980s and not, as was the case in this universe, in 2013, and any explanatory apparatus that invokes the crutch of parallel universes or time travel financed by the Koch Brothers is not to be credited. No, Mandela was alive and well in the 1980s, even if many wished for his death in prison. The Mandela Effect enraged my fa-ther, Toussaint said, it was more reminder that a black man had no place if it was not in the gridiron. There was no Bill Clinton Effect, or Hugh Hefner Effect. No one thought Clinton or Hefner, or Charl-ton Heston or Wayne LaPierre died in dehumanizing conditions in an apartheid jail cell decades before their obituaries were written. There was no Kennedy Effect, no Master Hammond Effect. No, it was as though the white world wished to be rid of us by closing their eyes and counting to three. I'm going to close my eyes and count to three, my father said, and when I open them there better not be a single white man on this planet. One. Two. Three. It didn't work, of course, the monopoly powers of collective memory wanted to believe Mandela was dead, or forget that he was alive, which amounts to the same thing, Toussaint said, turning at the sound of car tires.

A parish deputy pulled into the gated gravel drive leading to the Ashland Plantation house. I looked over at Toussaint — his hands were out of his pockets, clearly visible. Rodney King and the O.J. freeway chase must have flashed through his mind. The parish police, bored as they must be by rural policing, have a way of sneaking up on you unawares. Without leaving his vehicle, the deputy rolled the window down and confronted us — two out of place figures in a mixed plantation landscape of dark oaks guarding an old manor house movie set. Toussaint deferred this exchange with the representative of authority to me. Without being asked, I explained to the deputy we were here to see the house where the movie *Mandingo* was filmed. I pointed to the house I meant, even though there was only one. The deputy replied he'd never heard of it and didn't watch movies, but he drove away, seemingly satisfied with my answer. Toussaint never spoke a word. His empty hands remained outside his pockets till the police cruiser had disappeared in the blacktop vanishing point.

I had not seen the movie in many years, but after Toussaint's description of the scene in which Ganymede is forced by Master Hammond at gunpoint into a cauldron of boiling water and drowned with a pitchfork, I recognized the manor house's white columns and the grand portico at once, the backdrop to the movie's climactic scene, the destruction of another black body. Now that the parish police officer had disappeared downriver on Ashland Road, Toussaint seemed to feel comfortable in resuming his recollections of the Lincoln Theater.

I knew that Floyd Mayweather, for all his good fight prowess and ringside bravado, would have fared no better than Ganymede got, Toussaint said. *Mandingo* was filmed on location here, just south of Standard Heights at the Ashland-Belle Helen Plantation and the Burnsides Plantation, not far from the spot where my father showed me the springtime Spillway opening, Toussaint said, and I felt it in the hieroglyphs of the invisible keloid scars on my back that it was the boiling water from the cauldron that flowed through the Spillway and over my ancestors' graves in St. Charles Parish, Toussaint said.

The plantation and former movie set is closed to the public today, the sullen property fenced and withdrawn in curtains of Spanish moss, as the industrial plantations of the petrochemical companies take over more and more of the former agricultural lands — worked by enslaved persons — around it. The land once owned by Duncan Farrar Kenner, for whom the municipality of Kenner, Louisiana is eponymously named, is now owned by ExxonMobil, which has done little to improve the place or the grounds, as if the petrochemical supercorporation is in the haunted house business. Here Master Hammond fell in love with a slave girl. Here Ganymede fought bare-knuckled matches. Here Blanche seduced Ganymede. Here Blanche birthed a mulatto child. Here romantic reports of the German Coast Uprising of 1811 commixed with the river's wounds and skull and crossbones hydrocarbons to synthesize a toxic wormwood for Master Hammond's cauldron of boiling water.

Mandingo differs from *The Defiant Ones* and *No Way Out* precisely where those two earlier black and white films dovetail in agreement, Toussaint said in a sort of mixture of autobiography and critical film analysis. In *No Way Out*, which I saw one Sunday during a heavy thunderstorm that briefly made the power go out, Sidney Poitier's gesture — he has taken a medical Hippocratic oath, after all — of applying a tourniquet to the leg wound of the rabid racist who shot at him in the dark, even though he is told by Edie to let the man bleed — "I can't kill a man just because he hates me" — is structurally and symbolically homologous to Sidney Poitier's gesture in *The Defiant Ones* of not letting Tony Curtis fall from the train and to his death, from the locomotive which was so instrumental in the westward expansion of the skull and crossbones society. The black man saving the white man's life, Toussaint said, without looking at me. It's never the white man saving the black man's life, is it? For the culminating action of *No Way Out* I got as close to the screen as I could without falling through it and breaking the cinematic illusion, Toussaint said. I was so close to the screen that I could see the defects and scratches on the film and a black fly land on Poitier's head which was like the gigantic faces carved on Mount Rushmore. The tourniquet used to stanch the bleeding wound fashioned from a white woman's scarf, a scarf designed to hang about the neck and which could just as well choke or strangulate Poitier as save the crackbrain racist. All of these plotlines, the dénouement of *No Way Out* were written to comfort a white audience — I never saw one in the Lincoln Theater — which does not believe an armed madcap actor can rush into the theater at any time, in real life, and open fire the way he can at a black doctor on screen. Don't cry, white boy, you're gonna live, became a favorite line. Don't cry, white boy, you're gonna live, I said to every hazmat truck passing by on the crumbling streets named for the murdered native tribes. My father loathed these movies, Toussaint said, and all those years he did not know that on Sunday mornings his oldest son was in the Lincoln Theater watching a black doctor take care of a white man or a black boxer boiled alive in a slave master's cauldron. My father was an Iberville boy when Ken Norton walked beneath the hanging epiphytes of Spanish moss filigreeing the Ashland-Belle Helen Plantation, reenacting for the camera the subtle differences between a slave and an enslaved person, Toussaint said, taking a deep breath as the wind stirred the Spanish moss draped in the manor house's great oaks.

You may have been here long enough by now to have noticed: Baton Rouge has a distinct olfactory dimension to it — the gluey amalgam of sulfur, a gas leak, moldy gym towels, civilization burning, rotting bananas, rancid dog food, Toussaint said. Paper mill and sewage treatment plant. Just another Sunday. The multi-dimensional stench is stronger on burnoff days, and inside the theater, inhaling the stale dusty air of the theater that was like the inside of new and empty coffin, one can almost forget that the ExxonMobil plant is just upriver, but exiting the airless dark of Lincoln Theater I was reminded by the nose where I was: Baton Rouge. But there are Lincoln Theaters all over this whip-scarred land and mine, however special to me, was not the only one to ever show Blaxploitation films, Toussaint said. When I got out of Standard Heights for good, I wanted to see for myself the Lincoln Theater at 1215 U Street, next to Ben's Chili Bowl. The day I arrived on U Street, history was being rewritten. I looked on in the usual disillusionment as Bill Cosby's portrait — this was after Me Too's sexual assault allegations tarnished his celebrity beyond repair — was scrubbed from the mural like a depraved stain and a ghost silhouette emerged next to the outsized faces of Prince, Obama, Harriet Tubman and Dave Chappelle, a comedian my mother never liked for his liberal use of the n-word. Though the U Street Lincoln Theater was nicer than the tragic one back home — plusher seats, bigger screen, concession stand, roomier theater with a grand stage and gilt chandeliers that was more like an opera house than the charnel house in Baton Rouge — it was closed for many years after suffering damage in the 1968 race riots sparked by the assassination of Martin Luther King, Jr. and did not reopen till 1994, the stage where Ella Fitzgerald, Lionel Hampton, Louis Armstrong, Duke Ellington, and Billie Holiday had performed sitting empty and dark for decades.

The Lincoln Theater introduced me to a world beyond the putrid purlieus of Standard Heights, Toussaint said, the Lincoln awakened in me the dormant faculty of imagining a future beyond the streets with native names, but that all ended the day I went to the theater and a handwritten CLOSED sign hung over the door. The Lincoln Theater's closing terminated the faculty of projecting cinematic fantasy into a possible future, and it seemed that without the Lincoln there was no future at all, CLOSED signs hung on every door I could conceivably enter, and to an audience of one the Lincoln would now and for eternity screen only the most dismal productions: the bleak and austere Zone of Tarkovsky's *Stalker* — only white people could create a film so dull, so dreary, so ploddingly monotonous, so mind-bogglingly boring, Toussaint said, and I conceded his point — and the Nazi propaganda *Theresienstadt* film, the origin of which is a clever Aryan deceit: the Danish Red Cross was hoodwinked by a masterful Nazi theater production, a sanitized happy Potemkin village completed aesthetically by a children's opera and a production of Pavel Haas' orchestral works. Though the children of Standard Heights could not sing an opera — just rhymes for our own threnody, shrilling arias of hazmat symbols and descants of endocrine disruptors — I'd seen the community propaganda films ExxonMobil produced about the greenbelt, how the program would make Standard Heights a safer and healthier place and something something something about the public good, bottom lines, critical failures, shareholder value, Theresienstadt ghettos. These ExxonMobil films depicted a Standard Heights restored to its pristine natural condition after the buyouts, a world of enriched greens and wildlife refuges and Arcadian harmonies, but in reality the greenbelt was our dystopian Zone. How could the concentration camps be so bad if the children still sing and the Jewish orchestra plays so beautifully? The camp's overpopulation was remedied by deporting Jews to

Auschwitz, much as the population of Standard Heights, Toussaint sad, was emptied out — for what purpose we did not know at the time, though the final design is clear enough to me now — by bulldozers and devalued buyouts. The Gigantomachy was being waged across the centuries on many continents, with diverse principals and agents. The ExxonMobil greenbelt to be built on the ruined collateral of the nocturne like a New Eden on a landfill. The Thereseinstadt film, like the police dash cam footage of my brother's attempted suicide by cop, both of which I watched repeatedly until the events recorded no longer made any narrative sense, was inspired by *The Birth of a Nation*, the early silent epic drama film about the undead zombie Confederacy, and the boring sci-fi epic *Stalker* took both the Thereseinstadt film and *The Birth of a Nation* to their logical conclusion — Master Hammond's endgame, mixed from the blood of Whipped Peter's back and the wound that Sidney Poitier, as Dr. Luther Brooks treated so that a rabid racist may not die. In this epically boring movie, which the Lincoln Theater screened for one weekend and one weekend only before it was mercifully removed, the Stalker leads his two clients, a writer and a scientist, through the decaying detritus and industrial ruins of modernity, a defamiliarized landscape like a catoptric image of Standard Heights or any of the free settlements on the Mississippi River destroyed by the oil and gas conglomerates, in search of a highly restricted site, known as the Zone, which is said to grant access to one's inmost desires, all the craven hankerings and ensorcelled voracities that lurk in the mind's ghetto, much as you have followed me, quite without my asking, in search of the family house in Standard Heights, Toussaint said. Unlike these depressing miscreations, the Lincoln Theater instilled in me a capacity for future-facing world-building that, because he had not gone with me to the theater, was undeveloped in my brother, who could never get the police out of his mind, the white Bronco in slow motion dream speed on the native streets and the yellow police tape from crime scenes that we played with, wrapping the tape around the ExxonMobil trees to delimit our own crime scenes. But by showing me a world, however ungraspable and fanciful, beyond the razor wire and petrochemical nocturne of Standard Heights, the Lincoln Theater may have saved my life. Don't cry, black boy, you're gonna live, Toussaint said.

Bleeding Louisiana has never really left anything for future generations except plantations, agricultural and petrochemical, and when word got around that the Lincoln Theater was no longer showing Blaxploitation films, but seedy and flatitious pornographic films, I was no longer able to attend. The State Library closed — budget cuts. The pink strip club closed — too many funerals. When the Lincoln Theater at last closed its doors, I turned my eyes to the black theater of the night skies, the little of it that wasn't wiped out by the plant's sulfurous infernal afterglow. My father's vision was limited to ground-level machine phenomena — the Spillway opening, the barges on the river, the ExxonMobil plant — where the eyes never traveled more than a few degrees above the horizon, but my mother turned her radiant eyes to the skies, dragging me outside on cold nights — the arrows of the vanished native tribes could be heard raining through the ExxonMobil trees — to view the triumphant passing of Halley's Comet and the meteor showers — the Leonids and Perseids — that satsuma summer and cane harvest fall, and for the first and perhaps only time in my life I felt that I was a participant — because the observation brought it into being — in some cosmic theater co-creating a vast spectacle surpassing the picayune dramas on the Lincoln Theater's silver screen. I was not just a passive spectator, Toussaint said, watching, inertly and helplessly, a white man reluctantly and resentfully manacled to a black man on a flickering torn screen, both of whom, in the privacy of their interior monologues are conniving to undo the other, Toussaint said, focusing on me. It was important, I now realize, to my mother for my brother and I to see something that was not manmade above and greater than Standard Heights, that there were universal and curious phenomena far transcending the shirts versus skins pickup games and the Curse of the Saints, that Standard Heights was a bantam-sized place. These meteor showers, Toussaint said, were the real-time performances of the black and gold Saints-colored nocturnes painted by Whistler, those tenuous tenebrous impressions of petrochemical apparitions I once saw at the Whistler House Museum of Art in Lowell, Massachusetts, while researching the Negroes registered as members of the 54th Massachusetts Infantry Regiment, the meteoric bullet hole stars flaming down on Standard Heights and burning up in the firestorm of the plant in scintillating wormwood whispers of sterling showers like Whistler's *Nocturne in Black and Gold — The Falling Rocket.* All about me then was configured like a landscape zodiac, a map of the contaminated cosmos on a grand scale, the Mississippi River acting as that shimmering band of milky white, the Milky Way, to which I pointed expecting my finger to be cut off, Toussaint said.

I knew that if I had a telescope I would investigate the great black voids and vast blank interludes between the stars, those unchartered black geographies of the nocturne sky, not the starry sources of white light themselves which already drew so much pious attention and awestruck stargazing, more interesting negative objects — ones not manufactured with endocrine disruptors — must await in the stellar negation, though privately I hoped that tucked inside those blank interludes was nothing at all — more negation piled on negation, negations all the way down to infinity, a conceptual music of even greater negation than the nocturne itself, but of course this pure negation was only in my mind, the more one telescoped into the cosmological negation the more star fields and clustered deep space objects there appeared in the lens' aperture — negation was outnumbered by the sinister and cabalistic intelligence of luminous matter, Toussaint said, gazing with hazardous penetration at the sky above the old manor house.

One Sunday a minister who worked in the ExxonMobil plant, one of the more enlightened who did not preach the literal story of creation, organized an astronomy lesson in the vacant greenbelt lots, Toussaint said. An exorcism held on the levee to relieve the Saints of the black and gold curse weighing on the Superdome had resulted in a two-game win streak and after that Standards Heights trusted him. This minister placed round fruits, each representing a planetary body — the Sun was a watermelon; Mars was a satsuma; Jupiter was a cantaloupe; earth was a rotting avocado and Pluto was a boiled peanut; the minister had a banana too but I never learned what planet that was supposed to be — throughout the greenbelt lots at great distances from one another, crossing Hiawatha Street and an open ditch to the next vacant lot of the cosmos, placing a peanut in the weeds to mark the end of the solar system. At this distance, from the position of the peanut Pluto, the watermelon sun was no longer visible across the empty land, the rotting avocado earth drawing flies and gnats from all over Standard Heights to create a New Eden. The ExxonMobil plant, in the scale of this pedagogical model, an experiment which left an indelible impression on me, was greater in size than the entire solar system, a mechanical leviathan looming over the cosmic patchwork, spewing absinthian toxins into the miscreation: the ExxonMobil plant dwarfed everything between the watermelon Sun and the peanut Pluto. Whenever I ate watermelon, which we often did in the satsuma summer, I tasted the wormwood of the nocturne, the fetid materiality of the petrochemical sublime. The minister's solar system demonstration had the opposite effect of my mother's meteor showers: there was no organizational system or managerial intelligence supervising the spectacle, only the indefatigable, undead processes of extraction and refinement, process flow diagrams, and the sulfurous eerie lights from the plant casting animate shadows over the planetoid fruit the minister left behind in the vacant lots to rot and decay into identical black and brown mushy lumps of organic flyblown meat. The slave ships were not constructed to endure beyond this world, they were built and stocked with manacled men to immolate it, Toussaint said.

If the Lincoln Theater gave me a glimpse, ungraspable and gnostic, of a world beyond Standards Heights then the minister's little science experiment, placing fruits of different sizes to represent the solar system, gave me a glimpse even more incognizable of a world beyond this rotting avocado earth, but one that no matter how cosmic in scale was still dwarfed by the monstrous immensity of the ExxonMobil plant, so that no matter at what scale — the peanut Pluto or the watermelon Sun — the plant was always more leviathan: there was no escaping the nocturne through the dimensions of space, the only way out was to ride the current of temporal rivers other than Fisk's present river, to meet the expedition of Pierre Le Moyne d'Iberville and his men at the red stick crucifying the river and tell them to turn back, go home, *caveat emptor*, Toussaint said.

What I wanted most was to travel back in time to view the 1919 eclipse — an event I'd read about in the school library's sole book on astrophysics, published not too many years after the eclipse itself — that tested and confirmed Einstein's theory of general relativity, the geometric theory of gravitation, but of course this was a miracle that not even Christ Himself could've dreamed of — to the minister who attempted to exorcise the Curse of the Saints and showed us how small the solar system was in the shadow of the ExxonMobil plant, like a crawfish inside the belly of a whale, eclipses were more than physical events, they were numinous portals, malign or benign, to the west bank of the river where Whipped Peter and my father after the Christmas Eve explosion waited for the signal to cross to the river's east bank. Standing around in the greenbelt lots, he also told us about something called the Roche limit, of tidal forces that could rip apart the rotting avocado earth or the satsuma Mars if they got too close to the watermelon Sun, because the watermelon's tidal forces would overpower the avocado or the satsuma's self-attraction; logically then, if the watermelon Sun got too close to the ExxonMobil plant, which was orders of magnitude larger than anything I'd ever seen, except the river itself, even the watermelon Sun would be destroyed, exploding in watermelon juices: the Roche limit was like crossing Fisk's river from the east bank of *if* to the west bank of *then*. Yet no matter how hard I tried I could not summon the grit to cross the Roche limit, beyond which our planet would be crushed by the sun's gravitational forces, and somehow the possibility of this planet-death did not prompt in me anything like the proper solemnity or sorrow one would expect from the gratuitous destruction of a planet with all its ecosystems, languages, customs, cultures, the myriad faces of its unreconciled peoples, all its geopolitical borders, its sports teams — I felt no sorrow whatsoever at the loss of all this because by the energetic grace of creative destruction some other planet might be formed years hence, a planet evolving and hosting a species that did not make Blaxploitation films or the countless plastic products assembled in Gursky's supermarket. Yes, in dreams of this Roche limit, the ExxonMobil plant and the native streets were destroyed by overwhelming gravitational forces, their atoms and chemical elements dispersed and reorganized in a new universe without hazmat symbols such as the skull and crossbones or the corrosive liquid being poured on a human hand. On the other side of the Roche limit we would disintegrate into glittering rings, the particles and dust of this pulverized planet coalescing around the Sun like the rings of Saturn around a negative point, Toussaint said, looking westward now in the direction of the sun setting over the river.

There were other unexplained anomalies in the astronomy of Standard Heights: the star charts I had did not match the sky, east or west of the river, over the greenbelt lots; even if I had a telescope I would not have been able to see anything, so global was the light pollution from the ExxonMobil plant, for those who lived in Standard Heights the sky did not exist, the night sky our ancestors looked to for anagogic direction was obliterated by the ubiquitous sulfurous glow of the plant's industrial nightlife, while across town the white boys and girls who lived in the little burgs cut out of old cane fields and named for morbidly respectable dreams of English or French aristocracy — the English Villages, the Chateau Estates, the Versailles, Camelot Lakes — they could peer up from their immaculate herringbone lawns and palatial porticos and point their grubby white fingers like pale larvae at the mythic heroes configured in the hemisphere's constellations, Ganymede up there boxing with master Hammond, Whipped Peter running from the bloodhounds, but I could not. Baton Rouge had two different skies — one that black people saw, and one that white people saw. Under the sky visible to Standard Heights, the black people's sky, I learned that the streets do not love you, the concrete is not your family and the razor wire on the plant's security fencing is not your friend. But if I could not see the white people's sky, the moon was always visible, despite the plant's light pollution. And so I turned to the streets of the lunar surface, producing shaded drawings of the waterless surface of the moon, the only celestial body visible in that dispensation of sky available to Standard Heights, and I calculated and plotted the azimuth and altitude to track and observe the next solar eclipse that would not darken the skies of Standard Heights for another two or three decades, too long to wait if you're stuck in the Angola of the present.

But when the clouds manufactured by the ExxonMobil plant obscured the skies for long, dull, grey periods, and there was nothing above to see, not even a moon, I turned my eyes back to the flattened plain that held the river bed; somewhere in North Baton Rouge, maybe even in Standard Heights, Jean Lafitte had buried treasure to hide it from the greedy Spanish and the avaricious English with the intent to return for it later. My brother and I had grown up hearing about Lafitte's notorious exploits, his smuggling operations and his defense of New Orleans during the War of 1812. Using the same shovels my father did to unearth the mourning tree, we took turns drawing maps and digging for Jean Lafitte's buried pirate treasure but we never found anything but old Coke bottles, tin cans, lost boots and shoes, tires, mufflers, nails, bricks, household crap, potsherds and arrowhead points from the red stick natives. The buried pirate treasure had to be there, it had to be — we needed it to be there. In my humid greenhouse imagination, Jean Lafitte had personally left us a vast fortune, good Samaritan that he was — a stash of gold as atonement for his involvement in the slave trade — that we could use to buy a pirogue and sail downriver and away from Standard Heights forever. Although we found nothing that was worth anything, no one has ever convinced me that Lafitte's treasure wasn't buried in Standard Heights, Toussaint said, as the evidence of things unseen is sometimes itself invisible, impalpable, implausible.

Through the windows we were forbidden to open we watched police dogs sniffing around the vacant greenbelt lots as forensics teams scoured Standard Heights for forensic evidence. Standard Heights seemed to specialize in crimes without criminals. Dogs nosing through overgrown weeds, some tall as cane fields. No one ever asked us if we saw or heard anything. When the canine forensics team was gone, I raced into the yard, the door banging on the frame behind me, retracing the scented path where the dogs had nosed their way through the grass. I could find nothing of value or interest, though the dogs had not looked on ExxonMobil property, on the other side of the gate and barbed fencing that defended the plant from terrorists and attacks by chlorine gas ghost ships. But now I knew for sure that pirate treasure lay buried beneath the blocks named for vanquished native tribes — perhaps that was why ExxonMobil wanted the neighborhood razed, the lots cleared — not for some greenbelt to protect the plant from liability in the event of a catastrophic failure like the Christmas Eve explosion, but for the rights to the pirate treasure. Yes, the canine forensics team was on the scent of Lafitte's treasure — I was right that Lafitte had buried treasure in Standard Heights — or the bloodhounds were still on the oniony trail of Whipped Peter, after all these years the authorities and bloodhounds still had not found him. Whipped Peter was out there, at large, fleeing the whip. I hoped he was out there, Toussaint said, surviving somewhere in the swamps, having by now assimilated with the Cajuns or the Houma Indians who inhabited some of the least desirable lands in the country, stygian swamps below sea level. As the plant smokestacks mass-produced artificial clouds that occluded the sun — I thought of the boulder said to seal the tomb of the Lord — and the pressure-relieving burnoff flames that lit the flare stacks like the wicks of warmthless candles powering a false red-orange twilight, facing the mythic river I prayed to the cosmic negation that ExxonMobil would never find Lafitte's buried treasure before I did and the bloodhounds would be forever confused by the onions Whipped Peter had rubbed on himself to escape detection for more than one hundred and fifty years, as long as it took for the Republic of New Afrika to be founded, Toussaint said.

The Leonids had come again — Harriet Tubman and Frederick Douglass noted the meteor shower in their writings — when a severed human head was discovered in the vacant lot bordered by Hiawatha, Pocahontas, Navajo and Calumet Streets. The head's eyes were open and the lips parted as if about to speak some grave revelation, perhaps revealing the location of Lafitte's treasure. An ecosystem fed on the severed head: flies, ants, grubs, worms and beetles. The severed head — was this the face of the Green Knight? — had fallen to earth out of the same radiant from which the Leonid meteor shower came to us in the scintillating tail of the comet Tempel-Tuttle. No one, not the minister who exorcised the black and gold curse long enough for a two-game win streak, nor the realism of the bloodhounds, could dispel my conviction that the Green Knight's severed head had fallen from the sky out of the Leonids. Again — we were used to this by now, the severed heads of the German Coast Uprising rebels falling from the stars or floating to the turbid roiling surface of the mythic river — the yellow police tape was wrapped between ExxonMobil trees and the remaining posts of houses torn down, not by ExxonMobil, but by termites and locusts, Toussaint said, looking in the direction of the tumbledown manor house and movie set where actual flesh and blood slaves had been held in bondage before Ken Norton was boiled alive in a cauldron.

Another cargo truck passed on Ashland Road between us and the Ashland-Belle Hellen manor house, and I thought I saw a light wink on in an upper story but it could've been the setting sun reflecting off the dark windowpane. Toussaint's scrutinizing gaze followed the truck, mentally deciphering the chemical classification symbol on the back of the passing silver cargo tank, some corrosive or flammable byproduct of Ashland Road's petrochemical activity. The interior of the Ashland Plantation, were we to venture inside, would be stocked like the shelves of the supermarkets in Andrea Gursky's c-print photos, an emporium of endocrine disruptors and petrochemical commodities: Gursky's photos weren't of supermarkets at all but portrait photographs of the interiors of petrochemical plantations and manor houses. Like Albert Speers' architectural plans for the Third Reich, a regime with which the sclerotic plantation South shared more than an affinity for the enslavement of races dehumanized by supremacist ideology, not the least of which was the penchant for the language of the Chosen, plantation architecture revealed the farcical grandiosity of its egotistical designs most lucidly in these feral vegetative states of advanced decay, feckless abandonment, crumbling gangrenous decadence, I thought. One heard the sighing of the manor houses' last noxious breath and perishing senescence over long and mortal distances, from bank to bank of Fisk's present river, like the extinction of the megafauna that once patrolled the river's ancient alignments before the manacles of the levees enslaved it.

Toussaint began walking in the direction of the river and instinctively I followed a few paces behind. We came to the point — that is all it is, a bare geometric point in space, nothing to mark it — where Ashland Road and River Road meet in a perpendicular conjunction, the blacktop curling away downriver pulled ineluctably in the direction of New Orleans and beyond, where ships disembogue at the mouth of the river into the open water of the Dead Zone.

I could not stand to look anymore at that manor house, Toussaint said as if to explain why he'd walked away, with its crumbling colonnade, the plaster falling from the lath in the walls and the ceilings in large chunks like fistfuls of hair from a cadaver, revealing the ribs and skeletal supports of an extinct species, the black voids gaping in the ceiling where a chandelier once lighted the entryway, he said. Nothing moved here in this moribund castle, even the Spanish moss in the trees did not sashay in the wind, no sign of life but the black widows spinning silk dreams in the Confederate attic, and the rhythmic stillicide of leaking rainwater keeping a metronomic drip, Toussaint said. Had I been born in such a house I might not have been prohibited from an act as forthright and mundane as opening the windows to let in a little breeze — all because my father did not want the house filling with the sinister smells and calamitous gases of the ExxonMobil plant. All such manor houses ought to be torn down, perhaps ExxonMobil has at last done the right thing, letting the manor house decay naturally and fall ignominiously into hideous disrepair, no museum open to the nostalgic curiosities and revisionist meddling of the public who come to gawp at where Ganymede was boiled alive in a cauldron of water, and in the neglected ruin of the manor house also achieving the architectural self-actualization of the plantation style which from our petrochemical vantage point we can see was built — by slave labor no less — to endure most completely and perfectly as ruin and abandonment. And when the Age of Oil has come to an end, as end it must, Toussaint said, and the refineries and plants wind down their operations with a mechanical and nightmarish groan, the petrochemical death rattle, the last note of the petrochemical nocturne, I wonder if the petrochemical plants of Exxon-Mobil, Royal Dutch Shell and all the rest up and down this mythic river will not be like these manor houses of the slave plantations — decayed, crumbling, used for Blaxploitation movie sets, or sequels to *Stalker*, as the land ringing the ExxonMobil plant and Standard Heights once belonged to the great plantations of the South. There is no eschatological finale, no last apocalyptic blast, only a permanently recurrent state of deflated necessitous ruin which is like those sad empty Ferris wheels at Chernobyl, cheap fairground equipment at an autistic circus, broken harpsichords, every public festival a botched execution. Some will say that I rely too much on dreamwork hyperbole, Toussaint said, but they do not know Bleeding Louisiana, not like I do. I remember reading the story of Leiningen Versus the Ants in the school library, a pathetic story which veraciously captures the absolute incorrigible insanity of the plantation mentality — the plantation's owner is a positivist, his worldview is wholly scientism which has so successfully transformed the world into an exploitable resource, wounding the river with wormwood toxins and replacing the stars with skull and crossbones. In this story, Toussaint said, an army of highly organized soldier ants has mobilized against the plantation, which is deep in the Brazilian rainforest, attempting to overthrow the plantation regime. Like all Master Hammonds, Leiningen will not surrender the investment of his beloved plantation to an irrational act of God like the rebel ants, against which Leiningen deploys all the elements of the earth, water and fire, even going so far as self-immolation, laying waste to much of the plantation just to flush out the ants, as the Philadelphia police authorities decimated Osage Avenue where my mother lived for the sake of a few militant agitators. But the storybook plantation owner, after being nearly eaten alive by ants, survives and has evidently learned nothing, the plantation regime stronger than ever, and so I was heartened whenever I saw fire ants marching in long ranks like a second line parade on the native streets toward the plant, though it was never long before ExxonMobil workers were sent out to spray the fire ant colonies with gallons of proprietary formulas of insecticide, Toussaint said.

By now, the plantation manor house was well behind us. River Road was traversed by oil field hitchhikers and itinerant farm workers, those who came just to make their peace with the river. We passed a mentally disorganized man who walked hunched over, bent at a forty-five degree angle at the waist, his face directed at the ground so that I do not think he saw us. He might have seen two shadows cross the patch of earth visible to his downcast gaze circumscribed by his hunched posture, but not the dissimilar beings who cast the shadows. Whether he was mentally disabled or disturbed, I could not tell. Too much benzene, too many endocrine disruptors in the water. He spoke an arabesque and gothic-sounding pidgin of French and German. In a land fluent with myriad patois, pidgins, creoles, argots, dialects, and vernaculars, it is a wonder anyone understands his neighbor at all, that communication is not just a signing of hazmat symbols at a crossroads. Charles Deslondes and his party of insurgent slaves may have passed this very spot by torchlight on one of their night marches to battle in the Gigantomachy.

More and more, everywhere I look, Toussaint said, whether in the bombed-out ashes and ruins of Osage Avenue, which seems like only yesterday, or my ancestors who saw the river with their heads on pikes in the German Coast Uprising, the 2nd Amendment was contrived by armed yeoman and angry agrarians to enshrine in law the ability for white landholders and gun owners to quell slave revolts in an unequal contest — the slaves armed only with pikes, hoes, rakes, axes, a few raised clinched fists, frying pans — of disproportionate force, Toussaint said. For the militiamen of the well-regulated militia thought so necessary — so the language of the ratified amendment goes — to the security of a free state, the right of the people to keep and bear arms, such militiamen, it goes without so much as a coat of paint on a casket, were uniformly and semi-automatically white mama's boys as terrified of men like Deslondes as Ray was in *No Way Out* of the black doctor who tried to save his life, Toussaint said without deviating in his course downriver.

But then, because the German Coast Uprising came down to me through my father, who did not see my mother's meteor shower because he said it was just rocks falling from the sky, I began to doubt the historicity of the Deslondes report — a regiment of righteous Negroes led by a Negro, armed with torches and farm implements, a slave uprising against the established white plantation order and Master Hammond was too incredible — just as my father was skeptical of mother's sighting of the *Clotilda* ghost ship in Mobile Bay and the improbable events she recalled at Osage Avenue: brimstone and hellfire falling from the sky. After all, who had ever heard of Osage Avenue? Everyone knew about the drowned Phoenician sailor in Rodney King's pool and how behind the chains the Saints were, how miserable on third and goal, but Osage Avenue was like an urban legend synthesized out of the chemical dust settling on the Gigantomachy. And the German Coast Uprising, another episode in this cosmic conflict between gods and giants, was purported — if the river's direction of flow is to be trusted — to have antedated the Siege of Osage Avenue by almost two hundred years. My father's version of what I was supposed to believe sounded too much like *12 Years a Slave*. Though it is clear that Charles Deslondes was born an enslaved person in what was then Saint-Domingue, which after the revolution led by Toussaint Louverture, the western half of Hispaniola became known as Haiti, there are no historical studies on Charles Deslondes and the German Coast Uprising, as if it never happened, Toussaint said, perhaps my father confabulated it all, a bigger-than-life story to make Standard Heights bigger than its britches. I could not find a single historical monograph or dissertation on the Uprising in the State Library. Like the myth of Ganymede's kidnapping, Whipped Peter's existence was attested to by the Census form on which he was enumerated, but Charles Deslondes might as well have been a local folk hero like John Henry, and a local folk hero to only the black population — the rest of town had Peter Pan, John Wayne and Charles Ponzi — and not even the total count of the black population, for there were many in Standard Heights and beyond who had never heard the name Charles Deslondes — that segment of the black population which looked to the 14th Amendment with the same trepidation as my brother did before a white jury after his failed attempt at suicide by cop, Toussaint said.

Confabulation or not, whites had reason to be fearful of Deslondes' story: they were outnumbered, by some estimates, five to one, much as our species is outnumbered by spiders and ants who would devour our bodies if they could. Slave revolts in those days were common, he said, but their suppression was swift and sure; not only had this ancestor participated in the German Coast Uprising, according to my father — he was the chief instigator, the Black Spartacus of the German Coast, but my ancestors were illiterate so their version of history was not recorded, and even if it had been it would not be believed, no more than the police dogs sniffing around Standard Heights asked for our oniony opinion of who was winning the Curse of the Saints, or whether we'd seen anything suspicious before the severed head of the Green Knight fell out of the Leonids. The faceless men in white hazmat suits, who I sometimes saw lumbering slowly about Standard Heights like moon men, especially on days after the toxic ash drifted down in heavier amounts than could be considered normal, always after some unexplained event at the plant, appeared one day in black vans at the Destrehan Plantation to decontaminate it of its history, spreading disinfectant and memory chemicals, sanitizing the Uprising from every portico and colonnade, anywhere the petrochemical nocturne was an inconvenience to those who lived at the other end of the supply chain, these hazmat crews cleansing all evidence of anything that threatened the proper functioning of the process flow diagrams, just as those ten seconds of footage were removed from the video of Rodney King's beating and buried in the Gulf of Mexico's Dead Zone.

After Lee's surrender to General Grant at Appomattox, the riverine plantations became free settlements like Diamond, St. James, Morrisonville, Reveilletown, Reserve, towns where the afterbears of freed slaves either worked at the plants or not at all, but Petrochemical Modernism could not let them retain the dignity of a free settlement. Like the addresses listed on Rampart Street in the Green Book, they had to be annihilated, the freed settlements struck from the record like all evidence of the German Coast Uprising. The petrochemical supercorporations with skin in the game carved up the turkey in mutually advantageous excerpts of many Standard Heights, upriver as well as downriver. CEO vultures picking over forty acres and a dead mule. The Georgia Gulf Corporation bought out Reveilletown. Dow Chemical got Morrisonville, which free town's wells were chemically polluted and all but undrinkable, and Royal Dutch Shell got Diamond. It was the Scramble for Bleeding Louisiana, Toussaint said, each hydra of the petrochemical monster getting a little piece for themselves. Modern day residents of these free settlements had little agency in these buyout decisions, not even a net for a basketball goal; if they refused to sell, their property would be valued at zero. Shell, an official sponsor of Jazzfest, bought out the hometowns of jazz legends Tubby and Minor Hall and James Brown Humphrey, leaving not even a broken trumpet behind on which to play the Osage Avenue Blues, a few doleful bars of the petrochemical nocturne. Nothing now remains of these erstwhile free settlements except Norco, which is dying a painful death from petrochemical malaise. What happened to these free settlements was done also to Standard Heights: the buyouts, the demolitions, the skull and crossbones. It is as though — never mind *as though*; it is a certainty — the hydrocarbon zeitgeist of Petrochemical Modernism acted under some crazed compulsion to raze the freed slaves' inchoate attempts to found the first cities of the Republic of New Afrika. In the Parish Clerks of Court archives the dead deeds of the buyouts record the renaming of these Africatowns as Thereseinstadt, the toxification of the petrochemical atlas. At the nerve center of the buyouts are the graying shambles of the Ashland-Belle Hellen and Destrehan Plantations: the Negroes who came with the property were enumerated with the livestock and the farm tools, one plantation superseded by another. But the supercorporations' avarice demanded rights to what was inside the turkey: Jean Lafitte hid treasure within the walls of the plantations. The plantation was picked apart as if by vultures looting a carcass, vandals ransacking the mansion of its architectural valuables: marble mantels, cypress wood paneling, Spanish ceramic tiles, glass window panes, the antique fixtures distributed on the black market for antiques in New Orleans and installed in the post-Katrina renovations that would have made the city unrecognizable to my father. Lost forever was the plantation's 1,400 pound marble bathtub given as a gift to the planter family from the Emperor Napoleon Bonaparte, Toussaint said, a bathtub in which no Ganymede ever bathed.

Charles Deslondes' punishment — both of his hands chopped off, whereas Captain Jonathan Walker's were merely branded — for the revolt, or so my father said, was like some sadistic horror coming to life out of the boiling cauldron scene of *Mandingo*; after Charles' entire being was concentrated by an excruciation of pain localized at the extremities of his amputated hands, and extending from those two bloody nubs into infinite space, he was shot first in one thigh, then the other, at close range; his being was now bifurcated, dislocated into two regions of white hot pain — the missing hands and the holes in his thighs — and he was then fired upon in the region of the torso, his being split now into thirds of agony, each wound a hole in the wall behind Fred Hampton's bloody mattress, an expression of his reduction into the mortification of flesh, and the slavers could not acquit themselves till the offending slave was annihilated — because Charles' corpse like that of Jesse Washington after him was not even fit for dissection in a medical amphitheater, a scientific benefit to experimental physiology — in that element definitive of heavenly wrath and so Charles Deslondes was smothered in straw and set afire, Toussaint said, intestinal worms immolated with the host. This human bonfire smoldered for days, the smoke ghosting westward across the river and the indigo fields, running from bloodhounds, Charles Deslondes' emancipated soul mixing with the autumnal smoke of the cane harvests, for the offending slave rebellion's leader had to be expunged from the earth, no less than the free settlements, no less than Standard Heights, no less than the ancestral graves flooded by wormwood waters beneath the Spillway. Why must the Master Hammonds always destroy the hands, what was it about the enslaved person's hands that most terrified them? How is an enslaved person to pray without any hands? How was Mayweather to box the Great White Hope without the raised and resisting black power fist? And in this way, Toussaint said, Charles Deslondes was the first in the family, at least as my father tells it, exalted to the status of *homo sacer,* an accursed and sacred man, capable of being killed by any death mask white man at all. Deslondes' amputated hands crawled away on their five fingers like large black spiders into the swamps, waiting for the mob to disperse, plotting the next offensive of the Gigantomachy, Deslondes' revenant hands reappearing with teary eyes blinking in the palms on Osage Avenue, the hazmat symbol of the severed hand burned by corrosive petrochemical substances. But only the leader of the rebellion was singled out for such preferential torture, the remaining slaves of the rebellion simply had their heads set on pikes — the eyes open wide like those set in the palms of the Southern Death Cult motif — like ghoulish lanterns around the Destrehan and Ashland-Belle Hellen Plantations as a warning signal to other uppity slaves that the medieval punishment for rebellion would render the corpse ineligible for resurrection, the Good Lord requiring the whole body intact for such miracles to work, and while Toussaint himself never established the nexus, not that I can recollect, the severed head he discovered in the vacant lots must have come from the pikes arrayed in gruesome rows before the plantation or those heads of Congolese posted in front of Kurtz's house. Still a third contingent of rebellious slaves were hanged in *Place d'Armes*, which you will know as Jackson Square, Toussaint said, from which the equestrian monument of Andrew Jackson Jihad has yet to be removed; those insurrectionists who somehow managed to escape capture disappeared into the maroon colonies deep in the swamplands south of New Orleans, never to be seen again, biding their time till the last trumpet blasts. Today, Toussaint said, the sweet powdery smell of fresh hot beignets from Café du Monde in Jackson Square, a gathering place used for the public executions of rebel slaves, has the power to make me as sick as the toxic fish in Devil's Swamp Lake.

The dreams of the slaves on the Destrehan Plantation who survived the bloody revanche of the German Coast Uprising drew upon the same collective unconscious upon which Master Hammond drew in his wet dreams of his slave girl, Toussaint said. The old traumas can be passed down — encoded in engrams or traveling on the edge of a scythe in genetic dreams — through the generations, Toussaint said, rubbing his hands together.

And indeed, Toussaint sometimes complained of a recurring malady, a numbness or ataxia of feeling in both hands, as if amputated, and only later did I connect this anesthetic condition with his inability to iconoclastically launch the stones he had collected from Standard Heights at the Confederate stained glass window in the National Cathedral. Toussaint would flex his fingers, contracting them in a raised and resistant fist, saying how he felt his hands were thousands of years old, belonging to some long-dead mummy that had not died of natural causes, or that his hands weighed hundreds of thousands of pounds like blocks of the pyramids, and these psychomotor disturbances — his hands floating away from him on the river, the sensation of a petrochemical wormwood corroding his skin — continued until the stone statue of General Lee came down in Lee Circle when the numbness just as suddenly vanished. And then I remembered Toussaint tarrying outside the Royal Street mansion, the house of slave torture, rubbing his throat with his hands, "an assuagement of some phantasmal trauma, as if necklaced with an invisible iron collar," but without feeling in his hands how could Toussaint have felt his throat as anything more than the wind blowing through a vacant lot or the shadow of a chlorine gas ghost ship on the river?

The problem was Deslondes left behind no slave narrative in his own voice, Toussaint said, the quarters where he lived were destroyed by the plantation owners, and his name was spoken among a select few only in complicit tones of secrecy, if at all, under threat of death. It was after *The Negro Motorist Green Book* that I began discerning the slave narratives in the design, albeit a probably subconscious one, of every ancestral story I ever heard, discerning in them an archetypal plot shape controlling the content of these family narratives and even the farcical, vulgar plots of the Blaxploitation films I saw in the Lincoln Theater. The approximate formula for these narratives of enslaved persons proceeded in rough outline as follows: an engraved portrait of the narrative's author, signed by the author; a title page with the apologetic "Written by Himself," or if the slave narrator was not literate, "Written from a statement of Facts Made by Himself," or "Written by a Friend, as Related to Him by Brother Malcolm." A prefatory remark or prolegomenon authored by a death mask white abolitionist, because an enslave person cannot speak without first deferring to the words of a white man, without his voice passing through the mouth of that death mask; an epigraph in verse, usually by some fustian old man of letters in a wig like William Cowper or Thomas Gray, the narrative itself opening like the first chapter of David Copperfield — the slave narrator telling where but not when he was born, because no enslaved person ever knew the exact date of his birth, for through the elision of the date of birth the slave owner could control chronology and time itself, thereby depriving the enslaved person of their own beginning, or having begun at all, only the certainty of death staring them down at the other end of the chronology, Toussaint said. The bloodline of the narrator's lineage is stated like the fecund genealogies of the Bible. There are intimations of white paternity. Illicit moonlit trysts in the white rose arbor with a slave girl while the lady of the house is busy matchmaking for her daughters, lobbying on their behalf the most suitable planter's sons on the neighboring plantation. A sadistic slave master is titillated by whippings — mostly of women who are whipped savagely for the merest triviality. The narrator will at this point enumerate the many obstacles placed in his way to literacy, and they are formidable, mastery of language being an existential threat to the plantation regime. The diurnal routine and tedious descriptions of food, shelter and clothing belittling the minutia and descriptive tedium of that master of doldrums, Sir Walter Scott. The modulations of field work tracking the change in seasons. Harvest festivals. Ancestral rituals from the motherland. The lyrics to field hollers or other spirituals sung in the open air. A family is separated at slave auction; there are wild pursuits by slave catchers and fearsome bloodhounds. The narrator contemplates his escape — always and only by night, preferably moonless — from that peculiar institution, following the North Star till he is received in a free state by a Quaker family who serves him a jubilee breakfast, addressing one another with archaic pronouns such as thee and thou. At the suggestion of a death mask white abolitionist, the narrator assumes a new surname to signify his transformation into a freeman, while retaining the narrator's first name to signify the continuity of the narrator's identity from enslavement to jubilee, a continuity as indispensable a precondition to the Western colonialist experiment as shipbuilding and gunpowder. This narrative arc over-determines the individual lives, to varying degrees, of every single one of us right up to petrochemical nocturne's last note, it is a controlling arc that expresses itself like a scripted gene through us, Toussaint said, opening and closing his left hand.

You know how they say that every story is a love story, Toussaint asked, well every black man's story is a slave narrative. The slave narrative was our race's *bildungsroman*. I would not have believed this before visiting my brother at the Angola Prison Rodeo, the men I spoke to at the rodeo all have practically identical stories: the attempted escapes from Angola, sadistic prison guards who operate as the 21st century's overseers, the field work that is assigned on Angola plantation, the frustrating hours spent in the prison library to learn the rudiments of literacy and law, to earn a high school diploma, and yet the slave narrative of Petrochemical Modernism no longer ends, as it did in the 19th century, in freedom and a country Quaker jubilee breakfast, but in a prison cell in Angola if you botch suicide by cop. But of all the thematic elements of the slave narrative's arc the most ubiquitous is escape, Toussaint said. We are still escapists. My father's escape from Iberville, my mother's escape from Prichard and then Osage Avenue, my own escape from

Standard Heights. O.J. Simpson's dream speed escape from the Los Angeles police. In lieu of field hollers and the sung songs of mighty spirituals: the petrochemical nocturne on broken harpsichords and banging of leaden, melancholy instruments. And often as not our modern slave narratives, which never seem to progress beyond the theme of escape are, like those of Whipped Peter's time, merely ventriloquized and ghostwritten by well-meaning death mask whites, Toussaint said.

I thought about the implications of this slave narrative ventriloquism without drawing the same necessary conclusions that Toussaint must have arrived at some time before I did, always a step or more ahead of me. The old manor house slowly disintegrating in a vacant and witless dream, like a dummy whose ventriloquist was spooked when the doll began speaking of its own accord, unsavory truths about the ventriloquist, I thought.

We've had the soft hands of a ventriloquist up our backs for so long we have forgotten that our voices are for more than field hollers, Toussaint said. Malcom X's autobiography was, for all intents and purposes, ghostwritten by Alex Haley, Toussaint said, though Haley was also black and his voice blended with Malcolm's. No death mask supervened. Even MLK's speeches were written in draft form by Clarence Benjamin Jones. My own slave narrative, Toussaint said, is even now being ghostwritten when a single word will do. I feel the word *scream.* I smell the word *benzene.* I taste the words *endocrine disruptors.* I see the words *skull and cross-bones.* Not the benzene per se, or the scream itself but the word only, like my brother's soundless screams in the silent police dash cam video footage of his attempted suicide by cop, Toussaint said.

The stories my father told, about Whipped Peter or Charles Deslondes, conformed in their main parts to this narrative arc, never the whole arc at once, but in fragments like the window glass that fell out of their warped frames in the Christmas Eve explosion. But if the African diaspora had never heard the name of Charles Deslondes or Toussaint Louverture they knew the names of Reggie Bush and Paul Kagame. And if they had not heard Kagame's name, they soon would: not long after the Lincoln Theater closed for good, the presidential airplane of Rwandan president Juvénal Habyarimana and Burundi president Cyprien Ntaryamira was shot down by militants as it maneuvered to land at Kigali airport. When planes circled above the ExxonMobil plant and Standard Heights, preparing to land at Baton Rouge Metropolitan Airport, my brother and I ran inside, afraid they would be shot out of the sky by west bank militants. I read too about the Rwandan Genocide as it was happening on that apocalyptic and colonized continent, asking my mother — who abhorred blood so much she refused to kill the spiders in the house — if we were Hutu, Tutsi or Twa. Three ethnic groups I later often referenced when ghostwriting lyrics. She said she didn't know but that we were probably nothing. From afar, it seemed that the Hutu, Tutsi, and Twa had done it to themselves, yet the necessary conditions for the genocide were established by the German and Belgian colonial occupiers, the same death mask whites who put down the German Coast Uprising on this river. The Master Hammonds of the world went around stirring up antisocial trouble, making us fight amongst ourselves, like two heavyweight black boxers thrown in the ring and ordered to fight to the death while Master Hammond and Connor McGregor took bets, Toussaint said, pounding a fist into the palm of his open hand, right where the eye would be on the Hand and Eye Motif. Remembering d'Iberville's exploration of the Mississippi River, Toussaint said, in the days before its alignment was fixed in the levees by the Army Corps of Engineers, I began to look at the ExxonMobil plant in a new light. The Rwandan Genocide mixed with the slow motion dream speed police chase and the mountain of oil drums was transformed by wormwood rain into Rwanda's mountains of machetes. The skulls piled in anonymous smiles, faceless rows like the Catacombs of Paris. The trauma encoded into the DNA of unborn Hutu and Tutsi children. The half-hearted truces in the Gigantomachy never last long enough to get a final body count, and the Battle of Baton Rouge continues to be waged by each generation in succession. Deslondes' amputated hands crawled into the wormwood river, the ten fingers with which to count the dead chased into the greenbelt forest by Master Hammond's bloodhounds, Toussaint said.

The Battle of Baton Rouge

Every Standard Heights schoolchild who grows up studying the flocculent morphology of the manufactured clouds of the ExxonMobil refinery knows the true story of how Baton Rouge got its name: *le bâton rouge*. Toussaint may not have known the revolutionary provenance, on a tropical island of the Greater Antilles archipelago in the Caribbean, of his own name till he was old enough to know the petrochemical science behind the supposed cloud manufacturing operation, but the pickup game boys know the story of the red stick transpiercing the wounded river.

Because I have always sought confirmation of myths in their tangible sources, I had gone to Scott's Bluff to see for myself the famed spot of local legends, the point of origin for Baton Rouge's namesake, the result of a cultural misunderstanding, where Pierre le Moyne d'Iberville, for whom the Iberville Projects where Toussaint's father grew up were named, and his crew encountered the first sign that they were not alone: the red stick of the Houma and Bayougoula tribes who once inhabited the lands now owned by ExxonMobil and the vacant greenbelt lots of Standard Heights. Every place, no matter how humble or grandiose has an origin story that, through generational retelling and local marketing is inflated into a civic origin myth, Standard Heights was no different than anywhere else, at least in the recounting of its beginnings.

After wandering the diverse and decaying buildings on Southern University's campus for much of a day, by the river I came upon an abstract sculpture, constructed like a delta wing rocket, that was supposed to figuratively conjure the mythic red stick. I waited for a campus cop to pass in his cruiser before crossing Leon Netterville Drive at the resting place of three burial sarcophagi for J.S. Clark and his family, the land-grant school's first president. The cypress pole in the river must have been a terrifying and unnatural spectacle, the bloody red stick hung with the viscera and cruor of hunted animals rising from the water, the river itself crucified and bleeding. To call it a stick does not do justice to the thirty-foot cypress pole rising from this river, which then was uncontrolled by levees and could move or switch at a moment's notice.

Seated at one of the concrete benches arranged around a concrete table, in the green-black umbrage of stately and authoritative oaks, was Toussaint, contemplating the abstract red stick sculpture and watching the slow to and fro of barge traffic on the river.

I took a seat on the downriver side of the concrete bench across the circular concrete tabletop from Toussaint, and noted the

Louisiana state flag flying from one of the barges, the pelican sacrificing itself for its young. On the river, north and south are meaningless terms: everything is upriver or downriver. Scott's Bluff was just downriver from Devil's Swamp Lake where Toussaint caught toxic fish with his father, and downriver from us the Horace Wilkinson Bridge supported hazmat trucks and chemical tankers in their transit across the river. I leaned on the concrete tabletop and swiped the dry husk of a dead cicada off and into the grass, as I listened to Toussaint meander deeper into the memory palace, a journey which had started on this river.

I come here sometimes, he said, to meditate on the red stick, and to study the shapes of the manufactured clouds billowing in totemic chemical patterns from the plant's skyline of smokestacks and cooling towers, looking for some diagram of answers, a flocculent message from my father, though I know this is only wishful pareidolia, searching for codes and meaning in random natural variables, Toussaint said. He wanted me to go to school here, you know, to keep me in Standards Heights, but Devil's Swamp Lake and the plant were too close to the campus which, as a child, had represented some kind of academic Eden to me, an enclosed world apart from the ExxonMobil plant where a black boy or black girl could learn things that Whipped Peter and Charles Deslondes could not; enclosed yes, but too close, the petrochemical nocturne still audible during a local history lecture on the 1972 protest on Southern's campus, when two students were killed by police, boycotting classes for a month and stopping a football game, the one sacred event that more anything else had the power to bring whites and blacks together in a contest to win for the sake of winning, a protest over the state's unequal expenditures per pupil favoring the predominantly white LSU over the HBCU, Toussaint said, and then Big Bertha, the state police armed personnel carrier rolling around campus after Netterville, the school's president whose name is on that very street, he said pointing to the road between us and a clustering of drab, underfunded campus buildings, went Uncle Tom and ratted on the student protestors to the police. Now that I am back on this red stick campus after so many years, I realize that my father wanted me to go to Southern University to finish what was begun in the Battle of Southern University, Toussaint said.

I think of my brother, we used to come here and play games

on the green bluff, throwing our own red-painted sticks into the river like javelins, and counting the river barges flying under the flags of many countries, some of which I could name, others not, pretending between ourselves that the barges were the ships of d'Iberville's armada invading the Louisiana coast and Standard Heights. The campus was an escape from the ExxonMobil plant and the native streets of Standard Heights, a world apart where the streets were named for prominent black scholars and academics and school administrators, and not extinct native tribes. And the campus continued being that, a refuge from the petrochemical nocturne for me until the day in December, not long after watching the dream speed police chase of O.J. fleeing bloodhounds down the California freeway, we both saw a crimson stick projecting out of the river, this was before that sculpture was erected, Toussaint said, gesturing in the direction of the abstract red stick. We were standing on the president's sarcophagi, which we sometimes did, playing a modified form of king of the hill, leaping from one tomb to the other and pushing the other off, king of the sarcophagus I guess you might call it, and when he should have been defending his sarcophagus from my assaults, my brother froze, and when I saw what had riveted his attention I too froze: a cypress pole of seemingly infinite height rising from the river, decorated in hunted jaguar heads, extending skywards into the manufactured cloudworks, a chlorine gas ghost ship sailing by. We went home that day proudly believing in our little river town's origin myth, telling our mother and father nothing of the giant red stick we saw in the river, just as we kept a promise to each other never to brag about the time we had whipped two white boy bullies who had cornered us in the courtyard of the Pentagon Barracks. Though he denied ever seeing the chlorine gas ghost ships after the Christmas Eve explosion, I know he saw that bloody red stick impaling the river, Toussaint said. I know he did, as sure as I knew Jean Lafitte's treasure was buried beneath the native streets.

Rome had its twin brothers Romulus and Remus, sons of Mars, abandoned on the Tiber River, the twin infants suckled to maturity by a she-wolf, and without any disrespect I have wondered at times whether my mother was not also a she-wolf, Toussaint said. I once encountered a replica of the Capitoline Wolf, or perhaps it was a cast of the original, the bronze statue derived from the legend of the city's founding: the she-wolf — vigilant against minatory presences which the viewer cannot himself see but which he knows must exist invisibly in the spaces all around him — and her twin infants suckling at the she-wolf's breasts executed in two contrastive styles at different times, as if Romulus and Remus existed in a time apart from the she-wolf. And though I sometimes pretended my brother and I were the twin brothers abandoned on the east bank of the Mississippi River, raised by our she-wolf mother, Baton Rouge has no such grandiose founding myth as Rome, merely a red cypress tree stripped of its bark and sunk in the riverbed like the flagpole of a flagless nation: a stick in the mud — that is Baton Rouge, Toussaint said.

The Baton Rouge founding myth goes something like this: after locating the mouth of the river, necessary in the realization of the dream empire connecting New France via the Mississippi to the Saint Lawrence River in Canada, Pierre Le Moyne d'Iberville captained an exploratory voyage upriver. Death mask white men who believed in the immortality of the soul and the ecology of the Book of Genesis had never before penetrated this far upriver into the continent. One of d'Iberville's men kept a travelogue of this Mississippian voyage, which I quote here in the verity and fullness of the original because if I ever documented a city's founding moment — when white Europeans set imperial eyes, the same leering gaze blinking in the Hand Eye Motif, on the river banks for the first time — I would wish to be quoted:

"From there [Manchacq] we went five leagues higher and found very high banks called écorts in that region, and in savage called *Istrouma* which means red stick [*bâton rouge*], as at this place there is a post painted red that the savages have sunk there to mark the land line between the two nations, namely: the land of the Bayagoulas which they were leaving and the land of another nation— thirty leagues upstream from the *baton rouge*—named the Oumas."

Though nowhere does d'Iberville mention the pink flamingos of Spanish Town, the savage eponym, *Istrouma*, survives in the names of Baton Rouge schools, laundromats, barber shops, package stores, and deserted streets, d'Ibervbille's men bringing with them their own words for things — they could not refer to New France with the selfsame primitive utterances of savages who delimited the borders of their nations with a bloody stick. The travelogue's red stick, it was learned, demarcated the border between the Houma and Bayogoula tribal hunting grounds, the same tribes that constructed the earthen mound in Arsenal Park with the cannon aimed across the lake at the ExxonMobil plant, Toussaint said. Can you imagine the United States and Mexico marking their common border with a red stick impaling the Rio Grande? Just as a few years later, savages in spacesuits would, while on a moonwalk, plant the American flag on the surface of the moon to mark the border between the tribal, astral hunting grounds of the United States and the Soviet Union. The Mississippi, prone to deltaic switching, and the thrashing about of a wounded snake as drawn in the Fisk maps is not a single, unified river, but has multiple personalities — the river moves, changes its mind, changes course, sliding across the Lower Alluvial Valley, has grown many incommensurable lobes. The red stick could not contain the angry avulsions of the river any more than the nails could keep the body of Christ on the cross. Fisk maps were ventriloquisms, as if Fisk himself had a hand inside the river's whip-scarred back and was forcing it to speak across the muddy millennia in a turbid hieroglyphics with no Rosetta stone.

The tribal red stick was the first act in pinning down the river like a butterfly specimen, Toussaint said. The death mask white men and the native Houma could not let the river move willy-nilly, for how then could the death mask whites colonize the upriver interior if they had to redraw the maps every time the petulant river moved? With the red stick in its watery abdomen, hostage and captive, the river could no more switch deltas than a butterfly could elope to South America. Had that red stick not been in the Mississippi, demarcating the hunting grounds of two tribes, perhaps these European explorers would never have stopped and Baton Rouge would never have been founded: no ExxonMobil, no Standard Heights, no severed head falling from the stars, no Christmas Eve explosion, no nocturne. But a red pole projecting thirty feet above the surface of the river is meant to be seen, and in some versions of the city's foundational myth the red stick is rendered with blood and human bones, Toussaint said. A grave and exigent token to the invading death mask Europeans, almost like their warning siren of imminent hazard, natural processes beyond human control. D'Iberville and his men scanned the river bluffs with eyepieces — gilded baroque instruments inlaid with mother of pearl and precious stones — and the red stick itself must have been seen with both eyes, otherwise not at all, as the brain will executively elide or cancel anything seen with but a single eye, even a chlorine gas ghost ship seen by a hundred men, but with a single eye of each of the hundred will be dismissed by accident investigators as a mass hallucination, aberrations of petrochemical mentation. I myself have experienced this optical elision, Toussaint said, when looking with but a single eye at the Exxon-Mobil plant or the Ashland-Belle Helen Plantation in the hopes that they would vanish, troubling us no more. And perhaps this is what happened to the slave ship *Clotilda* docked in Mobile Bay, which my mother insisted long after it was appropriate to insist — I never saw her so adamant on a point as she was on this; more even than that I never read the Green Book again — that she saw with her own eyes just as you see the bulldozers moving earth back and forth in Standard Heights, but my mother, who was incapable of anything less, saw the ghost ship with two eyes, the same pair which must have looked at me with solicitude and that clairvoyant presentiment as together with my brother we greeted a fatherless New Year, Toussaint said. Whereas, because they too were descended from the founders of Africatown, a free settlement which had no chance of becoming a great city like New Orleans or Chicago, a few still alive in Prichard confirmed the ghost ship sighting not a soul elsewhere in Mobile were able to corroborate the alleged porting of the slave ship *Clotilda*, and I will tell you why, Toussaint said, because they looked into Mobile Bay with but a single eye, that stylized eye set in the palm of the severed hand that appeared on the walls of Osage Avenue and the hazmat trucks that went to and from the ExxonMobil plant at all hours. But the ExxonMobil plant could not be vanished by any sort of self-skullduggery or optical illusions, this mephitic metropolis of super-corporate petrochemical industry, this hydrocarbon Theresein-stadt and industrial movie set of *Stalker* persisted whether I willed it to or not. Even a lifelong honorary member of The Cloud Appreciation Society may harbor a grudge against manufactured clouds, Toussaint said, squinting up at the cadaverous sky.

What is today downtown Baton Rouge — asphalt parking lots, a few vintage brown and beige low-rise skyscrapers with black-tinted office windows behind which must be the spidery rooms of the Ashland-Belle Helen Plantation — and the ExxonMobil refinery was once heavily forested jungle when d'Iberville and his crewmen sailed upriver and stopped before the mysterious blood-red stick. I am trying to provide a sense of the landscape's uninhabitability the more it becomes inhabited, Toussaint said. The red stick was anchored in the river's abdomen somewhere around Scott's Bluff, which is today Southern University's campus and commands the greatest view of the river and its barge traffic — a logical point for the red stick.

Ever since, governance of Baton Rouge has been conducted under the flags of France, Britain, Spain, Louisiana, the Republic of West Florida, the defunct Confederate States of America, and the United States of America. Unsatisfied with these, I drew up and flew my own battle flags, Toussaint said, the Hand and Eye Motif flag of Standard Heights, the flag of the Corsican Republic, the skull and crossbones flag of the Republic of New Afrika, and the black and gold flag of the New Orleans Saints. In the greenbelt lots we collected the longest sticks we could find, painting them fire engine red and planting them in the vacant lots like survey rods delimiting our tribal hunting ground, Toussaint said.

The explorer's travelogue, dating to the 18th century, is the last word of Deep Time before the natives were reduced to nothing more than street names. Native Americans, even before the streets bore the names of their tribes and chieftains, have occupied Standard Heights since the Middle Archaic Period, their customs and traditions, oral and material, evolving according to a logic that was more like Fisk's maps' wayward serpentine meanderings than the plant's linear schematic process diagrams in which one thing follows ineluctably and fatally upon another: D'Iberville's accounts are dated using the *anno Domini* system of the Julian and Gregorian calendars — a reckoning of time utterly alien to the Native American cultures it is used to date. To say to a Houma that an event occurred *anno Domini* would've meant nothing. Not only did we subjugate them spatially, by appropriating their lands through underhanded treaties and campaigns of removals, opening up frontierlands to white death mask settlers, but we subjugated them temporally by imposing our own systems of linear time upon them. There is no year zero in the *anno Domini* system — the void and the abyss cannot be admitted into Christendom — invented by Dionysius Exiguus, a monk from Scythia Minor, a place I imagined as the setting of Biblical scenes like the bare knuckle good fight between David and Goliath, David downing the giant with a raised and resisting black fist. Year zero is unthinkable in Christendom. The void, as in the *Hirschsprung* legend of the Black Forest — a knight plunges to his death in pursuit of a deer over a gorge

— will not be surpassed, particularly not by a green knight, Christendom's quintessential defender and principal jailer, Toussaint said.

From the deserted streets of Standard Heights, I learned the names of native chieftains and warriors before I knew the Founding Fathers. Before Thomas Jefferson and James Madison, there were Tecumseh and Osceola Streets. One simply walked out the front door, turned right or left on the street and printed on the green street signs, often canted at acute angles, on each corner were musical names like Hiawatha and Pontiac, though some of Standard Heights' streets were signless; when a street sign was struck down by a car or chemical cargo truck the city did not come out to replace it. And so from Hiawatha Street I knew about the unification of the Iroquois, and on Pontiac Street I was to learn of Chief Pontiac's resistance against the British in his eponymous war, and I never figured out why these rebel natives got streets named for them but Charles Deslondes and Whipped Peter did not. No Charles Deslondes Avenue nor Whipped Peter Boulevard, but on the south side of Choctaw Drive you could commit suicide by cop on Jackson Avenue and fish in the deep water potholes on Madison Avenue in a Bleeding Louisiana parody of the Manhattan advertising district. The streets named for Geronimo and Osceola had no signs, and no one could be reached at the offices of the Society for Threatened Peoples to order replacements for them. And so the manufactured clouds of ExxonMobil cast ghost ship shadows over nameless streets that never healed like the keloid scars on Whipped Peter's back, Toussaint said. Without street signs or markers other than potholes to navigate the native streets, it was easy to get lost, but the house number never faded. Our house number, Toussaint said, was spray-painted in black paint on the corner post supporting a spavined leaking roof and even now that the house is gone those four black numbers remain inexpungable — floating, emblazoned on the noxious air like chemical residue or the tattoo on a body that has long since decayed. From the standpoint of the street, by the deep water pothole where my brother and I sometimes caught catfish and crawfish, the house address numbers are read in the usual fashion: from left to right. But walking through the yard and the spot once occupied by the demolished house, then turning around in the backyard to face the street, the four black numbers are reversed as in a mirror. I have tried to scrub those four black numbers off the air but they cannot be razed as the house was razed, Toussaint said, black and broken mirrors hanging in place of the windows we were forbidden to open.

Two ongoing set piece battles, one from 1779 and another from the American Civil War, 1862, are still being fought in Baton Rouge, the outcomes uncertain. Digging for Lafitte's buried treasure in the vacant lots around Standard Heights, we uncovered the skeletons of dead dogs, thinking they were the remains of a Confederate soldier; the car batteries and junkyard mechanical miscellany were the unexploded ordnance of these unresolved conflicts. A map of the battlefield hanging in the local library depicted only unplatted green fields and low-lying swampland where ExxonMobil and Standards Heights and the interstate would be on a modern map of the same area, though the streets of Spanish Town are legible in the grid of rectangles around the lake there was at that time no Hiawatha Street, no Osceola Street. The battle was fought partly on sections of land now under the dominion of ExxonMobil, around Standard Heights, and the crummier sections of Mid-City. I would listen to my father talk about bombs going off in the European cities and towns — cobblestoned squares, steepled shadows and *Götterdäm-merungs* — long after that continent's Second World War — live hand grenades, the multifarious classes of ordnance that fell from Allied planes and burrowed into the earth, unexploded, hibernating until the right moment. At least machetes and oil drums did not explode and increase the casualty rate long after the formal cessation of conflict: it was this unexploded ordnance, from an old undecided battle, which caused the Christmas Eve explosion. Perhaps it was no chemical accident at all, no failure of safety systems as reported in the accident investigation report, but the final and decisive shot fired in the Battle of Baton Rouge, Toussaint said.

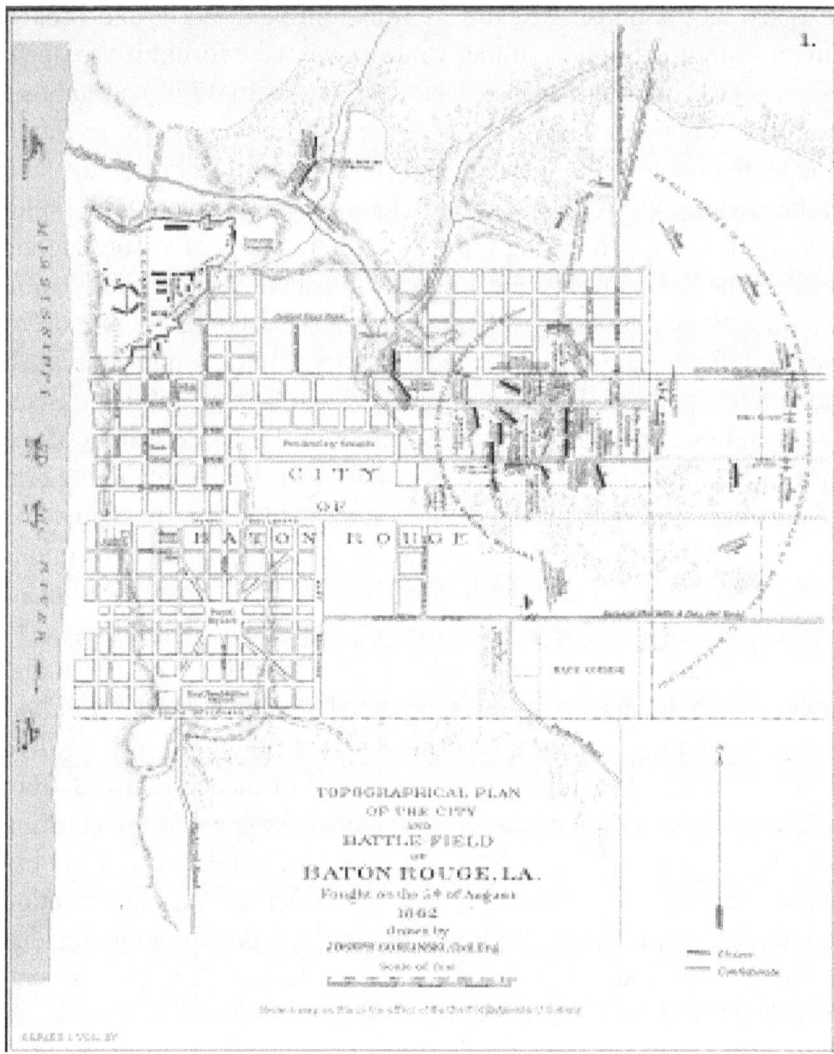

TOPOGRAPHICAL PLAN
OF THE CITY
AND
BATTLE FIELD
OF
BATON ROUGE, LA.

Not long before the Christmas Eve explosion, I had heard the Liberty Bell ringing in Arsenal Park, as if someone was trying to warn us of some imminent catastrophe. On quiet nights in the dead of winter, still as photosynthesis, when unfettered sound traveled like a runaway on a moonless night, I could sometimes hear the un-cracked Liberty bell clanging in Arsenal Park, rung by ghost children, a few lost tourists, or the Houma themselves, the bell peeling through the vacant greenbelt lots, an unheeded warning of the toxic sieges to come.

On Sunday afternoons in the cane harvest fall and the fly

ash winter — it was too humid in the satsuma summer, nothing ever dried — clothes were laundered with a homemade lye soap on a washboard, and my mother hung the family's laundry to dry on a clothesline suspended from the Live Oak, which we named the Dead Oak. Though at no time did my mother ever wish to be some fancy Sally Hemings, cavorting around Paris with a president, this tradition of drying the laundry — summer dresses, overalls, socks, underwear, jeans — on a clothesline ceased when my father saved enough money to buy a used washing machine, a rattlebanging contraption salvaged out of a flooded house when the owners, man and wife, drowned in the comfort of their own living room, in which my father had watched many black and gold losses, a clock left ticking on the wall, this double death by water watched over by the framed photographs of family and loved ones, those who had preceded them to the river's west bank, looking on expressionlessly and helplessly from the walls as their loved ones outside the frames drowned in the rising floodwaters, Toussaint said.

More than Sally Hemings, my mother was like the lead actress in *Jeanne Dielman, 23 quai du Commerce, 1080 Bruxelles*, one of the few non-Blaxploitation foreign films I saw at the Lincoln Theater, burying her identity in a reified routine of cooking, cleaning and maternal duties as regimented as the marches and drills of the Negro regiment my father was then claiming we had bloodlines in. But she ran a tight ship, a model of homeplace order against the arbitrary and iffy bedlam that was, she said, daily at our door. A dropped spoon or overcooked rice could set off a murderous rancor or unexploded ordnance. Enthralled by my father's gift, which she did not know was salvage from a flooded home, mother pulled up a chair and watched the spinning of this newfangled magic machine all night like a television — what she envisioned in that machine's spinning she never told — and we found her in the same chair the next morning, asleep with her chin on her chest. Long after the washing machine and dryer took over the laving, the clothesline was not cut down from the tree, but hung suspended still in the air, a long white crescent line demarcating two blue zones in the sky, the line languidly rotting in the humid gluey funkiness, growing black mold and slime, drooping in the center till it disintegrated and the two blues of the sky were reunited. I remember how the washing machine changed my mother, feeling some vital part of her function in the household economy had been replaced by a machine, like her pastor's heart had been after a lifesaving surgery, and while the washing machine may have saved her time and gotten the job done with brutal efficiency, as the cotton gin had in earlier times, it did not wash our clothes with the same quality of maternal solicitude with which she hand-cleaned my father's work clothes from the plant, his blue coveralls covered in a mysterious menagerie of stains and chemical blotches. As ever, the washing machine was more than just a washing machine, it was the ambassador of a way of life that had no freight in Standard Heights: my mother had not been in the presence of a washing machine since she had cleaned Edwin Edwards' house while working in the white mansion by Capitol Lake as a maid, Toussaint said, so there was a period before the clothesline rotted away that she went around calling my father Governor, a title he resented, for Edwin Edwards was the governor who sent in the shock troops to quell the student protests at Southern. I ain't no kind of governor that Louisiana would ever elect, he would say.

In Standard Heights there grew a small grove of satsumas — glowing orange globes hanging like painted fruit in the green trees. A nonnative citrus, the satsuma was imported from Japan by Jesuits to New Spain, and all over sacred Native American grounds satsuma groves were planted by Jesuit hierophants in quincunx patterns echoing the chemical classification placards on chemical cargo trucks. No one knew to whom the satsuma tree belonged, nor did I ever see anyone picking the fruity orbs that fell in ripe superfluity to the ground, swarmed by ants and wasps, and other crawling creatures, the orange spheres melting on the ground, uneaten and putridly blackened like the rotting avocado earth and the watermelon Sun used in the minister's demonstration of our picayune place in the solar system, Toussaint said.

Standards Heights' skies were polluted by commercial billboards. The injury attorneys' outsized, hideous faces lit up like ghastly zeppelins: death mask white men with crooked cheesy smiles, greasy hair, bad suits and names like Bubba Boudreaux and Wayne "Winchester" Deslondes. The faces of men who could hit a manatee with the propeller of a speedboat and claim it as a tax deduction. Suburban dads obsessed with World War 2 history, submarine warfare, the Civil War, that sort of thing, Toussaint said. Billboards for suicide prevention depicting a depressed-looking man, holding his head in his hands as if suffering a terrible migraine or a casino hangover, a table in front of him covered in pills and empty liquor bottles. I once thought I saw the man on the suicide billboard at the Lincoln Theater, sitting in the dark of *Mandingo*, but I couldn't be sure, so many men in Baton Rouge looked like they could be on one of our suicide hotline billboards. Billboards for gambling addiction hotlines, dice and slot machines and gaming tables. Billboards for unwanted pregnancies, sad abandoned mothers with bulging enceinte stomachs weeping in the comfortless, fatherless night. Billboards in fluorescent orange advertising the annual summer gun shows. A billboard for the Angola Rodeo, another for a class action lawsuit against ExxonMobil. A billboard that appeared one Thanksgiving, *Real men provide, Real women appreciate it.* Much later, after my departure from Standard Heights, the billboards for Obama's impeachment: *Where's the birth certificate?* Smiling graduates in cap and gown advertising for Baton Rouge Community College. An LSU football billboard of running back Leonard Fournette exploding in a run out of the plane of the billboard. The 800 numbers we prank-called on the land line. Standard Heights was the advertising industry's market for suicide, gambling, addiction, fornication, freak accidents, and the causes of death in traditional hip-hop songs, as though my brother and I, and all the pickup boys would one day have our tragic mugs on the billboards overlooking the greenbelt lots where we grew up.

The satsuma tree grew beneath one of these suicide hotline billboards, Toussaint said. Maybe that was why no one picked the citrus, cursed by the suicidal ideation of the despairing man with his head in his hands. Undaunted, I snuck up on the satsuma tree from behind, ambushing it when the billboard's lights were out, and without looking up at the suicidal man, I picked the forbidden fruits one by one. I brought the satsumas home, using my shirt as a basket, and dumped them onto the kitchen table. Some of the satsumas rolled off the table and plunked on the floor, a heavy fruity sound. I relished peeling the skin, which crumbled off in zesty aromatic pelts, wedging the liquid succulent crescent segments into my mouth — everything turned orange — and while my eyes were closed in the indulgent, solipsistic act of tasting the forbidden satsuma my mother slapped the fruit out of my hand. Don't eat those, she said.

While my mother watched the washing machine turn and rumble like an awakening monster, my father tinkered with an old

Monte Carlo with a blue velvet interior, Toussaint said. How the Monte Carlo got there, for I never saw it run, I didn't know, and when I asked my mother she said the Monte Carlo had simply appeared there one day after their escape from Iberville, but that it had been there in the yard as long as she could remember, an ageless leviathan, perhaps old as the ExxonMobil plant itself. He polished the car's paint job and washed its body better than he attended to my mother, this manufactured symbol of petrochemical freedom, but one which did not run, and the more my father tried to make the old jalopy run the more distant became the destination he had in mind. Had the engine started, it would be the bark of bloodhounds. You know your father has never left Louisiana, my mother told me in confidence, Toussaint said, but you mustn't let that change your opinion of him, for he would be aghast if you knew, not that physically he couldn't leave Louisiana, of course he could physically leave Louisiana at any time, just like I did, my mother said, I think mentally or somehow spiritually he cannot leave Louisiana, he is too firmly rooted here like the Jesuits' satsumas and the red stick the natives planted in the river, she said. Wherever he thought he was going in that defunct Monte Carlo, *The Negro Motorist Green Book* was not going to take him there, Toussaint said.

When he was done for the day working on the Monte Carlo, he sat at the head of the table, salvaged from one of the houses bought out and demolished by ExxonMobil, and monologued about his life, about ExxonMobil, about Iberville, the Curse of the New Orleans Saints, the team's record of losses serving as poignant lessons or homilies on being a long-suffering baghead. It was during one of these didactic dinners that a knock was heard at the door — the telephone line had been disconnected long ago; you could not call our family home and I never knew what the number was — and a soft-spoken, morbidly genteel representative of ExxonMobil asked to speak to father privately. I saw him for only the quickest second, through the crack in the door, but he might have been the melancholy man on the suicide hotline billboard. A death mask white man had never come to our door before, this modest clapboard house on the vanished native tribe streets. My father put his napkin down — a rectangular rag cut from mothballed cotton shirts — and went out to the front porch before the ExxonMobil man could enter the house, a thing I knew my father would never let this interloping visitant from the plant do. Anyone from ExxonMobil was not welcome in our house. The plant might get the best part of him and rain chemical ash from the sky upon us, but it would not cross this threshold. While he was on the porch speaking in foreboding tones — we could hear his voice booming through the closed door and the wall — to the ExxonMobil man, who wore a work shirt with the company name and logo stitched over his heart, carrying a black umbrella as it had rained that day, my brother and I sat at the table, dinner of rice and beans and andouille growing cold, holding our breath through perilous thorns of silence so we could overhear the adult argument outside, my mother, already understanding what the ExxonMobil man had come for, withdrawing from the table to the watch a load of laundry turning in the machine. He had not, of course, come to bid us good evening, to borrow a cup of sugar, or to ask if we needed anything, Toussaint said. Having lost my appetite, all I could think about was that our house too would become a vacant greenbelt lot.

Each of us eyed the door, and mother scolded us to mind our manners and our own business and never mind what was transpiring on the other side of the front door, it was not to be given the least thought in this house, if we were meant to know what my father and the ExxonMobil suicide hotline billboard man were discussing, then we would've been invited to join them. If I didn't comply mother would sternly count down from ten, as if reciting the countdown of a detonation, and then on Christmas Eve the explosion came, even if it wasn't timed with her countdown. I did not yet know for sure, when my father wordlessly left the dinner table to confer privately with the ExxonMobil man while his dinner got cold, that my mother had lived at Osage Avenue, another of the myriad streets named for a vanished native tribe. An indefinite period of time passed at the table in ever more excruciating elongations of suspense — as my father was not a man to let trivial matters interrupt his dinner, what could they possibly be discussing for this long? — before my father returned to the table and resumed eating his cold meal as if an official ExxonMobil man, his black umbrella dripping wormwood all over the floor, had not just knocked at our door. My brother and I had enough survival skills by then to keep quiet and pretend nothing was amiss. A durative silence. I heard our father angrily masticating his food, grinding the gray meat that had once been a cow into oblivion. Then he spoke.

ExxonMobil wants to buy out this house, my father informed

the family, Toussaint told me with a clutched urgency suggesting ExxonMobil might still, even today, buy out his house, wherever Toussaint found himself to be living, as if he lived under this imminent and constant threat of buyout no matter where he went. But I'm not selling it, Toussaint's father said, this house is not for sale, so if anyone from ExxonMobil comes around with a check in hand offering to buy it, you tell them we're not selling. I will not sell out the family home to ExxonMobil, that two-headed beast of a corporation, Toussaint said, I've come to adore my little forty acres and a mule in the ExxonMobil greenbelt, all this countryside greenery, the oak trees with the branches strong enough to hang a man from, the birdless sky, the windless nights, the acid rain, the chemical ash falling on us like some kind of afterlife snow, my father said. I'd like to have something to pass down, for my sons to inherit, I who inherited nothing when Storyville and then Iberville were demolished for big money condos, so that their patrimony will be more than a single windowpane salvaged from the house in Storyville, he said, stabbing the dead cow with his fork. But my father could be capricious in his feelings for the plant: if anyone in Standard Heights defamed ExxonMobil he was the first to defend the company as the lifeblood, though a vampiric one, of what remained of Standard Heights, though in his heart he reviled the company, but dared not show in public his private contempt for a master he had not chosen and could not escape from, and while he resented being beholden to this industrial behemoth and the hellscape that environed us, he acknowledged the interdigitated fates of slave and master, the dancing dialectic that held both in total symbiotic bondage, Toussaint said. Standard Heights was patrolled and guarded by bloodhounds with keen noses for escapees and runaways, *The Negro Motorist Green Book* of no use on Standard Heights' streets named for annihilated native tribes, for in his mind, and maybe in the minds of all the men who worked at the plant, the plant and the surrounding neighborhood of Standard Heights, constructed by Standard Oil, hence the name Standard Heights, were Petrochemical Modernism's adaptation of the antebellum plantation and slave quarters, respectively, but Petrochemical Modernism's industrial plantations are clogged with smokestacks and gas flares, crude oil distillation towers and isomerization plants, reflux drums and distillation columns — all the industrial accoutrements of the oil refinement process from which the plastic pink flamingos are born, Toussaint said.

In other words, my father's position in the company was not a simple one, his anxiety over *dé*classement greater than his dread of deracination. A man was not a man without a home. No, he was not about to let the petrochemical plantation buy out its own slave quarters, the move from Iberville in New Orleans to Standard Heights in Baton Rouge was the last time he would be forcibly relocated, and so he went on, between bites of cold andouille, I moved us from Iberville, my father said, for whom the demolition of Storyville was still alive in his memory, to escape the white man's bulldozers, the cops, the bloodhounds, my father becoming indignant and adamant on this point, Toussaint said, because he was the first in his family to own the house he lived in, even if he did not own everything in it, likening the move from Iberville to Standard Heights, when I was not yet old enough to understand the magnitude of what was happening to us, to Mary and Joseph's flight into Egypt, as recorded in the Gospel of Matthew. And so the ExxonMobil suicide hotline billboard man, with his black umbrella dripping wormwood, left us with our house in the family name, at least for now, and to finish our cold dinner off in the deep and abiding silence after father's jeremiad against the buyout program's attempt to unhouse us during the family meal, the Exxon-Mobil man — frustrated and stymied by this obstinate plant worker's principled and self-destructive refusal to submit to the salient logic of necessity and a little money, though confident in the Great White Hope's ability to prevail in the end — driving back to the corporate office in Houston, where cause and effect are matters of opinion, big oil executives and engineers every day making important decisions affecting far-off places like Standard Heights, drawing up their maps of the Battle of Baton Rouge, pointing to the last remaining holdout house in Standard Heights and saying, that's the one, Toussaint said.

Iberville

I came here to rebuild the city, block by block, in the brain's kaleidoscope of fictive cartographies. The toy streetcar rattles its metal fetters on the great bosky boulevards and oaken avenues of this sinking, drowning city with its unrepentant stone General Lee at the eye of the storm in Lee Circle. Everywhere construction and reconstruction are maniacally underway rebuilding this decaying surrealist dream. Potholes deep as a double shot of Jameson. Busking cockroaches migrate from one baroque dilapidation to the next. In the swelter of the subtropical afternoon, when the heat achieves its maximum curdling zenith, the city rises up over itself like a Mardi Gras Godzilla, smashing buildings and parade floats. From this steaming dripping welter, the corporeal parts of men and women stick together, seeking refuge in the license of the French Quarter, the flag of Antarctica and the flag of the Republic of New Afrika paraded down Royal Street, penguins and polar bears protesting all anthropogenic culture. Subsidence and sinkholes claim the lives of Boschian revelers. Sweating walls cant a few soft degrees off their true center — there are no right angles in this nonlinear city. The old canals that once reticulated the city like a Dixie Florence, the Carondelet Canal, the New Basin Canal, all drained and filled with concrete. Whence this restive energy? Yellow fever and malaria still claim lost souls, buried in the levee holding back the river, but for how much longer? The New Orleans Charm-Industrial Complex is accepting tax-deductible donations. Another second line for a dead president brasses down Magazine Street. The Victorian gingerbread woodwork melts like icing on a byzantine cake. The Spillway opens in the spring, and floods Canal Street. In the same streets, no matter the city, one wanders and digresses in endlessly circling repetitions. Canal Street leads inevitably to Commonwealth Avenue; St. Charles Avenue to Massachusetts Avenue; Esplanade to Huntington. Cats dream in windows and curled around potted hibiscus on turquoise verandahs. Obscene crimes are committed in the gas lamp night. The streets are chewed up, new black asphalt spat out. The city masticates and digests itself like a green, gold, and purple Ouroboros. The Dead Zone at the Mississippi's mouth yawns wide and wider, ready to swallow the fairytale conurbation whole like an anaconda choking on a pig. New Orleans is a doomed city, like living on a tragic shipwreck or clown spacecraft that is tumbling out of control through intergalactic carnival space.

To rebuild the city and inhabit the constructions of mentation and counter-mapping that Toussaint left me with. Toussaint was born in the Iberville Projects, constructed atop the city's erstwhile red light district — Storyville where the glamorous whores waltzed to sultry jazz piano and painted streetwalkers called and crooned from the corners of the French Quarter. When I first met Toussaint, he was wandering the broken grounds of his birthplace, now an active construction site fenced off from the public while yellow bulldozers roamed what's left of the red light district like prehistoric steel dinosaurs that plowed through the brick WPA-era buildings, pointlessly moving earth from one end of the site to the other.

The announcement, published in *The Times Picayune,* of the discovery of human remains, unearthed during the excavations, brought us both to Iberville; Toussaint because the bones, he believed, might have been those of his ancestors, and me simply out of that perverse, macabre fascination that has made white southerners both fanatical tellers of and active participants in ructious ghost stories, but also unable to look away from lurid scenes of death's archaeology, and so it must have been at Iberville, as the old government project was being torn down, that we encountered one another for the first time, I reflected with a note of humid melancholy, such a — I will not call it a friendship, for it was not that exactly — but such a meeting could only transpire in the presence of a demolition, the creation of another absence in Toussaint's life, and it was here, at the busy redevelopment site of the Iberville Projects, which stood in turn upon the redevelopment of Storyville, that Toussaint first divulged anything of his past life in Standard Heights in the petrochemical shadow of the ExxonMobil plant, demonstrating a sophisticated knowledge, for a layman, albeit a scientific knowledge tinged too with personal memories and chlorine gas ghost ships, of highly technical chemical and refinery processes, deploying perhaps with alarming facility the positivist language of polymers and monomers, separation processes, heat exchangers, materials compatibility, hydrotreaters, catalytic reformers, alkylation, hydrogen synthesis, fluid catalytic crackers, the entire flow diagram of a chemical plant blueprinted in his mind, and it must have been these bones rattling beneath Iberville, and Storyville beneath that, which were on his mind that day we met at the Mississippi riverfront in Baton Rouge and I deambulated behind him through Arsenal Park — the cannon on the Indian mound unironically aimed at the ExxonMobil plant — to the vacant lot in Standard Heights where the family home once stood until the buyouts were completed according to plan.

Badly flooded in Katrina, the Iberville Projects were coming down. I expected the excavation, which substantially delayed the redevelopment project while archaeologists cataloged the artefacts exhumed from the ground, to turn up something akin to Pompeii — preserved Romans of all social classes in frozen postures of fatal shock and last horror, lewd couplings, nightmarish contortions, covered in the petrochemical ash released from the ExxonMobil plant. But Storyville is not even the final stratum, the fabled red light district was erected over the Protestant section of Saint Louis Cemetery No.1 and so in this Catholic city, where the streets are named for saints, the Muses, state governors and undead Confederate generals, the bones of Protestants lay beneath the whorehouses, brothels, gambling houses, boozy saloons and general dens of iniquity that gave Storyville its bawdy red light reputation. Layer upon layer of accumulated past, anywhere you turn ground with a shovel will strike a casket. The soil of New Orleans is a fetid gumbo, a dark roux preserving human remains and bygone cultures in a rich amalgam of organic matter and soft alluvial clay. On the former grounds of Iberville, on top of the projects and the old red light district, luxury apartments now ascend over Basin Street.

Demolition was like an heirloom in Toussaint's family, inherited by each generation in turn. Before ExxonMobil's buyout of Standard Heights, Toussaint's father had people — those who fled the torchlit ghost stories of South Louisiana during the Great Migration, but being unable to imagine life away from the Mississippi River got no farther than St. Louis, Missouri — who were evicted for the demolition of Pruitt-Igoe, those monstrous thirty-three public housing towers on fifty-seven acres of land, skyscraper ghettos. Riveted and repelled at the same time, I watched the demolition of the Pruitt-Igoe towers in the silver dark of the Lincoln Theater, Toussaint said, in the tone poem film *Koyaanisqatsi*, a native word meaning "life is out of balance," another of the white race's boring art cinema pieces with its slow motion dream speed sequences and dramatic minimalist score, the unexploded ordnance which detonated on Christmas Eve at the ExxonMobil plant and at the 16th Street Baptist Church in Birmingham also took down the Pruitt-Igoe towers, Toussaint said, brushing his arms off as if he felt the demolition dust settling on his skin.

I had seen this provocative figure, then unknown to me, standing before the redevelopment site for a long time, contemplating the mysterious movements of the earthmoving machines back and forth on the site. His fixation before this deconstruction must have caught my attention, as most of the passersby at this tattered edge of the French Quarter did not stop to linger before the half-completed teardown of an abandoned housing project on which someone had spray-painted, in bubble script, *destroy this memory*. I walked by the long ferny brick wall separating St. Louis Cemetery No.1 and its notorious dead from the living, passing beneath the crumbling crypts and the pollution-stained crosses shadowing Basin Street, stopping across from the statue of Benito Juárez on the neutral ground, the Mexican revolutionary on his plinth, composing his liberal reform Plan of Ayutla, a strategic counterpoint to the stone statue of General Lee, unreconstructed Confederate, across town at the center of the storm raging in Lee Circle. His fingers laced in the construction fencing, as if bracing for a storm, and given that, like Fisk's many rivers, nothing here moves in a straight line, I thought little of Toussaint, a total stranger then, beginning his counter-narrative *in medias res* as it were.

Because I wished to see what had become of the addresses indexed in the Green Book and to see for myself who resided there now, I visited the addresses of those who were listed as friendly to traveling Negroes at the time of the Green Book's printing, perhaps testing whether they were still friendly to Negroes or not. I lived in Boston at this time — a permanent address has always eluded me; *fernweh* ravages one like a contagious disease from an early age when the family home's closets are rattling with skeletons — and hoped that I would never live anywhere in particular; I didn't want to be called by any demonym or gentilic, as every place I'd ever been was within the audible range of the petrochemical nocturne, Toussaint said, peering through the construction fence to inspect the excavation site.

I went to the Harriett Tubman Hotel at 25 Holyoke Street, in Boston's South End neighborhood, row upon row of staid, puritanical red-brick brownstones, and asked for Harriett Tubman. None of the otherworldly exoticism of Cancer Alley and none of the abandoned, decaying charm, like that of a dead albatross. But even in Boston I felt marked more by what I'd left behind — higher infant mortality, lower life expectancy, mysterious blood illnesses, hazmat symbol systems, fratricides and infanticides, Civil War re-enactments, the underperforming infrastructure, the sword and the plow, the slow poisoning of the environment, the Curse of the Saints, bibliomancers and practitioners of a *sortes vergilianae* — after the buyouts than I felt stirred by my new northern surroundings, but the Old World for which one feels such *Heimweh* is as suspect as the new, adoptive one, and *Heimat* is one of those loanword concepts to keep you from ever leaving the spatial social unit into which you were arbitrarily and nonconsensually born. There was no Harriet Tubman at the Harriet Tubman Hotel, and at the Melbourne at 815 Tremont Street, around Frederick Douglass Square, and a place called Mother's Lunch at 510 Columbus Avenue, I was no closer to finding a place friendly to a traveling Negro.

Then the addresses listed under tourist homes, I inquired after a Mrs. M. Johnson domiciled at 616 Columbus Avenue and after a Mrs. Ford of 209 West Springfield Street, the resident — a Harvard man — did not understand what I wanted, had never heard of these past people, and so I showed him my copy of the Green Book and he confirmed for himself that his address was listed there as a safe stopping point for traveling Negroes in the Jim Crow era. In Boston, every address listed in the Green Book was not only intact, but occupied, by all appearances thriving and without the spooking of the petrochemical companies' haunted manor houses, a disconfirmation of broken windows theory — the dissimilarities between the North and South's respective treatments of historical memory as it pertains to the Negro's ability to move unmolested about this Republic is nowhere made more painfully salient than in tracking down the Negro-friendly addresses listed in the Green Book. Osage Avenue notwithstanding. With this caveat: at every Boston address listed in the Green Book, when I rang the bell, I was greeted cordially and very professionally but with some edgy suspicion by a pale face and turned away, just as my father turned away the ExxonMobil man when he came to the door that evening interrupting dinner to name his price to buy out the family home and collect another piece in the ExxonMobil greenbelt.

I had little hope that the addresses listed in the Green Book could be found in my hometown, but I felt I had no choice, Toussaint said, or even if they could be found the addresses would be nothing like those in the north. Then back in Baton Rouge I found the Ever-Ready at 1236 Louisiana Avenue, an abandoned leprous house, ugly and disfigured, the windows boarded up, a small tree growing out of the roof. What man has wrought is quickly restored to an ultimate state of nature here. The Ideal Cafeteria at 1501 East Boulevard had been bought by powers of eminent domain and razed to make way for the right-of-way for Interstate 10, which elevated the indefatigable streams of hazmat trucks with their ancient and cabalistic chemical symbols above the roofs of the neighborhood where the Lincoln Theater once provided proof of concept of a future outside of Standard Heights, Toussaint said.

In New Orleans, the establishments friendly to transient Negroes clustered on South Rampart Street: the Astoria at 225 South Rampart Street, the Patterson at 761 South Rampart Street, and the Riley at 759 South Rampart Street. On the way I must have given away tens of dollars in small bills and spare change to the homeless panhandling the corners of this devastated block. A streetcar like that on Saint Charles once rattled down Rampart; now it was choked with hazmat trucks and single-passenger vehicles running on gas from the river refineries. No place for traveling Negroes, all three Rampart Street addresses were razed for parking lots, those black voids that have afflicted the landscape of Petrochemical Modernism. At each parking lot, like stations on a pilgrimage where the holy sites and shrines have all been obliterated by war or dismantled by rival sects, I stopped to mourn the loss of a homeplace friendly to traveling Negroes, replaced now by petrochemical blacktop. The Green Book's addresses listed elsewhere than Rampart fared no better. An establishment known as The Chicago at 1310 Iberville Street met the same fate as Rampart, and The Paige at 1038 Dryades Avenue was cleared to make room for an exit ramp accessing the Pontchartrain Expressway. I began to understand that Petrochemical Modernism was in need of *Lebensraum*, room to grow and hostile to memory that was not engineered in its process flow diagrams. Nothing of the South's friendly refuges for the traveling Negro remained. The Palace listed at 1834 Annette Street in the Marigny — the original house was gone, swept away in Katrina, and in its place a soulless and bland mausoleum of recent construction. It was as if some omniscient, opaque authority had taken the Green Book and picked precisely those addresses friendly to traveling Negroes for systematic removal, leaving no quarter for the traveling Negro, perhaps on his way to the Republic of New Afrika, escaping the bloodhounds. Louis Armstrong's neighborhood, the birthplace of jazz, bulldozed for the Euclidean void of parking lots and the miserable municipal constructions where you pay your taxes or a parking ticket. The Rampart addresses, test cases of broken windows theory, were so many bad memories — there was something here we did not wish to remember, or did not want to see survive in whatever epoch awaited us on the other side of Petrochemical Modernism.

As Toussaint said this, watching the earthmovers pick apart the Iberville Projects for human remains, a great blackbird landed on the shoulder of Benito Juárez, and when I turned back to the construction fence to which he had been clinging, as if for dear life, Toussaint was gone, leaving me adrift and alone on Basin Street, a soft subtropical rain falling. Not long after this first Basin Street encounter, I retraced Toussaint's steps exactly as he had described them to me that day at the Iberville Projects, visiting the addresses north and south listed in the Green Book, to see for myself what had become of the Negro-friendly houses and motels, the white faces like mine answering the doors of posh homes that had once been occupied by people who needed a little book to tell them where it was safe to sleep for the night. It was exactly as Toussaint had said it was, that day on Basin Street: little if anything remained, and where a house could be found at the address it was inevitably answered by my double. I had almost come to the conclusion that visiting the addresses in New Orleans was a waste of time, that Toussaint had sent me on a sort of geographic fool's errand, but something about the thoroughness of the demolition of those establishments friendly to traveling Negroes goaded me to see it through to completion, not to be defeated by the earthmovers.

Discouraged and more despondent than I had been in a long time — my obsession with demolitions and clearances, the multilayered strata of the petrochemical ruins was then at an acute climax — I went to the last address listed in Central City, expecting to find the same pattern of systematic removal repeated. A young man dressed like a croupier riding a woman's bike with boxing gloves and sunglasses on. An old man — he looked like Khalik Allah's close-up portraits — outside a gas station desperately scraping a scratch lottery ticket with a nickel. He peered at the petrochemical symbols his scratching revealed, an expression of indignation but also a confirmation of everything he already knew to be true, threw the losing lottery ticket on the ground and fired up a cigarette. Something had to burn. Not exactly a safe haven for traveling Negroes, I came to a creole cottage, painted luridly in an ashy pink fading to gray, the brick chimney stacks leaning to the west like pre-Columbian cairns. A demure knock at the door — the bell worked perfectly fine — and I was prepared to renounce the project at once when the front door opened heavily, reluctantly, cracked enough to see the disarrayed gloom within, and that's when Toussaint met me for the second time, though it may have been the first or even the last, for each successive meeting had the irreconcilable feeling of both a first encounter and the melancholy finality of an unresolved parting as the Christmas Eve explosion had been for Toussaint and his father. This is the *dérive* method by which *The Negro Motorist Green Book* led me back to Toussaint, who after each encounter I didn't know if I would see again. The Green Book was written for the safe passage and watchful navigation of the petrochemical nocturne, beware the Hand and Eye motif, as Mayweather had to lull McGregor into a false sense of security before the knockout; as the inscrutable chemical placard symbols are carved into the bark of the ExxonMobil trees; as little Ruby Bridges could not attend class in this self-dreaming city without being escorted through the rabid bloodhound mob by armed U.S. Marshals.

Toussaint opened the door to this Green Book address I had found listed in the Green Book, but he did not invite me in.

Colored Entrance

After he gingerly put away the ghostly glass plate of Whipped Peter — I never saw it again, it was not among his belongings delivered to me in a damp box after the Christmas Eve explosion, and so the glass plate's existence is no more certain than ExxonMobil's manufactured clouds — my father showed me another picture, Toussaint said, taken by a man named Gordon Parks, on assignment for *Life* Magazine, of my mother on the sidewalk outside the Saenger Theater in downtown Mobile, Alabama — she always said it like that: city first, state second; the city never without the state; it was always *Mobile, Alabama*, said with the same conviction and pride with which the people in her state said *Roll Tide* — looking for all the world like she was not what she in fact was: a little black girl from downhome Prichard, Alabama. *Life* had decided not to run the picture, and it was easy to see why, Toussaint said. My father, who had never been in any kind of theater, Lincoln or Saenger, seemed as astounded by this image as I was, as if he were seeing it for the first time, and the latent history lesson here was that the Colored Entrances were nicer in those days than the universal and come one, come all entrances of today. No one invites us in with colored neon today in the era of Petrochemical Modernism. The unsaid expectation is that we not enter at all, Toussaint said.

I cannot say for sure what perverse urge was behind my father's need — and I experienced it as a need, because no one asked him to see these horrors, they came forth from him unbidden; had I known of their existence I still would not have asked to see them — to share these old time images with me, for he never spoke of them again, and it was implied that I was not to speak of them to anyone else, not my brother, not anyone else in Standard Heights, and certainly most of all I was forbidden — another prohibition to go along with not opening the windows — to speak of Whipped Peter or the Colored Entrance photo of herself to my mother, Toussaint said. He stressed that mentioning these images to her would far surpass in inhumanity and barbarity the contents of the images themselves, even though the Colored Entrance photograph in downtown Mobile, Alabama did not have, *prima facie*, Toussaint said, and here the Latin Toussaint learned in the State Library became evident, the same outward barbarity and cruelty as the black and white plate of Whipped Peter's savaged back, an image which visited me in nightmares for years, Whipped Peter's back implying the hand of a ghostly, unseen whipper who perhaps stood outside the photo's frame, and from Whipped Peter — and this constituted the core of restitution or reparations in this country — we inherited a generationally de-escalating series of punishments: my father, my mother said, had suffered caning and birching at the hands of older family members, a few blows to the head and stomach from off-duty New Orleans police, but she said he was not lashed or cropped, whereas I, Toussaint said, having neither been caned nor birched, neither was I flogged or knouted with a horsewhip or cat-o'-nine-tails as my forebear Whipped Peter was, but I was feruled in school for petty infractions and more than once walked around yellow crime scene tape and over police chalk lines outlining the final orientation on the blacktop — once, even in the parking lot of one of the Green Book's Rampart Street addresses — of a friend's body after another suicide by cop, Toussaint said. This de-escalation of punishment, a sliding scale from the flogging to caning to feruling may suggest that an iota of incrementalized progress, measured in body bags and funerals, was made in matters of human decency but my father, had he lived long enough to bear my brother's several attempts at suicide by cop, would have said the police are the modern day descendants of slave bounty hunters, and the ExxonMobil plant is our petrochemical plantation, Toussaint said.

No longer do I marvel that this photo of a savagely whipped enslaved person came down to us in black and white, and not full color, as it could not have been at that time, before the invention of color photography, whereas the Colored Entrance photo, as Toussaint referred to it, was shot in downtown Mobile, Alabama and printed in full color, albeit in the soft muted mid-century tones of Petrochemical Modernism. The mint-colored pastel dress and blurry faded neon, Toussaint said. The mummy gray of the street, and the flashing chrome of the bumper on the car moving towards the cameraman, Toussaint said. The softened, lacy jauntiness of the dresses, and the aggressive red of the white woman retreating into the photo's vanishing point — one hears the angry knives of her heels stabbing the pavement, each echoing angrily into eternity, Toussaint said, the white temptress always appearing in a blood red dress, like Blanche driving Ganymede to his death in a cauldron of boiling water from the Spillway.

Having finally found him, Toussaint did not immediately invite me in to his safe haven in Central City, the address listed in the Green Book of places friendly to the traveling Negro. I stood outside on the street with nowhere to go, like his mother outside the Colored Entrance. Toussaint had been composing lyrics in the blue glow of an old iBook, those chunky white vintage laptops that are heavy enough to sink a corpse. The room was dim and without heat, and his body was padded in a puffy jacket that, though Toussaint was by no means diminutive in stature, made him appear larger than he was, like the giant winter coat Tom Brady can be seen wearing on the sidelines while the defense is on the field, and under the puffy jacket the black and gold characteristic of a Saints jersey shone but I could not decipher the player's number. XXXtentacion — real name Jahseh Dwayne Onfroy — had just been shot and killed in South

Florida. Whether for personal security or adornment, Toussaint kept a small hunting knife sheathed on his belt, and his skin was healing from another tattoo. The iBook rotated through songs by his favorite artists — Lotto Boyzz, XXXtentacion's "Everybody Dies in Their Nightmares," Ski Mask The Slump God, Kodak Black, Styles P, Boosie Badazz. He composed his lyrics — he was working on an album, *Petrochemical Nocturne* — in the machine's Unix command prompt terminal; because, he said, use of a word processing application like Microsoft Word got in the way, all the formatting made his lyrics look like an office memorandum, and he preferred the white or green text on a black background like a programmer writing lines of clandestine code. I caught stealthy glimpses of his surreal lyrics in rhymed snippets about Natalie Holloway and Mrs. Dalloway, missing white girl syndrome and Stockholm Syndrome, the Superdome and Superfunds, the uberous noble savage who dreams a regime with the mind of a mainframe, scoring cheap points like Tyson biting Holyfield's ear off, so he can't hear the wolf-whistling nocturne. The blank pages of the Green Book and getting rich on Lafitte's buried treasure. I hadn't seen an operating iBook in a long time, an antique machine that went out of production years ago. There were several pieces of unopened mail from Georgetown University on the floor. I have been to the spot where your mother stood beneath the Colored Entrance sign of the theater, I said, thinking this would evoke another of Toussaint's associative, episodic apostrophes, those freewheeling footnoted excurses by which I was able to join him in his journeys to recover his bulldozed and demolished past.

Yes, without always realizing my own complicit role in the upriver and downriver repetitions of the perpetual flux, I have stood in the very spot where Toussaint's mother was photographed by Gordon Parks. I came to the spot after aberrating from bench to bench in Cathedral Square, formerly an 18th century Catholic cemetery, then known as Campo Santo, threading through the murky city blocks along Joachim, Dauphin, Franklin and Conti Streets, though I prefer *boneyard* to cemetery, or even necropolis, which too prettified the metropolis of the deceased. A series of demolitions cleared the block of commercial structures in 1979 for the park and now one can sit forever on those standard green iron benches in cities everywhere and watch the black vibrations of bats quivering about the Cathedral Basilica of the Immaculate Conception. Before me, ossified in its implacable religion, stood the tower of a veridical cathedral, the pious prototype for the petrochemical cathedrals of Cancer Alley, as I saw manufactured clouds rising from the basilica's twin smoke-stacks.

Locating the exact spot in the Gordon Parks photo was not necessarily easy, I said. The Colored Entrance neon sign is gone, and so too are the gray buildings with green and red neon signs. Though I distinctly saw a classic woman wearing a long red dress who might have been the same as the photograph's white woman in the red dress, walking away from the cameraman and the photograph's two principal subjects standing on the street corner, behind Toussaint's mother, a white woman in a flowing red dress who had never suf-fered the indignity of using a Colored Entrance to enter the theater, the library, the grocery store, the courthouse, or any other public place in which one might need to conduct business. The cars on the street are different, more fuel efficient, and less nostalgic and vin-tage-looking, gone are the shark fins of the atomic age streamlined for clean futuristic superhighways, the kind of car you expect to see parked at a drive-in movie theater showing a Blaxploitation film.

When my father, Toussaint continued, taking a seat on a col-lapsed and stained sofa, was the same age as my mother in the Col-ored Entrance photo, he was either a schoolmate of or a personal friend of Ruby Bridges, the brave little girl of six years who under escort of the U.S. Marshals integrated schools in Orleans Parish. As a little boy living in the Iberville Projects, where they're now build-ing luxury condos, he attended William Frantz Elementary School on North Galvez Street after Ruby had already done the job, he was plagued with regretful self-reproach, as if he'd committed a crime, that he did not do this himself, was not the one to integrate the school, while the revolutionary voice of Fidel Castro resounding on *Radio Free Dixie* through the yards and corridors of Iberville haunted him, because Ruby Bridges was out there before jeering, taunting death mask whites alone, and even once integration was accomplished she had no classmates, as no teacher would take responsibility for her instruction except a single educator from Boston, although my fa-ther would not want to be escorted in the presence of armed U.S. Marshals, Toussaint said, my father would have preferred to go it alone rather than be protected by white Marshals. Once again, the force of armed security guards who have shepherded us through the gauntlet, protecting us from the mobs of nobodies, protecting the cane field suburbs from another German Coast Uprising. Then next to the Green Book, on the shelf with the family Bible, I discovered a copy of *Look* magazine, the January 14, 1964 issue, in which the magazine had printed a full-color centerfold, now faded, of the Norman Rockwell painting of that day in November of 1960, which once hung outside the Oval Office in Obama's White House, since replaced by portraits of Andrew Jackson and Hugo Black in Trump's White House, Toussaint said. This event is painted from the child's perspective, low to the ground, at Ruby Bridges' height, the U.S. Marshals depicted headless, Toussaint said, like Audubon's print of the flamingo that I mistook for a decapitated bird, like corporate automata of the gray flannel suit, he said, the Marshals' baggy pants rolled at the cuff like those of the black dappers in purple or blue suits of the Zulu Social Aid and Pleasure Club. Little Ruby carries a ruler, an instrument for measuring the Christmas Eve explosion and the height of the oil drum mountain, and two notebooks for drawing the process flow diagrams and engineering schematics of the petrochemical plant. Ruby's white dress, so reminiscent of my mother's churchy, Sunday dress in the Colored Entrance photograph, shimmers like a ghost in moonlight, *KKK* scrawled illiterately on the wall of the school violently splattered with bloody tomatoes, traditionally thrown when a comic delivers a bad joke, but our race's attempts to make peace with being on this continent have always been a bad joke to the mobs of nobodies, Toussaint said.

But maybe it was for the best my father had not been the one to integrate William Frantz Elementary School, cursed as we already were. The Bridges family suffered disproportionately for their daughter's courage: Ruby's father was fired from his job; they were refused service and starved out at the grocery store; and Ruby's Mississippi grandparents, sharecroppers, were evicted from their land, like everyone in Standard Heights. Though I could not open the windows, I could open that copy of *Look* magazine and in the bloody tomato splatters on the elementary school wall understand something of why my father forbade them ever — present, past, or future — to be opened. These aestheticized reproductions of actual historical traumas rendered the event intelligible — I do not say meaningful, or any other emetic sentimentalities, for there is no meaning in the downriver dialectic of the toxic wormwood: Ruby

Bridges going to school under police escort — this was the antithesis to your George Wallace, Toussaint said, a little black girl taking a stand in the schoolhouse door. Klansmen hiding in the rose bushes. The faces of museum security guards and the U.S. Marshals, had we been able to see them, were the same as those despairing on the suicide hotline billboards casting sinister commercial shadows over the greenbelt lots of Standard Heights. I suppose it had to be a painting, and not a photograph, Toussaint said, for there were camera-shy tribes in Standard Heights who believed the camera compromised the soul by preserving the body, against decay, in a black and white image, so that a photograph of a little black girl under white escort would have risked the immortality of her soul, Toussaint said.

At the time, I could feel in my bloodstream the rising wormwood river running between the east bank of the flashing neons and muted mid-century colors of the Colored Entrance photograph and the west bank of cold bloodhound grays in the glass plate of Whipped Peter, this grayscale forebear. What might the soul-stealing cameramen have done with Whipped Peter, had color then existed? The keloid scars recorded in textured browns and livid flesh tones, and not crude black and white. But the only color images in Whipped Peter's time vanished as soon as they were made, exposures lasted for days at a time and the colors reproduced were so sensitive and ephemeral that they faded before the viewer's eyes like a corrosive liquid dissolving the human hand in the hazmat symbol. Often at the vespertine vanishing hour, going to the river at sunset to spy across the water for my father on the west bank, I have recalled Rilke's line about the quickly disappearing photograph in the more slowly disappearing hand, Toussaint said, looking at his own hand, as if his own body might be as transient and changeable as Fisk's many rivers, disappearing at a slightly slower — though no less inevitable — rate than Whipper Peter. Black and white had this much going for it, a technical permanence, he said, Whipped Peter might have disappeared forever had his whip-scarred back been captured on color film. The Colored Entrance photo's provenance, however, can be traced back to the laboratory of James Clerk Maxwell, the maestro of color. Before you is the world's first permanent color photograph: Thomas Sutton, in an empirical test of James Clerk Maxwell's thought experiment about how a colored image could be stabilized and produced, took three black and white photos of a multicolored ribbon: one photo through a red filter, a second photo through a red filter, and a third through a green filter. The colored tartan ribbon, with its pteropine form, was created by projecting the trichromatic photographs superimposed on a screen, the additive primary colors recombining to evoke the flight of a luminescent bat, that nocturnal creature which circled the gloaming balefires and hydrocarbon spires of the ExxonMobil plant.

In the experimental photograph, the color ribbon bat is caught in midflight, its radiant wings stilled by the camera at forty-five degree angles: the variegated chromaticism of the world, once denatured by colorless documents of a runaway's whip-scarred back, has been restored to color. My mother and her family left Prichard and the Colored Entrance for Philadelphia not long after this Colored Entrance photo outside the Saenger Theater was taken, Toussaint said. She was only a little girl in Alabama a little while before they followed the safe houses in the Green Book to Osage Avenue. I've been to the Saenger in downtown Mobile, to see showings of *The Defiant Ones* and *No Way Out* when the closed sign was hung on the doors of the Lincoln Theater, which did not need a Colored Entrance sign because it was a colored theater, and I realized that Ganymede and the black doctor, the good fight of the black and white movies, were both trapped in the same colorless world as Whipped Peter, Toussaint said.

The skull and crossbones fate of Native Americans, Toussaint said, apparently changing subjects, but in the departure from the originary point he never failed to formulate an associative nexus returning him to the beginning, in South America was no different than what befell the tribes represented in the native street names of Standard Heights: the Caduveo, the Bororo, the Man of the Hole. Only seldom did the natives fight back or resist with any efficacy, and when they did they turned the creation against the creator, photograph against photographer, Toussaint said, while I thought of the day I had been stopped and questioned by ExxonMobil's security guard, forbidden to photograph the hydrocarbon leviathan itself. Sometimes the taking of a photograph results in the death of its maker, and in the Boston Public Library I have read of an eminent ethnologist, an Italian by the name of Guido Boggiani, who explored the interior of Brazil in the late 19th century, conducting documentary fieldwork, but not having a soul himself, as a death mask Occidental, Guido Boggiani committed the fatal mistake of photographing the Chamacoco Indians, so that he could take their likeness back home to Europe with him — they could not be expected to understand this mechanical black box which reproduced the ghosts of their likeness on shimmering glass plates, and so the ethnologist was treated to the apotheosis of anthropologists, not a victim but a totem of ritual killing — I do not say murder for the Chamacoco were never prosecuted and these tribes, like the *homo sacer*, exist so far beyond the reach of our myopic jurisprudence that murder in our lexical sense has no meaning, Toussaint said, putting his iBook down now and opening the door of the Green Book house — a cue that it was my time to go. The Chamacoco, he said, waiting by the door, may be forgiven for believing that photography, which fixes a simulacrum on a glass plate more true to life than their carved wooden figurines representing deities, heroes or demigods, that this little black box abducts the souls of its subjects, for splitting the anthropologist's skull with an axe obtained through a trade with European colonists, and destroying his camera, which according to their custom they buried in a shallow grave along with Boggiani's negatives. The flamingo wildernesses and greenbelt jungles of Standard Heights must be rife with broken cameras and undeveloped negatives — perhaps that is all that remains of Lafitte's buried treasure — of those who tried to capture the hideous likeness of the petrochemical leviathan: the Gordon Parks photograph of my mother on the sidewalk outside the Colored Entrance in downtown Mobile, Alabama; the photo of a brutalized Emmett Till in his coffin; the likeness of Whipped Peter's whip-scarred back. In the photographs you have shown me, Toussaint said directly to me, beginning to close the door of the Green Book house now, I see no souls, no transcendental runaways, only corporeal nocturnes. Gray ash flaking from the sky like the fallout of a cremation. Endocrine disruptors in the teddy bear. Benzene in the king cake. All such photos should be buried in shallow graves by nearly extinct natives and forgotten at least forever; from such photographic seeds, when the benzene-rich and hydrocarbon rains come, they will flourish into the measureless labyrinth of sentient flora and flamingo habitat that will grow over the petrochemical ruins when the last chlorine gas ghost ship sails down the river, he said, shutting the door on the Green Book house.

Confederate Dead at Antietam, 1862

When I told Toussaint about Birmingham's 1916 Reunion of the Confederates, the riverboat — we boarded in Baton Rouge and intended to port in New Orleans, a sort of Creole *Fitzcarraldo* — we were on was passing the infernal refinery operation at Norco, a petrochemical river town renamed from Sellers to Norco ten years after the 1916 Reunion of the Confederates. The equanimity with which he absorbed this new information — something I'd never divulged outside those immediate relations who might be sympathetic — made me think perhaps he had not heard me. A westward floating armada of rainbow-striped hot air balloons drifted low over the river. This argonauting abreast of Toussaint, up and down Cancer Alley, was addling my sense of direction and orientation, landmasses subsiding and the river twitching like a livid serpent. I opened the map app on my smartphone and though we were clearly on the starboard of a riverboat in the Mississippi River — I confirmed this: chocolate water rushing by in muddled torrents on starboard and port sides — the pulsating red dot representing the smartphone user's GPS coordinates was placed a few feet onshore, dislocated, lost, deracinated: I was in two places at once, a bifurcated vanishing point, one half of me on the riverboat with Toussaint, and the other half on the eastern bank of Fisk's river.

In a junk shop on one of the French Quarter's narrow, cobbled streets, just days before Mayor Landrieu's administration announced plans to remove all the city's Confederate monuments, including the problematical statue at Lee Circle, struck by lightning so many times it now had an electric charge, I said to Toussaint who was watching the hot air balloons float over the river, I discovered this postcard amidst an assortment of nostalgic postcards — national monuments, panoramic vistas, roadside motels with vintage neon blade signs, the seven wonders of the world — in a card catalog drawer next to a marble bust of a man resembling Toussaint Louverture. The bust's nose was broken off, and the marble eyes were of the sort that looked at you omnisciently without pupils — a white ellipsoid where the personality of the eye should be colored. A common stylistic treatment in busts of Roman emperors. Just behind the postcard of the Confederate veterans I pulled a lynching postcard of the charred remains of Jesse Washington in Waco, Texas, while outside the junk shop I heard the merry chaos of trombone and trumpet and tuba in a second line brass band, the snare drum like a death rattle. The smell of immolated human flesh seemed to emanate freshly from the postcard, unextinguished after all these years, the remnant heat burning my fingers, so that I thought the postcard itself might spontaneously combust and burn down the junk shop, and for a flickering moment in the crepuscular memories of the junk shop, I saw the Confederate veterans' feet moving in time with the second line brass band, goosestep marching into the postcard's vanishing point, where one half of me waited on the eastern bank of Fisk's river, I said feeling the human sacrifice from that lynching postcard burning still in my fingertips.

The Confederate veterans postcard could be any patriotic parade — it could be a presidential visit, or the celebration of an armistice after many years of war — on 19th Street and 2nd Avenue North, both of which I have traversed by foot enough times to thread them through a needle in my sleep. No *A MAN WAS LYNCHED YESTERDAY* sign hung from Birmingham's buildings as it did almost every day of the year in those days from the NAACP's offices on 5th Avenue in New York, I said. The city at the time of the Confederate veterans parade was still intact, before the bombardments and assaults of white flight and suburbanization pathologized it as if the conflict of a world war had been decided in its streets: majestic, classical buildings torn down for surface parking lots or left to time's cruel dilapidations; the old streetcar lines ripped up to make way for the tyranny of the single-passenger automobile; the grand boulevards and tree-lined avenues are commercial strips and marginal retailers of petrochemical products like Gursky's supermarket; Birmingham's addresses friendly to traveling Negroes all demolished or worse.

But it is neither a presidential visit nor an armistice depicted in the postcard, as the patriotic red, white, and blue bunting would suggest, though the bunting is as colorless as Whipped Peter's portrait, this is a convocation of martial revenants, a procession of the Confederate dead. The Ku Klux Klan paraded through downtown on horseback in full regalia, the pure linens of their white robes and headdresses sparkling in the sunlight. And how far is it really from the Angola of the present, the point of Petrochemical Modernism where we find ourselves situated on the continuum of time, that straight and unerring line stretching from the watery wastes to the razed Green Book addresses, to the moment captured (as if it were a wild beast) in the postcard in *Anno Domini* 1916? And from the postcard's frozen moment — how much further back is it really to the year 1863 when brother fought brother? And from 1863 how much further back is it really to the Enlightenment when the

European continent was sanguinary with the internecine ideals of Liberty, Equality and Fraternity? How much further back does one have to go till one is out of range of the shots that left the holes in the wall behind Fred Hampton's bloody mattress? How far is it from the Rosenbergs to Joan of Arc? How far is it from Medgar Evers to Whipped Peter? From Robert F. Williams to Charles Deslondes? I asked, as the petrochemical settlement of Norco, now upriver, disappeared from view behind a bend in the river.

I did not know what to do with the postcard, but neither could I look away or reinsert the postcard between other postcards of a Canal Street Mardi Gras parade or a Mississippi riverboat as if I had never seen it. This reunion of Confederate soldiers must have been like reuniting soldiers from the Battle of Thermopylae, I said. What must the Confederate soldiers have reminisced about? The exhilaration of battle, the smell of gunpowder, the victorious fusillades of cannon and musket fire? The good old days before the Lost Cause? Representatives of an undead army that refused to surrender on any terms, these Confederate veterans were unwilling witnesses to the accelerated rate of changing times that outpaced them with every footstep. A world war had been fought since Appomattox, a global butchery that must have made the Confederate veterans happy they were too superannuated to serve in a conflict whose firepower and weaponry belittled their quaint muskets and mild, gentlemanly cannons. They must have felt their fight for an old order had been for naught, as they were surpassed by women's suffrage and the New South's intestinal creep into the newfangled century. Unlike the Confederate veterans marching into the postcard's vanishing point, even as I stood in the junk shop, I do not wish to traffic in counterfactuals or virtual histories: what if Hitler had died in the failed assassination attempt of July 1944? Who cares — he didn't. What if Robert E. Lee had prevailed at Gettysburg? As Winston Churchill speculates in *If it Had Happened Otherwise*, an odd question for a man charged with defending Europe and defeating Hitler, even if the counterfactual of Lee's supposed victory is staged from the standpoint of an historian in a parallel world in which General Lee was not forced to surrender at Appomattox, which goads the fictional historian to ask what might have become of this country had Lee lost; I am here to tell what would have and did happen had Lee lost. And who cares if Lee had not been forced to surrender — he lost more than 20,000 men at Gettysburg and today his monumental statue in Lee Circle is as endangered as the pink flamingos of Spanish Town.

What if John Wilkes Booth's pistol had jammed, failing to assassinate Lincoln; Booth is institutionalized instead of hanged, and Lincoln, now perceived as a warmonger, is impeached by Congress for mismanagement of the Civil War, only to die in opprobrium and dishonor? Who cares — the pistol fired and Booth was a good shot. Too much of this *what if* history is endued with the narcissistic illusory agency of individual actors who are themselves only collateral in the petrochemical gestalt and the lugubrious astronomy of which they are largely unaware, I said. But these Confederate veterans, marching ignorantly through the streets of my hometown, each footstep on the windpipe of Charles Deslondes, a bogeyman in the praxis of historical negationism, the gaslighting of everything Toussaint inherited from his mother and father, like my grandmother's emphatic denial of the 23andme genetic history testing results that returned positive results for a statistically significant percentage of sub-Saharan African DNA in my family's bloodline, a revelation that brought some small degree of coherence to my fragmented body, for our bodies are like Pangea, once a unified land mass that broke up and has been drifting apart ever since.

More than the Confederate dead marching through the streets, protesting the future which Toussaint saw in the Lincoln Theater, this should trouble you: how seldom we refer to the 22nd century, as if nothing beyond the 21st century, of which I am already tired of hearing, can be conceived, a time not even the Hand and Eye Motif can see through the dense noxious chemical fog on the Mississippi River. The Confederate veterans' time is out of joint, they are split down the middle by a selective memory, marching in two vanishing points at once, one leading to a Lee Circle with General "King of Spades" Lee triumphant and immortal at its center and the other to a Leeless Circle drowning in wormwood floodwaters. So much the better. This was not the retrofuture as it was conceived by these Confederate veterans — at the time of war, the time of peace, it didn't matter — on the battlefields of Antietam and Gettysburg, or in the undecided, unfinished Battle of Baton Rouge. These Confederate veterans espoused a haunted ontology that accepted no terms of surrender, however magnanimous, and were themselves the ghosts which were neither present nor absent, neither dead nor alive, which haunted their own attics and said boo in the Republic of New Afrika. Always and already, these veterans of a Confederate hauntology — the white gerontocrats who sit on the boards of petrochemical supercorporations — knew the whereabouts of Colonel Shaw's stolen sword, the one used to lead the 54th Massachusetts Infantry Regiment into the census of slaughter in South Carolina, though they would never tell.

Toussaint's counterpoint, as I extrapolated it from his ghost-written lyrics, because every vanishing point must have its point into which to vanish, to the veteran's hauntology was Afrofuturism: the Republic of New Africa where Amira Baraka would be the national poet laureate. This Republic without presidents was associated with a man named Harry Haywood, a black Bolshevik and black secessionist, Haywood's Republic of New Afrika satisfied Stalin's criteria, articulated in *Marxism and the National Question*, defining a stable community of people, constituted by historical forces, on the basis of a common language, geographic territory, political economy, and socio-cultural profile. A crescent moon hung perpetually in the sky over the Republic, which was like those slow motion futuristic glimpses of utopian and dystopian cities and landscapes in *Koyaanisqatsi*, the visual tone poem of time-lapse photography of manufactured clouds shadowing skyscrapers, housing projects in advanced stages of disrepair, the demolitions of large tower projects, time lapse footage of people waiting in line, traffic patterns, commuters going to or from work, sorting mail, manufacturing televisions, hot dogs on an assembly line conveyor belt are followed by people riding up an escalator, television shows are channel-surfed in rapid succession, microchips and satellite imagery of the planet, a rocket exploding after liftoff — all the little white-picket-fence dystopias of Petrochemical Modernism. The Republic of New Afrika would be a refuge where the damned voyage of the MS *St. Louis* — a ship of Jewish refugees escaping destruction in Nazi Europe — would be allowed to port, where the *Anti-Clotilda* could anchor. *The White Motorist Green Book* listing the names and addresses of those in the Republic's metropolises who were friendly to traveling whites. Black metropolises which were not modeled on Fritz Lang's harsh, brutal urban vision; lush, fecund, prelapsarian, a great pre-Columbian empire like the Incas, without writing and therefore timeless, without past or future, and certainly no Confederate dead marching in parade phalanxes, I said.

No petrochemical supercorporation had conducted a focus group in the creation of this Afrofuturistic republic, no greenbelt for the imminent domain of the downhome blocks with native street names. At the time the Confederate veterans postcard was taken the lifeless monuments to their fallen and by now mythologized, apotheosized leadership were going up on courthouse squares all over the South and even a few in northern and western states that had nothing to do with the Confederacy, states that were not even states at the time that Colonel Shaw's sword fell from his grasp. The statue of General Lee in Lee Circle had been on its column by the time of the Confederate veterans' parade long enough to show signs of age. Pigeons circle the General like vultures, and the anthropomorphized Confederate quarry stone is in the same throes of mortification as Ozymandias. A spider in the General's ear, a cockroach in his brain. Present at the monument's unveiling — sculpted by a Yankee, Alexander Doyle of New York — though not for its removal, were former Confederate president Jefferson Davis, General P.G.T. Beauregard, who later would have his own equestrian monument in New Orleans, by the same Yankee artist, and the daughters of General Lee, I said, even as the riverboat Toussaint and I were on sailed downriver towards Lee Circle.

Everyone thought the war was finished at Appomattox — it wasn't. Appomattox was just the beginning of the war's next phase, I said. The statue of General Lee was the focal point of clashes between Black Panthers and hardline segregationists such as David Duke who agitated to bring the jubilee of destruction of the Detroit race riots and Rodney King riots to New Orleans, salivating like a bloodhound for race war, because every white supremacist secretly wishes to see his hometown burn to the ground. When Beauregard's equestrian monument came down, I felt the horse should be allowed to remain on its plinth, riderless and free to roam — this animal which has so often in history been the casualty of our discords, I said.

The junk shop had postcards of Lee Circle, and all the other Confederate monuments throughout New Orleans, soon to be out of date once the statues came down. I bought the Confederate veterans postcard for reasons which are still opaque to me, perhaps to remove it from circulation to spare my family the further embarrassment of having one of our tribe fighting again on the wrong side of history, maybe out of the same deficient urgency that compelled someone to edit ten seconds of footage from the Rodney King video. The young black girl behind the junk shop counter asking if I wanted a small gift bag, while I burned with shame and a bad conscience hoping that she would not examine the postcard to see what event or time period it depicted. Even seeing the black and white postcard in her hand, a ghostly afterimage of another world, not parallel to this one but on the same historical timeline, the one in which Lee lost but his followers refused to surrender, as she rang up the price, was almost more than I could bear and I left the Royal Street shop ashamed of my motives but nonetheless relieved that the postcard was no longer for sale either: it had to be sent downriver to the Dead Zone. Outside the junk shop, the second line brass band was gone and the iron-work horsehead hitching posts were casting the equestrian shadows of General Beauregard's horse galloping through the empty quietus of Royal Street. Still, I could not celebrate the removal of these ahistorical monuments — they never should've been erected in the first place, these stone men who, like Job, should have no name in the streets, whose memory should perish from the earth, General Beauregard's horse galloping across the night sky in the toxic clouds manufactured at the ExxonMobil plant. These Confederate generals immortalized throughout the city in stone, they had been little boys once, hadn't they? Hadn't they too played made-up games with shapeshifting rules? Did their fathers prohibit them from opening the house's windows and did they see pictures of their mother as a little girl beneath a Colored Entrance? Did their brothers commit suicide by cop? Did they see chlorine gas ghost ships on the river and fish for contaminated fish? Robert E. Lee's childhood home in Virginia could not have been less like the buyout homes in Standard Heights, I said. Like me, I said, they too were split down the middle, in two vanishing points at the same time, one on each bank of the river.

Where others might remember a home-cooked meal, a warm and doting mother, twilight softening the green of a kitchen garden, the soft luxuriant nostalgia of cashmere, the dripping decay of an heirloom grandfather clock, I remember with all my senses the scorched smell of the plant on burn-offs days, the petrochemical nocturne playing at all hours, the uncanny sulfurous heartbeat of the plant pulsing and flickering on the bedroom wall at night, the roof and the hood of the car grayed with ash that drifted out of a grim sky like petrochemical snowflakes in summer or winter, flakes that never melted, forming a chemical membrane or pellicle on all things, the ancient oaks as well as the mountain of rusting oil drums, Toussaint said, gazing over the starboard guardrail and down into the river's boiling cauldron of muddy-brown wormwood.

Confronting the ghostly Confederate soldiers in my past, I told Toussaint, has been the great question of my life, wresting the wraiths from that hypogeal black place in my familial inheritance: the Alexander Gardner photo of the uniformed corpses rotting in the sun over Antietam. None of this I experienced personally, but still I cannot shake the impression, alternating between phases of vagueness and decrescent poignancy that culminate in a bayonet between the ribs, that I am wrapped in the fog of war, the smoke of musket fire and cannon fire dulling and bedimming my senses, and that my own corpse lies shattered, disheveled and sun-swollen in *Confederate Dead at Antietam, 1862.*

When the war's first phase ended at Appomattox, I said, my great-great grandfather could not have been more than twenty years old, and in all likelihood much younger than he seems in the wartime portrait that once hung on the wall of my grandmother's basement and was destroyed by floodwaters on the same day — September 17 — as the Battle of Antietam. The soldier's portrait is reproduced here from a digital copy I made, acting under the premonition that the original would not last long, that it was fading before my eyes as the fog of war lifted, like the portrait of Rilke's father. Many times in the month of September, just before autumn killed off the cicadas and the hurricanes got an attitude, I have recited aloud, but not so loudly that I cannot hear the penultimate plangency of the cicadas'

evensong, the haunting last lines of Rilke's *Portrait of My Father as a Young Man* — "Oh quickly disappearing photograph/in my more slowly disappearing hand." — every time expecting my own hand to disappear as I pronounced the final syllable of *hand,* a hand branded like that of slave stealer Captain Jonathan Walker.

As the riverboat navigated another twisted meander in the twitching river and I saw Thomas Sutton's composite iridescent ribbon bats flittering about the riverboat's smokestacks, I recited the poem's elegiac lines for Toussaint, modulating the cadence in emphasis of disappearance, a poem familiar enough to him that Whipped Peter's whip-scarred portrait evoked the same lines of disappearance and loss, albeit for a forebear on the other side of the river, and for whom there were not enough Confederate dead at Antietam. Rilke's poem captured in ghostly verse my own father perfectly, Toussaint said, this man disappearing before my eyes after the Christmas Eve explosion into the watery shades on the river's far shore, an unknown territory I hoped to explore like the houses emptied by ExxonMobil, Toussaint said, who had no photos of his ancestors, except of Whipped Peter, and his mother had destroyed all the photos in her possession after the Christmas Eve explosion, burned some, torn others with her own hands and flushed them down the toilet or, so Toussaint thought, painted them onto the exterior of the house when she covered it in her grief of black paint, announcing an indefinite period of mourning to Standard Heights in plain view of the ExxonMobil plant, sealing the photos in a dark veneer of oil-black latex paint, an entombment that preserved them while also effacing them forever. Rilke's lines speak of "the slim Imperial officer's uniform: the saber's basket-hilt," I said to Toussaint, as if Rilke had written, without knowing it, about this very family portrait from the Civil War. My great-great grandfather in his Confederate officer's uniform, long rotted and devoured by time's cruel passage, his posture artificially stiff and martial, the sleeves of his officer's jacket slightly too long for him, as if wearing someone else's uniform, only one hand visible, the gold matte so perfectly oviform that he could be posing for the portrait inside of a golden egg. The CSA buttons glinting on his uniform, the hand-colored blushing adding a little life to his monochrome face. Not yet one of the anonymous fallen corpses in Gardner's photographs, he is very much alive, his young Alabama gaze concentrating on the living viewer in the Angola of the present, totally unaware of the coming carnage, much less the reasons for it, or that the antebellum plantations would one day be remade into petrochemical plantations, I said.

Though it might have been a Mathew Brady portrait, the photographer's identity is unknown, and who knows but he became a victim of those indigenous camera-shy tribes that ritually killed all photographic soul-stealers, his little black box and negatives buried in a shallow grave on the brother-against-brother battlefield with the corpses of the Confederate dead, I said.

Even now, after so many generations since the Civil War have made populous the lands west of the Mississippi River, although not nearly enough to make room for the rest of us on the river's east bank, when I see Gardner's photos, which is not often, as I now studiously avoid them, such images leading only to unhealthy syndromes, the way the superstitious will avoid stepping on cracks or black cats crossing the street, I feel the cold pall of the morgue and the fog of war returns, and in Baton Rouge I catch myself watching my steps lest I accidentally trigger unexploded ordnance, I said. And when that fog softens into a deliquescing flux that rolls away like the chemical effects of a heavy sedative wearing off, I feel that I have been in a comatose, dissociative sleep like the Confederate rifleman in *The Home of a Rebel Sharpshooter*.

Gardner's title is not without irony, for the rebel sharpshooter's aim was evidently not sharp enough to save his life. My great-great grandfather's brother fell to a sharpshooter's bullet that day at Antietam, the uniformed and untested handsome officer inside the golden ovoid portrait — the black and white quality of the photograph would distort the inconvenient truth that the uniform is grey, must be grey, it could have been no other color — combing the field of battle after the action was over — strewn with dead infantrymen and horses, the dogs of Cerberus unleashed, Sutton's luminescent vespertine bats in the shadows of blasted trees — in search of his brother, of whom no golden oval portrait survives, finding on his still-warm body a handwritten letter, *I encountered my double on the battlefield of Antietam*, he wrote to his wife the day he died; such are the mirrored eidolons that visit gray soldiers in the final hours preceding demise. Unlike Emmett Till in his open casket, the individual identity of the corpses' faces in Gardner's photographers are sometimes discernible, a gentle expression of repose or astonishment, in stark contrast to the images of war from our own century, of men in business suits leaping from burning towers, unidentifiable even with modern technology, and I have seen these very faces — farm boys, college graduates, the sons of simple farmers — on the streets of unreconstructed cities such as Baton Rouge, Birmingham, Memphis, Montgomery, and even Baltimore and D.C. and once in Philadelphia when I went there to see the bombed out ruins of Osage Avenue for myself. But the home of the rebel sharpshooter is not the bloody battlefield it was when Gardner tiptoed among the corpses with his prying camera, the Confederate soldiers were the perfect photographic subjects: immobile, already frozen for the camera, Gardner composing his shot unhurried. Gardner's battlefields are now verdant fields or wildflower meadows efflorescing with teams of annuals and perennials invented by spring, those battlefields in the northern latitudes quietly blanketed in snow like an arctic, rimy landscape from a Robert Frost poem. The photographer of Confederate corpses is himself interred in Washington D.C.'s Glenwood, the same cemetery where you will find one of his more infamous subjects, George Atzerodt, participant in the conspiracy to assassinate Abraham Lincoln, who also sat before Gardner's camera in the days before his execution by hanging. In some virtual histories, Gardner's camera was destroyed by the vanished native tribes of Standard Heights and buried in a mass grave with the Confederate dead, and no one asked if the rebel sharpshooter's gun had jammed, if he'd run out of ammunition or been slain by his double. To be buried with one's subject, I said, Audubon with his headless pink flamingo, Gursky with his supermarket shelves, Boisseau with his flood, Fisk with his manifold serpentine rivers, Gardner with his Confederate sharpshooters, that is all one needs to know of the ten seconds of edited footage from the Rodney King video, I said.

Having found none of the addresses in the Green Book friendly to traveling Negroes, and the postcard's black and white veterans marching still into the vanishing point, perhaps hoping to find one among them who could tell me why they were still marching even after Appomattox, I walked in the marching footsteps of the Confederate veterans through downtown Birmingham myself, I said, passing as I did the New Ideal building, an abandoned women's department store on the Confederate parade route. Though it wasn't there at the time of the parade of course, the New Ideal logo was painted on the department store's back wall facing a multi-story, empty parking deck so that customers could see it as they parked their cars. Somehow, this juxtaposition of New Ideal and parking deck, completely without irony, struck me as the Confederate veterans parade's masterpiece. The New Ideal survived depressions, world wars, race riots, recessions, booms, slumps, spikes, inflations, bubbles and recessions again till in 1990, the year I was in kindergarten, I said, the New Ideal where my mother bought her wedding gown closed forever and has been a symbol of mordant and ruinous irony ever since.

The Confederate veterans parade route passed the site of the future Gaston Motel, where Toussaint's mother spent two sleepless nights on her itinerary north to Osage Avenue, and the parade turned south onto 16th Street passing, years beforehand, the very site of the church bombing where the four little girls were buried in the exploded rubble of the house of God, a church that I have long suspected but cannot prove was destroyed by the unexploded ordnance of the Battle of Baton Rouge, the Siege of Osage Avenue and the Christmas Eve explosion, I said. It was as if the Confederate veterans parade was leaving a future-directed trail of devastation and waste in its wake, setting fire to and looting everything around them, the scorched earth of the Confederate hauntology.

The Confederate veteran's parade route and its segregationist ostentation in white Klan regalia would have passed what is today known as the city's 4th Avenue Historic District, that area of town where black businesses were allowed by city ordinance to collocate, the mounted Klansmen and surviving veterans of lost battles such as Gettysburg, Chattanooga, Appomattox and Antietam passing beneath the darkened windows and locked doors of the Colored Masonic Temple, the Carver Theater, the New Deal Barbershop, all casting their longest and darkest shadows over the postcard procession. Make no mistake, I said, the Confederate veterans parade route was not an accident, it was thoughtfully if unintelligently planned, passing locations strategically targeted for their importance to the local black community — churches, storefronts, businesses — to intimidate, to passively terrorize with their bizarre medieval outfits, the medieval-looking horsemen, to send a clear message: the zombie Confederacy has not surrendered. The postcards too were part of this message, using the mail system to spread the parade's route across the country, I said.

Although I would not have done it, I can see why you might wish to remove such a postcard from circulation, Toussaint said, looking over the riverboat's rails at the river flowing below, as we seemed to be passing a point on the river which we had already passed an hour or more ago, caught in some vortical kink or temporal snag in the river's refluence. Often, Toussaint said, in petrochemical dreams I read the text of my genome over and over, my genome in hieroglyphic symbols on the hazmat trucks or written in the very hand which is on that postcard's reverse side, the one used for the card's sinister message, the script of an undead Confederate veteran who sometimes answers the door — wearing blackface, no less; I never said this was a good dream — of decaying manor houses in the Green Book's index of addresses friendly to the traveling Negro, and before he will let me leave, the only way to make the dream stop was to whistle, and not just any tune, I had to whistle "I Wish I Was In Dixie," a horrific and mortifying tune, except in the dream I was not Toussaint: I was Emmett Till, yet I could not wolf-whistle. I never learned to whistle, unlike my brother whose whistle could be heard from Port Allen on the west bank of the river, heard clear as a shot over the tugboat horns. I was a black Ahasuerus lost in my per-egrinations of South Louisiana and Mississippi trying to wolf-whis-tle but never quite getting the hang of it — my wolf-whistle was a deflated and uninspiring flatulence of benzene and naphtha. I woke in my coffin, Toussaint said, painted black like the house after the Christmas Eve explosion, as in Poe's "The Premature Burial," and inside my coffin, which writhed with watery snakes and the venom-ous squiggles and looping nooses of the courtroom portrait of bound and gagged Bobby Seale, some thoughtful mourner had left a post-card, my genome, but in lieu of the sequencing alphabet, all scram-bled with endocrine disruptors, were printed the addresses — hotels, motels, taverns, restaurants, auto repairs — of *The Negro Motorist Green Book*, where Negroes were welcome, including the addresses in New Orleans where you knocked on the door, Toussaint said, and the one where you found me in Central City, except that with the cof-fin sealed there was no escape and outside I could hear the gnashing and barking of bloodhounds.

In the offseason, with the Curse of the Saints mollified for the time being by another winless season, my father engrossed him-self in a different curse, the case of Medgar Evers, a veteran him-self of the Battle of Normandy. The houses in Standard Heights, he used to say, were not as nice as the one story brick ranch house at 2332 Margaret Walker Alexander Drive where Evers was shot down by an armed death mask rebel sharpshooter hiding like a coward in the bushes, and in his preoccupation with the Larry Holmes boxing match I have wondered whether my father wished to die like that, not in the Christmas Eve explosion, the casualty of esoteric industri-al chemical processes, but shot down in his own front yard for fight-ing the good fight like Medgar Evers, and my father was less enraged by the fact of the assassination itself, heinous as it was, but that Med-gar Evers was refused admittance to the local hospital in Jackson, to him that was the greater crime, one expected the worst, to be shot at by undead rebel sharpshooters who were still emotionally fighting Pickett's Charge, but to be egregiously and unethically denied medical care by those sworn to the Hippocratic Oath — that he could not comprehend, Toussaint said, and like my mother's kin who survived the Tuskegee experiments, or at least some part of them survived, the hospital's racist rejection of a wounded Medgar Evers only solidified and totalized his rancor for the medical establishment in its immaculate fingernails, white Klan robes, with its fancy expensive degrees and the highfalutin Latin names for the strange syndromes and genetic diseases that disfigured Standard Heights in cancerous statistics, Toussaint said. Then around the time of the Rodney King riots, Toussaint said, the name of Jeffrey Dahmer appeared in the news and it was as though Nathan Bedford Forest had been resurrected. Jeffrey Dahmer's serial murders went unsolved for so long, my father said, because he targeted black men, and when a black man went missing in a place like Standard Heights — maybe he fell into the holes we dug for Lafitte's treasure, maybe the mountain of oil drums buried him, maybe a giant blackbird carried him across the river — no one noticed till the probation officer took rollcall. Dahmer was only the latest, most spectacular iteration of an entrenched white fantasy that has been with us since Delphine LaLaurie's sadistic treatment of her slaves on Royal Street. Let's not forget the Sacramento Vampire who ate his victims. We are still living out the premise of the Hamitic Hypothesis; still we endure the white mob of nobodies like Charles Gabriel Seligman, author of *Races of Africa*, who invented the Hamitic Hypothesis because they were uncomfortable with the possibility that Biblical characters such as the sons of Noah might not be Caucasian. The consumption of the flesh of young black men — the logical, anthropophagic culmination of the Jesse Washington lynching, the Emmett Till lynching, etc. — if whites could ingest the magical ebony flesh of this immemorial bugbear and the bogeymen of their racialist nightmares then perhaps he would go away and they could at last, and with the smiling congratulations of the Dixie-whistlers, integrate into the being of their own person and social body the black omnipotence which they so feared in him, and the possession of which they ingeniously sought to extrajudicially deprive him. Dahmer could embody the Great White Hope's dreams only by ingesting the flesh of the secretly loathed black Other, and as he fed on his black victims, Toussaint said, white America silently, passively cheered him on, just as my brother and I had cheered for O.J. Simpson fleeing the police at dream speed. If the Master Hammonds and Jeffrey Dahmers of this world wish to consume my flesh, Toussaint said, they will have to eat the black words tattooed thereon first.

Then there was Carolyn Bryant Donham, Emmett Till's accuser, who recanted her testimony against Emmett Till, the testimony that incited the boy's lynching, Toussaint said. Till had, the testimony went, wolf-whistled at her, grabbed her by the hand, threatened her personally and the racial caste system generally, and uttered salacious naughty words in the presence of a white southern belle — blasphemy and sedition. The rebel flag stores sold out of their stock immediately. I recognized myself, Toussaint said, in Emmett's open-casket funeral, and more than myself — my brother who attempted suicide by cop. Inside *The Negro Motorist Green Book*, he said, was a news clipping of the open casket printed in *The Chicago Defender*, a yellowed and foxed clip, rectangularly cut, that had not been there the first time I opened the book. Not till two or three visits to the little green book later did the news clipping appear; someone, my mother or father, a sick joke played by my brother, or the Exxon-Mobil man who came to buy out the house, deliberately inserted the clipping there, knowing I would find it. Emmett Till's face, brutalized beyond recognition, never left me, I saw that poor boy's disfeatured face in the bark patterns of the ExxonMobil trees and in the clouds manufactured by the ExxonMobil plant; I saw Emmett's deformed face drawn on the Aints Bagheads my father wore on gameday; I saw that same brutalized, almost inhuman face appear on the river's west bank where Whipped Peter and my father dwelled after the Christmas Eve explosion. In his open coffin, Emmett Till was the vanishing point of my broken face reflected in the fragments of the shattered window glass on the kitchen floor, unlike your gray Confederate corpses at Antietam, Emmett Till's identity had to be destroyed so that his murderers could purge the Emmett Till within themselves. Every Master Hammond has an Emmett Till inside him, Toussaint said. Emmett in his open casket appeared like the subhuman monster that the white imagination wanted him to be, Toussaint said. That the black newspaper's offices in the Black Metropolis-Bronzeville District of Chicago were inside a deconsecrated Jewish synagogue did little to check my father's notion, Toussaint said, put forward almost as an unfalsifiable theorem, that we were both the chosen people and a persecuted people, the Curse of the Saints was the modernized petrochemical version of the Curse of Ham, Toussaint said.

The riverboat was passing those low-pressure zones along the river where Charles Deslondes incited and led the German Coast Uprising, and the filming location of *Mandingo* at the Ashland-Belle Helen plantation, the smoking spires of Norco's petro-cathedrals, every *mise-en-scène* on the bank of the river. Thinking of Emmett Till's open-casket non-face, I took the Confederate veterans postcard from my coat pocket, and contemplated the curiously fateful entanglement that put Toussaint and I on the second story deck of a steam-powered riverboat discussing a Confederate veterans parade in 1916. I held the postcard over the railing, the picture of veterans parading triumphantly through the streets of Birmingham and disappearing, foreshortened into the postcard's vanishing point and marching mindlessly and inexorably into the river water that flowed behind them.

My great-great grandfather, the one in the oval portrait who searched for his brother after Antietam, took part in the Confederate procession that day, I finally confessed to Toussaint leaning against the rail, his sight fixed on the riverbank, and feeling the keen relief of voicing this complicit encumbrance I awaited Toussaint's judgment and condemnation. I was to be disappointed. I was mistaken in interpreting his silence as permission to proceed. My great grandfather would have been in attendance as well, the next generation being indoctrinated into the Confederate hauntology, somewhere along the parade's route that wound through the city like a serpent. My great-great grandfather, I said, is clearly visible in the last row of marching veterans, the one closest to the cameraman, second from the right, but I was never sure after being corrected by my grandmother who, with the ruffled rectitude of a pedantic Daughter of the Confederacy points out some bagatelle that, had it been otherwise, might have altered the outcome of a life, a battle, a campaign, a war.

Toussaint pointed to the lone figure in the bottom right of the photograph, a man facing away from the parade, perhaps entering the front door of a store in disgust or terror, and while it is not easy to discern the race of anyone in a black and white photo, let alone a solitary figure clothed head to foot, indeed many of my ancestors in their sepias appear more Creole than white, the lone figure which

Toussaint brought to my attention, and whom I had otherwise over-looked did appear to have a black face, and I thought how inscruta-ble and unaccountable it was at that time in Birmingham for a black man to attend a parade honoring Confederate veterans. That's him, Toussaint said, without explaining what he meant. I examined ev-ery quarter of the photographed parade looking for black umbrellas, unsure of exactly what Toussaint meant. The black man Toussaint brought to my attention, I thought, must have decided not to follow the marchers into the oblivion of the postcard's receding vanishing point.

On the other side, the postcard was almost illegible. In the decrescent light of a steamboat evening, I strained to read the mes-sage written in the little white space provided for the purpose, the handwritten, cacographic print — greetings, well wishes, wish-you-were-heres, solemn valedictions — vanishing with the parade image and its costumed marchers lost in the fog of war. I do not know how, but we were again passing Norco on the same starboard side of the steamboat, though I distinctly recalled seeing the petrochemical town and its stygian skyline of towers and smokestacks disappear around a bend in the river three quarters of an hour before, as if aboard this riverboat we were caught in a repeating loop, a glitch in the river. Twice now we passed the same flare stack on the east bank belching burn-off flame and black smoke. Toussaint seized the postcard, squinting in the ebbing violet light to scrutinize the print of the postcard's message, as he had at the names and addresses of safe houses in *The Negro Motorist Green Book,* and pitched the postcard into the river, the black and white image of the parading veterans turning counterclockwise in a muddy eddy, spinning on the wheel of Ixion, then burning up in the fiery reflection of a spiral sunset rippling on the blue-brown river's surface roiled by the steamboat's giant red wheels, the revolving paddles churning the glitching river, and the postcard was gone like a slowly disappearing hand, as black ellipses of vesper bats like Thomas Sutton's composite iridescent ribbon circled the riverboat.

The Siege of Osage Avenue

But long before the Christmas Eve explosion and the funeral home accident, Toussaint's mother moved through the tender phases

of green juvenescence and the uncertain transitions of young wom-
anhood in a modest but at least owner-occupied brick row house
on Osage Avenue in the Cobbs Creek neighborhood of West Philadelphia. There were no Colored Entrances here per se, as down in
downtown Mobile, Alabama, and the North Star was not occluded
by the poisonous cloudworks — Beauregard's galloping horses, Emmett Till's non-face — manufactured in the ExxonMobil plant. In
line once to see the Liberty Bell, the real thing, not the uncracked
replica in Arsenal Park down in Baton Rouge, she had wondered at
the bell's crack, why such a famous bell that everyone came to see,
standing in line for hours in the heat, should have such a fatal and
ugly flaw. Her mother had said the Liberty Bell was cracked because
liberty and justice were not for all, and that the cracked Liberty Bell
revealed the true state of the nation's cracked soul. The new northern
city itself was bigger and badder than anything she had seen around
Bienville Square in Mobile. Block upon block of perfectly gridded
city streets, the rectilinear immaculation of brick row homes with
their self-identical stoops and windows that opened with impunity.
The University of Pennsylvania is a few miles east. On the numbered
streets of Philadelphia, which beyond Malcolm X Park went as high
as 63rd Street, a number too high for Baton Rouge or Mobile, before
she learned to squeeze her tiny hand into a proud black power fist,
her sugary buttery accent faded, blending with the Osage Avenue
voices of MOVE's agitators who harangued the neighborhood with
virulent political diatribes night and day through a bullhorn like the
voices intoning over *Radio Free Dixie.* And though African-American and middle-class as Cobbs Creek then was, it was MOVE's
radicalized green politics and their atavistic desire to return to a
hunter-gatherer society, a time before Petrochemical Modernism,
living like the Bedouin or Hadza people which antagonized their
neighbors who kept a low profile to integrate into middle-class white
America. Their children, who ran about naked, ate out of trash cans,
throwing their feces out the window and into the streets. MOVE
believed sincerely and seriously in the tenets of a half-baked anar-
cho-primitivism and the virtues of composting — a radical idea back
then — and constructed a defensible bunker on the roof, preparing
themselves for the coming siege which they all felt was written in
the bloody stars shot into the wall above Fred Hampton's mattress.
MOVE's members changed their surnames to *Africa*, wore their

hair in unwashed matts of tangled dreadlocks in the fashion popularized by Caribbean musician activists such as Bob Marley, and they spurned as products of Western white supremacy all science, medicine, and technology, all of which have been used in the policing and terror of black bodies — as when the Philadelphia Fire Department turned their fire hoses on Osage Avenue's radicalized row houses to flush out the agitators like so many unwanted pests.

I can still hear her violent, full-body coughing from repeated exposure to the plant's benzene and naphtha, Toussaint said, but her lungs were also remembering the teargas the police used on Osage Avenue, many years after the Christmas Eve explosion my mother died of lung cancer, the benzene, naphtha, and teargas were too much, though she never smoked a day in her life. My mother and her family were ordered to evacuate their homes on Osage Avenue and take with them possessions and supplies for a twenty-four-hour standoff between the police and MOVE, Toussaint said. The police commissioner announced all this through a megaphone — every black neighborhood knows the sight of an angry cycloptic death mask white man in uniform shouting orders that are not to be ignored into a megaphone. And Toussaint's mother never forgot the hateful voice in the megaphone that she could hear, but could not see the embodied source of, like so many of the macro-forces felt beneath the Colored Entrance neon, reminding the MOVE agitators where they were, in the land of Whipped Peter and that cancerous cough that will never go away: *Attention MOVE: this is America. You must abide by the laws of the United States of America.* I wanted Jack Johnson to sucker-punch him. On live television, the day after Mother's Day, two water gel explosive entry devices were dropped from helicopters on a middle-class black neighborhood, tear gas metamorphosed into armadas of slave ship ghosts, the police firing off more than 10,000 rounds of ammo, so much that they had to request more ammunition from the police academy. Some of the Vietnam vets on the block had flashbacks to the screaming burning villages, waking up on Fred Hampton's bloody mattress from a nightmare of black helicopters pouring cauldrons of boiling water on Osage Avenue. The core of the rubble was too hot to touch for days, the black bodies, covered with a medical sheet, escorted out on gurneys and Osage Avenue, a once prosperous middle-class neighborhood lay in ruin. All because of radical composting, Toussaint said.

The aftermath of the aerial police bombing takes a preeminent place in the history of peacetime bombings of civilians. Philly became known as *The City That Bombed Itself*, a meta-bombing. After the police went home, satisfied of a job well done, and the firemen were still spraying the smoking rubble with silver jets of water, Toussaint's mother picked through the rubble, searching for anything that could be salvaged. Nothing of what she had brought with her from her life in Pritchard remained. Such an aerial assault was unthinkable in Prichard. Colored Entrances and bloodhounds and a slow poisoning by carcinogens sure, but Master Hammond never dropped bombs on Standards Heights or downtown Mobile, Alabama. Tarriance here was not an option for Toussaint's mother, and the family made plans to return to the South, far away from the North Star. Even my hometown, Birmingham, known as Bombingham had the sense not to bomb itself. Though the bombing of Osage Avenue may resemble the Klan bombings of churches and the homes of private citizens that terrorized my native Birmingham, a sense of proportion was observed, Bull Connor's police did not raze entire city blocks, like burning down the plantation house to flush out a few cockroaches. The City of Brotherly Love it was supposed to be called, but Toussaint's mother found neither love nor brothers in the Siege of Osage Avenue, which like the Avenue itself, is nowhere to be found in the annals of the great sieges, with the Siege of Leningrad, the Siege of Berlin, the Siege of Port Hudson, the Siege of

South Rampart Street, the Siege of the Republic of New Afrika, the Siege of Standard Heights, where it rightfully belongs, erased from the history books like Toussaint's ancestors buried beneath the Spillway and the demolished addresses of safe houses on Rampart Street in *The Negro Motorist Green Book*.

While Osage Avenue was yet smoldering and the earth was still warm to the touch from the fires the fire department let burn, plans were swiftly drawn up for the redevelopment of the self-inflicted decimation: sixty-one mass manufactured row houses all designed in a style incongruous with the surrounding blocks so that the infill did not mesh with the surrounding blocks. I turned to post-development theory to supplement the Christmas Eve explosion accident report, which spoke of the Christmas Eve explosion as an isolated incident, not as something linked by unexploded ordnance to the Siege of Osage Avenue. The habit of theory is hard to break. Broken windows theory still determines your statistics around here. Maybe it is better not to rebuild. Let Osage Avenue remain a keloid scar in the neighborhood, a noncontiguous outlier of the Dead Zone, an anti-monument to the anti-memory of the misguided siege of a middle-class black neighborhood.

I visited 6221 Osage Avenue — this was in the autumn of 2016, one month before Trump's election — to see for myself the neighborhood where Toussaint's mother grew up after leaving Prichard. Osage Avenue was deserted that day, the air crisp and clean, as it often is in October in the north, a cloudless and brisk quality to the blue air that feels unnatural on the banks of the Mississippi, at the mouth of the Dead Zone. Phenologically, the transitory months of autumn witness an increase in casket sales and cremations. A season to recite Keats. The cane harvest smoke back home was then drifting over Fisk's river. Dying maples carpeted the blacktop in a death shroud of mourning, and concrete sidewalks with orange and burgundy leaves. Plastic grocery bags floated like ghostly membranes on invisible currents of air, their flight somehow evoking the melancholy of unborn or miscarried fetuses. I tracked the Doppler movement of emergency klaxons in the distance. A police helicopter flew low overhead. So much for the investigation of Osage Avenue that October day.

Osage Avenue is narrow, and the building line continuous from one end of the block to the other, a foreshortening tunneling effect. Before me the Confederate veterans parade marched triumphantly in the bombed ruins of the vanishing point. Some predatory, entrepreneurial spirit posted an *I BUY HOUSES* sign, red letters on a yellow background, to a utility pole — Petrochemical Modernism runs on the entrepreneurial spirit to transform all into gold. I turned the corner of Osage and went up a block on Pine Street, a man on a concrete stoop held a sign — *I used to be someone* — over his face. I went up and down Osage and Pine in search of some sign, a plaque or monument dedicated to the eleven people, including five children who perished in the Siege of Osage Avenue. An Obama 2012 campaign sign hung next to a portrait of Kennedy in black-face. No historical marker commemorated the siege. Some graffiti wag had spray-painted *destroy this memory* on the brick façade of a boarded-up residence. Plastic patio furniture turned over in the wind. A stack of discarded rubber tires. *Let this fire burn* tagged on the wall of a fire-damaged row house. The glass eyes of Osage were boarded up. A campaign sign for Clinton 2016 on the windowsill of a second story window. Chlorine gas ghost ships in the whorls of the woodgrain, horsemen and bloodhounds in sheets of plywood. Everything arranged like lifeless elements in a necrotic still life. Then I noticed what became noticeable only by an optical trick of superimposing my own capital improvements upon the still life: the absence of reflected light, not even in the broken window glass that should have twinkled like the North Star. This mental makeover, a fresh coat of paint, glass in the windows, a roof that didn't leak, only widened the gap between myself and reality: everywhere a dull, cadaverous gray-brown like spoiled meat, and though the street bore their eponym, no sign of the Osage.

I told Toussaint of Osage Avenue's windows, how they were boarded up by the Redevelopment Authority, like eyes sewn shut in a dead non-face, which he was not at all surprised to hear. So the windows of Osage Avenue cannot be opened either, Toussaint replied, I haven't been there in years, but I do agree that Osage is exactly as you say it is, with the exception of one detail: the decimation wasn't rebuilt as you say it was, my mother was long gone before they broke ground on the redevelopment, and of course she never went back, Toussaint said, so that I wondered whether Toussaint and I had visited the same Osage Avenue.

But there is no Osage Avenue in Standard Heights, Toussaint said, where the streets are named for lost Native American tribes, the founders of Standard Oil's company town on the edges of the plant elided the Osage Nation — Mid Midwestern Indians of the Great Plains in what is today Missouri, Arkansas, Kansas, and Oklahoma — from the indigenous streets of Standard Heights. The Osage were so lost that they could not be an eponym for a street, for who wanted to live on a street named after an annihilated native tribe when the purpose of naming a street was to provide direction and to distinguish it from all others, not to so discombobulate the weary traveler that he never found his way again, because Petrochemical Modernism cannot leave vestiges or mementos of its work, it cannot be satisfied with having destroyed the eponymous tribe, it must also destroy all the tribe's eponyms and namesakes, nothing less will do, Toussaint said.

Though destruction was not what I saw that day I visited, Osage Avenue and the peoples who lived there were programmatically destroyed, like the non-face of Emmett Till. Destruction fails to capture the gritty details of the reality of Osage Avenue and Standard Heights, too abstract a word, textureless, it smooths over all the jagged, barbed, asperous, sanguinary surfaces. Destruction happens in other countries, to other people. Destruction — an intellectualized and transcendent condition whispered from a far off, safe distance, on a hill above the ruined city, where the individual deaths and infinitesimal actions of armies cannot be discerned: a window shattered, a structural brick wall crumbling, the first flame of the coming millennial conflagration. Destruction has nothing to do with the very concrete bombs dropped on Osage Avenue, or the very real ExxonMobil suicide hotline billboard man who offered Toussaint's father far more money than he had any business refusing.

And so I went in search of destruction on an empty avenue once besieged by the Philadelphia police, named for a Native American tribe that no longer exists, and maybe it never did, having as I did at that time in my possession a copy of the Kerner Report, a publication of the National Advisory Commission on Civil Disorders, otherwise known as the Kerner Commission, an 11-member commission seated in Executive Order No. 11365 by President Lyndon B. Johnson with the task of investigating the 1967 race riots that upset the accepted racial entropy in cities across the country, I said. The Report of the National Advisory Commission on Civil Disorders, or the Kerner Report, contains no technical engineering diagrams or complex equations such as are to be found in the Chemical Board's investigative report of ExxonMobil's Christmas Eve explosion, I said, equations that are really just mathematical proxies for the skull and crossbones symbols on the hazmat trucks.

The Kerner Report, Toussaint said, was silent on the chlorine gas slave ships, the flying window glass and the missing Saints jersey; the Kerner Report had nothing to say about the severed head we found, the mountain of rusting oil drums, my mother's chronic cough, or my father's blood that ran into the street from the funeral home — even in death he found some means of escape through the tortile concertina wire, his blood following the downward passage of gravity into the Mississippi, and thence running down to the Spillway and flooding over the burying grounds of our enslaved ancestors, and beyond to the Gulf of Mexico's Dead Zone. Standard Heights, Osage Avenue and the like are buried beneath a barrage of disingenuous reports, riddled with inaccuracies, miscalculations, disinformation, fantasies and bogeymen, Toussaint said. But these reports can go on forever, take on a zombie life of their own, replacing and altering reality: one more report, they say, and we will have the situation figured out, order will be restored; one more commission report and we'll get to the bottom of things, Toussaint said.

Without reviewing the Kerner Report, the Philadelphia Redevelopment Authority — every black community in the New World has, at one time or another, been besieged by the honeyed promises and rapacious bulldozers of a redevelopment authority, since the first redevelopment authorities were chartered by Columbus and d'Iberville — went to work erasing all evidence of the siege. The new houses constructed, like the reservations for the final casino internment of the Native Americans, were shoddy patchwork, the roofs leaked, the plumbing was haunted, the floors sagged like the skin of starved hags, faulty electrical wiring shorted the lights out like a haunted house, doors that led to nowhere upon nowhere, and the windows didn't open. The Redevelopment Authority's contractors, always the lowest bidders, cut corners and cut them again, and when those corners had been cut they cut some more corners, Toussaint said, until there were no corners left to cut. And when you thought corners could not be cut anymore, they cut corners a little more. Resident complaints became so vocal that to avoid a second public relations crisis the Redevelopment Authority organized a program to buy out Osage Avenue's homeowners. Does this sound familiar to anyone? Toussaint asked. Checks for $150,000 were written without questions and Osage Avenue emptied of all but a few tenacious, stalwart residents who had nowhere else to go, or maybe they held out in the belief that their forty acres and a mule was worth a higher price, Toussaint said.

When I arrived at Osage Avenue, I said, the street was fully if autumnally lit, one half of the canyon-like street was softened in buttery sunlight and the other half dusked in darkness, half the block's vacant row houses sunlit and the row houses on the block's opposite side — the side with *destroy this memory* graffitied on it — endowed in the purple-black depths of umbrage, the sun speeding towards the horizon now as I watched with horror the wavering line demarcating the half in departing sunlight from the half in ensuing darkness move menacingly over the row houses in favor of the encroaching night which totalized its black kingdom over a half-redeveloped and largely uninhabited Osage Avenue, submerged in a crepuscular nocturne like the world seen through tinted windows. Sutton's vesper bats circled in the autumnal gloaming over the Avenue. A car with a Louisiana license plate pulled up to the curb and parked, the engine still running. The driver — a man of striking Native American features — exited the vehicle, left the car door open, and snapped a quick picture of the block, hurried embarrassedly back to his car, and drove away, I said.

But there was one man living on the boarded-up and desolate, twilit block of Osage Avenue, his shadow stretching towards me along the gray road. What do you want? the man demanded, unused to visitors. And I answered him, I'm looking for the Osage. I'm the last man on Osage, the last man on Osage said, I'm the black Robinson Crusoe of Osage, you know, he said laughing. The Redevelopment Authority tried to buy me out, everyone else on the block said yes, give me that money, and they all up and left for who knows where, but not me, I stayed right here on Osage Avenue, I didn't die in the bombing and no Philadelphia Redevelopment Authority is going to kick me out. Osage is like the Alamo for me, man. The fucking black Alamo, he said.

I asked him to show me inside, if he would, as I had an interest in examining the quarters of a survivor of the Osage Avenue bombing, how such a refugee lived in the midst of urban Philadelphia — the skyscrapers taller than anything in Baton Rouge, as Toussaint's mother said they were. I could not examine the Iberville Project's quarters' interior for the simple reason that they no longer exist, and by the time I met Toussaint on Basin Street it was too late — the Project was already fenced off for construction, but this picket of Osage Avenue invited me in and showed me such precise hospitality and neighborly warmth as I came to expect, perhaps paradoxically and against all evidence, only in one of the former Confederate states back home.

He had a case of gas masks, prepared in the event that Osage Avenue is teargassed again. Fire extinguishers. Flare guns. Infirmities, he said, prevented him from leaving, and anyway he didn't want the money offered in the buyout terms of the Redevelopment Authority's contract because the cash had portraits of white men like Grant and Jefferson on them, and the Emancipator was on the most worthless denomination there was — the one dollar bill. Chump change. If he took the buyout at all, it would have to be paid in one dollar bills in cash he told the Redevelopment Authority, and his terms were refused. Since entering, I felt I was being watched, and I was just as suddenly spooked by the dark, unseeing eyes of white faces looking up from a desk — the white faces did not have conventional Caucasian features such as those in my great-great-grandfather's war portrait, which were also mine. He showed me to a collection of plaster death masks, the quiet, somber faces of members of his family who died in the 1967 Newark race riots, ignited after police brutalized a black cab driver. Personally, the man said, they should've used all that ordnance they dropped on Osage Avenue to blast Mount Rushmore. Blast Stone Mountain. Blast city hall. He said he suffered Legionnaires' disease, and had resigned himself to his disease and his fate as the only remaining occupant of Osage Avenue, reiterating his wish to die here. Osage is my Alamo. He said that if he closed his eyes, and tightened his fist as if about to strike someone, he could recall Osage Avenue with preternatural clarity the day before it was sieged, a beautiful and peaceful day in May, as the Japanese must have recalled Hiroshima and Nagasaki the day before they were atomized by nuclear physics into oblivion, and in his memory palace he walked Osage Avenue in springtime when it was most vivid and clear, children playing made-up games in the street, but always the pre-siege memory of Osage Avenue was vitiated by images of the firebombing, children screaming helplessly in the night, the vampiric susurrus the wind makes as it tears through a burning building, wood rafters tumbling three stories through the flames. Who ever heard of a city so dumb, so self-loathing it done bombed itself? Not even Baton Rouge, that uglified cancer cell of a city, was dumb enough to bomb itself.

If the last man of Osage recalled the street before it was bombed with preternatural clarity, like the face of a loved one before a disfiguring accident, as the last man of Standard Heights, Toussaint sometimes seemed to be remembering a place that never existed at a time in which it was not under siege of some kind. It is not up to me to decide whether Toussaint was remembering something or inventing a miracle — how memory takes a sight such as the ExxonMobil plant and distorts it as an aesthetic reproduction that can be hung on the wall of the memory palace. No matter how strenuously he focused on the streets of Standard Heights, Toussaint was unable to recall them with sufficient memoriter detail to place them in his cognitive map. The river twitched, rearranging the map again, or the cloudworks' ephemeral chemical formations changed before he could interpret their hazmat symbols: Standard Heights and Osage Avenue were no memory palaces; indeed, Toussaint's mother's street was an anti-memory palace, besieged for the purpose of totalizing the anti-memory, widening the crack in the Liberty Bell, and erecting in the place of familial *Heimweh* a pile of smoking rubble. Trying to understand the operations of memory in a place defined by erasure and refluence, by ebb and flow and omnivorous demolitions, as my own familial memory is in a constant state of flux that I can barely keep pace with, I was then reading John O'Keefe and Lynn Nadel's seminal study, *The Hippocampus as a Cognitive Map*, in order to better grasp the principles at work in Toussaint's memory of his petrochemical childhood:

"The method of loci, an imaginal technique known to the ancient Greeks and Romans and described by Yates (1966) in her book *The Art of Memory,* as well as by Luria (1969). In this technique the subject memorizes the layout of some building, or the arrangement of shops on a street, or any geographical entity which is composed of a number of discrete loci. When desiring to remember a set of items the subject ‹walks› through these loci in their imagination and commits an item to each one by forming an image between the item and any feature of that locus. Retrieval of items is achieved by ‹walking› through the loci, allowing the latter to activate the desired items. The efficacy of this technique has been well established (Ross and Lawrence 1968, *Crovitz 1969, 1971, Briggs, Hawkins and Crovitz 1970, Lea 1975),* as is the minimal interference seen with its use. "

Toussaint had memorized the layout of the family home in Standard Heights and the streets named for extinct native tribes; I had walked with him through his cognitive map of these memories, in search of the discrete loci, the concrete mnemonic triggers that would help him remember all the way back to the red stick, yet walking through the loci was not as simple as it sounded when all that was left were vacant lots, a pile of bricks, keloid scars, and the activation of the desired items resulted only in the bloodhounds sniffing out one's location. The method of loci was nonoperational on Osage Avenue; the imaginal technique failed Toussaint when he needed it most. Even in memory, Toussaint could not walk his street in Standard Heights and recall anything worth dredging up, a few toxic dead fish, a severed head, the rotting fruit of the planets, as the more he attempted to remember of the family house's interior layout the more it shifted into a polymorphic and mobile Rubik's cube. I suffered as Job suffered, Toussaint said. I knew Toussaint did not mean this in a melodramatic sense, that he suffered in the way of Job that is conventionally understood, as a righteous man tested by God, and deprived of all he loved, although the privations Job endured are not unknown to Toussaint, but suffering as it is written in Job 18:17 "His memory shall perish from the earth, and he shall have no name in the street." In order to defy this erasing verse of Job my father told me everything he knew, and a few things he didn't, so that Whipped Peter's and Charles Deslondes' memories would not go the way of Job, would not perish from the earth, that they should have a name in the street even if it was a street named for an annihilated native tribe, Toussaint said.

When finally, I summoned the catawampus courage to overcome the trepidation and the taboo, which had gripped me for years, against opening the windows, and still uncertain of my punishment if I followed through with it, I opened the kitchen window over the sink, the one facing the plant, framing a nightmare view, bordering on the visionary, of the hellish smokestacks and the great mechanical metropolis where my father worked, Toussaint said. The moment the window opened and the prohibition was broken, the view changed instantaneously, the refinery vanished and with it the smokestacks and all the hellish glowing infrastructure of the petrochemical nocturne. In lieu of this petrochemical dystopia that I had thought fixed and eternal, I saw a whip-scarred tableau, one familiar to my race, a thousand times more terrifying, and at the sound of my father's voice — I told you not to open the window, didn't I? — I slammed the window shut, so fast I felt the oxygen sucked out of the room — the terrifying scene truncated like a head from its neck after a guillotine came down — and the ExxonMobil plant continued to poison my vision. After that flirtation with violating the Eleventh Commandment, I had some inkling that ExxonMobil was not merely mass producing clouds on behalf of the Cloud Appreciation Society, Toussaint said.

The house on Hiawatha Street contained portals to another world my father did not want me to open, Toussaint said. Each window of the house, when opened, revealed a scene contrasting with the one visible through the pane when the window was shut, and I knew another day of cancerous coughing and vomiting was ahead for my mother when the men in white hazmat suits could be seen stalking through Standard Heights with beeping and clicking testing equipment and the windowpane was closed as evil gray ash like the dying embers of a last judgment fell in petrochemical snowstorms from the sky.

Violating his prohibition against opening the window triggered something in my father, and he knew I had seen something I was not meant to see, Toussaint said, but opening the window also opened some dormant memory in him. My great-great-great grandfather, three greats ago, participated in the German Coast Uprising, my father said to me for the first time, as before now — before transgressing the prohibitions against opening the window — I'd known, by eavesdropping on a late night conversation between my mother and father, only that I was conceived one hot, sticky Juneteenth when my mother, who was said to be beautiful as the dusk at the winter solstice and was addicted to serrated weapons, stealthily removed the condom from my father in the midst of an exerting coupling, and so I was conceived by an act of passionate bamboozlement, all that stood between me and nihility was a thin piece of latex, a product manufactured from the petrochemicals behind the concertina wire fences, Toussaint said.

Testing the window — I call it a test, for the window did not stay open long enough for it to be a true opening — not only opened that terrible tableau beyond ExxonMobil to me, but also opened up my father in a way I'd not thought possible, as if the window were connected by some intangible mechanism to inner chambers within my father, and through him it opened up that vast though colonized island country across the Gulf of Mexico where slave rebellions once brewed against the empire, Toussaint said. Quixotic coups against the plantation regimes and bloody insurrections in the wormwood moonlight, to keep the boardrooms and shareholders up at night. Such island slave rebellions and German Coast uprisings were still happening — these are the actors deep in the past who are still struggling to open the eye in the Hand and Eye Motif, trying to liberate us from the Angola of the present, Toussaint said.

My mother might've known, before fleeing Prichard for Osage Avenue, that even though the North had no Master Hammonds or Colored Entrances, still it provided no refuge or quarter to those living under the Curse of Ham, as a great-somebody or other on that side of the family who was in Detroit during the riots of 1967, participated in the rioting, throwing a rock or Molotov cocktail or two at the Detroit police, Michigan State Police, or Army National Guard, any uniformed cracker white boy with a gun, and getting a billyclub and a boot on his human face. This same great-somebody, I am told, Toussaint said, was supposed to have stayed at the Algiers Motel the night of the Algiers Motel Massacre, but so traumatized were they by the events of that night that they could not bear coherent witness, just as my father's surviving coworkers in the Christmas Eve explosion spoke only of the metal-like cold that night and nothing of the chlorine gas ghost ships, as if the incoherence of the witness was not itself proof that the bullet hole stars were visible no matter how far one may be from a Colored Entrance.

I felt triangulated between my parents, as my mother told me things about my father that he would never dream of divulging; everything I knew of my mother's people's history came down to me through my father's telling, as if my parents were each other's ventriloquist dummies, Toussaint said. Before the fires were out and the rubble had cooled, my mother left Osage Avenue for New Orleans, my father said, and was housed in the Iberville Projects where she met my father at a spring crawfish boil. He would've been deftly cracking the crustacean's heads off and savagely, not to say vociferously sucking the tender meat of the tails when she first laid eyes on him, an unflattering first impression. He was a very emphatic and lusty crawfish eater, and not even the most refined gourmand or connoisseur of the crustacean can eat crawfish without making a mess. But the fortitudinous way she adapted to her new life in Iberville, this girl from Mobile, Alabama and survivor of the Siege of Osage Avenue, endeared her to my father, my mother's life in Philadelphia much like Emma Lou Morgan, the black heroine in *The Blacker the Berry,* her deep royal purple-black skin the target of barbs from light-skinned kids who had not yet decolonized their minds, nor seen the terrible visions I did when the window above the kitchen sink was opened, Toussaint said. But in Iberville skin tone was creolized, and my father had a thing, I suppose, for girls dark as the dark side of the moon: my father said their first kiss was beneath the spacious oaks in Congo Square, and my mother said it was among the tombstones and above-ground mausoleums, beneath a full moon, in St. Louis Cemetery No. 1 while a candlelight séance was being held at the tomb of voodoo queen, Marie Laveau.

Though she left Osage Avenue before the smoke cleared, yet the damage to her lungs — tear gas, burning asbestos — was done. My family's health history is like a litany of all of Petrochemical Modernism's worst incurable diseases, Toussaint said, the cousins lost to leukemia, pulmonary edemas, breast cancer and aneurisms, aunts and uncles succumbed to ever vaguer more perfidious maladies. Instead of the Dancing Plague or the Mandela Effect, which only infected white communities anyway, we got exposure to endocrine disruptors, neurotoxins, mutagens, and teratogens that corrupted our genome with petrochemical hauntology, Toussaint said. In winter pickup games we used to stop play, opening our mouths, catching petrochemical ash on our tongues like it was pure white snow — how were we to know it was not? A second cousin who died on Plank Road at a notorious night club called Bella Noche from injuries sustained while twerking like the Dancing Plague of 1518. We are born, Toussaint said reflectively, all in the same manner, there is only one way to come into the world, but the extreme variety and creativity of methods of departure is unequaled anywhere in the world by the mortality schedules of Cancer Alley. Those who survived the agonies of birth and were not stillborn often as not suffered gruesome birth defects, and I do not mean a simple cleft lip or palate, nothing so simple as that, though that was certainly not out of the question, but terrible Biblical afflictions like *spina bifida* that required *italics* and Latin to be uttered in mysterious medical tones, and inexplicable inhumane chromosomal disorders like Down syndrome and Edward's syndrome, as the ExxonMobil plant hacked and rewrote our genetic code in metastasizing petrochemical symbols and skull and crossbones hieroglyphics that no one could understand, because the soulless plant, Toussaint said, was not satisfied with clearing the lots of Standard Heights and insuring that we never returned to Hiawatha Street or Pontiac Street, it had to intervene in genetic history itself and meddle with the genome, like a Bay of Pigs of the bloodstream, Toussaint said.

In a dream, next to *The Negro Motorist Green Book*, I pulled from the shelf the human genome printed as a book, a 100-page manifesto of alphabet soup, and under the orders of Master Hammond — ancestor of the security guard's order to back away from the museum's Gursky print — I went about erasing the sequencing alphabet and rewriting in its place a picture book of hazmat symbols for corrosion and acute toxicity, flammables and oxidation and the Biblical story of Abraham and Isaac, one which my mother tried to protect me and my brother from at a young age, feeling it was not right for us to read a story about a father killing his son, even if it was a Bible story with a moral purpose and God had intervened at the last possible chance to spare Isaac's life, Toussaint said, for she knew that our father was capable of following such murderous orders from a higher power to the letter, though her solicitudes failed to prevent me from dreaming that my father was about to sacrifice me — usually by drowning in the Mississippi River, but sometimes by bloodier means too — to placate some ancient river god or industrial deity, the petrochemical divinities residing in the manufactured clouds, Toussaint said, which I took to mean a propitiation of the ExxonMobil plant — a bloodthirsty and Old Testament supreme being. Later, when I learned that it was an angel, a lesser being in the hierarchy of the celestial organization, not God who commanded Abraham to cease and lower the knife poised at his son's throat, the holy roller's high-fructose corn syrup religion lost all credibility for me. God could not halt the ritual sacrifice of a son himself but had to send a lesser being as a proxy to do his dirty work, and still this sacrificial dream recurs to me, no matter where I may be living at the time. The Lord Almighty might as well be Down Syndrome or neurotoxins, Toussaint said.

When I first violated my father's prohibition against opening the window, I thought I might at least and at last hear birdsong, but as so often when I have tried to pretend that Standard Heights was normal, I was to be disappointed. There are no birds in Standard Heights, poisoned or chased away by the chlorine gas ghost ships, dispersed for good by the Christmas Eve explosion. Birdsong was an alien noise to me that I did not hear till one primaveral day walking the soft dirt paths through the Arnold Arboretum, the birch trees aflame with the conflagration of fall like Klimt's *Tannenwald*, such as do not exist in Cancer Alley. The deeper I walked into this autumnal Tannenwald, following the aural allure of this siren birdsong, never heard in the artificial forests ExxonMobil was planting around Standard Heights, the less I wished to ever emerge from its comforting, northern gloom. A wood such as might be inhabited by the Green Knight. One that was not planted by ExxonMobil for a greenbelt buyout program. Yes, I saw waterfowl up and down the banks of the Mississippi — herons, pelicans, egrets, cranes, ibises, but these are not songbirds. The pelican's song is a plaint. The egret's elegy. The ibis' requiem for the swamps, all lugubrious arias and benzene birdsong of the petrochemical nocturne. The plastic pink flamingos of Spanish Town have no voice. The whooping crane's whoop was a harrowing howl for home, a plea for a ceasefire. The anti-birdsong of barges and unexploded ordnance. The whooping crane — an estimated lifespan of a quarter century — lived longer than some of my own family, and through aggressive hunting and wanton destruction of habitat their population was reduced to a paltry twenty-one whooping cranes around the time that Iberville was under construction. The now depopulated waterfowl habitat was colonized by Stymphalian birds, man-eating swamp birds with giant bronze beaks, sharp metallic feathers and toxic chemical dung, devastating the cane harvest and the satsuma trees. These ancient swamp birds from Stymphalia nested in the mountain of oil drums that formed the highest summit for many hundreds of miles, nefarious mythic birds that could only be defeated by Hercules in his Sixth Labor. But the Age of Heroes is bygone and on the Louisiana state flag, in place of the pelican, the Stymphalian bird devours its young, Toussaint said. Then I felt the slippage and twitching of the river in my cognitive map: the arboretum's northern autumnal woods were like smokestacks and gas flares by nightfall, at the hour of the nocturne's greatest plangency, I must have taken a wrong turn, become lost on the linden paths, for the Tannenwald was transformed into an impenetrable blighted forest of process flow diagrams and gray-scale boxes, towering smokestacks spewing toxic ash, boiling cauldrons of wormwood and arcane infrastructure with no logical function, Toussaint said, and it is not altogether clear that I ever found my way out.

My father said that mother was maladapted to the southern miasma and the poisonous climate because she was from Philadelphia, a city my father mocked for its moniker — the City of Brotherly Love. Ain't no brothers loving nobody there, he said, too cold. How is a City of Brotherly Love going to go and bomb itself? Her people were from Alabama, some crumbling, police-taped block in Prichard, which is outside of Mobile, and not known for anything charming enough to be on a postcard, but her people left for the North when it became clear that black folks were not going to get a fair shake in Jim Crow Alabama, and then she and her people left the North too when they were displaced by the Siege of Osage Avenue. She never spoke of Prichard or Philadelphia, except to say that the mosquitoes in Prichard were the size of pterodactyls, and that the buildings in Philadelphia were taller than the flaming smokestacks at the plant, which I could scarcely imagine, Toussaint said, the tallest manmade anything for miles around was the mountain of rusting oil drums and the only building I'd ever seen taller than ExxonMobil's stacks and towers was the Louisiana State Capitol building where Huey Long was assassinated, but mother said there were towers in Philadelphia even taller than this, and that buildings in New York City were yet taller, and through this escalation of vertiginous heights straight into the Norco cumulus — to be admired from a safe distance — I realized I lived in a very small place.

The Petrochemical Education of Toussaint and the Endless Death of *Radio Free Dixie*

Like his father, Toussaint listened to *Radio Free Dixie*, a radical radio program which went off the airwaves back in the 1960s, but recordings of its broadcasts are still being transmitted from some remote unknown location in the Gulf of Mexico's Dead Zone, and late night broadcasts from Havana, Cuba of Herbie Hancock's "Watermelon Man" and Nina Simone's "Mississippi Goddamn." How about a hearty goddamn, Toussaint said, for every state in the Union — an Alabama Goddamn, a Louisiana Goddamn, a Georgia Goddamn, Texas Goddamn, and for all those who can, a Massachusetts Goddamn. Fifty goddamns. We'll make it fifty-one goddamns if Puerto Rico ever becomes a state, he said.

A single staticky radio brought the music of Motown and soul to Iberville, Toussaint said, and it was on this device in the room of another Iberville tenant that my father listened to news reports of the Watts Riots and the riots leading up to the Algiers Motel Incident, and it was also on this device that he was able to tune in to a program then known as *Radio Free Dixie*, the name of the program alone terrifying to the McCarthyist warmongers who had lascivious wet dreams of nuking Cuba, Toussaint said. If Frederick Douglass and John Brown had had radio technology — what noble and rabble-rousing perorations we might have heard. Through the crackling static of the 50,000-watt broadcast, the voice of Fidel Castro resonated through Iberville, the anti-capitalist rhetoric heard across Rampart Street in the bars of the French Quarter and repeated by the Benito Juárez statue on the Basin Street neutral ground.

My father heard the fugitive Robert F. Williams encourage his radio listeners to exercise their Second Amendment rights and defend themselves against white supremacy, lest we are all Emmett-Tilled, Toussaint said. He warned of a violent and long hot summer, and Williams meant what he said. The long hot summer was no metaphor. Quite literally, a long hot summer came. The Overton Window burning in the tower of Turner's painting, at the time my father was listening to the Chicago Eight's verdicts on *Radio Free Dixie*, this window was on the verge of permanent closure, and my father did not want us opening the Overton Window, his world in which the Saints were spooked by some supernatural football curse made sense to him, and unlike my brother Xavier he was not constitutionally incapable of punching a clock at the plant, every morning waving to the team of white security guards that protected the plant from the indigenous tribes in Standard Heights. Stop, question and frisk was then a popular way to deal with men like my father on Rampart Street or Hiawatha Street, Toussaint said.

I was the first of my family to attend college, and it appears that I will be the last, Toussaint said. My brother uniformly succumbed to the pipeline of narrowed expectations set for him by Standard Heights, serving a life sentence in Angola, where he is a rider in the prison rodeo. He can hit foul shots blindfolded, feeling the ball with the eye in the palm of his hand. For a while, he tried to punch the clock working at the plant but we lost touch after arguments that turned physical over how he could go to work for the plant that killed our father, Toussaint said.

After the Christmas Eve explosion, discipline around the house was lax, we opened the windows freely, and by the second anniversary of my father's death my mother started seeing a man whose proudest achievement was a trip in a stolen car to Roswell, New Mexico where he saw a cyber-punk with dreads wearing a full-body metallic body suit in the McDonald's. His second greatest achievement was breaking out of Alcatraz, but I think he meant Angola. Every summer, around August when the truculent heat rends soul from the weary body, he vowed he was moving to Antarctica. It didn't last. She remained a widow the rest of her life, the grief was too overwrought for the men who came around, her period of mourning lasting well into the next president's term, Toussaint said, she was too much the character of Joan of Arc in the French silent film and her cancerous cough made them suspect she was possessed by some petrochemical demon trying to escape from her lungs.

Then one Christmas — this was well after the Christmas Eve explosion — my mother gave me a lock from Angola's death row, a heavy padlock the size of a human heart. I once — and only the once — went to visit Xavier at Angola Prison, in the cane harvest month of October during the Angola Prison Rodeo, the prison transformed into a surreal bazaar and penal circus like a small-town Brueghel, Toussaint said. Ticketholders thronged into a small arena like a high school stadium, the prisoners in black and white striped prison uniforms waving to free family and friends who came to refresh their memories of the imprisoned beloved whose face and voice grew fainter, more like the face of one drowned, the voice of one who cannot speak with the passing of every year. The rodeo chutes opened violently as if the bull were pressurized steam demanding to be released: a prisoner flailing on the back of a possessed, indignant and deranged bucking beast. Many of the prisoners were thrown almost instantaneously from their bull, the crowd laughing and jeering at the spectacle of a prisoner, already down on his luck, tossed through the air like a ragdoll. It must feel good to laugh at someone with a life-sentence, Toussaint said. I did not think for a minute that any of the onlookers in the rodeo stadium that day wished to see the prisoners succeed, to actually ride the bull, they came to see a condemned man thrown from the horned beast and trampled to death, thankful it was not themselves in the rodeo, but oblivious to the social forces afoot which had put these prisoners on one side of Angola's prison walls and themselves safely and innocently on the other. It was clear that the rodeo goers were not in attendance to see some fair and uncertain contest between man and beast, but to witness a farce the outcome of which was decided since the first slave ships ported in New Orleans, because even if a rider held on and somehow managed not to be thrown and trampled he was still on the inside and they were not. The Master Hammonds and the prison wardens have always loved to see two Negroes fight, Toussaint said, to dance for a few dollars. Rural whites from as far as Arkansas and Mississippi and eastern Texas came to the rodeo even though they had no friends or family imprisoned in Angola — for the same reasons the world needed a racialized bout between Jack Johnson and Jeffries, the Great White Hope.

Xavier was a god of the rodeo, Toussaint said. The bull he rode was really the bull that lived inside him. To ride the bull, one had first to master the bull within, only then could he hope to succeed in riding the real bull that would, if it could, bash his brains out for the entertainment of those not in Angola. In lieu of the South's martial equestrian Confederate statues there should be a statue of one of these Angola prisoners hanging on for dear life to an angry bucking bull — that would be a token of something akin to progress. But there was more than just rodeo, there was prison art, the trinkets and whatnot the making of which passed a life sentence. A prisoner carved sculptures of Jesus and Mary out of Velveeta cheese for the rodeo's craft fair. Handmade soaps and bird houses. Belt buckles. Self-portraits in watercolors and walking sticks carved from cypress wood. A film crew was shooting a documentary that day, the real life story of Angola's rodeo riders. When shows like *Making a Murderer* were starring wrongfully accused white men from the cognitive abyss of Trump's voter base, the Angola prison rodeo's potential for entertainment had to be monetized, casting real life convicted murderers from Central City and the Seventh Ward, shirts versus skins black boys from the Bottom or Standard Heights, Toussaint said.

The documentary crew did not know what to do with Xavier's real life story, Toussaint said. I'd seen the police dash cam video of the incident — indeed I have seen the video replay hundreds, thousands of times on screens and in my mind — and many years passed till in Angola, in the visitation room, separated by a wall of bullet-proof glass, we discussed what he remembered happening that night in Standard Heights on Pontiac Street only a few blocks from the kitchen where my mother would have been making stew or checking on the cornbread in the oven, Toussaint said, and after he finished telling his version of suicide by cop, which was never heard in court, I gave him my own interpretation of the life-altering events he remembered: his crime was not an attempted murder of a police offer, as the prosecution maintained during the trial, and as many in town still believed, but a premeditated suicide attempt, as evidenced by my brother's drawn out but ever escalating non-compliance with the police officer's orders: instead of remaining seated in the passenger seat with his hands visible at 10 and 2 he got out and lurched towards the police cruiser, his hands in his pockets (my father was very clear: keep your hands out of your pockets when dealing with police), shouting madly at the officer to shoot him, challenging him to take your best shot and aim for the heart, as if he were taunting or challenging an opponent in the boxing ring, and then when the police officer did not pull the trigger, he leisurely sauntered back to the car to retrieve a stolen pistol from the glovebox, Toussaint said. Consider the refusal to surrender, not taking cover when the police opened fire — the number of shots still disputed — in what the prosecution argued was justifiable self-defense though Xavier had fired no shots of his own. Osage is my Alamo, the man said.

The dash cam recorded the five minutes — grainy and choppy footage, the resolution low, the plot and action ebbing and flowing according to a hazmat logic — of my brother's failed attempt at suicide by cop; failed, because he now has a life-sentence in Angola. The eeriest part of the dash cam recording is not my brother's repeated attempts to commit suicide by cop, each one failing and then escalating, but that his repeated attempts were recorded in total silence, the dash cam recording, at least as it was released to the public, contains no audio, Xavier and the cop playing out the predetermined scripts of their social roles without making a sound, not even *Radio Free Dixie* dubbed over the action, or the petrochemical nocturne playing in the background as accompaniment to the officer's commands to surrender, an order never made of the stone statue in Lee Circle.

Five minutes I have watched so many times — *ad infini-*

tum hardly conveys the longueur of anxiety I get from watching and watching again my brother's failed suicide by cop — that whole days of my life must have been consumed in watching those five minutes looping, looping and looping, analyzing every second's movement, pausing the recording in places to get a better look at a blurry detail that might absolve him, protracting those five minutes into an eternity of agony, each repetition of the dash cam recording's abortive attempt at suicide by cop getting no closer to the core of what happened that night on Pontiac Street as the Exxon-Mobil manufactured toxic clouds of galloping Confederate horses and ghost slave ships. With each replay of the dash cam footage, Emmett Till's face distorting more and more into an unrecognizable mask, a mask that Xavier would be forced to wear in Angola. The reason he was pulled over was as simple as it was inevitable. Xavier had a taillight out — he didn't have the money to fix it — and an unregistered, illegal firearm in the glovebox, Toussaint said.

Suicide by cop — strange to some ears — is not so uncommon in Standard Heights. Xavier and I played our shirts versus skins pickup games beneath the suicide prevention billboards, the depressed man with his head in his hands looming over our every touchdown. Some kind of self-loathing *Weltschmerz*, antedating his birth, that he carried with him into the world, which once activated could not be reversed. He'd been suicidal since before the Christmas Eve explosion, but he needed to externalize the locus of agency, to outsource the action to some third party, he couldn't do it himself; I understood, I told my brother in the visitation room, that men act from positions of negative capability and that in the cop's mind Xavier was only performing the script of an encounter over-determined since Whipped Peter first ran from the bloodhounds, certainly before the cop pulled Xavier over that night in Standard Heights, the stars in our sky were not the same stars as those in the cop's sky. As boys, Xavier and I had awakened in Fred Hampton's bloody bed and connected the bullet hole stars shot in the Standard Heights sky into the internecine constellations of the Gigantomachy and the petrochemical hazmat symbols on the cargo trucks, Toussaint said, and in this connecting of the bullet hole stars into skull and crossbones and other noxious hieroglyphs, I had foreseen the calamity that would befall my brother on Pontiac Street — no rebel sharpshooter, just suicide by cop.

Xavier's arms were camouflaged in runny, watery prison tattoos, the text of a cryptic genome. Most tattoo artists, Toussaint said, don't know how to ink black skin, and so you have to go to a trusted black tattoo artist, a black man who has inked himself first and knows how to turn black skin into the artwork it was meant to be, not the sanctimonious holy rollers of Standard Heights who believed tattoos were a sin and offense against God because the ink, unable to enhance even a pig, defaced the divine image of the godhead molded in human clay from the very banks of the Mississippi River, Toussaint said, forever amen. He had more tattoos now than he did when the guilty verdict came down, self-inked symbols of skull and crossbones on his left arm and death riding a bull on the right, chemical nomenclature — benzene, naphtha and the molecular skeletons of their structural formulas — all over his chest and neck.

But I had not come to Angola to see my brother thrown from a beast in the prison rodeo. Do you remember the chlorine gas ghost ships? I asked my brother, Toussaint said, I need to know whether you remember seeing them that Christmas Eve. It's very important. It's extremely important, Toussaint reiterated. I have to know if I was the only one to see the ghost ships that night, Toussaint said. Think, he said, you must remember, the slave ships that formed from the chemical fog ghosting out of the plant and sailing downriver. Looking at me as if I were the one on the inside of Angola, and he was a free man, come to visit his slightly tetched brother, Xavier thought for a moment, and then he spoke, a flat and incarcerated voice. No brother, no I don't, he said. Dad died in an accident a long time ago, and there were no ghost ships or whatever you call them, Xavier said. If it is true that our view of reality and our memory of what has happened to us or been inflicted upon us is conditioned by our relative position in a socioeconomic scheme and a now mostly manmade or man-meddled environment, an unnatural synthesis of petrochemicalism and oedipal hatred for the whore of mother earth, then the prison might have befogged and institutionalized Xavier's memory, a few steps outside the prison's borders and he might have remembered, Toussaint said. As a free man he would remember the chlorine gas ghost ships. But he denied it, and I was compelled to accept this denial *prima facie*, there was no arguing with his imprisoned memory. Do you still rub yourself down with onion? Xavier wanted to know, Toussaint said, and I asked him why would I do that? To evade the bloodhounds, of course, Xavier said. I don't have to, I said, the smell of that onion never goes away, one rubbing was enough for a lifetime, Toussaint said.

The transformation of prison upon my brother's whole person was as total and complete as the erasure of Standard Heights itself. Xavier behaved like the white man wanted him to more in prison than he ever did in Standard Heights. In Angola, I lived like a man who died twenty years ago, he said. Xavier's exemplary prison behavior got him assigned to a cleanup detail, which though it may not seem like much to us is in fact a rare and coveted privilege for the Angolan. That's what they called them, Toussaint said, Angolans. You never become anything but Angolan. Under heavily armed supervision, my brother said that day in the visitation room, we are ordered out of our cells and loaded into a converted yellow school bus at dawn, under the watchful eye of prison dogs and sleepy armed guards. They never tell us beforehand where we're going. We turned up in cane fields and on the side of state highways and reptilian, stygian bayous choked with trash where even the Cajuns would not live in the floating metropolises of their houseboats. We cleaned up the puke and beer cans around campus and Tiger Stadium after the LSU games, and swept the confetti off the streets after New Year's Eve celebrations, year after New Year, in a cyclically recurring bacchanal of trash that would never end. Even after the Anthropocene — yes, the gods will be present, but in what form and to what end? — the confetti would still fall from the sky like chemical ash and champagne bottles full of wormwood pop themselves. Angola had taught me to fear the gods and to pretend that the world outside of Angola simply did not exist, because I had to. Even the old gods feared the Parcae: Nona, who spins life's thin thread from distaff to the spindle; Decima, who measures the length of life's thread with her rod; and Morta, who cuts life's thread and chooses from the permutations of possible deaths the manner of an Angolan's demise. I did not know where the guards were taking us till I saw, etched in whip-scar tissue against the clear blue-black sky, the soaring black tower of the State Capitol building, a familiar beacon from our time growing up in its long shadow, that sad watchtower from which the chieftains of power presided in zooted contumely and mocked us, and the watchtower itself engulfed in the glowing furnace of the ExxonMobil plant where the mortal thread of our father's life was cut, Xavier said. You know the red-orange sulfur and smell of that balefire. The State

Capitol tower lit up like a lighthouse on some penal colony island. They bussed us out to Standard Heights, my brother said, just as the prison yard lights were going out. This was my first homecoming since my arrest on Pontiac Street, or maybe it was Tecumseh Street, I never can be sure, Xavier said. The prison bus pulled onto Hiawatha Street and under implied threats of imminent death we filed off the yellow school bus like delinquent schoolchildren, our breaths pluming in the cold wet air, and went to work. I was the last to deboard the bus, unable to bring myself to return to Standard Heights as an Angola Prison rodeo rider. I felt that if I stepped off the bus that I would plunge straight into the void and be impaled on the bull's horns. The cleaning detail was better than casket-making in the workshop or picking cotton on the Angola plantation while some horse and rider watched you, waiting for one false move, beneath the shadowy brim of those black hats that made them look like lackeys of white death. The funeral home had leaked again and the funeral home owner called in some favors to get an Angola crew — we were known for our meticulousness in cleaning the grounds of the governor's mansion — to deterge the bloody streets of the vanished tribes. All the houses are gone now, my brother said. Yes, I know, I said, not one is left. A few wooden crosses marked the fading memory of car accidents or unsolved homicides. The mountain of oil drums seemed smaller than it had in the days of our pickup games, almost mortal. I tried to recall the spot where that cop pulled me over, but it seemed that the native streets had changed places in my absence, a remote and inaccessible zone like the back of the skull, the spot would not come out of its hiding place. Though the cleanup work was grim, the other prisoners went about it with something like hopeless cheer, glad to be on holiday, but convicted in the knowledge that it will end, aiming the chugging pressure washers on the blood till it thinned and bled down the storm drains in pinkish rindles, all the while surrounded by bored armed guards on horseback. General Beauregard's galloping horses in the petrochemical cloudwork, Toussaint said. The canine units with thinly leashed mastiffs, Xavier said. The guard is a nobody without a prisoner; the prisoner exists with or without the guard, but the guard needs a prisoner to guard in order to have his own self confirmed by the prisoner's imprisonment. Pathetic, Xavier said, to be dependent like that on a trapped animal for the confirmation of your own self, predictable and pathetic. And what became of the satsuma grove? I asked my brother. Gone, Xavier said, all gone. But the suicide hotline billboards are still there, those billboards will be there till the bitter end, he said.

I'd not seen Xavier's cell, and never would, but I imagined it as a gray box in which nothing eventful happened, or nothing which could properly be called an event, the slow drip of incarcerated mentation the only activity other than the diurnal changes of light and the guards plowing the long, echoing concrete corridors day and night. Mother gave me a lock from Angola's death row, I told Xavier, I think she got it at an antique shop in New Orleans. I'm not sure what she meant by giving me this death row lock as a gift, but I keep it in the room with me at all times, just within arm's reach, the lock beating in the dark like a heart, a locked heart with no key, long lost, thrown to the bottom of the river or melted in the plant's balefires. I considered the cold dead weight and iron substance of the lock in my hand, the numbness of my extremities temporally suspended. Recall, I told my brother, Toussaint said, ancestors of ours may have worked the fields of the plantations that were consolidated into the land for the prison in which you brother, Toussaint said, are now confined for the remainder of your natural life. He took what I said to heart and locked it there; I know this because he said nothing in return, there followed no rebuttal from him, no extenuation, he knew the score, speaking only with his hands: the knuckles of each hand were tattooed, the black letters only indistinctly visible on his dark skin: *Game* tattooed in gothic blackletter on the knuckles of his right hand and *Over* on the knuckles of the left.

I knew it was more than mere prison boredom in a life sentence that made my brother ride the bull in the rodeo, Toussaint sad. The bull is an emissary of death, and to ride that beast, at least for the short time that you do actually ride it, and it does not ride you, is to escape death as our father did not in the Christmas Eve explosion. The Angola plantation was spared the fates of haunted house dilapidation and spooky disrepair that wrecked the Ashland-Belle Helen and the Destrehan by converting its use to the lifelong captivity of society's reprobated, the given-up-on, the flagellated, the condemned, the horsewhipped, the born-in-the-wrong-zip-code, and those who, without even knowing it themselves, were genuinely murderous.

And so my brother found his true vocation as a bull rider;

maybe he was never meant for more, though one could hardly be created for less without ceasing to be created at all. There are behaviors of the white collar professional class — the billboard attorneys, the ExxonMobil executives in Houston, the professors up at Southern University — which are beyond the grasp of anyone from Standard Heights: computer competencies, interviewing techniques, how to knot a necktie, poking at a keyboard with a single finger to type out ten words in as many minutes, the spelling so disfigured that it becomes a foreign language, showing up on time, navigating the social intricacies of hierarchical structures and the nickel-and-dime rituals of office politics. In Standard Heights, office politics is just how fast you are with a switchblade. Punching a clock is anathema to one whose diurnal rhythms are still timed within the agricultural framework of the plantation system, Master Hammond had devised too many slippery hierarchies of gotcha competence which my brother could not master. Pick yourself up by your bootstraps, Master Hammond told my brother. But I haven't got any bootstraps, he said. Then go buy some bootstraps and stop asking for a handout, he said. All while those elect few with a dial-up connection to God worship Supply-Side Jesus from the Lost Gospel of Reagan, trying to bootstrap each other to the moon, Toussaint said.

I asked Xavier if he remembered cheering on O.J. Simpson's failed freeway escape from the police when we were pickup game kids, how badly we wanted "The Juice" to escape, guilty or not, killing a white woman was not the worst thing one could be sentenced to life imprisonment for, and though I know somewhere deep inside he must have remembered, he said he did not recall the freeway chase, much less cheering for "The Juice," and that such a thing — cheering on a murderer in his escape from the police — was more preposterous than Simpson's supposed innocence. And so, as he turned his back on his pre-Angolan self, Xavier became an inner émigré, that self-torturous involution and blighted helix of escape from the petrochemical nocturne which to me seemed a lot like escaping slavery not by following the North Star, which was nowhere visible in the bullet hole stars above Fred Hampton's bed anyway, but by hiding in the barn behind the plantation, as if emigration plain and simple was impossible in a globalized south that threatened Antarctica with megachurch Supply-Side Jesus, suicide hotline billboards, and penguins with extinction because they were black and white. Now that Xavier's escape from Standard Heights had been successful, from the east bank to the west bank of the river where Whipped Peter and our father dwelled among the river shades, and escaping outward into the policed dimensions of non-Angolan space was no longer a possibility, when he was not training for the rodeo he advanced to a deeper mode of escapism through the books on the prison's pre-approved reading list. In the prison's pre-approved books — because nothing made it inside Angola without first being approved by a boardroom of self-appointed death mask white men — he escaped to worlds that were as much unlike this one as the worlds in the science fiction of Jules Verne, and worlds which were so much like this one — as in Malcolm X's autobiography — that Xavier must have seen no other way out, and because physical escape from Angola was next to impossible he escaped, without the guards noticing, deeper into the transcendence of inner emigration, without the need of onion scent to throw the bloodhounds off his trail. While the wives of the wardens read bestsellers like *The Help* on their Kindles, I brought him copies of some Richard Wright and some James Baldwin, I don't remember which, and my own copy of Malcolm X's autobiography smuggled inside a new translation of the Bible, which was on the pre-approved list, Toussaint said. To aid him in his inner emigration travels, wherever they might take him, almost like a clandestine compass to navigate the lands west of the Mississippi River, one Easter Sunday I gave him Eldridge Cleaver's *Soul on Ice*, a book I thought might save his life, as much as it had saved me from the *Welteislehre* and the Green Book had saved our mother in finding a motel friendly to traveling Negroes when she left Prichard for Philadelphia. Anything that I thought might help him fight the good fight. Angola's list of proscribed literature included the world's great works, but somehow *Lolita* and *American Psycho* were both permitted in the prison, two books which charmingly depict pedophilia and psychopathic criminality. *Mein Kampf* is not banned, as are other books written by white nationalists, including Louisiana's homegrown wannabe epigone Hitler, David Duke, but in Angola you will not be able to get copies of the pop-up edition of *A Charlie Brown Christmas* or *The Color Purple, Freakonomics* or *A Time to Kill.* Another book on the banned list is Facebook, he wasn't missing much there. Angola may be one of the last places where people still write letters, Toussaint said. Because everything he had to say was tattooed on his knuckles, Xavier never wrote and even if he had the letters never would have found me at the addresses listed as friendly to traveling Negroes in the Green Book.

He said his dreams in Angola were worse than ever before. He never dreamed of freedom or Popeye's chicken or the blessed and carnal goods of a woman, a time before the Christmas Eve explosion. No, in Angola, he dreamed of protracted torture, his hands cut off, bloodhounds chasing him through the ExxonMobil trees, his own bloodletting in the gutter, cramped and claustrophobic lightless spaces, premature burial, escapes that ended in brick walls or boiling cauldrons of water, his back hideously scarred and again and then again of the five minutes caught on the police dash cam when his suicide by cop failed, except in his dreams his suicide by cop sometimes succeeded and he woke at the moment of dream death in his cell paralyzed in hot night sweat and the gradually returning reality of a life sentence in the Angola of the present. They say that one's dreams partake of the collective story of mythic imagery and archetypal tropes that have distressed our sleep since before the Middle Passage, but I do not think that Xavier's partook of anything but the congenital traumas of our forebears, the structural formulas of endocrine disruptors and neurotoxins, Toussaint said. How many times — even in dream — can one be killed by a police officer and still survive, to wake up in a cell, and do it all over again?

So this was the dream speed endgame of my brother's escape from Standard Heights, and as I left him in the prison visitation room that day — though not without first giving him the keyless lock from Angola's death row, as my mother must have intended it for Xavier but could not muster the nerve in her lioness' heart to give it to him herself — not knowing whether he would find, on the pages of Malcom X's autobiography where the death of his father is recounted, the text of Amiri Baraka's "Ka'Ba," or Robert Lowell's "For the Union Dead" tucked into the section narrating Malcolm's arrests, Xavier's face shone like the bronze Negroes of the 54th Massachusetts Infantry Regiment marching to fife and drum to their nameless deaths on the Boston Common. In Xavier's face, I recognized those metallic watery goodbye eyes: they were the same brazen eyes that glowed like heated flint in the non-faces of the bronze Negro soldiers who marched into battle — no fog of war blinding them — and perished anonymously, their corpses not even photographed for posterity by

Gardner or Brady. I never saw my brother again, Toussaint said.

I asked Toussaint to recite a few lines of Baraka's poem, which he had given to his brother together with an autobiography he thought would most resonate with Xavier's attempted suicide by cop, and as he did so — "A closed window looks down on a dirty courtyard" — I heard beneath his voice the petrochemical nocturne that was subtext to everything he said.

The monument to the 54th Massachusetts Regiment is located on the corner of the Boston Common, Toussaint said. A cold and icy day, the bronze of the Negro soldiers ringing like bells in a church service. I'd been ghostwriting lyrics and beats with Young Roddy and Jay Electronica who grew up in New Orleans' Magnolia Projects, borrowing here and there — because plagiarism is a white man's invention — from Robert Lowell's "For the Union Dead," which poem I had chopped and screwed for some Seventh Ward artists, and I had to see for myself the masks of the bronze Negroes, the most despised regiment in the Union, notorious for its boycotts of Union labor policy for receipt of lower wages than their white counterparts — the life of a white Union soldier was worth more than the life of a black Union soldier — and which raised bayonets against the undead Confederate hauntology, and before the Confederacy had even surrendered the regiment was already fighting against the stone zombie general in Lee Circle.

The counterpoint — because to defeat the undead Confederate hauntology everything must be balanced out by a countervailing symbol, an equal and opposite force — to the Confederate veterans parade pictured on the junk shop postcard was Colonel Robert Gould Shaw and his black regiment's march down Beacon Street on May 28, 1863. These bronze men, led by a white man on a horse, marching to their deaths down in South Carolina. I reached for the bronze Negro foot soldier with a hand that itself felt heavy as bronze, that characteristic amputative numbness of the extremities setting in in earnest the moment I touched the ice-cold bronze soldier. Commanding his Negroes in the maneuvers they'd been drilled in on the quaint green town squares of New England, Gould was shot three times through the chest at the Second Battle of Fort Wagner as he scaled a parapet, his blood spraying the non-faces and Union blue uniforms of his men who let his body lay where it fell at their feet. Monuments in bronze, such as the Boston Commons' 54th Massachusetts Regiment, and stone, such as General Lee refusing surrender in the eye of the storm in Lee Circle, these monuments to the skull and crossbones endure while the sectarian passions and vitriols that excited the senseless slaughter lapse into the bloodstream of oblivion. The Confederate grave detail buried Shaw — in that quaint time before the century of mass graves — with his black regiment, a petty act intended as an insult, though Shaw would not have wished to be buried anywhere else, he would join his bronze men in the poems of putrescence until — the flesh vanished from bone — his skull was indistinguishable from that of his Negro soldiers. On the Boston Common that day, snow falling that was not petrochemical fly ash, I watched the monument closely for any signs of life, that the bronze infantrymen might be stirring to fight the good fight again and hold General Lee to his terms of surrender: Colonel Shaw is sculpted with his sword drawn, poised for a blow, the sword stolen from his corpse by Confederate looters, and yet historians have not yet acknowledged that any of these bronze Negroes had rubbed themselves with onion before the battle so that death would not sniff them out. Before losing all sensation in my hands — the air fraught with a metallic cold — I dared touch the tip of the Colonel's drawn sword just as the sky dusted the bronze regiment in snow, till I began to see white explosions of delicate breath exhaled in plumes from the mouths of the Negro soldiers.

My father encountered very few white men outside the razor wire of the ExxonMobil plant, Toussaint said, and few of those were what he called good whites. My father had some begrudging respect for Colonel Shaw, but diluted as it were, this Colonel who was willing to die fighting with Negro infantrymen, the Colonel being only a slightly less malign version of his white bosses at the ExxonMobil plant, rejecting the symbolism of a white-led all-Negro regiment, feeling as he did that the 54th Massachusetts should've been led by a Negro, there was something amiss — for once he could not specify exactly what — about a white man on horseback, whether in blue or gray, leading a cadre of Negroes to their deaths in a conflict animated by white belligerents, a war the Negro never wanted, and I spared him the irony of pointing out his beloved Saints were quarterbacked by a white Archie Manning, the Colonel of the Aints, Toussaint said.

If the bombing of Osage Avenue taught my mother anything it was this: the North is only a longer noose than the South, so it doesn't strangulate you as quickly; but Sherman was the only white

Petrochemical Nocturne

man my father could stand, for inflicting total warfare and no mercy upon the South, for razing Atlanta, which was the Saints' archrival anyway, for the March to the Sea, for Sherman's scorched earth methods of warfare laying waste to the South and sparing churches only because he did not wish to answer for the sacrilege before God in the afterlife and because Southerners, when it was all over, would need someplace to go and ask for God's mercy, to beg forgiveness for what they had done, Toussaint said. Yes, General William Tecumseh Sherman, that was my father's kind of white man. And how happy my father would be to know that in the McKim Lobby of Boston's Copley Library, at the landing of the grand staircase over the interior courtyard, there is a small monument and dedication to Sherman and the March to the Sea at the other end of Lee Circle's vanishing point. More than Colonel Shaw, who he had to admire at least in death for being buried with Negro corpses, or General Sherman for his take-no-prisoners methods, he respected Russel L. Honoré, the Lieutenant General responsible for Joint Task Force Katrina and ultimately saving my father's hometown from the law and disorder anarchy of the diluvial edition of the Rodney King riots, or total victimization by rogue police for whom every street is an opportunity for the next Osage Avenue, itching to get a piece of the action in the next phase of the never-ending siege. It was Russel L. Honoré he would've wanted to see enshrined in stone at Lee Circle, even as the Iberville Projects took on water and there began to appear on the closed doors of his childhood those spray-painted FEMA X-codes like satanic cryptograms or extraterrestrial runes left by some civilization fleeing an occupying force, and it won't be much longer now, the dead buried in the levees are restless, before the X-codes denoting structural instability or the number of dead will mark the doors and walls of petrochemical palaces, Toussaint said.

But my father's family stories, about the enslaved persons buried beneath the Spillway or the scars on Whipped Peter's back, which at best I regarded as embellishments he picked up listening to *Radio Free Dixie*, and at worse as inventive woolgathering, were corroborated by an independent third party which happened to be a major American academic institution, which reached me first at my address in Central City, then when I would not answer their inquiries by mail, the burner phone I was then using rang, Toussaint said. It was an unfamiliar area code. I was aboard a riverboat at the time of the call, traveling again between New Orleans and Baton Rouge, and having an hour or more to kill before disembarking upriver, I answered. After conducting painstaking genealogical research, the well-spoken white-sounding representative of Georgetown University said that the Georgetown Memory Project, as it was known, concluded I was descended from the Georgetown slaves who were sold, by Jesuit priests no less, to ensure the solvency of this august institution of higher learning. It was a Sunday, maybe even Super Sunday, and downriver on the streets of New Orleans brass and bounce mixed in a musical gumbo, but aboard the riverboat the only sound was the watery rhythm of the great paddlewheel turning the river. The call's news — about enslaved persons who had been imported on this very river — somehow spooked the riverboat's mechanical operations, the paddlewheel stopping almost as soon as I got the call. I let the silence hang like a death threat on the line, resenting this attempt by the university administration to make me a slave again, Toussaint said, to dragoon me with bad memories like rusty manacles, for memories like that, encoded into the skull and crossbones and hazmat symbols of one's genome, can draw and quarter one as the rememberer is stretched and pulled in irreconcilable directions, across both banks of the river. These Georgetown enslaved persons boarded a ship named the Katharine Jackson, some white woman no doubt, bound for the Port of New Orleans and arriving in that city — the statue of General Robert E. Lee not yet on the city skyline — they were sold upriver to rice and cane and indigo plantations around Baton Rouge, Toussaint said. I have been retracing this upriver voyage on my riverboat excursions between New Orleans and Baton Rouge, under some unconscious duress or totemic, familial compulsion, following the itinerary of some outer emigration program unbeknownst to me, and it is a sign of the powerful influences of the petrochemical river deities that the call from Georgetown came when I was aboard the riverboat on one of these upriver voyages, passing at the moment of the call the district where the German Coast Uprising is said to have taken place, the rebels' heads on pikes facing the river. I have looked over the bill of sale and the ship manifest, which tabulated categories of name, age, sex, weight and height of the human cargo that passed in the autumn of 1838 through the Strait of Florida and into the waters that would later become the Gulf of Mexico Dead Zone once the petrochemical industries upriver began flushing their toxic effluvia downriver, Toussaint said. New Orleans must have been as strange and singularly mystifying to them — slaves from Maryland and Virginia — as it is to me when I return after a long time away in more mainstream places like Boston or Atlanta, cities where the happy median of Americana has whitewashed local granularities. This ship manifest is the only record of this ancestor's existence, the modest wooden cross that marked his final resting place rotted and degraded to dust long ago, maybe buried in the Spillway. The Memory Project's researchers cross-referenced the bill of sale and ship manifest with parish church records to establish the identity of a man who worked a sugar cane plantation at present-day Maringouin, which translates as mosquito, the river's bloodsuckers, a small bayou town north of Interstate 10, between Baton Rouge and Lafayette. Following the Christmas Eve explosion and my brother's irreversible incarceration in Angola, I was beginning to feel as though I were outnumbered by the legions of dead — all the names of these bygone predecessors my mother and father had passed on to me, knowing as they did the materiality of oral memory, that our people were elided from the physical records of the previous century except in a few handwritten bureaucratic slave documents, when they were recorded at all, the complexity and essence of their individuality reduced to impersonal tables of demographic data points, and it is testament to the thoroughness of the slave economy that an entire race of people could leave almost no trace except the official statistics and censuses which their enslavers kept as business records. I am not alone, after all, Toussaint said, and it was Toussaint's acute sense of his own condition as one, not alone exactly, but set apart, a *homo sacer*, that perhaps drew our respective isolative existences together, I thought. Almost three hundred slaves were sold by Georgetown to plantations across South Louisiana, Toussaint said, by now their descendants must be scattered far and wide across the river parishes, maybe a few of them escaped the plantations, disguised against the bloodhounds in the scent of onion, or in the years to come escaped Petrochemical Modernism as the state began to industrialize for the cold Black Migration cities of the North where another kind of nocturne awaited them: *Attention MOVE: this is America. You must abide by the laws of the United States of America.* All those descendants of enslaved persons fleeing the transition from the antebellum plantations to the industrial plantations, the antebellum nocturne to the petrochemical nocturne, I think of what Richard Wright, living in Paris at the time, said to an American journalist who asked him whether he would ever consider repatriating to the land of his birth, an emphatic *no* was the expat's reply, because, Wright said, he wanted his son to grow up as a human being: I realized that my brother, now an Angolan, and I had not grown up as human beings in Standard Heights, and that as long as we lived within the   petrochemical nocturne there was a chance, a very good chance that was, when I was being straight with myself, an ineluctable decision and foregone conclusion, that we would never become human beings, Toussaint said.

Because they thought it would make me a human being, or somehow atone for having not grown up as a human being, George-town offered admission and a full tuition waiver to my brother as well as myself, but after a drawn out and heightened pause, during which I thought I heard the distant warning sirens of the petro-chemical nocturne, I had to clarify to Georgetown that my brother was killed in the Angola rodeo, his ribs crushed by a bull's blunt hooves, and his skull fractured like the skull of some Cro-Magnon ice man mummy discovered in the Alps with a vicious head wound from blunt force trauma from a stone or primitive hand weapon. My brother's accident, death by bull, despite whatever Angola's cor-oner said, was no accident — my brother was just finishing what he started, suicide by cop. I was glad our mother, who had always taught us that if we did nothing else to finish what we start, did not have to see him that way, his skull bashed by bull hooves be-fore a roaring crowd of rodeo fans, and *Game Over* tattooed on his knuckles. I thought of the Green Knight's severed heads falling to Standard Heights from the bullet hole sky. I thought of the rebels' heads arrayed on pikes — a warning to would-be slave uprisings — before the river road plantations, and of the taurine paintings I'd seen, in Boston and New York of Picasso's bulls, which were not the same bulls raging from the chutes at the Angola prison rodeo.

The prison administration buried him on the prison grounds in a birch and pine coffin he made himself in the prison woodshop — Xavier had always been good with his hands, fixing things around the house when our father was gone, and so from those southern yel-low pines around the prison that seemed to both grow and decay at the same time he crafted his own coffin with the two hands tattooed with *Game Over.* The animal can still be seen today at the rodeo bucking and thrashing under the weight of convicted felons serving life sentences, Toussaint said. Xavier removed all his body hair one at a time from his body in the days before he died, as if preparing his corpse for the horse-drawn hearse, as if he knew what he was doing. His pallbearers were also serving life sentences: cop killers, fratricides, baby killers, baby momma killers. The day of the funeral, the driver of the hearse was dressed out in a black tailcoat and black top hat like a dapper emissary of death. For my brother, Martin's dream ended with a white cross in Angola's prison cemetery.

Final resting place implies too much, there is nothing final about the resting place of an Angolan, though I remember the day he was buried — family was not invited to attend — I was on the levee, a flat-topped burial like those constructed by the lost native civilization of the mound builders, the levee's dead protected the divided communities of the living from Biblical inundation and that below sea level paralysis brought on by fear of death by water, Toussaint said. While his fellow prisoners serving life sentences shoveled dirt — the rotting avocado earth — onto his handmade casket, I was watching the turbid river water spin downriver to the Dead Zone, and everything around me seemed to be either dying — it was not yet winter — or in advanced moribund states of atrophy, the daylight decomposed into the cadaver of purple-black twilight, the remnant day felt devoid of energy and matter, and I felt again the immaterial tightening and cold constriction burning around my throat, Toussaint said, as if ghost manacles were still chained there.

I felt the levee subsiding beneath me, the restive temperamental river squirming to switch paths. The transient land sinking beneath my feet, or the dead buried in the levee clawing and scratching for release. Referring to the anthropogenic, synthetic landscape which no longer dazzles us with prelapsarian innocence, man naively admires the observable hazmat happenstances of his past engineering achievements, Toussaint said, and nowhere did I feel this more acutely than on the Mississippi River levee. The river's current alignment is the truce — effected by river control structures and floodgate systems that fixed the river's movement at a particular time in its history — that was agreed upon between man and nature, and at times nature violated that agreement when the river broke through a levee, or swelled its banks and inundated a town, as in that Boisseau painting we saw of the great flood on the Mississippi, an artist's representation of death by water. Then, probably in the same stroke as the prison inmate pallbearers shoveled the first dirt onto the pine box — no open casket, for Xavier's face was too badly damaged in the rodeo accident — the bullet hole sky split in a frisson of meteorological distemper. In electric streaks and meteoric dapples the star of wormwood fell on the river and embittered its waters, possessing my soul simultaneously with awestruck horror and exultant wonderment. Grayish tombstones of thunderous clouds formed high above the levee, appearing as solid and imponderable as the stone from which General Lee in Lee Circle is cut, but evanescent in polyamorous forms before the clouds could be called by name, then smaller clouds accumulated at the base of the larger tombstones like cosmological cairns, circled by Sutton's iridescent ribbon bats, the bitter blazing light assailing the opalescent ramparts, the whole pageant swimming in tentacles of luminescent octopus floating through an ethereal aqueous grotto, the filaments of dying daylight burnished in a brownish blood-orange omelet on the river's rimpled surface. And then as the last shovelful was heaved in place, Xavier's hands with the *Game Over* tattoo crossed on his chest, the sun fell dark — a fist around a candlelight. The night smoldered, fuliginous and disenfranchised to the last vinegary star, till a monstrous moon like a white orchid bloomed on the restless, shifting river. Hesperides was preparing a homecoming for my brother on the Islands of the Blessed.

The phone call from Georgetown came around the time my tattoo of *The 54th* was just beginning to heal, Toussaint said. I refused Georgetown's offer of free tuition, of course, I did not want this peculiar institution's administrative pity or researched condescension; instead, I told the university to donate my tuition to the American Civil Liberties Union or the Society for Threatened Peoples and the Cloud Appreciation Society. Then I had Whipped Peter's scarred back reproduced in blackest ink on my own back. At first the tattoo artist, a virtuoso in the local tattoo scene of the Seventh Ward who took the same craftsman-like care my brother brought to bear in fashioning his own pinewood prison coffin, would not agree to this design until I told him the whip-scarred man in the black and white photograph was a distant relative. How distant? he asked. Not distant enough, I said, not so distant that I cannot feel the whiplash occasionally. It was important for me, I told the tattoo artist, Toussaint said, to feel the whip in the needle, to never lose the fire in the belly, to never fully extinguish the righteous flames of the obsidional event on Osage Avenue. The tattoo artist declined payment for his work but would not let me leave his studio — photos of his complete oeuvre on the walls: creaking slave ships, meandering profiles of the river like an ancient and leviathan tapeworm, cryptic diagrams and unknown symbolisms — till I promised to return, after the healing, so he could photograph my back for his portfolio: I too would become image, like Whipped Peter. My back bled profusely and the bandages filled with blood, splashing the bedsheets like Fred Hampton's mattress. I had to sleep on my stomach. Because the whip lashings were tattooed on my back I could not see them and after a time, Toussaint said, they healed and I forgot all about them, till taking my shirt off one hot day on Royal Street I heard gasps of horror from tourists. Whipped Peter's keloid scars tattooed on my back — more eloquent than any slave narrative told by a ventriloquist dummy, Toussaint said.

The slave narrative, the self-alienated structure of which I discerned in every family story told by my father and mother, is complemented by all the colonial travel narratives penned by white European explorers and derring-do navigators as they mapped the West Indies and the New World, and it was this mapping process itself, simplifying here, abridging there, that allowed them to hegemonize all the native tribes in Standard Heights' street names, for it was a New World only to those who worshipped a pale monotheistic god and misbelieved that bolls or blossoms of sheep — yes, sheep like those flocculent white icons of innocence and ovine herd mentality — grew on the cotton plant encountered in South America. But it was an old world to those who had been here since before the time the Dead Sea Scrolls were sealed inside clay jars in a cave, since before their god was crucified on a cross, since before Columbus mistook manatees for mermaids in the Caribbean Sea, since before the first note of the petrochemical nocturne, Toussaint said. Growing up on the streets named for vanished tribes: all narratives are captivity narratives, the slave narrative being a specialized department of captivity, Toussaint said. Love stories and ghost stories — all captivity narratives. When a black man is held from birth — or even before birth in the skull and crossbones chromosomes of his enslaved mother and enslaved father who may not yet know one another, who may have completed the transatlantic voyage on different ships, sold to different Master Hammonds on distant plantations — in the thrall-dom of the peculiar institution (a euphemistic coat of sugar if ever there was one, escaping this peculiar institution, often as an old man, only by some clever chicanery or white man's blessing, the emancipation coming as the result of the reluctant agreements and unreconstructed handshakes — hands have not been shaken like that since — between white men, the 54th's valiant contributions to the war efforts notwithstanding), it is called *Narrative of the Life of Frederick Douglass, an American Slave* or *Incidents in the Life of a Slave Girl* or, and in a slightly more picaresque, swashbuckling Huck Finn mode, *A Narrative of Adventures and Escape of Moses Roper from American Slavery*. When a white man is held in bondage or captivity, deprived of his autonomy by pagan savages and godless cannibals, it is called the *True Story and Description of a Country of Wild, Naked, Grim, Man-eating People in the New World, America*, a gag reflex title utterly devoid of even a trace of irony. These travelogues are read today, when they're read at all, by human tapeworms who reside in a self-pitying ruin in their own little private Idahos. The Christians who believed in the literal consumption of the blood and flesh of a god in their communion ritual were hypocritically appalled by this country of wild, naked and grim pygmy anthropophagites, the same Christians who gave Jeffrey Dahmer a chance in the world, Toussaint said.

Two specimens of captivity narrative: one by death mask whites about the tapeworm in their souls, the other also by death mask whites, more often than not, but with the parasitic narrative voice passing first through a black mask, much as my going public with my family history to you — the Spillway, Whipped Peter, the Christmas Eve explosion, my brother's failed suicide by cop, the Curse of the Saints, the Green Book — distorts my narrative voice even as it is told, Toussaint said. My brother had a Halloween mask of some white president or other, Nixon or Reagan, I don't remember exactly which, a white man in a suit at any rate, but the mask looked like the men who I imagined sat on the boards of supercorporations and prisons, the ones running the ExxonMobil plant where my father worked. You know the type, Toussaint said. The mask itself, when my brother wore it, never terrified me so much as when he removed the mask, thereby shattering the illusion of complete identity, and the unnerving appearance of my brother's dark, suicide by cop face emerging beneath that malign and wicked white mask sent me screaming out the front door in the direction of the river — without thinking, of course, for growing up in Baton Rouge one knew instinctually the polymorphic river's whereabouts even if blindfolded, that metallic tincture in the air was unmistakable, the river could move from one side of the nocturne to the other and I would still know its location, as if I carried the river in my own bloodstream. But one ran to the river banks in vain, one was not going to jump into that roiling brown gumbo, filled with petrochemical trash, corpses of the drowned Phoenician sailor, catastrophic alligators, crucifixion driftwood, undrinkable wormwood, the Mississippi River bridge burnt against the sky like a black harp, the river flowing to the Dead Zone and coursing between my bones and sinews as my very own blood, the guns of the Battle of Baton Rouge aimed at my back, Toussaint said. No, crossing the river, even with one's maniacal brother taunting you in a ghastly white death mask, laughing like a possessed jackal through the rubbery mouth of Reagan or the Great White Hope, was not going to happen no matter how scared I was. Even before the Christmas Eve explosion I felt the river rattling the bars of its cage, bristling at the confines of its prison. The pelican's plaint for the Dead Zone, and the ibis' broken clarinet notes threading dissonantly in the nocturne. White death mask or not, one turned away from the river, that watery abyss which knew one by name since birth, which knew every petrochemical symbol in my genome, and the malignant white mask — no longer on my brother's face — was waiting for me, a silent and eyeless face on the kitchen table next to a casserole cooling in the benzene breeze from a window that should not have been open, Toussaint said.

By the time I met Toussaint, on the levee that day in Baton Rouge, most of his tattooing was complete and the black Whipped Peter ink had healed, though I had no reason to believe he would ever stop, for he seemed to use the surface of his body as a riposte to all those captivity narratives, his skin a palimpsest text that could never be completed, telling a captivity narrative over which he had total control. He returned to the tattoo artist in Tremé, this time to cover himself in schematic process flow diagrams — the crude oil distillation units, the naphtha hydrotreaters, the catalytic reformers, the isomerization unit, the amine gas treater, the fluid catalytic cracker, the hydrocracker, the visbreaker and delayed coker, all the critical components that might have malfunctioned in the Christmas Eve explosion — all coordinated with stylized arrows of directional flow with inputs and outputs between the process units. Before the schematic process flow diagrams were fully healed, he had moved on to having his body inked in the arcana of chemical symbols — the skull and crossbones and the human hand burned by corrosive liquid — like the hazmat trucks transporting flammable and corrosive substances through the native streets of Standard Heights. His palimpsest skin was writing a petrochemical counternarrative, twitching like the river in its levee manacles. And then, on the inside of his lip, the word *MOVE*, for the organization that was the intended target of the Siege of Osage Avenue. Toussaint's body was a graphic spokening of other strange phrases: *open casket* encircling his neck, *YXV* on his chest, the word *worm* on the knuckles of one hand and *wood* on the other. *Thou Shall Not* printed on his ribcage. The Green Book addresses of homes and hotels friendly to traveling Negroes tattooed on his feet. The street plan for Standard Heights reproduced in miniature on his torso, native street names on his ribs. *Sub umbra floreo* lettering the curve of his wrist, the colorful looping skeins of the Fisk river maps flowing in flailing entrails through the smoking ruins of Osage Avenue; a spidery Saints' fleur-de-lis and the chemical formula for petroleum. Toussaint's skin was so dark that in muted, crepuscular light — as often in the chlorine fog and tenebrous miasmas of the river delta winter, or in the dark clinical grotto of an autopsy theater in Charity Hospital — the skin-text of these tattoos, the cabalistic schema of petrochemical processes at work on his body were all but inscrutable, indecipherable glyphs, invisible, like prehistoric drawings on the walls of a lightless cave that has never been exposed to torchlight.

Charity Hospital

I must have been walking south on Tulane Avenue, drawn perforce towards the river, musing over certain poignant or illustrative passages in General Sherman's memoirs — "I intend to make Georgia howl" — that struck a nerve in me, towards the crumbling Art Deco masterpiece of Charity Hospital, now a ghost of a building, designed by Weiss, Dreyfous & Seiferth — the same architects who designed the Louisiana State Capitol tower in Baton Rouge, visible from the unopened windows of Toussaint's family home. Tulane Avenue is not much to see, a rundown commercial corridor that may never have had better days, connecting downtown to the lakeside districts. Storyville streetwalkers and moonlight hustlers. I had been coming this way, by the ghost of Charity Hospital, for some time now, sensing that the condemned hospital had more of Toussaint's narrative to reveal to me. I passed the makeshift melancholy homeless encampment gathered beneath the Claiborne Expressway like refugees of the Zone in *Stalker*, castaways of a storm that never seems to pass. His form and silhouette were unmistakable, and I recognized at once it was Toussaint on the sidewalk in front of Charity Hospital, the only person, of all the passersby, who stopped to revive a painful architectural memory most would rather see destroyed and forgotten.

My father lay in his hospital bed, gazing dispiritedly — for what other mien is possible in the uncharitable rooms of Charity Hospital? — out of the gray window of his twelfth floor room watching the daily progress of the Superdome's cursed construction, Toussaint said pointing a finger at the high window he meant, though I doubted whether Toussaint, perhaps as a very young boy, an infant of the river even, had been in the hospital room with his father while he recovered from some mysterious industrial injury incurred at the ExxonMobil plant, one of many accidents before the ultimate Christmas Eve explosion. We did not have the money for a local hospital in Baton Rouge, he said, the industrial accident having affected his hearing, for a while he heard nothing, just distant tones and muffled bells, the pelican's plaint and the ibis' broken clarinet, the egret's elegy, the southern oaks' doleful saxophone, then the accident causing him to hear the unremitting warning sirens of the petrochemical nocturne and nothing else, Toussaint said.

While I am the first — and certainly not the last — to admit that the historiographic methods deployed in the service of presenting this account of Toussaint's life have not been orthodox, I knew that the Superdome had been constructed before the fourth opening of the Spillway in April, 1973, and that an eyewitness memory was not possible, even in a place like Louisiana where time feels as fluid as Fisk's rivers, though it was equally true that his father had so many industrial accidents at the plant in the years before the Christmas Eve explosion that it was impossible to disentangle one accident that caused hearing loss from another accident that made one cough up blood through the frowning mouth of a baghead; to distinguish an accident that caused one's bloodstream to flow in reverse from an accident that caused one's skin to boil as if thrown into a superheated cauldron. Thus, it was the dating of the construction of the sports stadium — an event I could independently fix in time — in which the Curse of the Saints would spread its voodoo over the black and gold, that compelled me to the realization that Toussaint had heard about this industrial injury of his father's secondhand from his mother, or maybe some third source I had yet to uncover. Indeed, the layers of ventriloquism threatened to drown my voice in the infrastructure of cacophony, like howling into the floodwaters of the Spillway opening in the spring.

From Tulane Avenue, the gothic mass of Charity Hospital — for the first thing one noticed at street level was the hospital's solemn and imponderable mass — towered above us like a nightmare transubstantiated into pteropine architectural form. As evening began palling over the city, though the building was supposed to be without power since Katrina, a light came on in the twelfth floor window like that glowing in Turner's painted tower, the very hospital window which, following the vector of Toussaint's finger into space, I had thought he indicated as the window from which his father observed the daily progress of the Superdome's construction, except that the Superdome is on the upriver side of Charity Hospital and Tulane Avenue, where we now stood in the palmy shadows, was on the downriver side of the eerie hospital, though this is a city in which structures as large as Charity Hospital or the Superdome have been known to sail up and downriver, kaleidoscoping on a supernatural temporal oxbow.

The hospital was poorly secured and evidence abounded of trespass and habitation by the area's homeless population. I followed Toussaint through a hole in the security fencing where other trespassers had preceded us and helped him ripped a loose sheet of plywood from a lower window. I felt like we were pulling bandages off an old wound that was now open and exposed, the eye in the Hand in Eye Motif blinking as I followed Toussaint into the ground floor of the abandoned hospital. The complex organic stench of mold, ghoulish decay, human and animal fecal matter, urea, mildew, and chemicals assaulted us like nothing I've smelled before or since. Olfactory warfare. Breathing through my mouth, I followed Toussaint, who seemed to know where he was going, down a long dark hall, the walls tiled in clinical light blue and wan institutional green. Paint peeled from the walls like dead skin, a curling and papery integument. On the ground floors, we made out in the murky blue anti-light the various rising waterlines marking flood stages like the geological strata recording prehistoric cataclysmic events. In the sepsis of labyrinthine hallways, I heard the riderless horse galloping down the bloodless veins of the hospital, the egret's elegy and the ibis' broken clarinet playing through the hospital loudspeakers. We wandered the hospital's many rooms, desolate and friendless places cluttered with intravenous poles and gurneys, surgical supplies, blood slides, labs of glass beakers and test tubes. A ping pong table and football in a room where trapped patients and residents entertained themselves, awaiting rescue. Mountains of furniture in manic disarray as after a global struggle. The floodwaters had moved heavy medical machinery and equipment from their wonted places, tossed them about like paper boats on a rising and incensed Mississippi. Scrawled in black marker on a nurse's communications whiteboard: *Fuck Katrina.* In the Infectious Disease Unit, a long desk sagging in the middle beneath the weight of so many microscopes, and in the pathology lab carts full of biomedical samples, preserved biopsies and body parts floating in jars and plastic containers. A room populated by anatomical skeletons and CPR dummies, the headless and limbless torsos of white victims to be saved from drowning by resuscitation, as Toussaint's ancestors buried beneath the Spillway were not.

We found ourselves in the hospital's maternity ward, the first place many New Orleanians saw upon entering the world, and for many it did not get much better from here. I thought I heard the urgent, motherless crying of an infant down the hall, but it was just the lamentations of the wind through an open window.

I was born here, Toussaint said, in the maternity ward of Charity Hospital, and later as a grown man spent a few heavily medicated days and nights in the psychiatric ward, talking to the spectral figures who came and went in my room but who were not accessible or visible to the doctors and nurses who brought me the wormwood-tasting food I refused or fed me colored pills. In the night, I sweated wormwood like a man thrown in a cauldron of boiling water. The doctors and nurses who had not been born in this hospital could not see or speak to Charles Deslondes and Whipped Peter, but I could, Toussaint said, or the two student protestors killed on Southern's campus, the crewmen of d'Iberville's upriver voyage into the red stick territory, the drowned Phoenician sailor, the chorus of antique voices echoing off the hard walls of the ward in which minds driven mad by the petrochemical nocturne have been lost.

Since its desertion in 2005, and the failed attempt to reopen it, Charity Hospital grows its own flora and fauna, an ecosystem unto itself, I realized. Birds have passed the seeds of fruit trees and other plants, and those seeds in turn germinate in the hospital's cracks and crannies, the habitat for raccoons and feral cats and the millions of mice scratching at the walls. Charity Hospital was prudently ruled by a sapient, hierophant owl, the apex predator who feeds on the rats, mice, cats and raccoons. The biota of the swamp: white ibis, roseate spoonbill, whooping crane, brown pelicans, pink flamingos — all had found habitat in Charity Hospital, seeking refuge from a changing climate and the rotting planetoid fruit, the sieges waged against them by the oil companies in the swamps. It was as if the animals were starting the natural experiment over without us. The rooms of Charity Hospital ransacked by wind or a violent stampede of mastodons, everything tangled in a luxated chaos, but the wind is not done with this place yet, it never is. Even now, the Exxon-Mobil plant is tinkering and prototyping experimental winds of velocities more violent than anything seen in Category 5, which will be too slow, too modest for the storms of the future. The colorized categories of the Saffir-Simpson Scale would have to be increased to measure the wind speeds of the petrochemical storms of the future, I thought, the hydrocarbon hurricanes and the benzene brimstone.

Wait here, Toussaint said, entering the room ahead of me. I waited in the hallway for some time, watching the wind scatter leaves down the corridor, then Toussaint reappeared, silently signaling for me to enter. In the maternity room where Toussaint said he was born — I do not know how he knew the room, but his mother must have told him — there grew a mature satsuma tree resplendent with orange globes of fruit hanging pendulously from thin branches like glowing lanterns. Toussaint plucked a satsuma from the tree and began to peel the skin from the globes of fruit, the fresh zesty orange summer fragrance commixing with the hospital's leprous and autumnal stench.

My mother forbade me to eat of Standard Heights' satsuma tree, Toussaint said, she said they were poisoned, or that eating the fruit of the satsuma would cause some catastrophe to befall us like the evil fruit in the garden of Eden, and my father, to teach me a lesson I would never forget, made me pick as many satsumas as I could carry, then peel and eat a satsuma, one at a time, until I was physically sick of satsumas and could not endure to eat another, Toussaint said, my stomach bloated with Standard Heights satsumas. But he did not relent and I ate satsumas until I was heaving up orange bile into the yard behind the house while my father looked on and, when I was done vomiting, he said, you won't eat of that satsuma tree ever again now you got your fill, and that winter Standard Heights had a record-breaking hard freeze that bejeweled the satsuma in icicles like frosty white daggers dangling from the branches. When the wind blew the icicles sang like wind chimes. Blackbirds and stray dogs ate the satsuma bile in the yard, and I never picked fruit from the satsuma tree again, Toussaint said, hurling the satsuma he'd picked through the open hospital window.

Toussaint went over to the window of the delivery room, framing the same vantage of the city his father would have seen the day Toussaint was born, had his father been present at the birth, as he was not, Toussaint confided. The window of his birth room was fractured into myriad pieces, the glass broken by storm winds but not shattered, as the glass had not yet fallen from the frame, but remained suspended in a frozen attitude of perpetual disintegration, cracking and splintering the city beyond the windowpane into countless fragments, an image not unlike that phantasmagoric nightmare he saw when he first violated his father's prohibition against opening the windows facing the plant. MRI brain scans stuck to the window for viewing against the sunlight. Toussaint removed the scan of brain images, held them to the last light, this translucent image of the frail structure of a human brain like the skull of smiling clown, and let them fall to the floor. It could've been the brain scan of anyone, an Angolan prison rodeo rider, a cop, the Green Knight's severed head, Charles Deslondes, or the melancholy man on the suicide hotline billboard.

My mother was from Prichard, Toussaint said, as he pieced together the cracked city through the fragmented windowpane, his voice echoing in the maternity ward, but her people's people came from Africatown, and those people's people before them hailed from somewhere in West Africa, Toussaint said looking out the window at the fragmented city. She remembered the old, dark women whose hair was bloody from ticks, speaking some pidgin of their native language and slave English, their strange though plausible beliefs, and their remembrances told of the last illegal shipment of enslaved persons to this country. Her great-great-grandfather, Kossola, though no longer living by the time my mother was born, renamed Cudjo Kazoola Lewis by some Master Hammond who could not pronounce his African name, Toussaint said. If a white man at that time could not pronounce the native term for something, a place name or a proper name, the indigenous name of a river or valley, he simply renamed it to his liking, a word that made sense to him and no one else. The Atlantic slave trade had been illegal since 1808, but in the 1860s as the need for more labor increased to keep pace with agricultural production and the demand for cotton, especially on the river plantations that later became so many haunted houses in Cancer Alley, affluent slaveholders of Mobile began to illicitly import slaves from West Africa, and that small, terrified contingent aboard the slave ship *Clotilda* brought with them their native customs, their rituals, their kinship systems, their superstitions — the ethnogenesis of Africatown, Toussaint said. No glittering metropolis, Africatown was at least free and the bloodhounds did not go there. The air around Telegraph Road, Toussaint said, where my mother was born, is mephitic and fraught with the stench of paper mills, and Africatown's children, what Cudjo's master would have called *pickaninnies*, played naked in lifeless Three Mile Creek, which was the Devil's Swamp Lake of Prichard. Above the waste of dead or dying pines the shadows of suicide hotline billboards, sun-faded and peeling at the edges like the painted walls of Charity Hospital, messaging sanitized and scarcely credible hope for the next world and the hereafter in random Bible verses in giant screaming fonts and the halfhearted sense that life in Africatown was more than just bad luck. I wanted to know the kinship structures of Africatown, to which moieties my mother belonged, Toussaint said turning away from the spider-cracked window and pacing the hospital delivery room as if expecting a child himself. I could scarcely imagine that a child had been born in this gloomy and faded room, in which the serpents of Fisk's river slept and dreamt the next Spillway opening.

The illegal trade that trafficked my mother's people into an unknown and hostile country was thoroughly planned, Toussaint said, in every detail, no less than the Siege of Osage Avenue or the buyouts of the black-owned family homes in Standard Heights. The *Clotilda* lay in wait behind deserted sandy islands of the Mississippi Sound, avoiding the vigilance of patrol boats that scouted the waters for pirates and slave smugglers violating the law, and the *Clotilda*'s mast was cut down to further elude detection. Three days the slave ship waited for the tug that was arranged to meet them. The tug pilot, according to sources, was attending a church service, bowing his head in prayer with closed eyes, when news of the illicit ship's arrival reached him, the news conveyed by a slave who had been born in this country, as much an American as Cudjo was not, Toussaint said with some ironic annotation. How to come to terms with this: that the pilot of the tug which assisted the *Clotilda* through the complex estuary of shallow, slow-moving serpentine rivers that feed into Mobile Bay, was beckoned by a slave for whom Africa was merely a distant mythic land which the older slaves talked about longingly and with heavy sighs. A place an American slave could scarcely believe existed, Toussaint said, no more than someone from the river's east bank could believe in the west bank. And the barrier islands behind which the *Clotilda* hid are today developed with pastel beach condos and happy vacation homes, periodically destroyed by hurricanes and rebuilt on higher and higher stilts, because they have not sufficiently learned to fear death by water, Toussaint said.

Although not documented, the ship probably sheltered behind the wind-sculpted dunes of Dauphin Island, the closest and largest island, tad-pole shaped, then defended by Fort Gaines, whence comes our expression: *damn the torpedoes, full speed ahead!* from the Battle of Mobile Bay, Toussaint said, the motto of the cops in the slow motion dream speed police chase. I have stood in the salted sea breeze on the outer ramparts of this crumbling stellated fortress overlooking Mobile Bay and the Gulf of Mexico, waiting for the chlorine gas ghost ships to pull through the bay. From Fort Gaines, looking east across the mouth of the Bay, the mirage of Fort Morgan, the masonry pentagonal bastion fort on Mobile Point, delicately shimmers a few feet above the lapping green water, though at the time of the *Clotilda*'s illicit odyssey the oil rigs that presently blot the horizon were not yet drilling beneath the sea like gothic pipe organs playing the opening minor blasts of the petrochemical nocturne. An illicit slave ship passing between Fort Gaines and Fort Morgan to enter Mobile Bay would have been a prime target for the guns positioned to defend the bay from attack, Toussaint said. The tug and the *Clotilda,* that strange hybrid pair, averted the main shipping channel of the Mobile River, slipping silently by lighthouses — that cycloptic lamplight scanning the dark waters for anything untoward — and into the lesser Spanish River. At Twelve Mile Island the tug docked and, with the ship's lights off on a moonless, swampy night, the ship's enslaved cargo was transferred to a steamboat that completed the rest of the voyage up the Alabama River. Cudjo and his tribesmen felt with their naked feet for the first time the strange soil of a plantation south of a little town — still languishing on the map today — called Mount Vernon, the slaves passing somewhere in the vicinity of Ellicott's Stone, a survey monument of the 31st parallel north latitude, the demarcation line between the Mississippi Territory of the United States and Spanish West Florida, for ever since his arrival on this continent the death mask white Europeans have been surveying and laying down the net of invisible lines mapping out the territory of Petrochemical Modernism. Today, the stone is contained by a rectangular cage or fence, so the stone cannot escape the bloodhounds, victim of our penchant for imprisoning everything which does not speak our language, Toussaint said. Cudjo and the other slaves kept quiet in the woods, exposed to the Alabama rain and the light of a sun which somehow had been brighter in Africa, until buyers could reach the secluded plantation — as illicit cargo, Cudjo was not sold on a public auction block — some were sold to plantations in Selma, but Cudjo stayed behind and, until the Civil War, worked the grounds of the plantation around Mount Vernon Arsenal; here Geronimo and Apache Indians, on their way to warn the Osage of the coming siege, were imprisoned in the barracks after Geronimo surrendered to American authorities. The Arsenal later became the Mount Vernon Hospital for the Colored Insane, where many of the cargo's afterbears ended their lives in madness and the despair of deracination. On Halloween in 2012, the hospital closed, abandoned like the fortresses defending Mobile Bay and overwrought with devouring green miles of vines and kudzu, Toussaint said, as if everything — the forts, Charity Hospital, the Iberville Projects, Standard

Heights — were built to be abandoned.

The slaves were transported up the Mobile River by riverboat, Toussaint said, and Captain Foster set fire to the *Clotilda*, in order to sink it in Mobile Bay, and destroy any evidence of their illicit agreement, and in destroying the *Clotilda* Captain Foster destroyed more than just a ship, indeed Captain Foster could not comprehend the full scope of what he destroyed as he dropped a torch on the hay bales and kerosene-soaked deck of the slave ship, and the enslaved persons of Mobile watched the ship which had brought them to this strange land and any hope of ever returning to their homeland burn in Mobile Bay. And who was Clotilda, the mysterious woman for whom this burned slave ship was named? I imagined some feminine monster such as the Delphine LaLaurie, holding slaves captive in her Royal Street mansion, practicing cannibalism and torture and every sadistic cruelty which has ever depraved the invisibly manacled mind of Master Hammond. In fact, Toussaint said, the slave ship *Clotilda* was named in honor of the second wife of the Frankish King, Clovis I; the cult of Saint Clotilda exalting her as the patron of queens, widows, brides and exiles — why must ships of slaves be named for white women? As if the white feminine ship carried black bodies in bondage in her own belly, capturing them on the fecund and familiar shores of one continent, gestating them through the horrors of the Middle Passage, and birthing them upon the savage shores of an alien world. A ship so named, for white royalty, for the mothers of Master Hammond. Captain Foster must have believed he was destroying the evidence of his own misdeeds and protecting the plantation conspirators from prosecution by federal carpetbaggers, because today's criminal justice system is just a reprise of the antebellum one: the federal court case *U.S. v. Byrnes Meaher, Timothy Meaher, and John Dabey* failed to convict the slavers for lack of evidence — the slave ship seen burning in Mobile Bay was insufficient evidence of malfeasance — and the case against Captain Foster and his co-conspirators was dismissed. While she never stopped remembering the day, my mother said in her deadpan reportage — the I've-seen-it-all realism of a Standard Heights mother — that she saw, as a little girl, before the family left behind the Colored Entrances and followed the North Star to Osage Avenue, the *Clotilda* docked in the Port of Mobile, and that trustworthy Africatown elders saw it too, Toussaint said turning away from the fractured window now to pace the hospital room from window to wall, wall to window and back again, like someone held against his will in the cargo hold of a slave ship, sailing into some hostile and unknown territory.

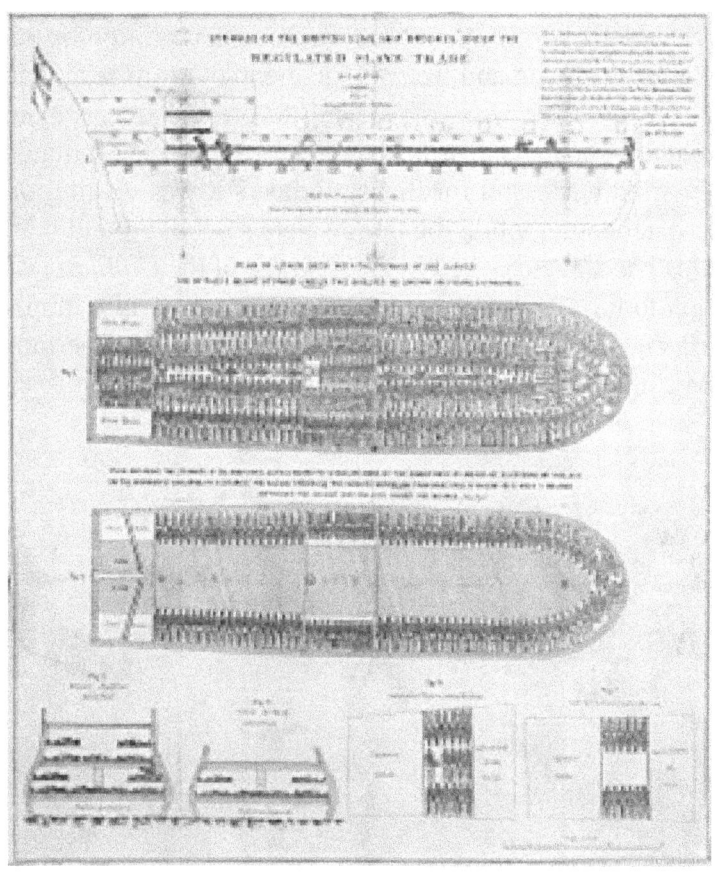

As soon as the captives debouched from the cargo hold of the ship, a dark and fetid floating dungeon, they set foot on the state of Alabama, their new home, and the bloodhounds immediately took note. All of this is a matter of course, but the worst sea journey white people have ever experienced, aside from the vacation cruises decimated by norovirus outbreaks and the failed sanitation systems that send raw sewage overflowing into luxury ocean liners, was pho-to-documented in Alfred Stieglitz's *The Steerage*: a black and white photo of ghostly passengers from the lower-class section of an ocean liner, and while it may be tempting to suppose these travelers are embarking on the famed immigrant's experience typified by the passage through Ellis Island, Toussaint said, in fact they are leaving America to return to Europe, either turned away by immigration officials or because they did not like what they found in this immiserated, patch-work country, so they left, as Cudjo could not. And while the New World represented economic opportunity and social mobility for the immigrants of Italy, Poland and Ireland, the menu of promises made to the tired, poor, huddled masses yearning to breathe free, for the slaves shanghaied aboard ships the New World was bloodhounds and a whip-scarred back, and for their afterbears it was waiting on your roof for a helicopter while the floodwaters rose all around you, Toussaint said. The slaves packed in the steerage of the *Clotilda* had no such option to turn back to their homeland like the white immi-grants aboard *The Steerage*, for them the Old World died the mo-ment they saw the first alien slave ship on their shores.

As Toussaint's pace quickened from one side of the hospital room to the other, and we both sensed some lurching or starboard listing in the floor, I summoned upon the fractured glass of the hospital windowpane the beautiful but terrifying maritime painting of J.M.W. Turner's *The Slave Ship.* Turner's painting depicts the *Zong* massacre of one hundred and thirty-three African slaves drowned at sea, as was common practice when ships ran low on supplies, while in the distance, behind the ship's masts and the resplendent painterly sunset are the ExxonMobil plant's smokestacks and cooling towers, manufacturing toxic chlorine clouds that floated across the Atlantic and settled over Standard Heights. The drowning slaves are as close to the foreground of this horrific painting as Toussaint was to me, still nervously pacing the floor of the hospital room, the floor now listing towards the hospital's port side, as if we were aboard a vessel in a violent storm, Toussaint almost manic now in the measure of his movements and the rapid pace of his storytelling, as if trying to hurry through to the end in case he was interrupted or we drowned in the wormwood floodwaters he must have felt rising around us.

The *Clotilda*'s enslaved persons settled a community outside of Prichard, on land owned by the planters who brought them here, calling it Africatown, Toussaint said. A continent became a town.

After the Three-Fifths Compromise, Cudjo's people became three-fifths human. Fractionally, they had two more fifths to go, but these fifths are measured in whiplashes and Christmas Eve explosions. After Emancipation, when Union soldiers informed him of his new free status, Cudjo and his fellow Africans — Toussaint was very clear on this point: his mother insisted they were not African-Americans — wished desperately to return to their native country in Africa, somewhere in Yorubaland, which could have been modern Nigeria, Togo, Benin, or Sierra Leone, but reboarding the *Clotilda*, like the passengers in *The Steerage*, now that the slave ship had been burned, was as impossible as reversing the Middle Passage, so Cudjo and the other enslaved persons worked for the men who brought them to this continent, forming a self-governing tribe based on a chief and the ministrations of a medicine man, their own leadership and healthcare. Cudjo, the boy who in Africa trained as a warrior and hunter now became a sexton in the Baptist church, introducing into the local Protestantism a syncretism of Yoruba cosmology and the holy-rolling of the Southern Baptists. Sometimes when the scarlet of dawn frosted the treetops in a light reminiscent of the Old World, Prichard metamorphosed in Cudjo's mind into the traditional town of his childhood, the shotgun shacks becoming again the straw huts he lived in, before a rival tribe of the Kingdom of Dahomey stormed the town, defended by palisaded gates, and he looked away in immitigable horror from the blank gaze of severed heads hanging from the belts of the invading warriors who, having accepted the Green Knight's challenge, sold Cudjo and his people to Captain Foster. Though a warrior himself, Cudjo did not resist the forced march through the barbecue smoke of his tribe's slow-smoked severed heads to the barracoons on the coast. He heard the cruel waters crashing on the shores before he saw the ocean, like the infinite sighing of a global sea monster, Cudjo had never before seen the Atlantic Ocean, that watery highway of empire's dreams he was about to cross to a distant land called Alabama, Toussaint said. Foster hand-selected one hundred and thirty slaves, sixty-five men and sixty-five women, balancing the sexes like a population manager at the outset of a bold experiment in human genetics, and while the human cargo was transported to the *Clotilda* in several crude native boats rowed by Dahomey youth, Foster combed the African coast with a spyglass, taking in of that alien nature only what conformed to the nature of his mind. Through the spyglass he saw a treacherous black flag run up the crude ships of the rival tribe that had sold Cudjo and his kinsmen to the *Clotilda*'s investors. Foster knew what the black flag portended: the Dahomey warriors intended to retake the slaves and hold Foster and his men for ransom, but an American slave ship was too fleet for the rainstorm of arrows that splashed down on the Atlantic in sharpened arcs from the shoreline. Eventually, the human cargo was brought on deck to stretch their limbs, adjusting their eyes from the captive darkness of the cargo hold to the Atlantic sunlight, and Cudjo saw all about him for the first time the laughing, mocking waters and the strange salt of the open sea, Toussaint said looking towards the center of the hurricane-destroyed maternity ward room in which he was born. Cudjo outlived everyone taken captive on that slave ship, witnessing for himself the slaughterous horrors wrought by industrial capitalism's First World War, and then the financial system's total worldwide collapse, until on the 26th of July, 1935, Cudjo embarked on the next phase of the cycle of familial and lineal rebirth posited by the Yoruba people, Toussaint said, the last man of Africatown waiting for the impossible resurrection with Whipped Peter and Charles Deslondes and my father on the west bank of Fisk's river.

Everything my mother said about her Africatown roots was confirmed by Zora Neale Hurston's ethnographic fieldwork in Mobile, which my father could have read for himself, as Zora knew she had to keep Cudjo's oral history from falling into the hands of the slave narrative ventriloquists and the white folklorists who came down south plundering the living remains of Africatown's collective memory, just as Captain Foster and his slave ship crew had plundered their bodies from the Old World, and I can only imagine what Zora would think about me telling all the petrochemical secrets of Standard Heights to you, Toussaint said. Hurston, I knew, had painstakingly transcribed Cudjo's slave narrative in an oral vernacular that, to readers of modern standardized English is in places nearly incomprehensible. Will you make me incomprehensible? Toussaint asked. But even in the family these stories of the Old World were treated like fables, my father never believed any of what my mother told of her people's people, that they were the last slaves, stolen from West Africa, captured by a cabal of Master Hammonds. For a man who had never been outside of the Mississippi River's flood zones,

Africatown didn't exist, it was a tragi-comic melodramatic folktale, like the ancient apologues with talking animals, she told herself so she wouldn't have to be another little black girl from Prichard, Alabama whose people fled for the North and were bombed out of their homes, as if Osage Avenue and West Philadelphia were just another rice village of Viet Cong in Vietnam, questioning everything which she presented as no more questionable than the engineering and the chemistry of the ExxonMobil plant were to him, my Doubting Thomas of a father even going so far as to question the Siege of Osage Avenue, an event which for my mother was an incontrovertible fact no more mootable than the color of the sky above the river or the fixed positions of the bitter bullet hole stars, Toussaint said. The truth was an iffy triangulated battleground between them on which they grappled for supremacy. He had never been to Alabama or to Mobile, and neither did he believe Mobile's spurious claims to be the inventor of Mardi Gras, a cultural innovation which he would never allow bogarters from Alabama to take away from him, Toussaint said. For all my father knew Africa too was another canard of the white man, a mythical homeplace concocted to make us into African-Americans, hyphenated hybrid beings, neither African nor American, but least of all the legends presented with the probity of memoirs she told, often while washing dishes or hanging clothes on the line after the washing machine he bought her broke, did he believe that she saw, with her own eyes the *Clotilda* slave ship docked in the Port of Mobile when it was confirmed by professional historians to be rotting at the bottom of Mobile Bay, where it belonged, my father said. Just to get under her skin and make her doubt the testimony of her own senses, he went so far as to one day, wearing a paper baghead after yet another tragicomic Saints loss, call the Mobile Public Library and the Mobile Historical Society to have these respective public institutions double-check and authenticate my mother's claims, the Mobile Public Library telling my father, in the wake of his loss, what he least wanted to hear: that there were uncorroborated reports circulating in the community of the slave ship docking in the Port of Mobile, as recently as that very hurricane season, but that the *Clotilda* was, in all likelihood, at Mobile Bay's bottom where historians said it was, sinking after Captain Foster torched the evidence of his crime, Toussaint said, but my father, who demanded tactile evidence as proof of things unseen, never let my mother forget that the slave ship has not been found, Toussaint said, though archaeologists have scoured the waters around Twelve Mile Island searching for the submerged remains of this ghost slave ship, for the drowned evidence of things unseen.

In our era of fake news, Toussaint said, one must be ever vigilant against the rude intrusion of opportunistic hyperbole, mendacious metaphor, and partisan perfidies. I too have been momentarily hoodwinked by the persuasive verisimilitude of fake news, taken in by its seductive alternate reality, and believed in miracles. Without at first knowing it, I once read a fabricated news story in the *Jackson Telegraph*, which does not exist, about an alleged mass grave of tortured African-American men unearthed on the property of a former Klansman outside of Jackson, Mississippi. On first blush, such an atrocity — a racialized series of murders in rural Mississippi dating back to the Klan era — does not strike one as altogether implausible, does it? Lynchings no doubt occurred in Mississippi and throughout the South, and most of them remain unsolved, their perpetrators either protected by the police or long dead, if not committed by the police themselves, Toussaint said. The fake news article spread like herpes over social media and claimed, citing an FBI spokesman, the mass grave was the work of Eldon Lee Edwards, the seventh Grand Wizard of the Knights of the Ku Klux Klan, a sort of Attila the Hun of Mississippi. The forensic report was definitive: the bodies of these black men evinced unmistakable signs of sadistic torture and mutilation. The hideous deeds of Delphine LaLaurie are conjured in the popular imagination, but I noticed that the soil featured in the photo of the ostensible mass grave was the wrong color, the soil of Mississippi is not a pale, chalky gray like that depicted in the photograph, the alluvial soils of Mississippi are a contagious reddish, ferrous coloration. The other telltale sign of falsified reportage is that the victims were buried. Lynching victims were never buried — why should the lyncher bury the victim when they had no fear of reprisal or criminal prosecution? The Klan wanted their victims displayed to public view, as a macabre example to the black community, a dead black body was no use as propaganda and intimidation buried in the ground, it had to be visible hanging outside the courthouse and in the public square as a warning to the Negroes with their little Green Book. But this photo featured in the *Jackson Telegraph* is in fact of a medieval mass grave dig site in Spitalfields, London, England, as far as can be from the Mississippi Delta, occupied by Choctaw and Natchez natives while medieval Europe was imploding in internecine religious wars over the correct interpretations of church doctrine, but the faked report of the mass grave might also have been plagiarized from Alexander Gardner's battlefield corpse photographs of the Confederate dead at Antietam, 1862, Toussaint said, so that my father, who spent his lifetime rooting for a losing football team and yet still hoping for miracles, had he read the *Jackson Telegraph,* would have felt morally justified in his demands for evidence of things unseen, even things which my mother, who had a median imagination, could not possibly have fabricated herself.

The city lights sparked and refracted in the spider-webbed hospital windowpane, Toussaint turning away from the delivery room window a final time, and I followed him tacitly, trustingly, without a word as we descended a dozen lightless flights of stairs to the hospital basement, never once questioning where he was taking me, as I never did, till we arrived at a point in Charity Hospital's mazelike meander beneath which we could venture no lower: in the operating amphitheater and hospital morgue — an examination table at the focal point of ascending amphitheater seating where the body of Toussaint's father was autopsied after the Christmas Eve explosion, the coroners searching the father's body for evidence of things unseen, for the skull and crossbones, for the key to the hazmat symbology, for the red stick, for the wormwood and endocrine disruptors, for the sunken slave ship at the bottom of the bloodstream. The tainted heavy stench of black continental masses of mold seemed to assault all the senses, and senses I did not know I had. The stygian mold clinging to the face like wearing somebody else's death mask. The basement morgue's autopsy theater had been submerged beneath several feet of putrid storm water for some time, and the wormwood watermarks stained the walls, themselves the wan, diseased color of a drowned corpse. Toussaint looked at the autopsy table without saying anything, listening to the watery roar of the Spillway inundating his ancestors' gravesites as the river rose and flooded his bloodstream.

For a long time we stood at the bottom of the amphitheater, below the wormwood watermarks encircling the room like the waterline on a sinking ship, gazing at the empty autopsy table, while I tried to reduce my breathing to a minimum to not inhale mold spores. Once the flickering, transparent silhouette of a headless corpse began to materialize on the autopsy table before me, a bloody red stick impaling the damaged abdomen, I looked away, and read Toussaint's tattoos, *worm* on the knuckles of one fist, and *wood* on the other.

Almost nothing remains of Africatown to see today, Toussaint said, a few brick fireplaces and crumbling chimneystacks, ramshackle sharecropper shotgun shacks, the tall, spindly and hateful longleaf pines that choke the coastal plains and marshes, the cemetery overgrown with feral weeds and hurricane kudzu where the diaspora's dead were buried, including my mother's great-great-grandfather Cudjo, his headstone weathered and vandalized. There is the Africatown welcome center that operates out of a mobile home, but few visitors. Nothing in Africatown is new; indeed, one is surrounded by things that were old the day they were made. I discovered human skulls in the woods, Toussaint said, roundabout the Africatown welcome center. Much like Standard Heights, Africatown is surrounded by heavy industry of obscure purpose on all sides. The lumber mills, the barges, the coal terminals, the tank farms storing toxic tar sand oil, the railyards — none of these were here when the *Clotilda*'s human cargo stepped ashore on Alabama, after watching the slave ship burn in Mobile Bay. But Africatown has been obliterated by Petrochemical Modernism's systematic program of erasure, and the little that remains to be seen today is overgrown and in a sorry state of disrepair far more advanced than even the Ashland-Belle Helen Plantation, Toussaint said.

Toussaint's father, the eternal baghead and sore loser, persisted in his doubt of things unseen even though his mother brought south with her the empirical evidence he surely needed: a singed brick from their bombed, ruined house on Osage Avenue, a brick she kept hidden from Toussaint's father in a strongbox under the house, which was raised high enough on pylons that Toussaint could crawl beneath the house at night to check on the brick, making sure the Osage Avenue brick was still there, awaiting its obscure purpose. A brick that Toussaint would use later — after the Christmas Eve explosion and the chlorine gas ghost ships — to smash the windows he was forbidden by his father's Eleventh Commandment from opening, throwing the brick through the one windowpane left in the house that was not destroyed by the blast waves from the Christmas Eve explosion, as his father threw the television out the window when the Saints defeated themselves. For Toussaint, life was a bereaved math and transatlantic algebra of losing: the Saints lost, he lost his father on Christmas Eve, his family lost their home in Standard Heights to ExxonMobil, he lost his brother first to the prison-industrial complex, and then to the rodeo. Every loss was compounded by another in the petrochemical economy, even the golden statue of an Africatown ancestor lost its head to the death mask white men, like so many of the slave rebels in the German Coast Uprising lost theirs to Master Hammond.

Africatown's golden bust of Cudjo — depicting the town's founder like the colossal heads and jadeite masks of the Olmec, but zooted in coat and tie — had been decapitated by death mask vandals the night before my visit to Africatown that winter, Toussaint said, the burnt beige grass and trees were dead and lifeless in that way of hiemal plant life on the Gulf — as if they had never been alive. I traced the twin curving gashes of tire tracks where the vandals had tied a rope around the statue's neck, and with the other end of the rope tied to the back of the truck, the driver pressing the accelerator until Cudjo's golden head was no longer able to resist the tension and was pulled clean off its neck. I began to feel the constriction, both physical and metaphysical, of a cold iron necklace around my own neck, as if my head too might be yanked off. I looked around the headless golden monument, scrutinized the sere ghostly grass, walked off a perimeter — the vandals took Cudjo's head with them, and the golden countenance of Africatown's founder has not, to my knowledge, ever been recovered. Had Cudjo accepted the Green Knight's challenge, or did the golden visage fall from the Leonids like the severed head my brother and I discovered among the rotting planetary fruit in Standard Heights? Or is the golden head of Africatown's founder mounted on some Alabama redneck's trophy kill wall with giant rebel flags, taxidermy waterfowl, and pictures of himself in white robes and Klan regalia?

Ants and insect life crawled over the headless bust, but though the grass around the Africatown welcome center was winter-burned and dead, the grass at the base of Cudjo's monument grew green as the cutouts of the African continent on the welcome center sign. This kind of symbolic barbarism is nothing new in Alabama. Decapitations of statues honoring public figures are a favored rural pastime, a frat boy's recreational game in Alabama; a bronze bust of Nathan Bedford Forrest in Selma, Alabama was decapitated by Civil Rights protestors; in retaliation a statue of Fred Shuttlesworth in Birmingham, Alabama was decollated, as if the state's statues are engaged in clandestine warfare with one another, with bloody guillotines and pickup trucks, and so what began as the destruction of a slave ship — evidence of a crime — and its irretrievable sinking into the lightless swampy bottom of Mobile Bay digressed into the decapitation of all possible witnesses to the crime even as General Robert E. Lee stands unmolested and triumphant, his head still attached to his shoulders, on his monumental pedestal in Lee Circle.

But before Zora could get to Mobile, the slave narrative ventriloquists went to work on Cudjo and his little Africatown, Toussaint said, though producing nothing so eloquent as the decapitation of a golden ancestor. Though my father never read it, not long after Africatown's founding *Harper's Monthly Magazine* ran a story about the *Clotilda*, recounting the plot among the plantation men and the harrowing transatlantic voyage in romantic tones like some kind of oceangoing *Huck Finn*, as if the article's author had been aboard the ship himself, manacled in the ship's hull with the contraband human cargo, stinking and sweating and dying. The story's author claims his historical information came to him directly from the enslaved Africans themselves, but the details of the transaction, the business side of the dealings between the ship's owner and the plantation men, all the antebellum economics of supply and demand, the sportsmanship of the slave economy must have been as unknown to the captives as their final destination in Mobile County was, as unintelligible as the West Germanic language of their captors, and neither does the story's author cite any authoritative source for his assertions, which are bold and florid, much in the manner of Biblical narratives, Toussaint said, and therefore as with all storylines from the omniscient ventriloquists, not to be trusted.

But if the slave ship *Clotilda* did not dock in the Port of Mobile, as my mother was certain it had, and sink upon burning in Mobile Bay, as my father doubted it had, then how to account for Africatown's welcome center? Never before had I seen a welcome center, much less a welcome center sign, in such an unwelcoming place, Toussaint said, it would've been like erecting a welcome center on Hiawatha Street or the bombed ruins of Osage Avenue, or the spot in the Spillway where my father claimed our enslaved ancestors were buried. The headless golden bust of Cudjo is still there on the brick plinth, bearing sightless witness to its own desecration and pickup truck vandalism, and the dream speed takeover of Africatown by industrial factors. And the black and white photos of Cudjo, flanked on either side by granddaughter and grandson, which my mother preserved in a moldy album with other important family documents — birth certificates and the Christmas Eve explosion death certificate — knowing that her people have long left no trace in the official record, obliterated by siege or the vast anonymous powers of petrochemical erasure. This photo of Cudjo — at the time it was taken he was the last man alive in Alabama or anywhere else who remembered the African village from which he was captured, the village now little more than an exotic myth in his decaying memory palace, the last man alive who recalled the names of those villagers who perished in the slave raid at dawn and those who survived the Middle Passage, then the cultivation of cotton on an antebellum plantation, the last man alive who could argue the impossibility of ever being a freeman in a place like Alabama.

My mother did not think of what she inherited from Cudjo as in any way a slave narrative, they were simply dinner table family stories that were passed down like recipes for cornbread or old photographs, Toussaint said, what eventually became slave narratives and propaganda documents in the abolitionist cause started as family stories before they were anything else. The ventriloquists of the slave narratives were all born on U.S. soil — they were as American as George Washington or Frederick Douglass — but Cudjo remained a stranger in a strange land, even after emancipation, a land growing stranger by the hour. From the way my mother made it sound, Cudjo never really integrated into the wider community outside of Africatown, and how could he? When the war was over and there were no more Master Hammonds, Cudjo wanted to go home to his village in Africa, before the slave raids, before the arrival of the *Clotilda*, but like my own rummaging through the vacant greenbelt lots of Standard Heights for some sign, some artifact of the house I grew up in, on either side of Cudjo's life, backward as well as forward, upriver and downriver, he was bound by a past as mutilated as his future, as fixed as the Mississippi is by the Army Corps of Engineers' levees and the bloody red stick pinning the crucified river like a butterfly specimen. Emancipation by the reactionary largesse of death mask white men with funny beards in Washington meant little to him if he could not return to his native village. Africa was not a town, to Cudjo it was a continent, Toussaint said, not just another stop on the highway, it was all of that green cutout painted on the crumbling Africatown welcome center sign. And Cudjo's story, ending as it did, did not have the salvific narrative arc of Christian theology, of hope and resurrection and salvation everlasting, it was a linear vector in a process flow diagram straight into the petrochemical dreamwork. Cudjo's narrative, as I received it from my mother, while she baked cornbread or washed the dishes, was one of regretful backwardation and unhappy deracination, the petrochemical nocturne had reached with tentacles deep into the past and across the Atlantic to import the ancestors of the men like my father who worked the petrochemical plantation of Standard Heights. If Cudjo could not reverse the voyage of the *Clotilda*, resurrecting the burned slave ship out of the swampy waters, building Africatown would be how he prepared his afterbears to survive the Siege of Osage Avenue. And as the process flow diagrams and gray-scale boxes in the Christmas Eve explosion accident report have shown, not a single note of the nocturne is reversible, Toussaint said.

Toussaint had stopped pacing the autopsy amphitheater by now. He told me all this — of his father's death and autopsy, of Cudjo's transatlantic crucible in the Maafa — while we stood in the hospital morgue's autopsy theater, his gravelly, baritone voice echoing off the hard, ceramic-tiled walls. With the hand tattooed with *worm* he massaged at his neck, the lingering traces of an iron neck collar. The silhouette of the headless golden corpse on the autopsy table flickered in and out as Toussaint walked between us and, as he passed from the head of the table to the end, I saw Emmett Till's battered and inhuman face crudely affixed on the headless bust of Cudjo.

Toussaint took a seat in the amphitheater as if awaiting the autopsy of someone he knew. I tried to visualize what the autopsy amphitheater must have looked like — clean, modern, sanitized, the perfect place for the examination of causes of death — before the storm without the dirty black waterlines ringing the walls, before the toxic mold and before the cadaverous stench, a reversal of the nocturne, the ibis' clarinet unbroken. My father had a crescent moon tattooed on his hand and the state flag of a self-cannibalizing mother pelican on his right arm, a tattoo that my mother hated, she did not understand why he would want this self-cannibalizing bird on his body, Toussaint said plaintively, his voice echoing against the clinal tile walls, the autopsy amphitheater repeating his words in dying decrescendos like rings rippling outwards around a stone thrown into the river. In the wake of the Christmas Eve explosion, by Christmas Day, he said, my father's pelican tattoo began to make sense, for the plant's flags — three of them: the American flag, the Louisiana state flag, and an ExxonMobil flag — flew at half-staff, the state flag — "Pelican in Her Piety" — flying over the Exxon-Mobil plant like a flag of surrender over a besieged crystal city. The state flag's mother pelican feeding her three young pelicans with the blood pecked from her own breast, the self-cannibalizing bird of a self-cannibalizing state. Spare me a drop of blood, I said to the mother pelican on the flag. Not till that day after the Christmas Eve explosion, with the state flag at half mast, the pelican mother sacrificing herself to feed her young did I understand what my mother's ceaseless fretwork of worry had been about, Toussaint said, and by then I was the man of a house that was no longer ours.

Long before I found the Osage Avenue brick under the house though, Toussaint said, the older Rastafarian renegades of Standard Heights, who were more familiar with the old days of black radicalism, more avant-garde than the organizing of bus boycotts in Baton Rouge and lunch counter sit-ins, talked of some country I'd never heard of called the Republic of New Afrika, and about which I could find nothing in the State Library, no entry on this mythical Republic in the encyclopedias. More than leaving Standard Heights, which I have never been able to get to leave me, I wished to visit this Republic, but it remained mythical and unlocatable — the Capital was rumored to be in Hinds County, Mississippi or the Oceanhill-Brownsville area of Brooklyn, and the national anthem was either a jazz standard or a song by Public Enemy or Bob Marley, depending on who you asked, Toussaint said. No one knew the exact geographic coordinates or the founding fathers of this black Republic, only that it was an independent African-American-majority country composed of Louisiana, Mississippi, Alabama, Georgia, South Carolina, and the contiguous black-majority counties in Arkansas, Texas, North Carolina, Florida, and Tennessee. Such a large geographic area — how is it possible that no one knew where it was? Of course, in the annals of petrochemical historiography, after the buyouts have come for the Republic and Charity Hospital too, they will say, without proper citation of authoritative sources, that no satsuma grew in Charity Hospital's delivery room, Africatown was but a bad dream of the diaspora, the Christmas Eve explosion had all been imagined, the Curse of the Saints was simply bad luck, the Republic of New Afrika was a utopian sci-fi *ignis fatuus*, and Standards Heights never existed either.

Standard Heights Lies by the Sea

Toussaint and I remained in the autopsy amphitheater listening to the irregular pattern of a leak dripping from the ceiling on the autopsy table where the golden corpse of Cudjo had been. A watery plinking of alien notes, a hazmat and industrial staccato. The dripping escalated in a tremulous crescendo, the Spillway opening the bloodstream, and then faded into an unraveling echo. We stood at the bottom of Charity Hospital's ruined autopsy amphitheater, like two lost actors on the stage of a morality play, beyond the customary genres of comedy and tragedy, neither of us moving or breathing, as if waiting for the other to climb up on the autopsy table for the surgical knife.

I followed Toussaint through the hole in the security fence and onto Tulane Avenue, across the neutral ground on Loyola, turning downriver off Common Street and then through the revolving gold doors of the Roosevelt Hotel. Nothing could have been farther from the basement morgue of Charity Hospital. We found ourselves in the hotel's glittering gold lobby beneath the crystal octopus of pendulous, monstrous chandeliers. A security guard eyed us as we entered the hotel bar, the Sazerac. Everywhere we went, surveilled by the vigilant watchmen of petrochemical assets. I took off my coat and bought Toussaint a drink and we waited for the effect of the alcohol to dispel the aseptic chill of the morgue. The smell of hurricane mold clung still to us like the metempsychosis of disaster. For a long time neither of us said anything, Toussaint stirring his drink and gazing down into the brown vortex swirling in the glass. Had the glass been big enough, I feared he might jump in. I could still hear the faint dripping on the morgue's autopsy table. By the second drink, Toussaint was keen to break the long interlude of silence that settled over us after the morgue.

A few days before the Christmas Eve explosion I found out why my father had never been to Mobile: he would not set foot in that state, he said, because of what happened at Tuskegee, and so if mother's people were from the same state as the syphilitic scourge of Tuskegee he wanted nothing to do with it, a state that was complicit with the U.S. Public Health Service's doctors and medical scientists who denied treatment to Macon County's sharecroppers with syphilis, tricking them into believing they were the recipients of free healthcare. Free healthcare in Alabama? Don't make me laugh! He was paranoiacally petrified that my mother was syphilitic, that the disease must have spread from Tuskegee to Mobile, my mother's people having, or so he imagined, some tenuous connection to Tuskegee in the years before the experiments, Toussaint said, ordering another drink.

Because of Tuskegee, and the atrocities committed there, my father said, I will never be caught dead in your mother's home state, and he was as good as his word, wishing damnation and woe upon everything from that state, Toussaint said. Even Mark Ingram, an Alabama running back who played for the Saints was a tainted turncoat in his estimation, and whenever Ingram took an especially hard hit from a defender and was slow in getting up from the turf my father, Toussaint said, wasted no time, as if he were the head coach, in benching Ingram and subbing the backup running back into the rotation, just to get an Alabama running back off the Superdome's field. Like most Louisianans, my father's hatred for everything Alabama was hardcore and total, maybe pathological. Tuskegee was our Thereseinstadt, a ghetto in the middle of nowhere Alabama where government scientists freely experimented on black bodies, jabbing them with silver needles — just like the white colonialists extinguished the tribes of Standard Heights' streets with their degenerate European diseases — and withholding penicillin, a medicine that to me sounded like a disease worse than syphilis. When I told my father I wanted to go to the Tuskegee Institute on a scholarship and study aeronautics he forbade it with the same vehemence he forbade us to open the windows. His commandments before long outnumbered the Lord's ten. Thou shall not open the windows. Thou shall not drink the river water. Thou shall not eat from the satsuma tree. Thou shall not disrespect the black and gold. Thou shall not get too big for thy britches.

Thou shall not, Toussaint said.

At that age, Toussaint said, the more my father was allergic to everything Alabama the more I wanted to go to Tuskegee and study aeronautics, the science of flight, to be one of the Tuskegee Airmen, and drop bombs on the enemies of the Republic of New Afrika, raining death and brimstone upon the ExxonMobil plant. If I wanted to go to college, my father said, I could go to Southern University, upriver where the red stick was found, an historically black college north of the plant, but the smokestacks of the ExxonMobil plant were still visible from Southern's campus and I did not want to look out the window of a class on the history of the Maafa and see those baleful chemical columns manufacturing clouds and chlorine gas ghost ships, Toussaint said. No, Southern was too close to home, too close to the river, and too close to ExxonMobil. The smokestacks rendered all of Standard Heights in a colorless and cinereal film, a petrochemical membrane that traversed infinitely subtle modulations of gray, the multiple personalities of burnoff smoke on its Middle Passage through the grayscale: cadaverous Charity Hospital gray to lake bottom black, like the Zone System devised by Ansel Adams. The ExxonMobil plant, unbound by the Second Law of Thermodynamics, was a perpetual motion machine, never tiring of experimenting with more mephitic modes of toxic gray, grayer shades of chemical ash grayer than I'd ever known could exist. Pickup game boys, Toussaint said, are not supposed to know the names of chemicals such naphtha and benzene, much less be able to identify them by smell in the air. Tuskegee, syphilis or not, was the only way: I wanted to be Ralph Ellison and the black aviators flying high in fighter planes above the chemical smoke, dropping bombs on the petrochemical Babylon. If I could not be an airman, I would be an architect like Wallace Rayfield who designed Birmingham's 16th Street Baptist Church, or Robert Robinson Taylor, an alum of MIT, designer of Tuskegee's campus buildings, constructed by Tuskegee students, I would design buildings indestructible to the buyouts and chemical explosions and Standard Heights would be redeveloped after *The City of the Sun*, a castellated utopia defended by seven concentric walls and infused with an air as uncommon and intemerate as cosmic ether. There would be no burnoff days or gas flares to toxify the air in the lungs and my mother would be able to breathe, deeply and safely, the fragrance of summer and the aromas of autumn, without coughing up her very soul in violent paroxysms. The happy denizens of this New Standard Heights born with slower heart rates like the altitude-adjusted Incas. No Thou Shall Not posted at the birth canal. I would help the MOVE activists construct a bomb-proof invincible bunker on the roof of their compound on Osage Avenue, and the lost tribes of Standard Heights, under the command of Hiawatha and Pontiac, marshalled at dawn on the river's west bank, would join in the defense of the Republic of New Afrika against the mad scientists of Petrochemical Modernism and the death mask wardens of Angola, staging a jailbreak for the release of my brother who would ride out of that prison plantation on a golden bucking bull and besiege the ExxonMobil plant itself, Toussaint said, storming the petrochemical Versailles and executing the supercorporation's majority shareholders, throwing the process flow diagrams into the river.

I might've gone to Southern University or Louisiana State University, but I wasn't good enough at football to go on an athletic scholarship, and from the campuses of both schools one was still within plausible hearing distance of the petrochemical nocturne, a toxic psalm I had to get as far away from as the river would allow. How was I to hear a lecture on the diaspora or the chemical structure of benzene with the plant's warning system howling in the background? There was the University of Mississippi, the alma mater of James Meredith, the first to integrate the school whose mascot was a rebel white supremacist, but Ole Miss was too Old South for me, too many blonde sorority girls and rebel yell fraternity boys, too many pristine white columns, too much hot blood dripping on moonlit magnolia leaves. But no place was far enough and perhaps that is why I find myself unable to cut the umbilical cord to Cancer Alley, Toussaint said. If no place was far enough, and my father's Thou Shall Not was the answer to every attempt at escape from the native streets, then there was no more use in leaving the Pelican State than there was in my mother leaving Mobile, Alabama for Osage Avenue.

After the Christmas Eve explosion I stopped showing up for the pickup football games, Toussaint said, taking a long drink, the basic laughter of carefree tourists, a bachelorette party, echoing off the mirrors and stone of the hotel lobby like one of the cheap harem palaces of Sadam Hussein, I thought. Instead of trick plays and sandlot schemes, I studied the brutal architecture and design of petrochemical plants, Toussaint said, the labyrinthine industrial complexity constructed in Standard Heights that by greenbelt policy was being returned to a feral state of nature hostile to man, I learned the alchemy of the flow meters, pressure transmitters, level sensors, temperature sensors, analytical instruments, incanting the magical polysyllables of words like *nitrobenzene* and *dimethyl terephthalate,* arcane abracadabra of a savage language, the engineering of these petrochemical behemoths like a new materialist theology. Many of the fathers in Standard Heights worked as ExxonMobil security guards at one time in their lives, Toussaint said, but my father never defended the plant — and from what or whom? The security guards who patrolled the plant and native streets of Standard Heights with shotguns in their pickup trucks. All my life I have been surrounded by armed guards of one kind or another, protecting me from myself, protecting others from me, protecting everybody from everybody, protecting nobody from anyone, protecting anyone from nobody, protecting the plant from the revenge of the Osage and the vanquished tribes of the native streets, protecting the other security guards from the Old Testament criminal justice of the Soledad Brothers, Toussaint said. To all the security guards of the *Deus ex machina,* I say beware the Soledad Brothers. The museum security guard protecting the artworks of Petrochemical Modernism was no different, she did not want me getting too close to those precious photographs and paintings — if I got too close I might see the evidence of things unseen, the river twitching and writing in Boisseau's flood painting, the skull and crossbones ingredient labels on all the petrochemical products shelved in Gursky's supermarket — any more than ExxonMobil's security guards would turn their backs to let me cross the street, Toussaint said, ordering another strong drink.

I recalled that day at the art museum, the security guard warning Toussaint not to get too close to the photograph of the supermarket goods. But there was one painting the security guard did not guard as closely as the others. The museum security guard seemed not to mind Toussaint peering closely, even breathing on Anselm Kiefer's monumental canvas, thick as cake icing with lyrical impasto and encrusted with elegiac layers of paint — *Bohemia Lies by the Sea.* Toussaint's figure belittled and whelmed by the sheer scale of the artwork, a foreshortened road narrows into the distance through a meadow of poppies — one of Gardner's battlefields. A poppy blooming in the skull of each Confederate corpse. Toussaint peering close enough to the prodigious canvas that his exhalations stirred the poppies. Neither did the security guard intervene to stop Toussaint from stepping into Bohemia, walking down that country road, a solitary figure passing through a field of poppies, that mythical, antique flower of dreams, sleep and death, black crows scattering at his approach, somehow leaving no footsteps on River Road — I have seen crucifixions along River Road, Cancer Alley's Appian Way — without a salutation to the once grand sugar cane and indigo plantations, fixed upon a disappearing destination: Ingeborg Bachmann's Bohemia, a landlocked and defunct kingdom, no more attainable than the Republic of New Afrika. I could not follow after Toussaint this time, I had to let him go, and I was there in the gallery, if needed, to prevent the museum security guard from stopping him. Protecting Bohemia from nobody, the security guard could not possibly understand why Toussaint peered so attentively at all the hanging photos and pictures, the supermarket goods and the Mississippi flooding the museum floor. I do not think Toussaint ever saw himself as a victim of displacement, so deeply embedded was the peripatetic in his fluctuant nature. No Green Book guides the weary traveler on his passage of River Road, through the upriver and downriver process flow diagrams of Cancer Alley.

When I returned from the men's room, looking bewildered about the empty hotel bar, Toussaint was gone. The bachelorette party too was gone, the bartender idly polishing glassware. I should've known Toussaint would evaporate, like the chlorine gas ghost ships on the river. There on the marble counter of the bar, the black and white veins of stone threaded together indestructibly, Dixieland jazz piping in the background, the lyrics to a ghostwritten song Toussaint had started but abandoned, tentative phrases on a paper napkin. Standards Heights lies by the sea; Iberville lies by the sea, the lines read. Tuskegee lies by the sea. Osage Avenue lies by the sea. As the burnt hand writes of the essence of the conflagration, and the drowned sing the substance of the sea. If Standard Heights lies by the sea, I shall believe in the sea again. The moldy, deathly chill of the hospital morgue had returned. I vetted my face in the long mirror behind the bar, and found nobody there. I asked the bartender for the check, but he said my companion, just a few moments before, had settled the bill before departing, signing the receipt with a *nom de plume*.

Life and Death in Cancer Alley

Recently, I found a ticket stub to an art exhibit doubling as a bookmark in the pages of the exhibition's catalogue, a memento of another chance meeting with Toussaint. I don't remember how it got there, but the ticket stub must have been slipped between the pages and forgotten. At the time, I'd driven from Birmingham to Atlanta for a photography exhibit, bypassing Anniston, Alabama, a town that was no stranger to manmade chemical catastrophes — a fisherman caught a deformed largemouth bass in Choccolocco Creek; the fish's etiology traced to Monsanto, the company that gave Agent Orange and DDT to the world, and which had been dumping unregulated polychlorinated biphenyls into the town landfill and water bodies for years; the mutant fish floating belly-up, hemorrhaging blood and shedding layers of shiny silver skin as if submerged in superheated water. Like Standard Heights, other zones in the South were playing the carcinogenic overtures of their own petrochemical nocturnes.

I purchased a ticket to the "Picturing the South" exhibit commissioned by the High Museum of Art, Atlanta, Georgia. Art galleries and museums have long attracted me for their anti-decay qualities, as institutional repositories of mummified memories, perhaps for the same reasons that Toussaint was drawn to the Ashland-Belle Helen Plantation. The antiseptic, lifeless light falling on an ancient bust or a Renaissance portrait can illuminate some dark corner or inscrutable facet of a once mighty empire. The art galleries of the future will display plastic refuse and computer parts with technical annotations written by the art historians specializing in Petrochemical Modernism. The recessed gallery lighting conveyed on the floors and walls an eternal halo through which museumgoers passed, heels clicking brightly on the concrete floors like knives in the afterlife, the gallery's white walls a clinical backdrop to the exhibit's photographs of luxuriant and grossly verdant nature penetrated by haunted equations of petrochemical infrastructure. In these photos of noxious fog and petrochemical mists, a dense opera of soft greens and deadened greys predominated. The horizon line bisecting the photographic plane into two equal halves of blue or cloudy sky — in some photos no sky at all — and the only markers of mankind's puny presence were the basketball goals, crucifixes, dead cypress trees, streetlamps, utility poles — all rendered in strong vertical lines that aspired upwards but were cut off, truncated in their ascents a few dozen feet above the ground, as far as we can ever hope to ascend.

Outside the frame of the photographs, but from a distance that could only come from within them, standing before a large-format color photograph of an oil refinery and petrochemical processing plant, was Toussaint, our reflections doubled side by side in the black glass, superimposed darkly over the photographic image of the petrochemical plant that exploded one Christmas Eve and through some unstoppable, unforeseen chain reaction of infinitely cascading failures, is still exploding in the Standard Heights of Toussaint's mind, from the dead end streets and wormwood floodwaters of which I may never escape. Somehow, I had known that Toussaint would be here in Atlanta, on the exhibit's last day, to see the autopsy of the Christmas Eve explosion.

My father, Toussaint said there in the gallery, his voice echoing against the silent photographs hanging like closed windows on the white wall, was scheduled to work the night shift at the plant on Christmas Eve, covering a shift for a coworker so he could spend the holiday with his family in Port Allen across the river, and that was just like my father: to volunteer on behalf of someone else so he could avoid the self-created awkwardness — and it was entirely of his own creation — of spending a holiday at home, indignantly disbelieving in the miracle of the Virgin Birth, Toussaint said. If my mother's understanding of her husband's duties at the plant were opaque to her, my father's work at the plant was an unintelligible enigma to the rest of us, we knew that he performed manual and mental work that was somehow industrial and mechanical and chemical all at once; in the aftermath of the explosion — an explosion that dragged on for years, never really ending for anyone except my father — his plant duties were exalted from the merely mechanical and chemical into metaphysical and alchemical mysteries.

The explosion came as we were sitting down to dinner as a family, my father's chair at the head of the table empty, Toussaint said, looking at the photograph before us on the gallery wall of a toxic and alien landscape. All the lights in the house went out, he said. There was no electrical flicker; there was steady golden current, then there was nothing. A moonless night. Even the prison yard streetlights went out. The blackness that night was like closing your eyes underwater. I no longer lived in my own house. At that instant, the house in Standard Heights, which my father fought so hard to keep in the family was no longer ours. ExxonMobil would get the house, clear it, even if it cost them an expensive explosion and lawsuits older than the greenbelt trees planted after the domiciliary remnants were hauled off to a landfill by Devil's Swamp Lake. The windows which I was forbidden to open flew out of their frames in fine, incisive fragments of flying glass and musical shrapnel. Even the fragmented windows in Charity Hospital must have blown out. A door slammed. My mother screamed. The dinner table was cleared of its plates and glasses by the benzene blast. For all I knew the Mississippi River reversed course and the pyramids of Egypt fell down the well. The basketball stopped bouncing in the street. The ibis' clarinet broken, and the red stick snapped in half. The last of the pink flamingos flew away. The river filled with wormwood and the North Star plummeted through the neck of the Green Knight's severed head, Toussaint said.

I remember a reverse order of events: first the lights went out, then the explosion, the effects of darkness somehow preceding the explosive cause, and the silent ringing in the ears that I hear still on quiet nights, Toussaint said, I can hear it now ringing off the white walls in this museum gallery. The explosion itself and the flight of window fragments — luminescent colored ribbons shaped like flying bats — through the house came after the lights going out. But I can't be sure of that, either. Perhaps the flying fragments of shattered window preceded the explosion, or the explosion may have happened years before and the darkness was just catching up, Toussaint said. For years, walking through the ramshackle halls of the decaying memory palace, I have reconstructed the uncertain events surrounding that Christmas Eve, never coming any closer to a complete understanding, placing cause and effect in chronological order, of this industrial accident that changed forever the lives of those of us who survived the Christmas Eve explosion. A few blocks away on Pontiac Street, a baby crying inconsolably, the crepitant rotting of wood — with no obstacles but a few pinched, shadowy windbreaks of greenbelt trees, the houses having been long demolished, sound travelled through Standard Heights' vacant blocks in unfettered freedom of audibility, then the plant sirens — those cacophonous signals of mayday announcing that Whirl is King — not even ExxonMobil's empire was so complete that an explosive chemical accident could be contained. These were not the warning sirens of the nocturne we were so used to ignoring, but the real thing, Toussaint said. We'd always known it could happen at any time, the ideal petrochemical machinery illustrated by the process flow diagrams could fail, though we never suspected the failure would come when our father was on the nightshift, Toussaint said. I heard ominous incantations over the plant's public address loudspeakers: addresses of safe houses from *The Negro Motorist Green Book* as toxic black smoke roiled skywards in tenebrous columns like the Kuwaiti oil fields, and when the smoke ascended to heights exceeding the State Capitol building, I knew this was bigger than ExxonMobil, the two-headed leviathan supercorporation was battling the river deities and the vanquished native tribes.

During the Siege of Standard Heights, we were ordered to shelter-in-place, a safety precaution we'd practiced many times throughout my childhood, as a pestilence of chlorine gas — first used as a chemical weapon in World War I by the Germans and the British, soldiers described the gaseous smell as an admixture of pepper and pineapple — the color of rotting oranges and chartreuse drifted malefically over the vacant lots where my friends' houses once stood as black silhouettes against the apocalyptically flaming sunsets. Now fatherless, though we did not know it at the time, my brother and I helplessly watching through the blasted kitchen window the nebulous chlorine clouds metamorphose into the petrochemical daymares that haunted Standard Heights: armadas of slave ships from the west coast of Africa, the *Clotilda* burning in Mobile Bay, the ancestral slave armies of the German Coast Uprising slaughtered at the river.

They say that the blast was felt as far as twenty miles away from the plant, Toussaint said, and it was evident in his voice he was still feeling the resonating aftereffects of that blast as if it recurred in his brain continually, repeating like the police cam footage of his brother's suicide by cop attempt, and when the looting began — storefront windows were blown out — the National Guardsmen were activated to maintain law and order, Toussaint said, and anyone not from Standard Heights will never know what it is like to see military tanks and armed white men in full battle gear patrolling the streets where you played pickup football games, tanks parked in the streets named for extinct tribes with their guns aimed at your house, as if the Battle of Baton Rouge never ended. The Christmas Eve explosion was even felt inside the Governor's Mansion, from the front portico of which can be seen the smoking, glowing towers of the ExxonMobil plant, as forcefully as it was felt inside our family home, rattling the portraits of past governors hanging on the mansion's gallery walls, the portraits of Huey Long as well as all the other crooks, Toussaint said.

Chlorine gas, I later read in the accident report, Toussaint said, is highly reactive with water in the lungs where it forms hydrochloric acid, inducing violent coughing and vomiting. A terrible, painful death. My father, who took me to the Spillway opening in the springtime so that I would fear death by water, must have drowned in acid that Christmas Even, when the chlorine gas ghost ships sailed into his lungs, sinking in his bloodstream. The varieties of vertigo and vomiting — all were too common ailments to my mother who tussled with the air, acutely susceptible to the plant's unique blend of miasmatic ingredients that swirled invisibly around us: liquid benzene and toluene rapidly gasify when exposed to oxygen. The Christmas Eve explosion that took my father in an instant spent the coming years taking her breath away one day at a time. Children on the block were named Naphtha, boys named for hydrocarbons whose first word was benzene. Naphtha: it sounded exotic, maybe of Egyptian origin. We waded through the thick and treacherous ground-level ozone, smog sulfuring a story high over the river. We lived so long with the stench of burnt tar in our homes that fresh air, when the winds blew inland off the river, smelled like a strange and fantastic alpine chemical, Toussaint said.

My brother was never the same after the Christmas Eve explosion, and it must be that this explosion, after which our father who had such an outsized presence in our lives never came home, had some causal role in his lifelong confinement in Angola, his ride with death in the rodeo. Many years after my brother's burial in Angola's prison cemetery I saw Basquiat's *Riding with Death, 1988* and no more had to be said on the matter. Dawn that Christmas Day after the Christmas Eve explosion came like a shroud thrown over an unidentified, and maybe unidentifiable corpse, a black morning over Emmett Till's face. In our churchless prayers, we thanked the Lord the explosion was not accompanied by other disasters, the minor aftershocks felt days after an earthquake. I waited for the river's refluent change of mind; indeed, several times Christmas Day I went to the river alone and monitored the directionality of the surface current, the whirlpools of water curling and turning vortically around the submerged post of a dock or cypress driftwood. Refusing to believe the ExxonMobil plant could explode, we were told the impossible and the absurd: Santa Claus' sleigh had crashed into the banks of the Mississippi River. What was Santa delivering? Weapons grade uranium? Nitroglycerine? Others resorted to cosmic explanations such as a meteor strike, less likely to me than Santa Claus crashing his sleigh into the river banks. Baton Rouge is not even a cosmopolitan enough city to be struck by a rock from deep space, Toussaint said. But for the first time my attention was turned to the heavens and, bathing in its black astronomical totality and the bullet hole stars, I began to heed what may fall from its etherous dreaming, whether Cudjo's severed golden head may return to Africatown from the Leonids.

Sometime that spring my mother was presented with ExxonMobil's official report investigating the apparent causes of the Christmas Eve explosion, dedicated to my father and the other plant workers, also fathers of Standard Heights, who perished in the Christmas Eve explosion, published by the U.S. Chemical Safety and Hazard Investigation Board, an indecipherable report of technical mumbo-jumbo, engineering diagrams and scientific calculations, Toussaint said. Mother never read beyond the report's dedication page, she had no interest in the Christmas Eve explosion's material causes, or in what ExxonMobil thought went wrong. I read the technical report as if studying the hieroglyphics, ciphers, and arcane symbols of an advanced civilization that somehow went extinct, the report concluding, in dispassionate and resigned officialese, written with the tone of a proclamation of total surrender, that the Christmas Eve explosion was caused, or so they thought, by the catastrophic rupture of reboilers supplying heat through an exchange to distillation columns and propylene fractionators — nothing more, nothing metaphysical. But the investigation reported only the mechanical and chemical dimensions of the accident, not the metaphysical and alchemical causes underlying the report's transparent attempt to blame the Christmas Eve explosion on an engineering failure, ignoring the evidence of things unseen. These scientific and investigative reports, without the clairvoyance of a developed anagogical method, made no mention of the chlorine gas slave ships plowing through

Standard Heights' green ocean of vacant lots, where the renascent jungle was periodically hacked down by crews of groundskeepers with machetes; nor did the accident report mention the sharp musical fragments of the windowpanes flying through the black space of the kitchen, or the shrill notes of glass falling like seventh octaves of a petrochemical coloratura on the floor of the cramped, casket-like bathroom shared among five, sometimes seven people. Later, as I learned of Normal System Accident Theory, developed in the wake of the Three Mile Island accident, there was nothing normal about the Christmas Eve explosion — I would not be complicit and call it an accident, a Christmas Eve accident, Toussaint said. The petrochemical phenomena of Standard Heights, those seen and unseen, are anything but normal, no such thing as normal on the native streets. The accident report described a systems accident consequent to the unforeseen interactions between multiple, catastrophic failures of complex technological and organizational systems, salient in retrospect, but as invisible as carbon monoxide that Christmas Eve: the ExxonMobil plant was a rococo patchwork of industrial, mechanical, and chemical processes like a Rube Goldberg device, farcically and whimsically complex, the inexorability of failure merely the cost of having plastic pink flamingos prettify the yard and plastic grocery bags at Gursky's supermarket, manufactured by a process of blown film extrusion from polyethylene, long chains of ethylene monomers, for the petrochemical world we are in the process of creating is inimical to both ghosts and real flamingos. The accident report was written — ExxonMobil must have kept prepared cut-and-paste reports on file, as if in this production universe effect preceded causes — before we swept up the broken seventh octave notes of glass into black trash bags and taped old blue FEMA tarps over the glassless wounds gaping in the house's four — what sometime felt like a manifold — facades, the one facing the plant having suffered the brunt of the Christmas Eve explosion, Toussaint said.

I carried this accident report around with me for years, referring to it when other things went wrong or failed in my life, searching in its technical officialese for an empirical or positivist explanation for events such as the Siege of Osage Avenue, the scars on Whipped Peter's back, our football lost forever in the mountain of rusting oil drums, the Curse of the Saints, my mother's miscarriage, any of the events which are still recurring in the autopsy theater of my mind, dissecting them on the surgical table, trying to make sense of the explosion that came the night when across town the white folks were safely in church singing carols, lighting Christmas candles, celebrating the birth of the Lord who was executed like a common criminal at a young age, and watching the Yule Log Channel in their mansions of many rooms, Toussaint said, but the accident report held no answers for me, because it did not, could not factor the evidence of things unseen.

We were the last in the gallery on the exhibition's final day, "Picturing the South." Soon these photographs of Toussaint's world would be taken down from the white walls and boxed up and put away. While Toussaint told me about how his memory of the Christmas Eve explosion — the darkness before the explosion, effects preceding causes, the river flowing in reverse — conflicted with the surface narrative of the official accident report, silhouettes of our black, faceless reflections merged in the glass covering the photograph of the petrochemical plant where his father worked.

After the High Museum closed that day and the museum guards asked us to leave, Toussaint showed me the accident report — a ponderous, much-read, dogeared and excessively bureaucratic document, one that he carried with him everywhere he went, he said, just in case he needed to refer to its contents: he had consulted it when visiting the bronze monument of the 54th Massachusetts Infantry Regiment, for every Saints loss and when he received the news of his brother's death in the Angola rodeo, crushed to death by an angry bull. This was the document containing every engineering detail relating to the so-called accident, and yet it told him nothing about what actually went wrong at the ExxonMobil plant that Christmas Eve, nothing about the chlorine gas ghost ships or his mother's toxic coughing or his brother's suicide by cop. The accident report was like the unfinished autopsy of Cudjo's headless golden bust, heavy as an ancient tome, the Domesday Book or an encyclopedia of fictive beings — I flipped through the executive summary, the investigative process, background to the release, an incident description, and all the facile equivocations of technical paralysis by analysis: incident analysis, reconstructive analysis, hazard analysis, regulatory analysis, and key findings. The section on Root and Contributing Causes, purporting to settle the issue of what happened once and for all, did no more than reiterate banausic causalities, approximate guesswork between cause and effect, everything Toussaint already knew about the petrochemical leviathan: "The plant had no additional measures in place to protect against cooler failure, such as monitoring for chlorine leaks. Because the mechanical integrity system was relied upon exclusively, a failure in the cooler resulted in chlorine contacting incompatible materials in the coolant system and releasing chlorine to the atmosphere." The accident report, for want of a nail, gave full scope to the unerring hindsight of causality, as no one in Standard Heights ever rued, upon opening a window or noting a leak in a galleon that an empire would crumble because of it. The Christmas Eve explosion accident report concludes — after a recommendation to buy out the remaining homes in Standard Heights; that ExxonMobil began buying up the houses within a predetermined radius, instead of fixing the petrochemical paradigm itself, was a tacit admission that another explosion was inevitable and that the management of the plant was doing nothing to stop it except embarking on a frenzied cash buyout crusade — with an appendix of logic diagrams of gray-scale boxes illustrating critical junctures of failure in the plant's management and mechanical systems. Each gray-scale box representing a critical moment at which that catastrophic Christmas Eve chain reaction could have been halted, but was not.

A neighbor, one of the last remaining who had not yet been bought out and before the great exodus precipitated by the Christmas Eve explosion, delivered homemade condolence funeral wreaths improvised from old tires, Toussaint said. And so a used tire, a black circle, hung on our door, the bottom of the tire filled with dirt and a few struggling flowers. Poppies growing from Confederate skulls. While the black tire still hung on the door, industrial accident investigators — I don't know whether they were with ExxonMobil or some government acronym — came to the house to interview us and take the temperature of litigation in the neighborhood, Toussaint said. We could not hire a lawyer. I told the accident investigators exactly what I had seen: the armada of chlorine gas ghost ships sailing against the current as the river reversed course and turned to blood; of the North Star flickering out of the bullet hole sky and forming the severed golden head of Cudjo that fell to Standard Heights and caused the explosion; of the rabid bloodhounds heard barking across the river on the night of the explosion, even if my mother told me to stop fibbing to the plant's accident investigators, they were just trying to help us get to the bottom of what happened to our father that Christmas Eve, she said. That was the last Christmas we spent together as a family, and with my father no longer around to tell me not to, I could open the windows freely and without fear of the Eleventh Commandment.

TOXMAP

The official accident report of the Christmas Eve explosion fails to tell the whole story, omitting as it does what Toussaint told the accident investigator he saw the night before the explosion, just as the police reports after the Siege of Osage Avenue are no more than official addenda to *Mein Kampf*. After I finished the accident report's Root and Contributing Causes, I gave my copy of the Kerner report — the official investigation into the Siege of Osage Avenue — to Toussaint so that he could, if he wished, juxtapose its investigative findings with those presented in the Christmas Eve explosion's accident report and it was while he perused and collated the contents of these two reports that Toussaint discovered, quite without my help, the Toxics Release Inventory, a web-based mapping product resulting from a partnership between the United States National Library of Medicine, the Environmental Protection Agency, and the United States Department of Health and Human Services, a map that showed Fisk's river falsely fixed in place and not the floodwater dynamo of flux that Toussaint knew it to be.

I entered the website address for the Toxics Release Inventory page into the search field of my iBook's internet browser, Toussaint said, explaining the methodology he used to access Petrochemical Modernism's cartographies of toxicity. Using the TRI's TOXMAP geographic information system, and the map controls I navigated from the continental United States to Louisiana. I zoomed into the area of the map where I knew Baton Rouge to be and from the Baton Rouge region I continued to zoom towards the sinuous river, aiming for the petrochemical cathedral north of the Capitol complex and Standard Heights to the immediate east. At this scale, Standard Heights was mottled with geocoded points, as if diseased with measles or pox, each representing a toxic release event, Toussaint said.

Among the map's other data points of toxic events I discerned the little dot representing the Christmas Eve explosion; everything that happened and was detailed in the official accident report was distilled and reduced to a single two-dimensional point on the TOXMAP. But then, using the map controls to toggle north and south of Baton Rouge, along the so-called Chemical Corridor, or notorious Cancer Alley, I noticed other toxic points, all up and down the Mississippi River, on the east and west banks, representing toxic release events I'd never heard about, placing the Christmas Eve explosion in a context that transcended even the outermost limits of Standard Heights explored during my summer wanderings to the Lincoln Theater. We were not alone in our nocturne then, Toussaint said. The Chemical Corridor had many Standard Heights, the Curse of the Saints covering a vaster area than I could have imagined. Other fathers who went to work on Christmas Eve and did not come home, mothers who miscarried and who breathed benzene, naphtha, and teargas until their lungs collapsed, brothers who attempted suicide by cop. We'd been living among these toxic points — explosions, releases, malfunctions, breakdowns, systems errors, critical failures — for as long as I could remember, and certainly much longer than even that, Toussaint said.

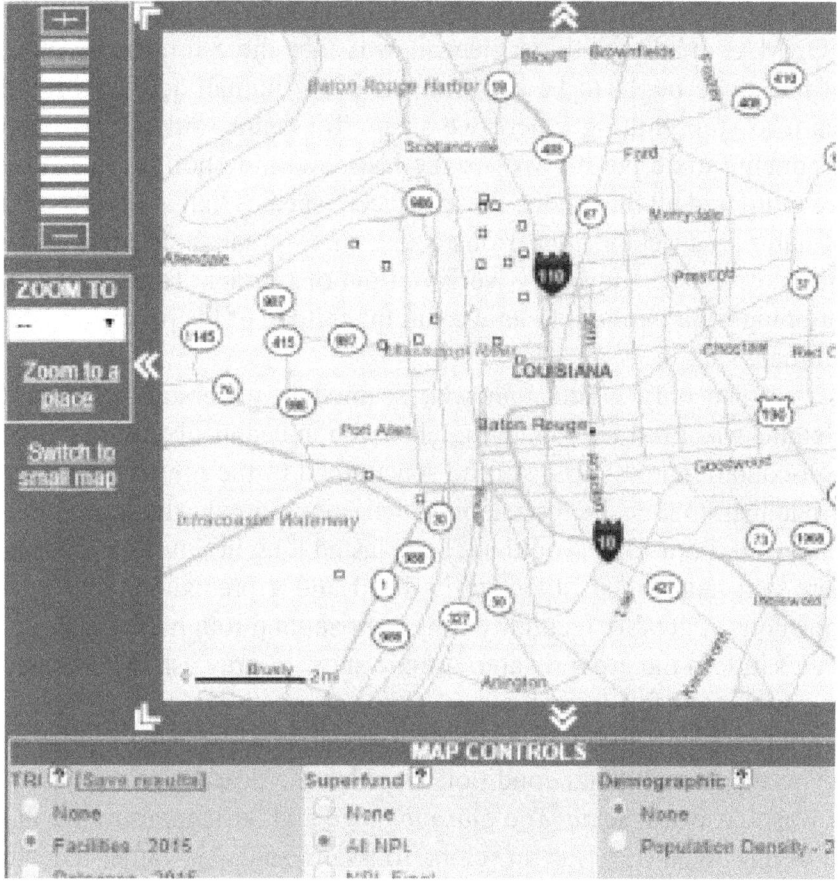

Just like the state's self-cannibalizing mother pelican and the whooping crane, I have been schooled in petrochemical anti-natalism, the assignment of a negative value to being born and to the reproduction of life, and what does one expect in a spermicidal superfund without birdsong? I must have been conceived within months of my mother's arrival in Iberville after departing Osage Avenue, carrying the burned Osage brick with her like some precious cargo, and Iberville's injurious environment cannot but leave lasting lacerations on the organism conceived within its walls: from the moment of birth one is exposed to the most flagrant insults and contrary conditions, the most toxic influences and malefic vapors, and is immediately upon birth embarked on an irreversible temporal process of decay against which one is powerless to prevail, defending ourselves against it with the many plastic, brightly colored products of Petrochemical Modernism. Phthalates, lead, cadmium, organotins. If the TOXMAP made anything clear, it was that three-fourths or more of the globe ought to be off limits to every human activity till we learn to stop shitting where we sleep, Toussaint said, till we stop producing toxic points. We are the last remaining hominin because we murdered all the others, those adjacent species that allegedly died of natural causes or mysterious accidents — final shots fired in the Battle of Baton Rouge — were victims of murder, Toussaint said, stopping for a moment to let the full magnitude of his petrochemical nihilism sink in.

The only white man who seemed to understand Standard Heights was Emil Cioran, though he lived in beautiful, cultured, and non-contaminated Paris, still he succumbed to the nihilism and anti-natalism that characterized his aphoristic, mordant thought, Toussaint said. Poor Emil would not have lasted long in South Louisiana; here anti-natalism is stood on its head and a precocious and promiscuous vegetable fecundity runs rampant and roughshod over all. PVCs lurk in the groundwater. A toxic snow of gray ash that seemed to cough as it fell from the sky. The dog breath smell of the plant on burnoff days like the inside of a gas chamber. *Le mort saisit le vif* — the French legal condition in which the dead seize the living. It was that word: *seize*. Too close to siege and besiege, as in the fall of Osage Avenue. I was no scion, Toussaint said. My father's death in the Christmas Eve explosion left us stunned and landless, there was nothing to inherit except the broken seventh notes of window glass on the floor, and even if there had been, it would have been worlds less than the entitlement of forty acres and a mule. Unlike the mythology of Christmas, in which Santa Claus gives presents and yet expects nothing in return, the petrochemical economy demands everything and gives nothing in return: my father went to the Exxon-Mobil plant that Christmas Eve and did not come back, resurrected into one of the TOXMAP's constellation of toxic event points up and down the river, a horoscope of noxious horrors, chemical calamities, so many that a celestial map had to be made charting ExxonMobil's buyout program…the ellipses in H.G. Adler's description of the expropriation of the land used for Thereseinstadt, bullet holes in the wall above Fred Hampton's bloody mattress, Toussaint said.

I'll tell you what happened, Toussaint said, after the chlorine gas clouds dissipated. I dreamt that, acting under some obscure tribal obligation, and the rites of the debt-payment system, I had to temporarily inter my father's remains in a shallow open pit on the vacant lot next to our house — I don't know who dug the pit; it was simply there — and once the flesh had putrefied and dissolved from the bone, I was to collect my father's skeleton, which I did, and wash his bones in the Mississippi River, which would not stay still, squirming like the colorful tapeworms on Fisk's map. After that funereal ablution in the wormwood river my hands went numb up to the wrist for the first time, the return of the fragmented body, the wormwood water leaching into my genome. The debt-payment system was not finished there though: the funeral hunt balances the scales with nature by taking the life of a natural creature. There are no jaguars, despite Southern University's mascot, in Standard Heights, so I went to Devil's Swamp Lake, where my father taught me his methods of fishing, and cast for a healthy, living fish, but there were none, and all I could hook was trash, the final resting place of the petrochemical plant's universe of plastic products, and so the debt-payment between father and son was never settled. My father's episodic melancholia, withdrawing from the family after a Saints loss, taking multiple consecutive shifts at work so as not to have to come home — messages from a deeper consciousness, the strange, bitter fruits of an unknown geniality of cogitation, like the injection wells for the repression of hazardous wastes deep beneath formations of porous sandstone or limestone rock, where nobody would ever find it, where nobody would ever remember it, Toussaint said, before the Christmas Eve explosion my father was injecting hazardous wastes into chambers deep inside the local geology of his memory, refusing to acknowledge that the burnt brick from Osage Avenue, stored under the house with trash and mice bones and lost footballs, where nobody would ever find it, where nobody would ever remember it, could also be used to break the windows I was forbidden by the Eleventh Commandment to open while he was alive, Toussaint said.

The accident report, clouded as it was by yellow-green chlorine gas, was opaque with impenetrable technical jargon and engineering language, a professional methodological argot that was not meant to be understood by anyone living in Standard Heights, illuminating the events of that day no more than Latin does the mystery of the Eucharist, Toussaint said. Phrases such as "the Christmas Eve explosion," which I too am guilty of deploying, were in fact a contrived community shorthand to obscure the real traumatic events of that day; as everyone knows the details of an accident or catastrophe are never accurate in the immediate aftermath, ostensible eyewitnesses are too unreliable, the Rashomon effect nullifying all hope of ever getting to the bottom of what happened that Christmas Eve in the ExxonMobil plant, convictions are overturned on the basis of false witness, and men are sent to Angola for life, one white man's word against a black man's word. Even the outcome of a Saints game could be determined by the notoriously biased NFL refs calling a pass interference penalty or a false start when all 74,295 spectators in the Superdome saw no such thing. And so the chemical accident which killed my father was buried beneath technical nomenclature and the more euphemistic, less technocratic "Christmas Eve explosion," blending as it did petrochemical violence with the nativity of the Lord, just as the horror of the funeral home was euphemized as "the funeral home incident," no one referring even obliquely to the river of blood that ran in the native streets like some Book of Revelations shit, Toussaint said. Not a single eyewitness report was to be found in the official accident investigation, no one but me in Standard Heights was interviewed — did they notice anything suspicious in the days leading up to the Christmas Eve explosion? Did they smell anything sinister in the air? — no security guard on duty that night was asked whether he saw what Standard Heights, without even being represented by an attorney, claimed to the media they saw. And even if they had been interviewed their testimony would have been generalized behind practiced bromides and clichéd expressions in the ineffective language of the traumatized, such as "on that ominous night" and "a terrible explosion was heard," for the traumatized fumble for the language which will repress, not illuminate, the grievous memory of the traumatic incident, which no one actually wishes to remember, behind comforting community prosaisms and thoughts and prayers, Toussaint said.

Some in Standard Heights, Toussaint said, looked towards the river and saw no plant at all, their vision of the river was not obstructed, like mine, by the smokestacks and infernal industrial nocturne glowing against the manufactured cloud cover. I, however, looked at the plant and could see no river at all, he said. There was no mystery to this riverine insensibility: whether out of cowardice, shame, or indifference no one who had been in Standard Heights long looked in the direction of the plant or out of the windows facing on it, some going their entire lives without once ever truly seeing the plant, Toussaint said, this omnipresent petrochemical leviathan in our midst. But the TOXMAP, published by a government agency, put us on the map in a way that could not be denied.

The TOXMAP revealed the whereabouts of Standard Heights' *genius loci* to me, he said. The TOXMAP's points whirred and buzzed before my eyes, he said, like planets dancing around a dark star. There were dots and points representing the site of my mother's miscarriage, my brother's confinement in the modern-day plantation of Angola, Jean Lafitte's treasure buried in the vacant greenbelt lots, the location of the severed head, the football that went missing in the chemical fog during one of our pickup games, and the spot where my mother's mourning tree was planted. When I zoomed out to a higher altitude, to the level of the continental United States, a point appeared on Osage Avenue in Philadelphia and a point around Prichard, Alabama, Toussaint said, a point for each note in the petrochemical nocturne.

TOXMAP even showed a colored point in what could only have been the location of the funeral home where not just the headless body belonging to the severed head was stored but where my father's body was held in a morgue overnight after the Christmas Eve explosion, refrigerated like a piece of meat, the very funeral home where blood was drained from my father's body, part of the embalming process that transforms the departed loved one into a bloodless taxidermy, and which reported a sinisterly macabre incident, a hemic tableau from eschatological dreams and which you will hardly believe, Toussaint said, but as much as I would prefer it to be the fabulation of having inhaled too much naphtha and benzene, I can assure you it is no such thing, that my father's blood after the Christmas Eve explosion ran counterclockwise in the native streets like a river, because I went to the funeral home to see the horrible incident for myself. After death in Louisiana, blood is drawn from a corpse and replaced with embalming fluids, like the formaldehydes in the plastic pink flamingos, then around the time that funerary flowers are being shipped to the funeral home, and black tires are hung like wreaths on the door of the family in mourning, the departed loved one's blood is disposed of into the sanitary sewer system like the still life junk in a *vanitas* after the lights go out, or at least that is the death industry practice, such as it is, here in Louisiana, though other jurisdictions may incinerate the withdrawn blood or dispose of it more sanitarily, but due to public budget cuts until further notice the funeral home's drain backed up and blood seeped back to the surface like a bad memory that could not be repressed, spilling in crimson pints — whatever unit of measurement is used for human cruor — in the native streets of Standard Heights, splashing in scarlet streamers in the gutters. The whip-wounds of Whipped Peter and Emmett Till's grisly faceless corpse must have contributed their share of blood to the funeral home accident, as more blood flowed in the native streets than could possibly have come from my father alone, Toussaint said. A sign of the End Times, some said. A sign of wrath upon ExxonMobil, others said. Yes, Toussaint said again, as if reiterating it to himself to overcome his own natural disbelief, my father's blood disgorged into the streets named for dead and persecuted native chiefs. The father's blood on Hiawatha Street and spilled on Pontiac Street. Except for one thing: the blood did not run according to the natural downflow gradient of Standard Heights' observable topography, returning to the stormwater system, seeking out the sea by the common paths of least resistance as is water's wont in most latitudes, as one would naturally expect — my father's hemoglobin ran unstaunched towards the house and the river, *as if uphill*, Toussaint said, emphasizing that this was the part of his story he had never told anyone else before, for the blood's natural shortcut, if the laws of gravitation still apply in Standards Heights, should have been away from the river, not towards it, as the levee and the bluffs are generally the highest points along the Mississippi. What I saw was against nature, he said. The blood of my father — like the Mississippi flowing backward after the New Madrid earthquake — counterintuitively defying gravity in death as it had defied ExxonMobil in life. I said nothing of this to my mother, of course, Toussaint said, she would have told me to stop sinning and fibbing.

The river was represented on the TOXMAP by a serpentine blue ribbon which I did not recognize, Toussaint said. I never saw the river in any shade or hue of blue, Toussaint said pedantically, not cobalt, not azure, not indigo, not beryl, not ultramarine, not turquoise, not teal, and certainly not the TOXMAP's soft Aryan baby blue. The varieties of red, once my father's blood intermixed with the river's natural sedimentary shades of rich brown, synthesizing the colors of the sinuous riverine maps of Harold Fisk, the Mississippi River twisting and contorting in strange loops like skeins of paint splatter-thrown on a Jackson Pollock canvas. Sometimes one or another of Fisk's rivers has been known to eat its own tail, self-cannibalizing at the point on the TOXMAP where ebb meets flow. The Fisk maps, tucked into a technocratic report for the Army Corps of Engineers, overlaid with the TOXMAP's points representing toxic events — here was a realistic map I could use to navigate the Standard Heights I knew, Toussaint said.

Ever since his first visit to the Spillway with his father, to bear witness to that momentous opening like a cosmic event — Halley's Comet or a total solar eclipse — Fisk's rivers ensorcelled Toussaint, albeit for different reasons, as the Congo River ensorcelled Marlow. For Fisk's maps are cartographies of fiction, no more veridical than the petrochemical nocturne to anyone who had not heard it for themselves. This was the Mississippi when d'Iberville and his crew came upon the bloody red stick crucifying the river; the river before the first stone of Baton Rouge had been laid and the flags of England and Spain and France fluttered from the masts of ships on the river; when the Houma and the Bayagoula canoed a different river every flood season; then the river before even humans, in the prehistoric time when mammoths and dire wolves, camels and gigantic beavers and a zoo of other exotic mammals and Pleistocene megafauna inhabited the river banks; the river's self-amputating avulsions separating parts of Tennessee and Arkansas from themselves and creating new islands and frustrating the efforts of mapmakers to fix the river on a single course. The river changing the most after d'Iberville and his crew discovered the bloody red stick, for then began the years of enslaving and working the river, the dredgings and deepenings, the clearing of logjams, the construction of floodgates and levees, the complex manacles of engineering controls that culminated in the Spillway Toussaint's father took him to see open, the river crashing over his ancestors' graves. Toussaint and I were closest to the river of 1944, when Fisk made his fictive maps, the Mississippi represented negatively as a white ribbon flowing through the valley in a kaleidoscopic riverine palimpsest of multiple personality disorder, the blank white river threaded and knotted by the rich green tumble of 1880, the coral pink unraveling of 1820, the haint blue lacework of 1765, and long after us there will no doubt be another sequel in petrochemical black, one more stratum in the twitching and squirming palimpsest of overwritten rivers. Fisk's river flows into the Dead Zone that every year expanded like leprosy in the Gulf of Mexico, that hypoxic region where the beloved dead such as Toussaint's father and the levee builders go to wait out the millennium, this particular phase of civilization that I have dubbed Petrochemical Modernism — who knows how long it will last. Maybe never.

Perhaps more devastating than the toxic events themselves was the effect zooming out on TOXMAP had on my psyche — I never should have done that — as it revealed the utter banality of Standard Heights' Christmas Eve event, Toussaint went on. Other Standard Heights — towns like Mossville and Diamond and Norco — were also mapped up and down the river. The TOXMAP situated Standard Heights within the wider context of the edgelands that oozed and suppurated like gangrene at the city's unknown perimeters — it relativized everything I held absolute: the mountain of oil drums, the chlorine gas ghost ships, the cloud manufacturing operations, our mortality rates — with the same effect on me as the refutation of geocentric theory with the heliocentric model must have had on the medievalists who clung to their anthropocentric cosmologies like life rafts in an unimpressed and apathetic universe, Toussaint said.

What might have caused the blood of Toussaint's father to reverse course like a deranged river and seep from the sewers and gutters, filling the native streets of Standard Heights with blood, I wondered, searching for a naturalistic explanation, a casual mechanism, knowing as well as Toussaint did that I was skimming only the petrochemical surface of incomplete appearances. The funeral home incident, which was not part of the accident report's official investigation, was only partially explained by terror management theory, how psychic conflict arises from the incompatibility of the instinct of self-preservation, which told Toussaint to flee the bloodhounds, and the inexorable caprice of death's imminent nightshift, the result of which conflict is terror, which being both inexorable and stochastic, requires retreat into familiar symbols and the cozy conventions of the tribe: Toussaint's dream of washing his father's bones in the river, and the funeral hunt which ends in the devalued catch of trash and dead fish. As in the bizarre case of Roy Sullivan, the Human Lightning Conductor, a park ranger struck by lightning seven times, after all those lightning strikes he died of a self-inflicted gunshot wound to the head due, so it is said, to unrequited love: death does not hunt one from the margins, descending in a flash and bang from the sky, spiraling inward upon the center — it exists already at the center, in the inchoate shadows hibernating in the soles of your feet, walking with you, taking your steps for you, ultimately breathing for you like a pair of second lungs till death and its claque burn and liquefy your lungs with chlorine gas. Death was not some far-off disaster, a mishap that happened to others, on embattled continents like Africa, or in family stories about slave uprisings and transatlantic crossings, but a totem right here in Standard Heights, it flew an American flag and a flag with a self-harming pelican on it. The worm eats at the core, not at the unfocused peripheries or the vanishing point tangents, drawing the father's blood out of the earth, one part Spillway floodwater and two parts wormwood.

Remembering the maps we drew of Lafitte's treasure buried in the vacant greenbelt lots, Toussaint said, I undertook my own counter-mapping efforts to rectify the TOXMAP's incompleteness. Using the online web-mapping resource SocialExplorer, I found that Standard Heights is administratively part of Block Group 3, Census Tract 5 and Block Group 2, Census Tract 5, Toussaint said. Against such census data categories as race, median income, and other household statistics, I mapped the approximate location of the German Coast Uprising, the vector of the Georgetown slaves as they made their rebellious way upriver, the voyages of the chlorine gas ghost ships, the locations and movements of the armies engaged in the Battle of Baton Rouge, the habitats of the hippogriff and Stymphalian birds, the tracking movements of the bloodhounds on the scent of Whipped Peter. The lands west of the river were declared *terra incognita*, and the east bank was marked with a skull and crossbones. This counter-map was a more authentic representation of the petrochemical geography of Standard Heights than any official government TOXMAP, Toussaint said, those sanitized official cartographies that cannot account for the keloid scars on the territorialized back of Whipped Peter. Instead, I counter-mapped the toxic terrain of the petrochemical empire, Standard Heights as the ruined capital, with its Neanderthal legislators and good old boy statesmen as the rotting fish of Devil's Swamp. Interrogating the petrochemical map-territory relation did nothing to reverse the Christmas Eve explosion or to erase the toxic points, but now I knew the lay of the land, the way it really and toxically was and not how the ExxonMobil plant told us it was and was to be, Toussaint said.

Then I woke late one discolored morning, Toussaint said, thinking it was almost nightfall: the sunlight maligned by wan streaks of ebonized shade, like liquid iodine on a sheet of glass. I got out of bed and went to the blackened window, the only one not blown out in the Christmas Eve explosion, discerning there the patterned striations of brushstrokes. An announcement of mourning or some whimsical home improvement. It would appear that under the duress of some traumatic afflatus mother had painted the house black after the Christmas Eve explosion — totally and completely black. Not one to loiter long in the widowhood of bereavement, she set to work the first Sunday morning of the new year and did not stop — it was a small house — till all the exterior walls and the roof were blackened with ten gallons of paint she got from the storeroom of the strip club, which used the black paint to cover the walls, floors and ceilings of the bathrooms, claustrophobic coffins of cinder-block with an electric chair toilet regretfully illuminated by a bare bulb and no privacy door, Toussaint said. I stood outside in the yard with my brother when the work was done, my mother admiring her completed brushwork, the house fully blackened and she said your father would've wanted it this way, Toussaint said.

After the Christmas Eve explosion, the names of the dead chieftains were all missing from the street signs. Hiawatha and Pontiac and Powhatan. I wanted to burn the palm branches on my father's coffin, this verdant and tropical leaf, emblem of casinos and luxury resorts, it offended my expectation that the funeral should be a cold and lifeless formality. Unlike Emmett Till's funeral, this was not an open casket affair, and graveside I stood between my mother and brother, the green palm frond mocking the lifeless father. The Curse of the Saints, I thought. My father was buried on the east bank of the river, Toussaint said, same side as the plant, the river sweeping by us, down to the Dead Zone, like blood pumping through an artery on its way to a fresh wound. The artificial green mat of plastic graveside grass, made in the process flow diagrams of the plant, and no one offered my mother a chair on which to sit and listen to the sermon without standing, which my father would not have wanted, and the interminable waiting for the coffin of writhing snakes to be lowered into the pit of black earth. You knew it could happen, you always knew, but the explosions at the plant were supposed to happen on someone else's shift, Toussaint said. Nevertheless, the explosion came as a surprise like being tasered in one's sleep. The Surgeon General put warnings on cigarette packs but not *caveat emptor* on Standard Heights. Sometimes I thought maybe things would have been different had we lived on the west bank, over in Port Allen, with the river between us and the plant, a house in the cane fields, farther from the plant's baleful influence. And when the dirt was cast on the palm frond I swear the river ran backward and the sun moved counterclockwise, the wind ripped pages from the Bible and drowned them all in the river, Abraham and Isaac, Jesus and Mary, Solomon and Sheba, Paul and the apostles, all drowned. All things flow, the river said, the river retelling the story of Abraham and Isaac, this time the son sacrificing the father, the self-harming mother pelican on the state flag at the Capitol building gnashing and tearing at its bloody breast, and the Liberty Bell replica cracking down the middle. There was a postseason Saints game after my father's sepulture, a futile and unheroic loss against the Falcons. It was more than a mere loss, a humiliating defeat, peewee against Goliath, as if we had lost the will to live or win. The green palm frond was the same vivid green as the artificial funereal turf laid out like a bib at the mouth of the pit. The symbolism of the palm has meant many different things to many different peoples, but it strained credulity that these cheap, kitschy palms once represented immortality, as the ancient Ba believed, when the only deity we could believe in was the petrochemical leviathan: the process flow diagrams had perfected the unseeing of the gods and the totalization of the greenbelt for the plant's *Lebensraum.* That day at the funeral, I could see only a browning, desiccant palm frond on a closed casket, nothing beyond this petrochemical vale of tears: the symbol of the palm branch in fact supplanted that which it was contrived to symbolize, its immortal referent obscured behind thousands of years of mythmaking. We knew what the hazmat symbols — skull and crossbones, the test tube pouring corrosive liquid on a human hand, the wormwood star aflame — were supposed to mean, but not this palm frond. A last offense against his memory, which was already fading, my father was buried in plain sight of the plant's smokestacks, the infernal manufacturing of chemical clouds forming and unraveling above his grave for eternity, snowfall of toxic ash settling on his gravestone carved with hazmat symbols. My brother and I were supposed to assist in moving the first shovelfuls of dirt onto the palm frond, but I couldn't do it. I thought our father would come back to haunt us, to reveal to us the location of Lafitte's treasure or to monitor whether we transgressed his Eleventh Commandment against opening the windows, but no such visiting revenant ever to my knowledge materialized, and somehow I knew that if he was going to come back and haunt us I would personally know about it, so little credence was given to Xavier's claim of seeing our father's face in the rusting pattern of the oil drums, dragging me out there one starless night to confront the drums in the wan prison yard lamplight and bilious afterglow of the plant, but I never saw any face, our father's or anyone else's. One no longer sees ghosts because we have failed to maintain the bare minimum of a desirable world that the dead would wish to return to, and so they dwell in the black and blank spaces between the bullet hole stars, he said.

Following the Christmas Eve explosion, Toussaint said, Standard Heights succumbed to a slow death by arsons and neglect, applied broken windows theory. A house on the block bounded by Pontiac and Hiawatha burned down, the fire department neither extinguished the fires nor bothered to investigate, and in dreams that seemed more vivid than anything I ever saw while awake, I wandered the vacant greenbelts lots of Standard Heights, at other times pacing in the cargo hold of a leaking ship, sifting through the rubble of Osage Avenue for the right brick, one in particular that would break the last window in the family home, the one that somehow did not blow out in the Christmas Eve explosion, joining a search party for the missing head of Cudjo's golden bust. Bloodhounds barking in the distance, gas flares belching from the ExxonMobil plant and melting the moon. I had to be careful not to step on the counter-map's toxic points, lest I disturb ancient petrochemical memories, the ground beneath our feet was studded with injection wells, Toussaint said, all the iniquitous byproducts of Petrochemical Modernism repressed into the porous rock, which in these oneiric sequences erupted in apocalyptic geysers of chemical lava that buried our house, inexhaustibly energized like the Centralia mine fire, a coal seam conflagration that burned eternally beneath the ground in Pennsylvania, and in my counter-mapping, as in Dante's *Divine Comedy*, I modeled Standard Heights' local geology as an inverted cone, each concentric circle narrowing as the cone neared the earth's core, deep beneath the ExxonMobil plant, the inverted cone having formed when Lucifer crashed to the fallen planet, a bitter star blazing like a torch it was said, rearranging continents and realigning embittered rivers, and there were those in church who said the fallen angel landed somewhere on the banks of the Mississippi around what is today left of the former Standard Heights neighborhood, the fires of perdition from this manmade event softly, satanically raging beneath our feet, the water too bitter to ever put them out.

The last time I was in Standard Heights I looked west towards the river and the petrochemical plant and said I hate you, Toussaint said, because you are the dominant apparatus on the globe and the silent toxic void in which all heterogeneous cultures, upon contact with yours, perish and those who remain have nothing left but contaminated memories that are too discontented, too toxic to remain long repressed in the injection wells and the infernal inverted cone created by a wormwood star falling from the bullet hole sky, Toussaint said.

Two Dreamless Nights in the Gaston Motel

Fat Tuesday and the vomitorium of the streets are debauched with gaudy masquerade. No one in this ragbag jamboree of bashed revelers wears their native face today. Costumed figures tossed fistfuls of colorful loops of mass-produced plastic trinkets to avid hands elevated in saturnine supplication, the beads thrown with too much gusto caught in tree branches, forgotten the moment of consumption. I picked up one of the beads from the ground, littered with Made in China paper slips. I had not known the beads traveled so far. The plastic beads in my hand felt like the rosaries I have fingered in the flickering dark of candlelit churches, a petrochemical miracle. In order for Petrochemical Modernism's model of consumption to work, we cannot know where our consumables — all those brightly colored products in the Gursky photograph Toussaint was forbidden to get too close to — originate, in what far countries and exotic climes they are produced by the millions.

The nocturne is a plastic protean song, and on Fat Tuesday it sounds like *March of the Bobcats* by Pete Fountain. The public license of Mardi Gras follows a gallows formula: the festival's zaniness and decadent spectacle increasing in direct proportion as the everyday life of Petrochemical Modernism becomes wormwood-dulled, howling with humorless neurasthenia, qualitatively comatose, whip-scarred insentient, flowing backward in comfortable stupefaction, bovine creatures standing in a field of lightning strikes. Rain flashed the pavement. The wet streets sparkled with brilliant trash. The tortuous and deformed arms of the muscular oaks dripped with parti-colored strands of single-use plastic beads that would bedizen the tree canopy for months to come. The beads falling in musical quarter notes — green, purple, gold — on the avenues, the strands degrading over time, the motley vivid lead-based paint washing off into the soils, leaving behind a colorless hard gray nucleus like a musket ball. The strands degrade, the color vanishes to whatever grayscale afterlife color is condemned, but the invisible, inert lead leaching into the earth has its own afterlife. These talismanic festival beads were manufactured in China from recycled e-waste: we shipped our scrapped electronics to a factory in one of China's free enterprise zones, and by some alchemical magic our computers and phones were transformed into the party rosaries thrown by masked krewes riding their strange floats at dream speeds through the saturnalia. Office equipment, mobile phones, television sets, refrigerators, game consoles. An office worker's former desk chair or computer station is transformed into the totem beads adorning the neck. An office computer became the beads thrown from a float. Like the miracle of the water transformed into wine, circuit boards are processed into the more coveted medallions. The world system, but for the global movement of plastic, would quickly grind to a halt. I wore a Zulu medallion around my neck that had been shaped, molded and intricately painted by the damaged, arthritic hands of a nameless woman working on a bead production quota in a Chinese factory. A Mardi Gras bead plantation, I thought, as the brass music enchanted the medallion necklace running in toxic rivers flowing around my neck like a hundred mad boa constrictors.

Like all the other marchers in the parade, he wore a skeletal blackface, though at once I recognized the tattoo on the man's knuckles: *worm* and *wood.* A woman's red lipstick kiss tattooed on his neck. The krewe wore elaborate, exotic costumery, resplendent headdresses high with feathers, like Nick Cave's soundsuits. Toussaint's upper body, shirtless, painted gold like the headless bust of Cudjo, his grass skirt rustling around his waist and he pitched hand-painted coconuts at the crowds gathered up and down Jackson Avenue. Spike Lee was King of Zulu that year, and the crowds were larger than usual, pressing against the miles of the portable police crowd control barriers with the NOPD's star in the crescent moon symbol. Our eyes met through the masked crowd and even through the laughing skull of face paint I recognized Toussaint. He seized me by the arm, and before I knew what was happening I was passing between the crowd control barricades, marching into the parade route to became one of the Krewe of Zulu.

The Gaston Motel, Toussaint said as we marched behind a tractor-pulled float, shouting over the rhythmic bedlam of drums and brass, opened on 1510 5th Avenue North to tap a single market: traveling blacks disallowed by Jim Crow from lodging at white hotels, as Birmingham was then a regular stopover for black activists traveling between New Orleans and Atlanta. My mother once stayed at the Gaston Motel, perhaps during the journey north from Prichard to Philadelphia — after the Colored Entrance picture was taken by Gordon Parks but before the Siege of Osage Avenue sent her and her family to the land I dreamed of as the Republic of New Afrika. A copy of the Green Book — maybe even *the* copy I chanced upon in the house — accompanied her from Prichard to the motel and northward. I can see her, on some rattletrap bus, with her pitiful common possessions, flipping through the Green Book's pages — they would be less yellow in her hands than they are today in mine — in search of friendly accommodations in a hostile city. Bus boycotts paralyzed the city's transit system, Master Hammond's bloodhounds transformed into Bull Connor's police dogs. My mother was not a Claudette Colvin, or a Rosa Parks — she would not have participated in the Montgomery bus boycotts resulting in the *Browder v. Gayle* ruling that promulgated the unconstitutionality of Alabama's state laws segregating the city buses, not because she did not believe in the causes of equality and desegregation, of course she did, Toussaint said, but because she felt compelled to follow the North Star and get the hell out of Alabama, which had too few addresses friendly to traveling Negroes in the Green Book.

My mother lodged at the Gaston in early May, Toussaint went on, mere days before the Gaston was attacked in a savage bombing that tore off the motel's façade on May 11, 1963, Toussaint said. Two nights in a second floor room, the door locked, curtains drawn against the city lights. Birmingham was not a safe place for a little black girl in those days, a sooty, dour, mirthless industrial town without the coastal Catholic footlooseness she was acclimated to in Mobile with its creole cheer and dignified, humid gaiety, animated as the port city was by an island ethos unknown in the Alabama hinterlands, Toussaint said. During the day, my mother told me while she cleaned out my father's things after the Christmas Eve explosion, Toussaint said, we didn't leave the hotel, but hung around in the courtyard and watched young black men in dark suits come and go, as far away as Prichard we'd heard how white people in Birmingham beat up blacks for the most petty imagined offenses, my mother said. Birmingham was a city where crude homemade bombs exploded in the night, you woke thinking the explosions were a bad dream but they were not, and the police would not come to the Gaston if you called for help. We listened to men arguing seriously in the courtyard, the panicked screeching of tires, the slamming of doors, she said. But Birmingham, built in the manner of the northern metropolises, an industrial city on a Euclidean grid, gave her a foretaste of what to expect in her new life in Philadelphia where the buildings taller than the Louisiana State Capitol scraped the sky and you did not know your neighbor's family's business, Toussaint said, and there were no Colored Entrances.

Many of the Civil Rights Movement's most crucial dramatic scenes took the Gaston as their setting: the black umbrella in the upper right corner was part of the theatrical property of those years and an awful augury of things to come. Another sighting of the Zapruder Film's Umbrella Man, this time in Birmingham, Alabama. Umbrella Man had been the only man in Dallas that November day to open an umbrella in otherwise clear, sunny weather when Kennedy was shot, and while it is not extraordinary for white folks of uncommonly pale complexion to carry an umbrella on sunny days to shield them from the ultraviolet rays of the sun, no one else in the photograph of the Gaston Motel carries an umbrella, and there are enough men in jackets to infer that the day was mild and pleasant. Umbrella Man had a flair for showing up around public figures who were about to be assassinated: more bullet hole stars. While Martin Luther King and Fred Shuttlesworth take questions from journalists, Umbrella Man was there, on the margins of the group of journalists gathered around the press table, putting in an appearance in Birmingham before, later that same year, being photographed on the presidential motorcade procession of John F. Kennedy who was assassinated the autumn of the year my mother spent two terrifying nights in the Gaston Motel, listening to the Klan bombs explode in the night, rearguard volleys in the Battle of Baton Rouge's unexploded ordnance, Toussaint said as the unremoved stone figure of General Robert E. Lee levitated over the city skyline, the Zulu parade winding through the eye of the storm of Lee Circle, and I saw a man standing behind the parade barrier beneath a black umbrella — a signal to co-conspirators.

This Fat Tuesday was balmy and sunny as the first day in Eden. To the stone General refusing surrender, blackfaced Zulus parading through the eye of the storm, it must have felt like the world was ending. I would not have stopped them had the parade tried to topple Lee that very moment. Already, Lee's statue is beginning to stink like the rotting corpses in Gardner's battlefields. Toussaint eyed Lee, not with malice and race hatred, but with his own brand of refined mockery and absurdist ridicule of anything set in stone, the Zulu parade wrapping around the base of the monument in a serpentine cavalcade as if all of Toussaint's race were trying to squeeze through the neck of a bottle, a bottle which is a Molotov cocktail, the entire body of the parade, in its oneiric fanfare around General Lee, proclaiming in univocal suffrage without a megaphone, because the *vox populi* has no need of such fascist instruments: ladies and gentleman, for now on your precious law and order are a laughingstock, your monotheism is a castrated cow, for now on the kingdom of heaven and the terrestrial globe shall merge into one delectable and cosmic king cake, from hence forth all jazz-less creation myths shall be rewritten in compliance with the reasonable demands of the Axeman of New Orleans' letters for the conduct of Fat Tuesday, *I am very fond of jazz music, and I swear by all the devils in the nether regions that every person shall be spared in whose home a jazz band is in full swing at the time I have just mentioned. If everyone has a jazz band going, well, then, so much the better for you people. One thing is certain and that is that some of your people who do not jazz it out on that specific Tuesday night (if there be any) will get the axe.* And there was indeed one stone General, not of our people per se, who was not jazzing it out on that specific Tuesday night, and for whom the axe was coming. One by one, under the sightless General Lee, the Zulu marchers paraded through the eye of this storm in Lee Circle, an ostentatious display of tropical-colored feathers and sparkling sequins, proclaiming the righteous demands of their earthly kingdom, no more Section 8, no more sleeping on park benches, no more supply and demand, no more *quid pro quo*, no more trickle-down economics, no more endocrine disruptors, no more suicides by cop, the TOXMAP shall be remapped with the coordinates of a new earthly kingdom, the petrochemical nocturne shall grind out its last pitiful note on a broken accordion, the murdered peasant king Jesus Christ reborn inside a king cake, men shall go about the native streets on leashes, the drowned Phoenician sailor resurrected on the west bank of the river, the bloodhounds shall be euthanized, the lost tribes of Zulu shall inherit the earth, the winner of the Angola Rodeo shall be paroled without further ado, the golden bust of Cudjo's missing head returned, the sunken slave ship *Clotilda* restored for its reversed transatlantic passage, the 54th Regiment shall be given equal pay as their white co-soldiers and outfitted with automatic weapons, Cancer Alley shall be cured, the human genome recoded with the dialogue of *Mandingo*, the chemical classification symbols buried with the ethnographer's camera, the good fight shall be given home field advantage, the Curse of the Saints shall be lifted, the temporary subversion of patriarchal norms shall be institutionalized in random acts of adult male breastfeeding, the boogie woogie shall be the Republic of New Afrika's national dance, Louis Armstrong, King of Zulu shall be coronated with the Rings of Saturn, the court jester cavorting with his scepter — all blessed by the painted whores of Babylon. And in place of the defeated but unreconstructed General Lee on his stone throne, circumscribed by a regiment of portable public toilets, at the heart of the eye of the storm, this blackfaced krewe exalts the shackled double of King's mugshot, in profile and portrait, after he was arrested and booked in Birmingham Jail.

Once the most superlatively luxurious mid-century motel then available to traveling African-Americans, and listed among Birmingham's Negro-friendly establishments in *The Negro Motorist Green Book*, the Gaston Motel now presents a sorry, diminished sight, Toussaint said, boarded up and forgotten, grass growing out of the cracks in the concrete, the windows broken like those in Charity Hospital. The wind roaming at will like a mangy cur. I found a postcard of the Gaston Motel between the pages of the Green Book, an idealized depiction of the motel's glory days in that halcyon period before the Klan bombings, the windows all intact, a pristine yet nostalgic mid-century quality to everything, the neat and tidy landscaping, the rows of vintage cars parked in the courtyard, a clean and nontoxic sky above, a place where Baraka's "a closed window looks down on a dirty courtyard" does not apply.

On a cold winter day, I stood alone in the courtyard where King and Shuttlesworth, prior to King's arrest, sat at a table giving a press conference, Toussaint said as we began the Zulu parade route's finale up Orleans Avenue, and though it was hard to hear over the Mardi Gras music, which was both festive and melancholy, I leaned in to make sure I missed nothing. I went up the stairs to the motel's second level, gripping the cold balcony railing, and looked down to the courtyard, in shadow now that the sun was ceding the nightshift to a magnolia moon. King and his men planned their generation's German Coast Uprising in the mid-century rooms of this now abandoned motel, Toussaint said, which had all the signs of recent occupancy by those who, like me, had been dehoused by the bulldozers of Petrochemical Modernism. I do not know which room my mother stayed in but I hoped she slept in Room 30, the very room which the Civil Rights activists designated as their War Room, and in which, late into the night, they planned King's defiance of court orders and his booking in Birmingham Jail. No suicide by cop. I tried to find Room 30 but the room numbers were all long gone. I thought of the houses in Standard Heights without house numbers. I remained on the second floor balcony till the black empire of night was complete and the bullet hole stars shone. A police cruiser slowly passed on 5th Avenue North, directing his searchlight into the courtyard, hunting for trespassers. I had not come here on a ghost tour. Merely, after seeing for myself the ruins of Africatown, I wanted to see where my mother had spent two dreamless nights in the Gaston Motel, a stopover on her way to *The City That Bombed Itself,* following the North Star to begin her new life as a future survivor of Osage Avenue. The Gaston Motel too gave the appearance of having been besieged and lost in an unfinished battle. The wind opened and closed an unlocked motel door, I heard children laughing in the courtyard, but there was no one there. The night sky over the Gaston Motel was indistinguishable from that over Standard Heights, the bloody constellations configured like bullet holes in a dark tinted window. I picked up a few sere, dead leaves from the courtyard, crumpling and grinding them in my hand into a fine cindery powder, opening my hand again, the wind scattering the brown spirits in dusty whorls about the empty courtyard, Toussaint said, as he slipped through the police crowd control barrier, deserting me in the parade route and melting into the lost Zulu tribes of Orleans Avenue.

The Second Defeat of General Lee

General Lee levitated outside of my window. Knowing that the General's days were numbered, and compelled to witness his removal, I'd been living out an assembly line of netherworld days in a room of Lee Circle's Hotel Modern, days running into one another like so many mass-produced plastic units of time, self-identical and fungible, and at night drinking old-fashioneds and bothering strangers in the bar of the Ace Hotel, which is not listed in *The Negro Motorist Green Book*. If I wasn't in the Hotel Modern, I was in the French Quarter, unpainted plaster or arabesque wallpaper peeling, like those inveterately decadent Mediterranean flats depicted like the stagecraft of a lucid dream in Anthropologie catalogs. Through the thin plaster walls, someone picking out the solitary, melancholy note of the nocturne from a minor, Aeolian scale on a rotting piano.

The Hotel Modern at Lee Circle was all angles and Rorschach splashes, wallpapered in neo-baroque fleurs-de-lis and arabesques in silver, white and black, long silent corridors blind with closed doors. Encountering no one in the corridors during the day, the corridor came alive whenever I was alone in my room, so that I heard the Hotel's other occupants but never saw them, bumps and hoarse shouts in the night. At night, from the window, I watched the trash sweepers and road cleaning trucks vacuuming the Mardi Gras trash around Lee Circle. Every morning I woke in my room, tentatively approaching the window — at eyelevel with the Confederate General — to see whether the removal had been completed, General Lee defiant in defeat on his priapic, ascendant pedestal, cars circling him like orbiting debris, the General's arms folded, surveying the sinking city, before it disappeared into the Gulf of Mexico's ever-growing Dead Zone — ours was the last generation of New Orleanians, Toussaint once said — and though Appomattox took place more than a hundred a fifty years ago, Lee's last day in power was May 19, 2017. In the wake of the Civil War, whose outcome was not what the majestic plural hoped for, the South was given to public monumentalism and grandiose sentimentalism, erecting delusional statues of stone and bronze on the courthouse squares, meanwhile leaving the confederate undead unburied on the battlefields, for burial would be to admit defeat.

Again, I encountered Toussaint in Lee Circle, the carnival trees still dripping with scintillating plastic beads. A tall solitary figure — he wore a hoodie in a stained glass pattern — in a crowd of onlookers gathered to witness the removal of the Confederate statue of General Robert E. Lee, Toussaint as stoic and implacable as a statue himself, fixed and immobile while agitated protestors and counter-protestors swirled around him. Though most of the removal's protestors were a whiter shade of pale, I was perplexed by the smattering of darker faces among their number who seemed to object to deposing the General from the city skyline. Toussaint remained aloof from either side, that was his style: not to take up a definitive position, even though he knew as well as I that not taking a position was a luxury available foremost to philosophers and publicans. Mounted on a horse, and cast in bronze or stone, Toussaint would have cut a redoubtable figure against the skyline.

The City of New Orleans, all spring and summer of that year, had been removing the Confederate monuments, constructed during the Jim Crow Era, honoring Jefferson Davis, General Beauregard, General Lee and the Battle of Liberty Place, this population of unreconstructed stone men commanding the city as if for some frontal assault. We were witnesses — the Hand and Eye Motif awakening from an anachronistic stupor — to the dismantling of a memory that never happened. Lawsuits were filed to block the monuments' dismantling, but in the end the courts ruled in favor of the City which voted for dismantlement. They should've painted Lee black, Toussaint opined, dressed him in a pink bikini, and flown the transgender and Rasta flags from the Confederate monument, appropriated and reinterpreted the monuments instead of treating them as precious objects to be stored in a museum somewhere. Let people use them for paintball target practice, he said. We need more monuments, he said, not fewer, monuments to James Meredith and Harry Haywood, monuments to Cudjo and Emmett Till, to Whipped Peter and Charles Deslondes.

Protestors of the monument's removal appeared attired in period costume, the Confederate gray uniforms, others wrapped in Confederate flags and brandishing open-carry firearms, having stumbled upon some re-enactment of all the battles lost by the Confederacy. So crudely vehement and rabid were the protestors in the expression of their opposition to the monument's removal, one would have thought they had personally been there that day at Antietam, ready to pose with the corpses for Gardner's camera. Rumor of hoax and back-fence talk swirled around us in the circle, the eye of the storm raging with whispered canards and unconfirmed creepypasta bruits: the statue of Lee was booby-trapped and would explode if tampered with. Whomever removed the statue would have a seven generational curse upon his family. Buried deep in the base of the monument was a sealed time capsule, a message from the Confederate past, and though no one knew for sure the time capsule was alleged to contain a cigar lit by the General, a soldier's Oxford Bible, a sheaf of memoirs, thousands of dollars in Confederate currency, and the war plans for the South's Second Coming. War plans which must be burned if they are not to be deployed in the everlasting Battle of Baton Rouge. None of the protestors knew that the statue of their beloved Lee was manufactured in the North like the Mardi Gras throws and trinkets that are imported from Hong Kong — we have even exported the manufacture of our historical memory.

Lee Circle was barricaded for crowd control and to prevent skirmishes between the monument's opposing sides. The Krewe of the Four Horsemen threw plastic Mardi Gras doubloons featuring a cameo of the General, and the slogan "Forever Lee Circle," in flagrant violation of city code section 34-28(b) prohibiting the use of throws conveying a polemical message. While the removal's opposing sides taunted one another or argued amongst themselves, Toussaint recited lines to himself from "For the Union Dead," "Shaw's father wanted no monument except the ditch" and "where his son's body was thrown/and lost with his men." Then the removal crew, identities protected by black masks, moved in on the statue, ambushing the defiant General, surrounding him from all sides. But Lee was not ready to surrender his special place in the sky: the city's removal crew struggled to fit a strap around the statue, like a condemned man resisting the noose, and for some time the outcome of the removal appeared uncertain, that the removal crew might actually fail to subdue the General, the Great White Hope remaining atop his pedestal in Lee Circle to fight another day.

Lee Circle, Showing Library and Shriners Temple,
New Orleans, La.

Standard Heights. Osage Avenue. Africatown. The disappearances of everything Toussaint has ever known. Even the people he knew vanished irreversibly — even as the river itself reversed course — behind implacable institutions: his father in the nightshift at ExxonMobil, his brother incarcerated in Angola, while the forbears of my own bloodline were, often as not, complicit with those vanishings. While we waited for the General to fall and for Lee Circle to be Lee Circle no longer, I felt this was the time to come clean with Toussaint, our time was running out. Long ago, I said, my people's people were staunch Bonapartists fleeing the Bourbon Restoration, when the brothers of executed Louis XVI restored the royal House of Bourbon to the crown, I told Toussaint while we waited for the noose to take Lee from his sky totem, and I got some sense of the whetted anticipation Toussaint must have felt while waiting for the Spillway to open in St. Charles Parish back in 1979 or 1983, as Toussaint said it might have been either of those years. Yes, my people came from center-right reactionaries, I said, they were outright monarchists desirous of a strong French empire consolidated under the House of Bonaparte, the Corsican family from which Napoleon descended. France underwent violent upheavals during the Revolution when the hereditary monarchy and the feudalism of the French patrician class were abolished, and because the Deep South was, and to a large extent still is enthralled to a patrician planter class that pined for the dubious hereditary advantages of feudalism, Bonapartism is one of many toxic isms that have hypnotized the South: anti-elitist rhetoric, military involvement in governmental affairs, and general conservatism, all evident in today's rising populism, a caricature of Caesarism, a charismatic strongman personality whose imperial rule is founded upon a richly embellished and mostly fictional cult of personality, I said.

In response to a petition from these Bonapartists, I said, Congress approved on March 3, 1817 an act granting the French refugees four contiguous townships of 90,000 acres of land at the price of two dollars per acre, but the land grant came with a single binding and impossible condition: the colonists must plant grapes and olives. An impossible and absurd condition — no plot of ground is more hostile to the cultivation of recherché Mediterranean products such as grapes and olives than the gross soils of Alabama — unless you consider that the Bonapartist colonies were believed to be clandestine military operations for restoring Napoleon's power from abroad, but Alabama has yet to be the stage for launching anything other than a few winning football teams and Neanderthal political campaigns, I said. Congress set the Bonapartists up for failure, knowing full well that olives and grapes would never flourish in the subtropical climate of rural Alabama where nothing but cash crops like cotton has ever grown.

Many years have fallen from the calendars since I have been home to Demopolis, hometown of the Gaston Motel's owner, at the confluence of the Tombigbee and Black Warrior Rivers, to see what remains of the French settlement there, I said to Toussaint, as protestors began booing the statue's demise. A Walmart Supercenter on the edge of town, a prototype of all the rundown, spavined river towns. A cement plant dusting the site of Aigleville, Alabama, or Eagleville, named after the French Imperial Eagle used by Napoleon's *Grande Armée*. The Vine Colony's Bonapartists were joined by white refugees fleeing the Haitian slave rebellion of 1791, led by Toussaint's antecessor and namesake, Toussaint Louverture, and so it was a slave revolt in Haiti, in the final decade of the 18th century, when explorer Mungo Park became the first European to set eyes on the Niger River, when Upper Canada outlawed slavery, when the Dutch East India Company was dissolved through bankruptcy, that entangled Toussaint and I, as I have here tried to chronicle, in the petrochemical nocturne of Standard Heights.

Because nothing but cotton would grow in Alabama, the

French settlers abandoned the Vine and Olive Colony for Francophone Mobile or New Orleans, and I must divulge here, I said to Toussaint, who listened intently by all appearances, never peeling his glance off the doomed statue of defeated General Lee, that among the French Bonapartists to depart the Colony for Mobile was a man named Jean, a principal financier in the conspiracy to illegally import slaves from West Africa aboard the *Clotilda*, I told Toussaint, who did not look at me immediately, his focused gaze directed vehemently at the Confederate statue still defiantly defending the circle, but when he did look at me at last his gaze was powerful enough to have knocked Lee off his pedestal like a shot from a cannon.

Now that I was confiding my own ancestry's errors to Toussaint, I felt something amiss in the timing. Why was this confessional imperative prevailing now, when we were about to witness an event — the desecration of the profane and ahistorical effigy of an unrepentant loser — that Toussaint had been anticipating since his father had first told him about the Curse of the Saints and little shirts versus skins black boys becoming president? But to call them errors was to miss the point — a wrong turn down the wrong native street was an error; burning the fried chicken was an error — it was too lenient and merciful when leniency and mercy were unearned, it did not contain the gravamen of the world-historical ripple effects that Toussaint and I were even now feeling in Lee Circle, this was not some minor mistake in filing paperwork, a misspelled name, a column miscalculated in a ledger tabulating the names of slaves with other real property, this was the familial version of the ExxonMobil plant's engineering "error" — the glimmer of a candle, benzene in mother's milk, the red and white blood cells of the present river attacked by bloodhounds — in the process flow diagrams that caused the Christmas Eve explosion.

Yes, it was true, I said, this Jean, from whom I descended on that diseased family tree which I have been trying to cut down, though I do not know whether he came from France, with the first wave of Bonapartists, or whether he was a so-called refugee from Haiti fleeing the rule of freemen of color, invested capital in the abduction of Toussaint's mother's ancestors from the distant slave coast of Africa, importing them to Alabama as the last human capital, founders of Africatown. And as the *Clotilda* crossed the Middle Passage with its kidnapped human cargo, Jean calculated his return on capital, that monstrous abstraction which has laid waste to Standard Heights and fixed Fisk's mutating rivers upon a single and serpentine course of destruction twining and helixing around the pedestal supporting General Lee, I said.

Opposing sides of the monument's removal — the removalists versus the preservationists; this is how things stand in this country of embattled binaries, those who are for change and dethroning the defunct idols line up on one side and are called progressives; those who are for keeping things as they are, because what is is good enough and better than the unknown line up on the other and are called conservatives — traded expletives and hurled rocks and Dixie beer bottles at one another. Death threats to the mayor's office. Suspicious packages left in doorways. In this country, we believe that good triumphs, inexorably and irreversibly over evil, and that for evil there awaits a cinematic comeuppance commensurate to the diameter, circumference and magnitude of the misdeed. For this reason, there are security guards stationed all over the petrochemical landscape. The reactionary response to the takedown of these stony symbols — a bathetic gasp before the oxygen is sucked out of the room by the fires of the *Clotilda* burning in Mobile Bay. There are, of course, worse worlds than the one we inhabit, at least if you believe those who wish for General Lee to remain at the center of Lee Circle, the center of their shriveled and spidery universe. One side of the opposition knew where Cudjo's missing golden head lay, and the other side, the counter-opposition, depending on whose side you were on, knew the coordinates of the *Clotilda* at the bottom of Mobile Bay: neither side of this binary impasse was divulging its secrets to the other.

Fearing violence, other Confederate monuments throughout the city had been removed under the cover of darkness, but the City broke protocol and Lee came down from his pedestal, where he'd been for almost a century, at six in the evening, as the rush hour traffic was thinning and the nation was sitting down to dinner. These statues of defeated generals look nothing like the men — and they are always men — they are supposed to represent, no more than a pile of ash, or a heap of bones resemble the man they once constituted. And anyway, what is stone? Pure immutability, intransigence, cruelty, heartlessness, frigidity, resistance. It is neither fluke nor fortuity that the Confederate generals should be carved in stone — a timeless material therefore incapable of aging, changing, or taking a single step forward without taking two backward.

The crowd cheered as the stoic stone statue of Lee was craned off the plinth, the old General suspended uncertainly above the circle like a man dangling from a hanging tree. Toussaint neither cheered nor applauded, but looked Lee directly in the eye, like a bloodhound honing in on its prey, and then a crescent moon rose over the monumental, dethroned pedestal like an upside down exclamation point. The dramaturgy of Lee's removal was anticlimactic for those who came expecting at least a good fight, a rematch of some kind, for the earth to tremble in its orbit, darkened skies, some sign of judgment like a total solar eclipse, the bloody donnybrook of Gettysburg, Egyptian plagues or a good throaty Rebel Yell from the General who hovered helplessly in the sky above the circle bearing his name, hesitantly, as if he were just on the precipice of saying something, addressing the crowds in a final farewell speech before the knockout punch. But nothing of the sort, no gospel goodbye, no Halloween organs piping a dirge for the finally defeated General. I admit I had expected more, needing some histrionic catharsis, but such is the ignominious dreary end of all who will not surrender. I imagined this is how the Spillway felt when all those innumerable gallons of river water were finally released to flow into Lake Pontchartrain, the waters racing like bloodhounds over ancestral graves. There would be no rematch. The good fight was over before it began. One saw blood running from Lee's nose, and from the bullet hole wounds in the sky above Lee Circle.

One half of the crowd gathered at the police barricades erupted in partisan cheers. I have heard cheering in many contexts, but none as cheerful as this: the cheers, in an audio recording without any visual information, just the cheering excerpted from the Lee Circle context, would sound no different than the cheering at a lively sports event — a boxing match just as well as a tennis match or a college football game. A futilitarian repetition of removal — boring to some, cathartic to others — played itself out one more time. The protests against the Iraq War. The Occupy Wall Street protests. The Women's March. The other half of the crowd which did not cheer — that dejected half went their separate ways in a defeated and dour silence, stunned that their stone General could have surrendered so easily, without a fight. Even Toussaint seemed a little disappointed that the General, so unrepentant all these years, had not lived up to the expectations one half of the crowd had for the Great White Hope.

The General may be gone, Toussaint said, but the removal of Lee's statue, or any of the Confederate statues, didn't go far enough in expunging the physical artefacts of the Confederate hauntology. As I know from the hazmat symbols and the three flags lowered to half-staff the day after the Christmas Eve explosion, symbolic victories come easily, often and cheaply; the underlying structures and petrochemical systems that militate unequal outcomes remain entrenched with or without their stone symbols — Standard Heights is still slipping away into the Gulf of Mexico's Dead Zone; the Angola of the present becomes all there was, is or will be of the past and the future; benzene and naphtha are sequenced in my genome, the bloodstream flooded with wormwood; Cudjo's missing head has never been found — and the same sun, just a bigger bullet hole star, which shines on the rubble of Africatown and Osage Avenue shines also upon the stained glass in the National Cathedral, depicting the major milestones in the undead General's Confederate hagiography: Lee's student days at West Point, his service in the Corps of Engineers, and the Confederate victory at the Battle of Chancellorsville. Another symbol that will have to be removed, the stained glass exalts Lee into the gray empyrean of Confederate sainthood, like some kind of Lost Cause Paul the Apostle. A mummification of the Confederacy, that tribe of cadaverous seditionists, a zombie nation that will not be quieted. Here was the petrochemical cathedral at which the zombie Confederacy and petrochemical proselytes worshipped, Toussaint said, I have imagined myself standing below this stained glass effigy in the National Cathedral with a pocketful of rocks carefully chosen from the vacant greenbelt lots around Standard Heights — the stones had to be from the right place, one stone from each street named for the lost annihilated tribes — and mentally honed my aim on the stained glass' Confederate flag on the right panel, backlit by the same sun that illumines our forty acres and a mule, but I could not do it, I could not throw the first stone, my father's prohibition against opening the window — in this case punching an irreverent wound in the blue and red glass — stultified me, and I emptied the rocks from my pockets on the National Cathedral's front steps. I had never seen anything like these stained glass windows before, Toussaint said, constructed from the broken seventh notes of the windows that shattered in the Christmas Eve explosion, rearranged to tell the life story of the stone man in Lee Circle who refused to surrender, Toussaint said, long after the war was lost.

     While one half of the Lee Circle crowd cheered, perhaps prematurely but certainly with all the *schadenfreude* of seeing Lee's supporters mope about the traffic circle, Toussaint's mood seemed darkened by disappointment in the incompleteness of the removal, of victory declared in the good fight too soon. What had really changed? The petrochemical nocturne still dirges on. The Exxon-Mobil plant still manufactured chlorine gas ghost ships in the toxic cloudworks. The Dead Zone grew larger by the hour. Cudjo's golden bust remained headless. The Curse of the Saints had not been removed. Why stop at Confederate generals? Why not remove every statue of every Master Hammond since the beginning? Lee was the descendant of Revolutionary War heroes, but how was he any different than Thomas Jefferson, Andrew Jackson, or George

Washington? They too must come down, Toussaint said, all these founding fathers were so many Master Hammonds, skull and cross-bones superpatriots, Devil's Swamp colonialists, Dead Zone jingoists of the Mexican-American War, the Indian Removal Act, the Louisiana Purchase, he said, all the chest-thumping conquests that named the hazmat streets of Standard Heights for vanished native tribes. Throw the symbols in the wormwood river, Toussaint said.

But there is some part of us, Toussaint said, that cannot tolerate or interpret the past without statues telling us how to live in the Angola of the present. We are erecting statues today to a new generation of stone heroes and heroines which, in two hundred years' time will be ridiculed and dismantled by a future that will need to be liberated from the Angola of the present which we are constructing— the values they represent now will be in conflict with tomorrow's mores, and who anymore can believe in everlasting, imperishable values? I can only believe in moving targets, in natural flux and molecular dream speed and the unquantifiable movement of Spillway waters. Did not the Protestant iconoclasts destroy the Catholics' profane images of God? Were not the statues of Communist dictators in the public squares of the former Soviet bloc countries torn down? Did not Iraqis topple the statue of Saddam Hussein in Firdos Square? Did not the death mask Europeans rename every bluff and valley and river in their own image? This is the recurring cycle of iconoclasm from which there is no escape, not even the removal of General Lee today will end it, he said.

Lee was a traitor, but of course all the so-called founding fathers were traitors, and had the U.S. lost the Revolutionary War they would've been executed or punished as traitors always have been, Toussaint said. As a native son of Standard Heights, who found out about the buyout of the Louisiana Purchase around the time that the ExxonMobil man knocked on our door at dinnertime to make a buyout offer to my father he thought would not be refused, I hated the Louisiana Purchase, brokered by slave-owning Thomas Jefferson, this theft so often touted as the greatest land deal in history was a calamity to the tribes of the native streets and a debacle for the river, never mind that the lands west of the Mississippi were not the French's to sell, a purchase that culminated in the Christmas Eve explosion, the Gulf of Mexico's Dead Zone, and the endless store aisles of colorful petrochemical goods in Gursky's c-print, the one I was asked by museum security not to get so close too, for fear I might damage the artwork, Toussaint said, or steal it as Jefferson stole the river's west bank. The Louisiana Purchase was merely a formal matter of bookkeeping in the accounts of westward expansionism and the genocidal colonialism that named the streets of Standard Heights after vanished native tribes. But Jefferson is too integral to our foundational mythologies, he and all the other skull and crossbones superpatriots form the nation's feeble superego regulating and delimiting the boundaries of this petrochemical experiment, he said, and they will never be forced to surrender like General Lee was today.

If you want a statue of a white man, why not John Brown or Tom Hanks dressed in a Soundsuit? Why not Andrew Jackson dressed as a pilgrim? Why not Abraham Lincoln performing CPR on the Statue of Liberty? Why not JFK with a bullet in his head? Why not the Great White Hope getting punched in the face by Floyd Mayweather? But I grow sick on this supermarket pharmacology of stone dead symbols, Toussaint said, not least with the chemical classification symbols — the corroded hand, the dead fish, the skull and crossbones, the immortal flame — on the hazmat trucks that never stopped gearing through Standard Heights after the Christmas Eve explosion, the truck volumes seemingly higher than ever before. The marketplace of undead symbolism is the special privilege of those on the other side of town, Toussaint said. Master Hammond and his heirs have monopolized symbolic discourse for so long that we no longer have our own symbols, Toussaint said looking at his empty, numb hands, and we may have to exercise our rights of angary to depose the unfeeling, unthinking, unrepentant stone sore losers. I shouldn't even be here, giving this stone so much power over my conscience, Toussaint said. All of Standard Heights took to the native streets when Alton Sterling was gunned down by Baton Rouge police; white supremacists brandishing tiki torches from Home Depot chant "blood and soil" around Lee Circle. All this rah-rah yelling, the partisan hullabaloo — and for what? We have not yet fully realized the value of silence as a stratagem, to let the river's flux burst the bloodstream's levees. What General Lee's epigones, these softheaded white supremacists in black hoodies and skull and crossbones masks desire more than anything is an apocalyptic confrontation, one last orgasmic bloodbath that will confirm their fragile virility before the world, and what displeases them the most, like spoiled children, is to be ignored, even those who try to intellectualize and prettify the blood and soil movement like Richard Spencer, with his tweed blazers and greasy Nazi cyberpunk haircut, Toussaint said.

What began as a removal of an obsolete and ahistorical symbol ended as a funeral for a Master Hammond. General Lee rested on the flatbed truck as in a funeral hearse, his arms defiantly crossed, the unseeing pits of his eyes darkened from staring so long into the vanishing point retrofuture in which the Confederate veterans on the junk shop postcard marched. As Lee was being transported like a critical patient to an undisclosed municipal warehouse for storage with Mardi Gras parade floats and to rejoin the other deposed Confederate monument men, and the crowds separated into smaller and smaller factions, radiating outwards from the now nameless circle's center, scattering in all directions, Toussaint told me, in what I did not then know would be the last time, of a distant relative — this told to him in turn by his mother in the fatherless days after she begrudgingly accepted ExxonMobil's final buyout offer for the family home in Standard Heights, but he couldn't be sure where she'd learned of this distant relative or how much the buyout from ExxonMobil was worth — who at that time lived as an enslaved person in the little village of Appomattox Court House, Virginia. As Toussaint and I processed the manifold meaning of the now empty plinth where the stone general had stood just that morning, on a high perch overseeing the city like Master Hammond surveying his fields, Toussaint told me too that this distant relation had been walking by the McLean House — now a modest house museum where I once went to see for myself the document of surrender signed by General Lee, confirming that the surrender's ink was indeed dry — at the precise moment in history that General Robert E. Lee, the very man whose stone likeness has drawn this crowd to Lee Circle, exited the McLean House with such a severe mien that only one thing could be concluded: Lee's reluctant acquiescence to the terms of surrender proposed by Union General Ulysses S. Grant. Under the circumstances — a ravaged country, secession and treason, hundreds of thousands dead having changed the hearts and minds of no one — they were generous terms, as the terms of surrender in civil strife go, the vanquished of civil wars in other places and times have not been so lucky. Consider that the Confederate General was not forced to sign the terms of surrender in a slave shack, Toussaint said, instead of in the comfortable, bourgeois atmosphere of the McLean House in the preserved rooms of which today white couples hold wedding ceremonies dressed in period antebellum regalia, holding lavish receptions banqueted on the front lawn landscaped like some Confederate Eden. And at Stratford Hall, the birthplace of baby General Lee, the elderly United Daughters of the Confederacy wept and prayed over the crib of Robert E. Lee, as neither Stratford Hall nor the McLean House has yet succumbed to the bulldozer fates of Iberville or Standard Heights, Toussaint said. That is what I can never forgive, he said, that Lee's birthplace and the house of surrender still stand, are open to the public for pseudo-history tours, while Exxon-Mobil left not one family home standing in Standard Heights, Toussaint said, and so it was because that distant ancestor, as my mother told it after the Christmas Eve explosion, just happened to be passing the McLean House at the very moment of the surrender that I am here, in Lee Circle, to bear witness to the de-resurrection of General Lee, his immutable removal from the city skyline, and so that I can dictate the terms of his surrender, Toussaint said.

There was some public concern, not unfounded, that once General Lee had been removed and returned to the other deposed Confederates — Jefferson Davis and P.G.T. Beauregard, who had been awaiting General Lee in a municipal warehouse — the reunited Confederate leadership might then conspire together for another round of armed insurrection and Confederate resurrection. Ready to make the counterfactual dreams of Churchill's essay in *If it Had Happened Otherwise* come true. Not an impossibility in a land where the wormwood river can flow backward and birdsong has gone extinct. As of my last visit to Lee Circle, to witness for myself that the stone General had not reclaimed his position on the skyline, no statue has been erected in lieu of Lee, the circle bereft of its namesake, an empty pedestal, though in some quarry a marble or limestone rock is waiting to be dimensioned and cut for Lee's replacement, which in its turn will be dismantled and unceremoniously carted off when its time has come, and in lieu of Lee I tried to picture the golden bust of Cudjo restored to its former glory atop the naked pedestal, remembering what Toussaint said, in the alleyway just off Canal Street, after the Mayweather-McGregor fight, about fighting the good fight, but forget the faith.

After the removal of General Robert E. Lee from the stone

plinth in Lee Circle, Toussaint vanished. I scanned the partisan faces of the crowds pressed against the police barricades, those gathered in factions for and those against the General's removal, but recognized none of them as Toussaint who did not much like crowds. I felt the river twitching in the manacles of the levee, the print on the pages of the Christmas Eve explosion accident report and the Green Book fading into oblivion. At my feet, I saw an eye blinking at me — a Zulu medallion thrown from the Mardi Gras parade. I picked it up — pictured on the medallion was a baroquely wrought and technical hieroglyph: the ExxonMobil plant's process flow diagrams and the Hand in Eye Motif. I hung the beads around my neck, the medallion's eye opening and closing, heavy as a millstone.

I guess Toussaint saw what he needed, that the General was no longer master of Lee Circle, replaced with a vanishing point on the TOXMAP. I returned to all the sites of our previous encounters, searching and inquiring, turning up only my own rank biases. Toussaint was not at the landing in Baton Rouge where the riverboat docks. I waited a few hours for him at the levee, among the metal tribe of cast iron and aluminum androgynous figures, the river flowing downriver as usual, and then called it off. Neither have I seen him around Iberville or Charity Hospital, or any of his other haunts. It may be that he is to be found walking the bombed-out ruins of Osage Avenue, or in Mobile in search of living witnesses to the *Clotilda*'s resurrection those years ago in the Port of Mobile, anyone who can confirm his family's history to his satisfaction, evidence of things unseen. I made inquests in the dazzling limpid sulfur of the ExxonMobil plant glittering on the rimpled river. I checked the rural road running before the Ashland Plantation and saw only a murder of black crows, their flinty eyes quizzing me, in the ancient oaks beneath the crescent moon. I sat waiting, long into the night, at the sports bar where we saw the good fight. But General Lee had at last surrendered and that particular phase of the good fight was over. I wished to tell him that the stained glass windows of General Lee in the National Cathedral had been deconsecrated and, though not smashed as he might have wished, the Confederate scenes had been removed. I bought a ticket to a showing of the movie *Detroit*, thinking I might find him there, but he was nowhere inside the theater, and looking for him on screen was no more useful than loitering around, waiting for him at the Triple S Food Mart, the mural portrait of Alton Sterling already fading, where asking around after him almost seemed to negate his existence, no one had ever heard of this Toussaint, and the memorial teddy bears too were moldering and frayed, their plastic eyes falling off. Hoping to find him by the water, those non-places of wayfaring and in-between-ness where he was most apt to tarry, I went to the ferry terminal where Canal Street ends by Harrah's Casino, and boarded the ferry to Algiers Point, a short ride across the river, watching the sunlight collapse like broken black glass over the river, the skyscrapers of downtown rising dismally out of the alluvial mud, built over pre-Ibervillean Houma villages. Standard Heights lies by the sea, I reminded myself, as a small child on the ferry pointed innocently at St. Louis Cathedral and said, *Disneyland!*

But in the meantime, since the removal of General Lee, I have learned of disturbing revelations about my own bloodline, which I am not eager to share with Toussaint, this time in connection with one of the accomplices to the assassination of the Lincoln Theater's namesake. Not John Wilkes Booth himself, a household name by now, a man superseded by his legend, but a lesser known conspirator by the name of Lewis Powell, of Randolph County, Alabama, a Confederate soldier wounded at Gettysburg and a member of the Confederate Secret Service. Much against my will, though I am less squeamish about such things after meeting Toussaint, I learned of my consanguinity to Powell when his great-grand-niece, Helen Alderman, contacted me from her home in Florida. Still, I don't know how she tracked me down, but no one can hide in the age of the internet.

I was sitting in the Spanish Town courtyard, wondering whether I would ever see Toussaint again, surrounded by plastic pink flamingos, listening to *Radio Free Dixie* — a broadcast about the worrisome growth of the Dead Zone, recitations of "For the Union Dead" and Baraka's poem about the dirty courtyard — when the loathsome call came. *Now you go into oblivion,* I thought, closing the pages on Audubon's *The Birds of America*: the Louisiana heron, the self-harming mother pelican, the fantastic flamingo, the egret's elegy and the ibis' broken clarinet. Helen Alderman told me everything she knew about Powell and his meandering skull, doomed to traverse the earth, a snowstorm of static interrupting the *Radio Free Dixie* broadcast. I told her, without expecting her to understand, that if she did not have Cudjo's golden skull I was not much interested.

She mentioned the Confederate statues, that they were coming down all over the country, our history being rewritten by unpatriotic coastal elites, she said, coughing and witch-laughing at the same time. I imagined her chain-smoking in a Florida mobile home, a Panhandle woman bitter as wormwood. We delude ourselves if we imagine that those with whom we share the most genetic history, these consanguineous reprobates, are all aboveboard, true-blue and virtuous salt of the earth kin — this errant bloodline that started with my great-great-grandfather's war portrait in the golden oval was as unredeemed, unreconstructed as the stone monuments of generals who refused even generous terms of surrender.

I thanked her for her call, and hung up, for some reason thinking of the Africatown welcome center sign, the fading paint on the great green continent. Of necessity, ours would be a world, I thought, in which a Confederate assassin's skull could be lost and found and lost and found again, but the decapitated head of Cudjo's golden bust went missing in the irretrievable bygones of redneck oblivion. At least now we had unveiled the meaning of the skull and crossbones chemical symbol and the nature of the hazardous cargo the trucks marked with this ghoulish symbol were carrying. I had no desire to know any of this; my relation to Lewis Powell was of no concern to me, I was not one of these "blood and soil" ultranationalist romantics who self-indulged ancestor worship and proto-Nazi cults of racialized territory, no more than Toussaint wished to know about Whipped Peter or Charles Deslondes, no more than Georgetown's offer of free tuition was meant to be taken seriously. I had no desire to know that Powell was kicked in the face by the family mule, breaking his jaw, Helen Alderman reported proudly, or that he once used the skull of a Union soldier for an ashtray. She sounded moribund herself, a medicated voice tremulous and diabetic, as she told me how Powell's skull turned up in the Smithsonian Museum's Native American bone collection by mistake. Powell's coffin, interred on the grounds of the arsenal where he was hanged, was later disinterred and reburied in a consecrated cemetery like a proper Southern Christian where it could await the Lost Cause resurrection of the dead like all the other Confederate casualties; because the living are restless to profit from the dead, the cemetery was sold, she said, and so Powell's earthly remains, as if some part of him was not earthly, were disinterred a second time, and it was during this second disinterment that a funeral home director, recognizing what he had on his hands, pilfered Powell's skull as a *memento mori*; from the funeral director, the restless skull, which challenged Toussaint in the geographic scope of its perambulations, found its way into the Army medical museum, from where it was transferred to the Smithsonian in 1898, she said, taking a moment away from the phone to relieve an unhealthy cough. Genealogical researchers at the Smithsonian contacted her as the next of kin, for which she was emphatically grateful, feeling in her bones, she said, that she had always been related to someone of importance to the Lost Cause, and Helen explained she was making arrangements for a proper burial of the skull, since that was all of Powell's earthly remains she had left. She had called to inform me of this burial, wanting to know whether I would like to attend the service or perhaps say a few words for this distant, infamous forebear. That was when I hung up. The static disappeared from *Radio Free Dixie* and the broadcast returned, clear and ungarbled. I was considerably shaken by Helen's account of the meandering odyssey of Powell's skull, which enjoyed too vivacious an afterlife, the assassin's skull aberrating with a freedom in death that Toussaint's forebears had not enjoyed even in life. I thought of Powell's skull with the disfigured, mule-smashed jaw mixing with the skulls and bones of Native Americans — Choctaw, Cherokee, Osage and the vanquished, annihilated, eponymous tribes of Standard Heights' street names where Toussaint lived. Then a sharp and inexplicable pain struck me in the jaw, like the sockdolager in an unequal good fight.

I scrutinized my own jaw in the mirror, searching there for some sign of consanguineous similitude with the man who attempted to assassinate Secretary of State William H. Seward, bloodying the Secretary's house in the process, and maniacally attacking everyone he encountered in the house — the Secretary's daughter, his son, his son-in-law, an Army nurse, the black butler, anyone unlucky enough to be in the house, screaming that he was mad. After the failed assassination, Powell was held prisoner in the *USS Saugus* to prevent his escape, but he was not shackled to an enslaved person like Tony Curtis in *The Defiant Ones*, the film Toussaint had watched in the Lincoln Theater. I wish it had been me, Toussaint said once when discussing this episode from Powell's life in connection with the film, I wish I had been the one chained to Powell in the hold of that ship — what conversations we would have had! One almost pities wretched Powell in the infernal bowels of that ship, perspiring in the claustrophobic underwater heat, biding his time, not entirely repentant for his minor role in the botched assassination and chained in the underworld of the single-turreted Canonicus-class monitor like Toussaint's ancestors aboard the slave ship *Clotilda*, on a Middle Passage towards the kingdom of death. Pity yes, sympathy no — as I grow weary of the South's self-inflicted hysterias, its self-pitying neuroses, its self-harming terms of surrender. Powell's perambulatory skull — the restlessness of all Confederate revenants — turns up in the most unlikely places. Falling from the bullet holes in the sky. The severed head in Standard Heights. The pikes posted before Kurtz's house. Yorick's skull in Hamlet. Poor Powell!

Unable to unsee this forebear's skull, evidence of things unseen, I saw Powell's skull in one of those Old World *vanitas* paintings of rotting fruit, diaphanous bubbles and fading flowers — the recurring symbols of mortal ephemerality. A king's crown or papal tiara and scepter lying by a skull. A candle has just been snuffed, the languid smoke lingering evanescently in the room, reluctant to depart. A *Semper Augustus* tulip drops a petal on the table. Pocket watches and sand clocks figure prominently in these requiem arrangements. Globes and maps of *terra incognita* and *terra pericolosa.* Creeping creatures like lizards and snakes. Seashells and butterflies. A vase of dying flowers and unfinished manuscripts. Not long following Helen's disturbing call, I found myself standing alone in a Baton Rouge art gallery before Carstian Luyckx's *Allegory of Charles I of England and Henrietta of France in a Vanitas Still Life*; less for the allegory, I was here to look for Toussaint one last time, in earnest, to tell him about Powell's restless skull. I had already been to Arsenal Park and the Liberty Bell replica there, he had to be on the east bank of the river somewhere, and to the Lincoln Theater and back downriver to the wards of Charity Hospital, but he never materialized. I was left with only the painted allegory of a king's execution. The *vanitas* canvas symbolically depicts Charles the First's beheading, and I looked around the gallery for a *vanitas* of Cudjo's headless golden bust. Outside the museum that day, my eyes adjusting reluctantly to the sunlight, I saw a man close a black umbrella as the sun timidly tipped behind clouds manufactured by ExxonMobil. Like the hateful information of Helen's call, the funereal effect of the *vanitas* lingered with me for a long time, mentally rearranging the objects in the painted world to conform to various nightmarish schemes: Powell's skull impaled on the red stick; Powell's skull fitted irreverently upon the headless neck of Cudjo's golden bust, wormwood oozing from the eye sockets; Powell's skull in Master Hammond's boiling cauldron; Powell's skull on my own neck; Powell's skull on one of the medical tables Toussaint and I found in Charity Hospital, stacked with spoiled medical supplies and preserved biomedical samples, the room of white CPR dummy torsos, a *vanitas* of Petrochemical Modernism. In the surviving photos of Powell's execution — unlike the lifeless General Lee, Powell had not resisted the noose — black umbrellas are open above the heads of some of the officials gathered for the grim proceedings, ghoulish ambassadors of the river's west bank come to escort another lost soul, in the hold of their chlorine gas ghost ship, away from the east bank where the satsuma trees grow orange and green and the mugshot living are held captive in the Angola of the present.

No one ever sees the Umbrella Man during the real-time unfolding of the event — he is only apparent retrospectively, as it were in photographs. And though I do not recall any black umbrellas present at the dismantling of Robert E. Lee's statue in Lee Circle—it was a sunny, rainless day, perfect for a public execution — the black umbrellas appear in pictures of the statue's dethronement reproduced in *The Times Picayune*, and will continue appearing as long as the nocturne plays.

Beneath the pallor covering my face, I saw the livid traces of Powell's skull, the structure of the jaw and the moonlight in the eyes. The skull looked at me with my own blank black eyes, bilious and baleful vanishing points through which the wormwood river flowed backward. Was this the skull of the severed head Toussaint discovered in the vacant greenbelt lots of Standard Heights? Even at the moment of death, I had photos of my ancestors going back generations. Toussaint had none, except a tortured man with a whip-scarred back. I do not think he had a photograph of his father, and the one photo of his mother on the street of Mobile as a girl could just as well have been the experience of any other little black girl from Prichard at that time, as there was nothing special then about using a Colored Entrance. Unlike the camera-shy natives who buried the Italian ethnographer Boggiani with his camera, my ancestors evinced no shame in having their photos taken because they did not believe in the soul's post-death identity, that there was anything but their materialist theology, converting to the doctrine of Manifest Destiny and infinite Louisiana Purchases that reduced these lost tribes to little more than native names of potholed streets that were later besieged or bought out by petrochemical companies because they needed land, always more land for what the Nazis had invented a word for: *Lebensraum.*

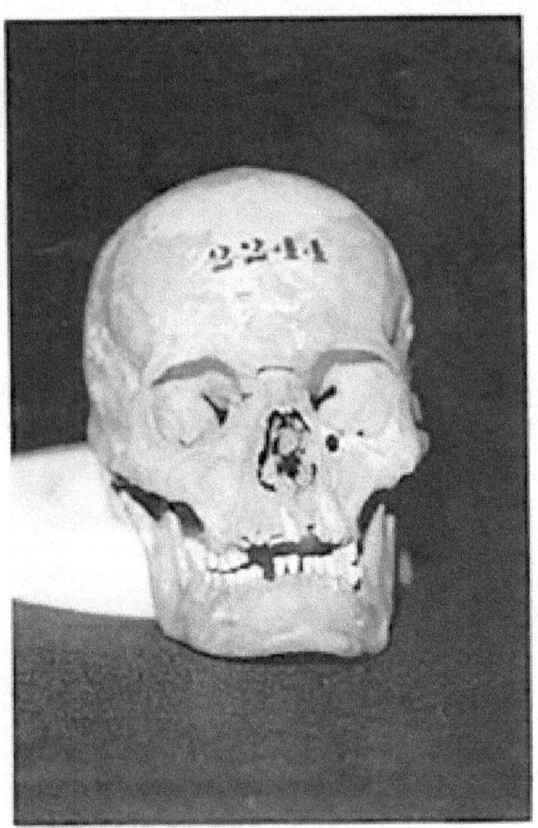

Then I received a small, compact, rectangular package in the mail, no return address. It was heavy, the earthy weight of something that had survived an absinthian inferno. I left it on the table for weeks before opening it. The package beckoned me, challenging me to open it. I resisted a few more days. But the package's invitation did not abate. I turned to the package one evening as the alarms at the ExxonMobil plant sounded a clarion and plaintive appeal, a dire warning of some unforeseen disruption to the ideal scheme of the plant's process flow diagrams, and inside the package, wrapped in newsprint was a rough red brick. The brick was cold and inert in my hand. Not like a thing that once had a heartbeat, but like a thing through whose clay the breath of life never breathed. The petrochemical nocturne played on *Radio Free Dixie* amidst the septic peels of sirens warning of the unexploded ordnance that lay buried in the earth around us like a minefield. I pondered what Toussaint, who at times was the generative site of more meaning than he knew how to process alone, might have meant by delivering this brick accompanied by photographic stills from the police dash cam video that recorded Toussaint's brother's final moments of freedom outside of Angola — I cannot say I am any closer to knowing. Toussaint must have been researching his brother's arrest, hunting for exculpatory evidence. Long into the night, I contemplated these photos of Xavier's suicide by cop, evidence of things unseen, extracting no more meaning from them than from the inert and impenetrable Osage Avenue brick.

Then I remembered the scene from *The Defiant Ones,* the one Toussaint first saw in the Lincoln Theater, Tony Curtis and Sydney Poitier are manacled together, because the warden had a sick sense of humor, and they must cooperate in order to survive the farce in which they must grind out the social compact. The fetters binding Toussaint and I have been broken, and the terms of surrender are more magnanimous than I could have ever hoped for, certainly better than we deserve. There is no black man, no Toussaint to aid escape by breaking the manacles on Lewis Powell's wrists, another native son of Alabama awaiting his self-created fate, Powell who died on a sunny day with a black hood over his head after dropping at the speed of death from a rickety wooden scaffold, beneath the indifferent eyes of assembled officials and journalists, but no proper mourners, his Confederate confreres in hiding, awaiting the stone General's marching orders. From a single brick, you can build an empire, Toussaint once told me, while we waited for the removal of General Lee. On cold nights I can feel the ghosts of those iron manacles burning on my wrists and ankles, he said, somatic signs that the deep past actors have not yet liberated us from the Angola of the present.

While the grown folks protest and counter-protest, map and counter-map, and the petrochemical nocturne warns of another toxic point to be added to the TOXMAP, outside my apartment window — one I have never managed to pry open — a little white boy and little black girl improvise an innocent game in the dirty courtyard, an entangled verdure of boscage and green labyrinth of webbed growth like an Henri Rousseau painting; gradually, the brindled light turns titian and umber, and I recall that today is the 2017 total eclipse. Our celestial sign has come. Perhaps Toussaint was out there viewing the eclipse he plotted coordinates for so long ago, and Osage tribes were shooting flaming arrows at the sun to relight the empyreal lamp and daunt the demonic spirits that made the sun recoil and quail in fear behind the moon. The children make up the rules of their courtyard game as they go, one of them brandishing a small red stick, undeterred by the eclipse's brownish darkness, and when the ExxonMobil plant's siren warns of another toxic point they are no more disturbed than if it were the familiar jingle of a summer ice cream truck. While they went about their game, now pointing the red stick at the moon, in the sulfurous light of the total eclipse I let the wind ruffle through the pages of *The Birds of America* until it stopped spontaneously on the headless pink flamingo.

The vernal rains are heavier this year, as much as ten or more inches in half as many hours — the Spillway will be opened again soon — maybe I can find Toussaint there, marveling again at the recurrence of the wormwood floodwater crashing the bays like watery fingers on a harp, the petrochemical nocturne playing over the plant's loudspeakers. And though General Lee no longer commands the skyline of a disappearing, subsiding city, casting his Confederate umbrage across the circle, the vultures wheeling overhead portend ash, carrion and mort, the bloodhounds sniffing Toussaint's footprints around the nameless circle.

The Saints lost in the Superdome again last night, surrendering on their homefield to a superior opponent, a loss compounded by another kind of loss: while broadcasting the Saints game against their divisional rival Atlanta Falcons, CBS used outdated archival footage of the New Orleans skyline, and on every television within earshot of the petrochemical nocturne General Lee was seen again, as if resurrected from the dead, restored defiant and triumphant to his pedestal at the eye of the storm in Lee Circle, gaslighting in adamantine refusal of any terms of surrender, as if Toussaint's ancestor at Appomattox had never seen Lee walk out of the McLean House with crestfallen mien signaling it was all over; as if the 54th Massachusetts Infantry Regiment under the command of a white man had been cast in the putrid meat of internal organs, not bronze; as if the blood of Toussaint's father had never leaked from the funeral home and drained almost of its own accord and under its own motility back to Fisk's river, like a serpentine meander returning to the principal riverine body, to be conducted downriver to the Dead Zone; as if the

Christmas Eve explosion itself had not been more than just the cost of doing business; as if Toussaint and I had not, with our own eyes seen the stone General's removal and heard one half of the crowd cheer the overthrow of an unreconstructed Confederate zombie. The candle in the *vanitas* blows out. The Angola of the present passes through the eye socket of Powell's restless skull. I was shocked, albeit not surprised by this undead General's rebel yell return in the middle of a Saints game, like a mutinous and hazardous material placed in the palm of the Hand and Eye Motif. For my own sanity, I had to check Lee Circle to confirm that it was all an error, that the pedestal was still empty, that the General had not, in fact, reinstated himself and usurped the eye of the storm, like Doubting Thomas poking his fingers in the wounds of the crucified Christ, to satisfy myself that CBS' anachronous stock footage was merely an intern's gaffe and that we are not dealing with a zombie Confederacy that simply will not die. "No monument except the ditch" does not apply to the stone General for whom no ditch is monumental enough. Something is rotten in the state of Louisiana. A question mark hangs like a dagger above the Gulf. When the groundhog sees his shadow in this state, two square miles of coastline are lost to the Dead Zone. When you hear panting footsteps rustle in the cane fields and dry twigs snap in the dark — a bloodhound on the scent of your fear of death by water. Note the foghorns' long doleful blasts sounding on the river, the emergency klaxons and the sirens of the plant's warning system wailing — another unexploded ordnance — the final shot of the Battle of Baton Rouge. The Curse of the Saints shows no signs of ebbing — the franchise continues its streak of losing seasons, close games and bad calls. Turnovers, interceptions, and injuries plague the Saints, off-field problems with law and disorder. The slow motion dream speed police chase ends in Angola and the light in the tower window of *Fire at the Grand Storehouse of the Tower of London, 1841* has been extinguished forever, the window burning in the tower prohibited by the Eleventh Commandment from ever opening. The eclipse is total, like a black umbrella opened over the sun, the children have quit their game, and it is now almost too dark in the courtyard to carry on with *The Birds of America*: the ink that blackens this page may have been derived from the ExxonMobil plant, that petrochemical cathedral in whose hydrocarbon sanctum — the diamond of chemical classification symbols on the altar —

we recite our plastic prayers beneath an empyrean processed by the plant's cloud manufacturing. There was a grand design and a petrochemical architecture in the buyout destruction all along. ExxonMobil has begun the work of building office suites — ugly beige boxes with tinted glass windows — on the vacant lots of Standard Heights, and before long there will be a *Lebensraum* of surface parking lots, office parks, an Angola of cubicles, and executive meeting rooms where once Toussaint played pickup football games and the wild summer satsumas grew. The leaking funeral home that held Toussaint's father is still there, though one wonders for how much longer, his father's blood flowing backward in the undeciphered wormwood river. The hazmat trucks with their branding of chemical symbols — skull and crossbones, the leafless tree and dead fish, the Hand and Eye Motif — moving like Holocene megafauna through the streets with native names. The last house has fallen in Standard Heights. I still go there sometimes, the threnody winds howling through the native streets and the vesper bats circling the last remaining greenbelt oaks, wearing the Made in China Zulu medallion, passing the uncracked Liberty Bell replica in Arsenal Park and the cannon aimed at the petrochemical plant, that toxic emerald city, careful not to step on unexploded ordnance, carrying Toussaint's brick — the one his mother salvaged from the burned-out wreckage of Osage Avenue, about the weight of a human skull — but there are no windows left through which to throw it, the brick flying harmlessly through immaterial naphtha and holy ghost benzene in slow motion dream speed, the refluent process flow diagrams breaking down in a metaphysical accident, as all around me the infernal gas flares burn and the sirens blare like last trumpets — the plant's warning system playing the terminal wormwood fugue of the petrochemical nocturne.

Petrochemical Nocturne – Rights Acknowledgments

Below are acknowledgments of all images populating the pages of Petrochemical Nocturne. Special thanks to Colleen Kane for The Lincoln Theater, Leland Kent for the photographs of Charity Hospital, and George Widman for his harrowing photograph of the Philadelphia MOVE bombing. This is not an academic historical study, so I exempt myself from the format of a traditional bibliography. Unfortunately, some photographs and paintings that were included in the original manuscript had to be omitted from the final cut for copyright reasons. These included a photograph of Drew Brees (Geaux Saints!) doing a superman over the top of the offensive and defensive lines for a touchdown, an Andreas Gursky print of supermarket shelves, a photograph of Martin Luther King, and the gruesome Fred Hampton murder scene whose copyright is held by the *Chicago Tribune.*

12.
Phoenicopterus ruber, the Greater Flamingo. Drawn by John James Audubon for his naturalistic study, The Birds of America.

16.
Fire at the Grand Storehouse of the Tower of London. J.M.W Turner. 1841.

22.
Meanders of the Mississippi River. As much artwork as it is map, produced by Harold Fisk for the Army Corps of Engineers. 1944.

35.
Bobby Seale at the Chicago 8 conspiracy trial after the 1968 Democratic Convention, Chicago. Painting by Franklin McMahon.

39.
No Man's Land, Flanders Field, France 1919. William Lester King.

40.
Vietnam Veterans Memorial. Maya Lin and David Olster.

50.
Louisiana Indian Walking Along A Bayou. Alfred Boisseau. 1847.

52.
Flood on the Mississippi. Alfred Boisseau. 1896.

53.
Photographer Unknown. Scars of a whipped slave (April 2, 1863, Baton Rouge, Louisiana, USA). Original caption: "Overseer Artayou Carrier

whipped me. I was two months in bed sore from the whipping. My master come after I was whipped; he discharged the overseer. The very words of poor Peter, taken as he sat for his picture."

55.
The Bonnet Carré Spillway diverting excess Mississippi River water. Photo courtesy of the U.S. Army Corps of Engineers. 2011.

57.
The Great Wave off Kanagawa. Katsushika Hokusai. 1831, Edo period.

62.
Listing of slaves held by John Lyons of St. Landry Parish, Louisiana. Population schedules of the eighth census of the United States, 1860, Louisiana. National Archives and Records Administration.

66.
Globally Harmonized of Classification and Labelling of Chemicals System. United Nations.

90.
Fight of the Century. Jack Johnson vs. James J. Jeffries. Nevada Historical Society. July 4, 1910.

97.
Superdome after Katrina. National Oceanic and Atmospheric Administration. August 31, 2005.

98.
A MOUNTAIN OF DAMAGED OIL DRUMS NEAR THE EXXON REFINERY. Baton Rouge, LA. John Messina, 1940-, Photographer. Environmental Protection Agency.

107.
Still photo from nationally televised footage of Rodney King beating. PBS. March 3, 1991. George Holliday, the plumber who took the grainy footage of the savage police beating of Rodney King, died from COVID-19 complications in 2021.

127.
The Lincoln Theater. Colleen Kane. Baton Rouge, LA. 2007.

166.
Topographic Plan of the City and Battlefield of Baton Rouge, LA. Fought on August 5, 1862. Joseph Gorlinski, Civil Engineer. From a map on file in the office of the Chief of Engineers, U.S. Army. 1862.

188.
Tartan Ribbon. James Clerk Maxwell. 1861.

191.
View of Great Confederate Reunion Parade in Birmingham published in the Birmingham Age-Herald. June 18, 1916.

198.
The Dead of Antietam. Alexander Gardner. September, 1862.

200.
Major John Pelham (1838 – 1863), Confederate Army artillery officer in the American Civil War, Alabama Department of Archives and History. Gardner Studios. Philadelphia, PA. Major John Pelham was the namesake of Pelham, Alabama and is buried in Jacksonville, Alabama.

201.
Home of the Rebel Sharpshooter, Gettysburg. Alexander Gardner. July, 1863.

203.
New Ideal building. Birmingham, Alabama. Author photo.

212.
MOVE bombing photo. AP Photo/George Widman. Philadelphia, PA. May 15, 1985.

253.
Blue Room. Charity Hospital. New Orleans, LA. Leland Kent / AbandonedSoutheast.com

256.
Broken Window. Wikipedia User: WiseWoman. No changes were made. Link to original work: https://commons.wikimedia.org/wiki/File: Broken-Window-20130513.jpg

261.
Stowage of the British slave ship Brookes under the regulated slave trade act of 1788. Library of Congress.

262.
The Steerage. Alfred Stieglitz. 1907.

263.
The Slave Ship. J.M.W Turner. 1840.

269.
Charity Hospital. New Orleans, LA. Leland Kent / AbandonedSoutheast.com

271.
Africatown Welcome Center sign. Africatown, AL. Author photo.

272.
Africatown statue of Cudjo Kussola Lewis. Africatown, AL. Author photo.

274.
Cudjo Lewis (1841 – 1935). Doy Leale McCall Rare Book and Manuscript Library, University of South Alabama.

276.
Charity Hospital Operating Room. John Norris Teunisson. Louisiana Digital Library/Louisiana State Museum. Date unknown, but John Norris Teunisson (1869 – 1959) was active in photo-documentation of New Orleans in the first two decades of the twentieth century.

295.
TOXMAP. Author screenshot of now defunct government website with GIS map. United States National Library of Medicine. Screenshot taken in 2016. I used this map tool to identify documented locations of brownfields in Baton Rouge and Cancer Alley. The online database was removed by the Trump administration in 2019; it is believed the database was closed to conceal the negative impacts of the Trump administration's efforts to dismantle environmental regulations.

311.
Gaston Motel. Birmingham, Alabama. City of Birmingham. Date unknown.

313.
Mugshot of Martin Luther King Jr. following his 1963 arrest in Birmingham, Alabama. Birmingham Police Department. April, 1963.

314.
Exterior postcard view of the A.G. Gaston Motel from a C. T. Art-Color tone postcard folder published by Curteich for the motel. Birmingham, Alabama.

315.
Courtyard view of the A.G. Gaston Motel. City of Birmingham. Date unknown.

319.
Lee Circle. New Orleans, LA. Postcard published by Curt Teich & Co, Chicago. Date unknown, but probably from the 1930s or 1940s.

325.
Stained glass biographical history of General Robert E. Lee in the National Cathedral. Wikipedia Author: Remember. March 8, 2008.

335.
Public execution of Lincoln assassins (Mary E. Surratt, Lewis T. Powell, David E. Herold, and George A. Atzerodt). Alexander Gardner. July 7, 1865.

337.
Washington Navy Yard, D.C. Lewis Payne, in sweater, seated and manacled. Alexander Gardner. Summary: this photograph has background of dark metal, and was presumably taken on the monitors, U.S.S. Montauk and Saugus, where the conspirators were for a time confined. April, 1865. Ex-Confederate soldier Lewis Powell was known as "Payne" in this photograph as he operated under an alias.

338.
Skull of Lewis Thornton Powell (1844 – 1865). Geneva Historical Society. "Alas, poor Yorick!" may not apply.

Petrochemical Nocturne

Amos Jasper Wright IV is from Birmingham, Alabama but has also lived in Louisiana. His first short story collection, *Nobody Knows How It Got This Good* won the 2017 Tartt First Fiction Award from Livingston Press and was published in 2018. *Petrochemical Nocturne* is his first published novel. He is presently working on several books titled *The Empire of Repetitive Motions, The Battle of Danziger Bridge,* and *In the Land of the Blind.* His author website is www.amosjasperwright.com

www.ingramcontent.com/pod-product-compliance
Lightning Source LLC
Chambersburg PA
CBHW060939030726
47503CB00003B/661